A WOMAN WHO KNOWS WHAT SHE WANTS

Ty pointed out across the ocean. "Look," he said.

She turned and saw that the sky had turned golden mauve; the ocean waves had metallic tips. The day was rapidly drawing to a close and nature was not going to let it go out without fanfare.

"Because of you," he whispered into her hair, "I've taken the time to appreciate evenings like this. And mornings. And every day."

Maggie's pulse raced. This man had a way of grasping her emotions and turning them inside out. "How did this happen?" she asked softly.

"I don't know." He leaned toward her upturned face, closed his eyes, and placed the brush of a kiss against her lips.

She opened her eyes. "That's not enough," she said.

"What?"

"I want more." Maggie had never said those words to a man in her life.

"I hope you won't be sorry you said that," he said.

"I don't believe," she said, "that sorry is what I'm going to be."

She slipped her hands up and felt his chest through the thin T-shirt, and encircled his neck with her arms. "Kiss me again," she whispered, "and this time I want to feel it in my toes."

CONSENTING HEARTS

GARDA PARKER

ZEBRA BOOKS
KENSINGTON PUBLISHING CORP.

ZEBRA BOOKS are published by

Kensington Publishing Corp.
850 Third Ave
New York, NY 10022

First Printing: September, 1994

Printed in the United States of America

*To
Shawn Kelly
a real hero with true vision*

*And
special thanks to Janice Piacente
she knows why*

*And
with thanks to
Frank Martorana, DVM*

One

"Come on Milford, help me out, here," Ty said into the phone. "I'm down to my last sou."

"Sorry, pal, no can do," Milford Jaris said from his Los Angeles home. "You're out of dough you can draw on."

"Well, then, think of something. We weren't partners for twenty years for nothing. We came up with a lot of creative solutions to problems like this in the old days." Ty took off his glasses and set them on the desk. He closed his eyes and rubbed the bridge of his nose.

"Those were the old days, Ty, this is now. We live in a litigious society. Everybody sues everybody. Even lawyers get sued these days. Can you believe that? People will take any crumb of what smells like a little manipulation and sue the jock off somebody. I can't take that chance anymore."

Ty easily pictured Milford sitting by his pool on this Sunday morning, probably sipping a Bloody Mary and reading the latest installment in his stock portfolio. He'd stretched out in a chaise lounge next to Milford, doing just that, on many a Sunday morning. Deals had been made and broken sometimes before the sun reached high noon.

This Sunday morning Ty had just returned from downtown, as the residents of Cape Agnes, New Hampshire, referred to their block of shops and restaurants in the business district, where he'd picked up a copy of *The New York Times*. He'd lingered for a moment on a corner and watched what he calculated was at least fifty percent of the townspeople streaming into the three churches situated in a triangle around the village green. Others, appearing maddeningly relaxed without a care in the world, were sitting on park benches facing the ocean and watching the tide, or reading one of the flyers, posted all over town, about the auditions for the summer theater production being held the following Sunday.

In sharp contrast to all of them, Ty now sat in a dilapidated beach house, wondering where he was going to scrounge up enough cash to buy food and get his laundry done, while pleading with his former law partner to save his life. He opened a bag of red-hot fireball candy and popped one into his mouth; his eyes watered for a second when the first wave of heat assaulted his tongue.

"Well what the hell am I supposed to do?" he said finally, hating himself the second the words came out of his month. He'd prided himself on his well-cultivated calm deliberation. In fact he'd made a pretty damned fine career out of it for a while, when he'd paid attention to it. The last thing he'd ever do is whine, but he knew Milford would perceive his words in just that way.

"Listen, pal," Milford said. "Grow up. You're forty-six years old. Figure it out."

"Don't use that with me, Milford. I've saved your antique butt a few hundred times and you know it."

"Okay, okay. What about that animal

clinic? Did you convince the rube vet to move out of your daddy's place?"

"Not yet. I just got here, remember?"

"Well, how long can it take to outsmart some small-town horse doctor?" Milford laughed, and Ty heard the unmistakable clink of ice cubes against glass.

He ran a hand through his hair. "If they find out the place is in receivership, they'll never move out of there unless the bank forces them. I know I wouldn't. I'd hang on until I could get control of the building myself."

"Well, then, get moving. Get them out, get your own company going, and make a token payment," Milford barked.

"I haven't got that kind of money. That's why I'm calling you, partner."

"I'm not your partner anymore, remember? You're smarter than they are, Ty. You know ways to get them out of the place. That's the best free legal advice I can give you."

"Will you listen to me? This may be a sleepy little town, but these types know how to go for the jugular. Nicely, of course. I knew some of these people when I was a kid. This won't be like some of the cases in the past where you and I have snowed them. And how is the new little ball and chain, anyway?"

Ty liked to raise Milford's dander by bringing up his twenty-three-year-old third wife. It was this last one of Milford's many dalliances that put the fury of hell into Ty's wife Sylvie and drove a permanent wedge into their shaky marital relationship. Guilt by association, that's what she figured. And she'd been right on some occasions. Almost as many times as he'd known about her extramarital flings.

Milford coughed, then cleared his throat. "If you saw Tiffany right now in this thong bathing suit she just bought, lying on her stomach out here in the glorious California sun, browning her delectable behind, you'd know exactly how she is."

Ty knew Milford liked to keep sticking it to him, too. Hanging onto his mansion through three wives had been a feat of creative jurisprudence, defying state laws that even the big-name alimony and palimony pundits marvelled at. He and Milford had worked it out together. There'd always been something a little crooked about Milford Jaris that, up to now, Ty had been willing to ignore. He'd managed to stay as straight within the law himself as he could and still pull off some pretty amazing solutions.

"Look, Milford, I know there's another chunk due me. You took care of this little transaction, remember? You said you'd handle everything and I'd be covered. So what's the holdup?"

"There isn't any holdup, Ty, baby. You're out of bucks, pure and simple. Get it through your head, will you? I don't appreciate having my Sunday mornings disturbed. Sundays are a time for reflection, meditation."

"Well, meditate on this, you thief. There's a holdup going on here, and you're the one holding me up. You owe me another hundred fifty grand, and you know it."

"I won't tolerate being called names," Milford said, infuriatingly calm. "You simply haven't received my final bill for services rendered. Actually, it came to about two hundred and eighty, what with your divorce settlement and your daddy's expenses from big-time living. But, I've decided out of the goodness of my heart and remembrance of a once lucrative partnership to overlook the loose change over and above your one-fifty. You got your freedom; you don't owe anything to anybody; you got the mutt; and you can get Daddy's building back. We're even and we're through!"

The line shifted to an annoying hum. Ty slammed the receiver down.

The golden retriever, who had been eyeing him from the moment his voice escalated into the telephone, got up from a spot on the hearth rug and plodded over to him. Ty looked at the dog with anger for a moment, then knelt down and hugged him around the neck.

"One of us has got to get a job, old boy. I guess you can't support me anymore. Kibbles are looking better all the time. Perhaps I'll be joining you in a bowl one of these mornings."

The dog slumped down at his feet and promptly went to sleep.

"You always were a little thin on moral support." Ty patted the already snoring dog, then went out on the deck that fronted the living room's wall of windows.

The Atlantic surf lazed in and out. The sand sparkled like a field of rhinestones, and the black silhouette of a sailboat cut along the clear blue horizon.

It was a beautiful early summer day at the beach, and he felt like shit.

His father had been missing for four years. He admitted he hadn't tried very hard to find him. He didn't miss the old buzzard. He hadn't been much of a father to begin with. In the aftermath of the publicity surrounding the old man's disappearance and while his marriage and law practice crumbled, he'd been forced to tell a lot of people a lot of things he never thought he'd have to say. But he never got around to telling anything to Michael Logan, Doctor of Veterinary Medicine of Cape Agnes, New Hampshire. Perhaps it was because he'd been born in Cape Agnes and there was some kind of stupid pride left in him about not letting the folks who knew him *when* know him *now*. Besides, he hadn't wanted to concern himself with trivial things like the clogged drains and rewiring and falling plaster which Dr. Logan had reported by mail with every rent check.

By the time Caesar the Wonder Dog had moved in with him, his funds and the life he'd known had moved out. If it hadn't been for the meager checks Dr. Logan sent to the bank for deposit in his father's account, and Caesar's dwindling television royalties, he'd have had virtually nothing to live on. And he'd been living off those checks for longer than he wanted to admit.

Caesar came up behind him, sat down and leaned against Ty's leg as he always did in his own gesture of comfort.

"Yeah, well you're not so innocent either, buddy," Ty told him. "All those free summers you spent here. The good doc even paid for the limousine without knowing it. Not to mention that new designer low-fat, low-cholesterol dog food you've grown a taste for over the past few months. You ought to be ashamed of yourself."

Caesar ignored the guilt trip that was being laid on him and sprinted off the deck and down the beach to scare up a

flock of gulls picking at a bunch of seaweed that had washed ashore.

"I know. You've paid your dues, too,"
Ty called after him. "Between you and
your vet I've been kept alive."

A nagging voice in the back of his head
told him he could keep himself alive if
he freed himself of this depression and
went out and got a real job. The whole
idea was distasteful.

But this wasn't L.A. And hadn't he
come back here determined to start life
over? Trouble was, he had no idea how to
go about such an undertaking.

He stepped off the deck and started
down the beach, wondering if he'd actually begun to acquire some shred of de-
cency in his old age.

He caught up with Caesar and they
romped together for a few minutes.

"Guess there's still some life left in
both us old dogs, eh, pal?"

Caesar barked.

"Well, then, suppose you figure out
how we're gonna go on romping?"

Caesar ran up onto the back porch and
flopped down in the shade.

Ty followed him and flopped down in

a green mesh hammock. "Great. I'm on my own. As usual."

Panic filled Priscilla's soft brown eyes as she looked up into the intent face above her. The doctor's hands carefully and gently pressed a stethoscope along her palpitating chest and delicate stomach, then lower. Her heart fluttered, and her legs contracted in involuntary response.

"Is it serious, Doctor?" The concerned voice came from the other intent face hovering above.

"Well, I think her upset stomach was caused by a combination of stress from the flight up from Miami and overindulgence in lamb kidneys for breakfast. I think with rest and time to get used to her surroundings, she'll be just fine."

"Thank you so very much, Doctor. I've been so worried about the poor little dear." The concerned voice relaxed. Everyone in Cape Agnes, New Hampshire, called Michael Logan "Doc," except Henrietta VanGelder, a summer-only resident who preferred the more formal "Doctor" when speaking to her favorite veterinarian. Henrietta's high regard for the doctor and her love for Priscilla, her champagne fluff of a toy poodle, was evident in her smoke-and-whiskey-aged voice.

Michael Logan folded the stethoscope and dropped it into the breast pocket of a whimsical patchwork-dog and calico-cat print lab coat, then brushed a streak of soil from her white skirt. Balancing a clipboard against her waist, she made a few notations on the dog's chart.

"It's my pleasure, Mrs. VanGee. I always enjoy seeing you and Priscilla here every summer." From a blue painted cupboard over a stainless steel sink, she brought out a fat brown bottle and shook several tiny pills from it into a small white envelope. "Give her a quarter of one of these every morning for seven days. And I suggest you put her on a strict diet of scientifically correct canine food."

Henrietta scooped up and clasped Priscilla to her ample bosom. She clucked over the poodle and kissed the pink bow-tied topknot, setting her own red-orange curls to bouncing. "I will take extra special care of her, Doctor. I can't thank you enough for restoring my little darling's health."

"I'm glad I could help. Priscilla is very special to me, too, you know. I'm sure she'll be just fine till you're ready to go back to Florida for the winter."

Michael Logan, known as Maggie most of her life, never ceased to feel rewarded whenever pets and their owners expressed trust in her. Their gratitude made it much easier to bear the financial finagling she went through to keep her young practice together. As owner of Critter Care of Cape Agnes, Maggie's hands had been more than full staying ahead of repairs to the rental property her business had occupied for almost four years.

Henrietta pulled her ever-present mink cape around her shoulders, covering the poodle, and flipped out the ends of her flaming hair. It framed her permanently tanned skin, softening the deep wrinkles around her eyes and mouth. Priscilla poked her delicate nose out from the folds of the mink, and Maggie scratched under the downy chin.

"Let me treat you to lunch," Henrietta offered.

Maggie checked her watch. "That sounds like a wonderful idea. I could use a break right now."

She ushered Henrietta out of the exam room and down the hall, guiding her over a pile of plaster chunks. Disinfectant and musty old lath, evidence of cleaning up after parts of the ceiling had fallen in, were particularly odoriferous in that area. At the reception desk, a bright green counter which separated the waiting room from an office arrangement of computer, file drawers, assorted pet foods, and grooming tools, Maggie handed the clipboard over the counter to the receptionist.

"Here you are, Jolene. Mrs. VanGee and I are going over to Mother Hubbard's for lunch. You can call me there if you need me. I feel the need for a bowl of Little Bert's therapeutic clam chowder."

Jolene Backus, the young and rather buxom receptionist, shook back her full long mane of tightly curled blond hair, the front of which stood straight up and didn't move, owing to the application of a cement-like gel. Mall hair, Maggie called it, but she had to admit she was impressed at how Jolene and all those other carbon copy beauties made it look exactly the same, day after day. She wondered how long it took them to accomplish such an architectural wonder first thing in the morning.

Maggie's own hair, once a dark auburn, had lightened with the advent of gray and faded to what she referred to as half-century-old colored hair. In the morning, it hung in a nondescript manner before she gave up trying to style it and hastily pulled it back in a tortoiseshell clip.

"You're feeling depressed, aren't you, Doc?" Jolene asked knowingly. Her eyes, tinted with contact lenses, expressed sincere care through a turquoise sheen.

"Does it show very much?"

"Only that you always go for a bowl of Little Bert's screamingly caloric chowder when you're depressed."

Maggie shook her head. "Some women cut their hair. I eat Little Bert's chowder. It's hereditary, I suspect. When I was a kid I remember my mother going over to

Mother's for a bowl of Big Bert's clam chowder when she was feeling down."

Jolene nodded with understanding.

"Something I've never been able to figure out," Maggie said, hanging her lab coat in the small closet near Jolene's desk, "is that Big Bert Hubbard was a skinny little man, while his son, Little Bert, is obviously one who enjoys his own cooking."

Jolene leaned forward onto the counter and whispered, "Mrs. Treen told me he has a fifty-two-inch waist."

"She ought to know, for all the sewing repairs she's done on his pants," Henrietta concurred.

Maggie smiled, grabbed her shoulder bag, and left the animal hospital with Henrietta, Priscilla riding inside her sumptuous mink sedan. Among the many things Maggie enjoyed about returning to her hometown as an adult was the sea air she'd missed so much while she lived in the Midwest, the feel of gritty sand on the sidewalk beneath her shoes, and the squawks of gulls circling overhead, competing with boat horns out in the bay.

"Isn't it wonderful about the Fisbees?" Henrietta broke into Maggie's musings.

"Yes, it is wonderful. She's due any moment."

That was another thing Maggie loved about returning to Cape Agnes, to be in on all the tidbits and important news she'd been excluded from as a child. sometimes she felt privileged now, knowing intimate details about the lives of some of the families she remembered who still lived here. Like the news about Vincent Fisbee, the police chief.

Chief Fisbee's wife, Maureen, was pregnant with their first child. They hadn't been using birth control for over seven years. And like everyone else in Cape Agnes, Maggie did not think of discussing it as being gossip. The Fisbees enjoyed sharing with their neighbors their desire to have a baby. The townspeople had been waiting to celebrate with them the moment they'd confirmed they were expectant parents, and were just as excited awaiting the newborn's arrival. Once the pregnancy had been confirmed, a huge shower had been thrown in the community center, and the couple was presented with every baby thing they would ever need.

People in this town cared about one another.

Maggie opened the spring-loaded screen door to allow Henrietta to precede her into Mother Hubbard's Cupboard. Another wave of smells assaulted her, and she breathed them in. Beef and chicken barbecue, spicy sauces, fish, coffee, cinnamon. The aromas were distinct in themselves, yet blended into a sense memory of childhood moments spent inside this wonderful old diner.

"Welcome back, Mrs. VanGelder. Hey, Doc!" Little Bert Hubbard called from his ever-present spot in front of the smoking indoor barbecue pit. A white vee-neck T-shirt stretched across his barrel chest to the last thread, the short sleeves strained around his beefy upper arms. A white apron made from a discarded tablecloth girded the middle of his massive trunk.

"Hey, Little Bert!" Maggie called back. "Got any of that chowder today?"

"Does a drug store have aspirin?" Bert

never could answer with a straight yes or
no.

"Well, as I live and breathe, who have
we got here?" a woman's voice drifted
across the room. Dottie Dearborn, a waitress who'd been at Mother's for over
twenty years, greeted one and all as if it
were the first time she'd laid eyes on
them. She waved, then ducked back behind the kitchen door.

Little Bert's son, Bert Hubbard the
Third, known as Bubba, a chunky boy of
about seventeen sporting a scanty black
moustache, peeked through the square
opening for bussed dishes and called
hello. Maggie waved and Henrietta nodded majestically, having perfected the dis-
tinctive wave of Queen Elizabeth the
Second, elbow, elbow, wrist, wrist, wrist.

Mother's looked exactly the same as it
had when Big Bert, the original Mother
Hubbard, ran it, like a shoreside picnic
spot set up inside a wood framed pavilion
with a massive stone barbecue pit and
copper ventilation hood dominating the
wall at one end. Ten red-and-white-
checked oilcloth-covered picnic tables
and their matching benches were placed

in a herringbone pattern down one length of the room. Along the wall just inside the door was a long white counter edged in chrome fronted by a row of matching vinyl-covered pedestal stools, remnants of a diner that had occupied the place in the twenties. Behind the counter was an old-fashioned soda fountain which dispensed gooey concoctions that Dottie or Bubba served up in tall plastic glasses.

Overhead, the wooden rafters were laden with ancient and near-modern fishing boat artifacts, from rusted anchors to deep-sea reels to green rubber boots to a rusted red-and-white Flying A gasoline sign.

Maggie loved this place. A single woman could feel comfortable walking into Mother's for lunch or supper. She could sit down at a table, and soon be joined by six or seven other people, men and women, all there for the same reason. No questioning glances as if she'd just walked into a bar looking to be picked up.

Except for today.

"Who is *that*?" Henrietta whispered,

pointing with her hair toward the lunch counter.

He sat on one of the low stools wearing denim shorts and a pale blue polo shirt. Maggie was being, well, *eyed,* she guessed she could call it, by a man she'd never seen before, a man with styled hair that was in need of a long-overdue trim, and was so perfectly tanned she wondered if he might be a has-been movie star summering at the seashore.

"I don't know," Maggie replied. "I've never seen him before now."

He turned back to his lunch and the two women sat down at the end of a table near the middle of the room.

"Well, we'll certainly have to remedy that, won't we, dear?" Henrietta peeked into her mink to check on her pet. "Thank you so much again, my dear, for taking care of Priscilla. I'll bring her by for a checkup next month."

"I hope we're still here then," Maggie said wistfully.

"What? Oh, dear, you're not leaving Cape Agnes, are you? Well, I'm not surprised, no, I'm not. This is no place to find a husband," Henrietta opined.

"Take my word for it, Florida's the place. You need to get away from here and find a good man." She sighed a tinkling arpeggio. "How romantic, running off in search of true love."

Maggie stifled a small laugh, and pushed a stray lock of hair into the clip at the back of her head. "No, Mrs. VanGee, it's nothing like that. Besides, good men somewhere in the vicinity of aged fifty are scarce as hen's teeth, and I'm much more interested in hen's teeth than men these days. They're more reliable."

The older woman's gray eyes reacted.

Maggie instantly softened. "I'm sorry. Did I say something to offend you? It was just my feeble attempt at a little veterinarian humor."

"No, dear, I was just thinking. When my poor dear Howard died last year, I thought there could never be another man for me. Howard was my third and best, you know. But, experience has taught me that I will find another. I guess I'm just one of the lucky ones."

"I guess."

"Now don't you worry, my dear," Henrietta went on without skipping a beat, "one divorce is nothing to be ashamed of. Look at me! I'm living proof. Two divorces and one widowhood. I'm not ashamed. I haven't given up the idea of marrying again. And you shouldn't either. For goodness sake, don't be depressed about that."

Maggie's mouth tipped up in one corner. "I'm not ashamed nor depressed about being divorced, Mrs. VanGee. My business, and that building, such as it is," she raised her eyes heavenward, thinking of the ceilings and the brown water stains spread along the lines where they junctured the walls, "take up all my time. That's just the way I like it. I don't want to get married again."

"Nonsense, child, of course you do. You have a grandson to consider."

"Tad has a town full of fathers and grandfathers," Maggie said, and tried her darnedest not to sound defensive. "He's very secure."

"How is the darling boy?"

"He's doing quite well. He's away at summer camp for a few weeks training to use a guide dog."

"Yes, of course, I suppose that's best," Henrietta said, nodding and not making eye contact with Maggie.

"Yes, it is. Blindness is a fact of life, and people learn to live with it every day."

"Oh, dear, is he completely blind now?"

"No, not yet, but the doctors have assured me he will be in a few years." Maggie busied herself unfolding a napkin. "I think this guide dog program is excellent for Tad. He has to learn to be self-sufficient. I won't be around forever to take care of him."

"You're still young," Henrietta said. "Plenty of time to catch a husband."

"Ha!" Maggie laughed out loud, grateful that Henrietta had moved the subject away from Tad.

"I'm over seventy, you know, even if I don't look it, and I expect to have at least one more husband." Henrietta kissed the tip of Priscilla's nose. "You should, too. Some wonderful man will just fall into your lap someday when you least expect it, and you'll want to be a wife again." She leaned close to Maggie and whispered, "Or close to being one, if you understand my meaning."

Maggie understood her meaning, all right. She marvelled at Henrietta Van-Gelder's stamina. Three husbands and prospecting for a fourth at seventy-four years. Maggie had barely managed one in just under fifty-two. If there was one thing she missed about having a man in her life, it was the *close to* part. Being close to one special man, connected to each other physically as well as emotionally and mentally, that's what she'd once longed for.

She'd numbed herself to the possibility over the last almost seven years since Tad had come to live with her. Sharing Tad's medical difficulties with a loving man would have meant a great deal to her, though how good she would have been at being a partner to someone over these last years was strictly hypothesis.

"That sort of thing happens only in fairy tales," Maggie said. "The knight or the prince rides in on a golden horse and saves the fair maiden. I'm not a fair maiden and I don't need saving. In any case, knights on golden horses are few and far between, and from what I read in the papers, princes aren't to be trusted either."

"Why, then, might you not be here, my dear?"

Maggie took in a deep breath. "We're being evicted. I received a letter from an attorney telling me our landlord—Dorian King, do you know him?—is turning the building into a fitness club. His son is moving to Cape Agnes to operate it, and he expects it to be a lucrative venture. We have thirty days, no, twenty-eight days to vacate the premises."

Two

"Pish tosh!" Henrietta bobbed her head to punctuate her words. "Dorian King needs more money like a hole in the head. Knew him in high school. Can't you find another place in town?"

"As far as I can tell there isn't anything suitable, let alone something I can afford. I believed Mr. King and I had an agreement, rental with option to buy. I guess that was a fairy tale, too. I suppose this is an unkind thought, but I visualize his son as being a directionless rich kid. Mr. King is probably just doing this to keep the kid busy and out of trouble. That isn't fair to us. I've paid the rent on time almost always, that is, when I wasn't broke from paying for all the repairs that he ignored. I've called him and written repeatedly, but he hasn't responded in over three years. My checks keep clearing at the bank, so I notice he's able to do that. And now this letter."

"Well, if you ask me," Henrietta said with an edge in her voice, "Dorian King is a swine if he closes Critter Care down, an absolute swine." She clasped Priscilla closer.

"I couldn't have said it better myself, Mrs. VanGee, but I suppose I can't say that to him in so many words."

"I suppose not. Priscilla will miss you, Doctor, and I will, too." There was a genuine note of sadness in Henrietta's voice.

"Don't start missing me just yet," Maggie said firmly. "I'm not giving up without a fight, that's for certain. I've worked too long and too hard to realize my dream. And Tad is happy here. This is home, this is where all his friends are. I will not uproot him and move to another town because of some rich kid's say-so." Her gaze shifted from Henrietta to a space rooted in another time, another place when she was a dutiful wife and mother. "Dorian King probably thinks I'm some weak female who'll meekly step back and let him have his way. Well, he has another think coming."

Little Bert brought a bowl of chowder to Maggie, gliding over with a smoothness that belied his girth and weight.

"Who is *that*?" Henrietta whispered to him, and motioned with her orange curls to the man seated at the counter.

Maggie stole a glance over her shoulder at him, just as he turned to look over his shoulder in her direction. By the deepening lines in his face and his salt-and-pepper hair, she judged him to be somewhere in his forties. She drew her gaze away quickly.

Bert shrugged. "Don't know yet. Hey, Doc, don't worry," he said in his gravelly voice, "things have a way of working out. If you get forced out of the King building, you'll get a better one."

"Thanks, Bert. You are ever the eternal optimist."

Maggie sniffed at the aromatic steam curling over the bowl. She was never surprised when anyone in Cape Agnes knew exactly what was going on in her life, or in anyone else's, so she didn't ask how

Little Bert knew her absentee landlord was trying to evict her.

Bert grinned and his mobile ruddy face fanned into countless pleats. His small gray eyes twinkled, and he blushed up to the dark damp hair that was plastered flat over his forehead. "Gee, Doc, you always talk so pretty. Must be cuz you're an actress. You know all them flowery things that make a body feel good all over."

"Just like you, Bert." She smiled with genuine care, then tasted the thick chowder. Chunks of clams and potatoes, the zest of garlic, a dash of nutmeg in the white broth, spread over Maggie's taste buds and slipped down her throat to warm her insides like a soothing embrace. "Mmm, gets better every time. You are a chef *extraordinaire.*"

Bert blushed again, snatched a white paper cap from his back pocket and plunked it on his head before heading back to the barbecue pit.

"Excuse me, Mr. Hubbard," Henrietta sniffed, "perhaps you didn't notice me sitting here."

"Couldn't not notice you, my dear Mrs. VanGelder," Bert said, turning back, bowing and scraping the paper hat off his head. "Dot's on her way with two glasses of your favorite. Fresh lemonade." He replaced the hat and returned to his pit.

"Speaking of acting," Henrietta turned toward Maggie, "don't forget auditions tomorrow. You are coming, aren't you? No Cape Agnes Community Players production would be the same without you in a leading role. You have such a lovely voice, dear."

A former stage actress, Henrietta directed the local theater group's annual summer production. From her own strictly amateur viewpoint, Maggie enjoyed working in the shows with her, for Henrietta approached them with as much professionalism as if they were Broadway-bound.

"I'll be there, but I'm not sure how much heart I have for it this year. Have you decided what show you want to do?"

Henrietta smiled broadly. "Yes, indeed. But I want it to be a surprise. It's going to be just wonderful, wait and see. The best production we've ever done. It'll do you good to be in it. Take your mind off unpleasant things."

Dottie rushed over with two tall blue plastic glasses filled with lemonade, and sat down on the picnic bench next to Maggie, her long legs crossed out in front of her. "You're looking smart, Maggie. Howdy, Miz VanGelder. Welcome back."

"Who is *that*?" Henrietta whispered to Dottie, nodding again toward the man at the counter.

"Don't know yet," Dottie whispered back. "Came in about a half hour ago." Dottie's even-toned blond hair swirled up to the top of her head and was decorated with a polyester bright red rose.

"Miss Willet certainly does wonderful work with your hair, Dorothy," Henrietta said, scrutinizing the elaborate coiffure.

"Don't she, though?" Dottie said, patting the back of her heavily sprayed hair. The coils didn't move.

Roz Willet, Maggie's friend and owner of Hairoics, a beauty salon as popular for its social gatherings as it was for hair styles, took care of Dottie's hair arrangement twice a week. She proudly displayed a sign in her beauty shop window that said, "Home of Dottie Dearborn's Do." Roz often gently urged Maggie to let her "fix her up," suggesting how she could cut her hair and make what she called Maggie's best feature, long-lashed large hazel eyes, stand out. Somehow Maggie had always managed to avoid a session with Roz. She was simply too busy working from early morning until late at night to bother with makeup and hair fussing. More than that. She deliberately chose not to do it. With beauty came a different kind of female responsibility that she didn't want to handle.

Dottie patted Maggie's arm. "Gosh, Doc, honey, I was so sorry to hear about you getting kicked out of your place. Mean son of a gun, isn't he?"

"I suppose the man has his reasons, Dottie," Maggie said, lifting the glass and taking a taste of the fresh-squeezed beverage. She sucked in her cheeks at the tartness that caused the glands in the back of her throat to contract. It was delicious.

"Don't they all, honey, don't they all? He should find out what it feels like to get his dreams yanked out from under him. What else can I getcha, Miz Van-Gelder?"

"The chowder looks delicious today.

I'll have a bowl for me, and an order of fried clams for Priscilla." On cue, Priscilla peeked out of Henrietta's mink. Maggie cast an admonishing look on Henrietta and shook her head. "Perhaps I'll eat them instead, dear," Henrietta added hastily.

"Pick up number four, Dottie!" Bert yelled from the barbecue pit.

"Right there, Bert, honey," she called back. "You just make the best of it, Doc. Someday he'll get his, you know what I mean?" She stood up and straightened her short skirt and checked to see that her panty hose hadn't bagged.

"Yeah, I know what you mean, Dottie." Maggie smiled as the waitress walked away.

A trim little man with wiry steel-gray hair and sharp, small, dark eyes sat down opposite Maggie. "Jolene told me you came over here for lunch, Colleague." He leaned over and planted a kiss on the older woman's cheek. "Welcome back, Henrietta."

Elmer Everett, a veterinarian who'd welcomed the chance to come out of retirement to work with Critter Care, always referred to Maggie as "Colleague." She'd come to adore him, even though he'd made it quite clear in the beginning he didn't think a woman had strength and stamina enough to be in veterinary medicine. He'd said he knew he couldn't trust her not to go all squeamish over the sight of blood and worse things. He'd been in the animal doctoring business, as he called it, for almost half a century and wasn't about to leave helpless animals in the care of these new veterinarians who were as wet behind the ears as a cow's nose. He'd been stern with her in the clinic, always checking her notes and questioning the reasons she chose one treatment over another. She loved discussing things with him, and knew he enjoyed playing the role of teacher. It had taken over three years, but Elmer had come around and now showed his respect for Maggie's abilities.

"Elmer, you're looking fit," Henrietta observed the man who was a good three or four years her junior, openly appreciating his stature. She leaned toward him, motioning in the direction of the man at the counter. "Who is *that*?"

"I take care of myself," Elmer said without a hint of smugness, his eyes bright. "Been on this earth longer'n I ever figured, so it's best I stayed healthy." He swung his head over his shoulder and read the daily lunch specials scrawled on the blackboard over the counter, then turned back to the women. "Don't know, don't care. Doesn't look like anybody I wanta know either," he said, referring to Henrietta's last question. "I'll wager his hair wouldn't move one whit in a good nor'easter."

Elmer smiled at Dottie when she came to the table and ordered his usual tuna salad on whole wheat, no extra mayonnaise on the bread, no potato chips, and an iced tea. Maggie sensed Elmer rather fancied Dottie, even though there was at least a twenty-year age difference between them, and the divorced Dottie never lacked for dates. She smiled inwardly. Everyone deserved to indulge in fantasy.

"Jolene said you'd be here," Lloyd Fitchen said, tapping Maggie on the shoulder. "Nice to see you again, Henrietta," he added, removing his United States Postal Service regulation cap.

"Who is *that?*" Henrietta whispered, cocking her head toward the counter. "Mailmen know everybody."

Lloyd took a long moment scrutinizing the man's back. "Don't know yet," he whispered. "Didn't see any mail for anybody new in town. Maybe he's just passing through. If he stays, you can bet I'll know who he is in twenty-four hours." He dropped his heavy mailbag at Maggie's feet, rummaged through it and came out with two envelopes and the *Cape Agnes Flea Market and Express Bulletin.* "Thought you wouldn't want to wait till tonight for your mail. Looks important." Lloyd sat down at the table with them and made a big production out of reading the day's specials on the blackboard.

Maggie accepted Lloyd's special mail delivery. He'd been a postman for at least thirty years and prided himself making special deliveries when he thought customers might want to receive priority mail before their usual delivery time.

She looked at the two envelopes, opened and scanned them quickly, then set them on the table while she continued to eat her chowder.

"They're important, ain't they?" Lloyd asked urgently, then looked up at the impatient Dottie when she tapped her order pad with her pencil. "I'll have the Eggs à la Tom Sawyer special, but I don't like the yolks runny. Can you fix that?"

"Don't I always?" Dottie said, writing furiously. "Something to drink?"

"A chocolate Coke." Lloyd closed the menu.

Dottie turned toward the counter and shouted to Bubba who cooked out back, "Two on a raft and wreck 'em, and a Pimple Pop."

"Woman speaks a foreign language," Lloyd muttered.

"It's a unique language all her own," Elmer countered.

Lloyd ignored the remark. He and Elmer zapped each other on a daily basis.

"Not bad news, I hope." Lloyd motioned toward Maggie's mail.

Maggie blew on a spoonful of chowder before sipping and savoring it. "American Express has offered me a gold card. All I have to do is charge five thousand dollars over the next twelve months. I'm sure it will seem like bad news to them when I refuse. The other one is a second copy of the eviction letter. Dorian King must have a pretty thorough attorney."

"Now, dear, things have a way of working out. I've always said that, haven't I?" Henrietta said, slipping a fried clam into her mink cape.

"Yes, Mrs. VanGee, you always have. I'm sure you're right," Maggie replied over the unmistakable smacking of Priscilla's dainty lips.

"Nobody's gonna budge me outta that place," Elmer vowed. "I worked in that building when I was a boy. And my father worked in the net business in there. And now it's my home. No, sir. I'm not budging."

"I've pledged to deliver the mail through snow and sleet and gloom of night, even if it's bad news," Lloyd said with a sad note of apology in his voice.

"You're all the dearest people," Maggie said, and knew if she didn't concentrate on her chowder she would start to cry.

The group shared lunch and conversation. Maggie dabbed at her mouth with a paper napkin, and looked at her watch.

"Well, I guess I should be getting back. Jolene will be sending Chief Fisbee to find me next." She stood up and slid around the end of the picnic bench.

"Well, then, I'll see you tomorrow at the auditions, Doctor," Henrietta said. "Do have a pleasant evening."

"Same to you. You, too, Priscilla. And thanks for treating me to lunch, Mrs. VanGee. I feel miraculously restored." Maggie started toward the door.

"Wait, dear." Henrietta tugged at her arm. Maggie bent down. "As soon as you find out who *that* is," she said with a toss of her curls toward the lunch counter, "do let me know, won't you?"

"Oh, absolutely." Maggie winked at her, wondering if Henrietta already had her eye on the new man in town.

She could admit that the new man in town certainly had his eye on Maggie as she left Mother Hubbard's Cupboard.

"I hope that's it for the day." Maggie let out a tired sigh and handed the last patient's records over the counter to Jolene. She closed her eyes and rubbed the back of her neck. "It's been one of the busiest days I can remember."

There was no response from the receptionist who stood motionless behind the counter. Maggie waved the folder in front of her face. "Jolene?"

"Who is *that*?" Jolene's gaze was fixed past her into the waiting area.

Maggie turned in the direction of Jolene's glittering stare, and met a cool blue one from across the room. The man from the lunch counter at Mother's. He held her gaze until Maggie tore hers away and slid it down over his torso, over denim shorts, down tanned legs, past dirty canvas deck shoes to a black leather dog leash attached to a choke chain that circled the neck of a golden retriever. The man's tanned hand scratched the dog's ear in familiar fashion.

"Caesar!" Maggie had never seen the man before lunchtime, but she knew the dog well.

Caesar the Wonder Dog gave her a half-hearted tail wag. He lay on the floor panting heavily, his tongue flopping on the tile, looking very little like the courageous canine hero he had portrayed for more than seven seasons on the television series bearing his name.

At the beginning of every summer since Maggie'd opened Critter Care, Caesar had arrived by limousine, was deposited by a liveried driver, and picked up by the same driver the Tuesday after Labor Day weekend. No one ever paid Caesar's room and board, but she'd never had the heart to say no to his eager face when he jumped out of the limousine, clearly glad to see her, Elmer, and Jolene. Cape Agnes's population of children loved to visit him in his own special run in the back of the Critter Care building, including her own ten-year-old grandson, Tad.

She narrowed her eyes and raised them to the stranger's face. "That's Caesar the Wonder Dog. You're not his usual driver."

The man inhaled a slow breath and straightened his back. "I know who Caesar is. I even know . . . the swine in question."

Maggie felt the heat of embarrassment rise over her face at the reference to her landlord. Earlier in Mother's she'd talked openly about her eviction notice, a manner she found easy in the friendly atmosphere of Cape Agnes. Right now she wished she and Henrietta had been more careful with their words.

"What's wrong with him? Caesar, I mean."

"Hot balls," the man said evenly.

Maggie regarded Caesar for a long moment. "I see." She motioned toward the hallway. "I'll take a look at him."

The man stood. With great effort and a long sigh, Caesar pushed himself to stand.

"Right this way. Jolene? Would you get Caesar's chart, please. Exam room two." She led Caesar and his sitter, aware that he hadn't offered his name, down the hall, over the pile of plaster chunks.

"Looks as if the ceiling's falling down," he observed without alarm.

"Mm-hm," Maggie responded absently, stopping for a moment to look back over her shoulder for the receptionist.

Jolene had moved to the other side of the desk and, clutching a folder in her hands, stared intently at the man, blatant approval registering in her bright red smile.

"Jolene?" The receptionist didn't move. "Excuse me." Maggie stepped around Caesar and tapped the young woman on the shoulder. "Caesar's chart in number two, Jolene."

"Uh, yes. Ten."

"No, Jolene, two."

"If you say so. I think he's a ten. For an old guy," Jolene said dreamily.

The blue eyes crinkled at their corners as an engaging smile lit the man's face. Momentarily flustered, Maggie shook her head to regain composure, then continued down the hallway to the exam room. "Lift him up on the table," Maggie said to him over her shoulder. "Roll him onto his back, spread his legs, and hold him down."

She heard the man groan and the breath go out of him as he lifted the hefty dog up onto the table. With her back to him, Maggie did her best to concentrate on going over Caesar's chart. There was something disconcerting about all this, this unknown man with a known dog star, and Caesar's hot balls. "Testicular inflammation," she wrote on his chart.

Maggie drew in a deep settling breath and turned around. The breath caught in her throat. Caesar lay on his back on the stainless steel table with the man's hands securing his front paws up over his head and flat like a wrestler holding his opponent down for the count. Caesar clamped his hindquarters together and shifted to one hip. His head flopped to the side, and his red tongue vibrated on the examination table as he panted. Clearly the dog was not enjoying the indignity of the moment.

"What is it you're doing?" Maggie worked to control her surprise.

"Holding him down with his legs spread like you instructed," he responded as if she should know perfectly well what he was doing.

"I thought you said he had—"

"Hot balls. A whole bag of 'em. I think he's got a third-degree burn on his tongue."

Maggie lowered her eyes quickly and studiously stared at Caesar's pitiful face.

"Tongue? Hot . . . you mean he . . . ingested *candy*?"

"Right." He inclined his head and eyed her, a grin tilting one corner of his mouth. "Has there been some sort of misunderstanding here?"

Maggie composed herself. "No, no, of coursé not."

She bent over Caesar and patted his head. His great brown eyes looked up at her with pathetic dejectedness, and she murmured soothing words to him. She put a stethoscope to his chest. Satisfied that his heart rate was in normal range given the extent of his discomfort, she dropped the instrument, letting it hang suspended from around her neck, and picked up Caesar's inflamed tongue. Her examination showed it was swollen and probably quite sore, but not severely injured.

"Is it . . . *terminal*, Doctor?" There was a smile behind his obviously feigned deep concern.

She straightened. "He'll live, but that's a mean irritation he's got there. I'll flush his mouth with sodium bicarbonate and water. That should take some of the heat out of it. You shouldn't give candy to a dog, you know."

"I didn't give it to him. He has a nasty habit of taking things from people."

"From you?"

"Yes. That stuff never affected me like that, though. At least I don't think so. Do you think you should check my tongue, too, Doctor? I mean, kill two birds with one stone, so to speak." When she didn't answer, he unsuccessfully tried to sound contrite. "Now, I hope I didn't offend you with my own attempt at a little vet humor. I thought your allusion to hen's teeth in the diner was quite good, myself. And then there was that poignant referral to a swine."

Maggie blanched. She leveled a steady gaze on the deviltry dancing in the man's blue eyes and lifted a wooden tongue depressor from her chest pocket. "Open wide," she said slowly, leaning toward him. A smile of amusement tipped his lips and he parted them and leaned toward her over Caesar, who panted even harder. ". . . and bark 'ah,' " she said, dropping her head toward the dog.

The man straightened up and let out

a laugh. "That's all he's been doing since the hot balls."

"I'm sure he has," Maggie said, opening and peering into Caesar's open jaws, "judging by how inflamed his throat is."

She opened the tap on the sink and filled a jar with cool water, scooped sodium bicarbonate from a tall clear container and mixed it into the water, then filled a dose syringe.

"He isn't going to like that," the man said knowingly.

"He'll spit it out." Maggie reached for paper towels. She opened Caesar's jaws, then squeezed the syringe, aiming the spray over his teeth and gums and the roof of his mouth, then around his tongue and the back of his throat.

Caesar spluttered and shook his head, then kicked out with his mighty back feet. The bicarbonate mixture flew all over the wall, all over the man, and all over Maggie.

"He should have spit out the hot balls," the man said, trying to keep Caesar pinned to the table.

Maggie blotted her face and the lab coat with paper towels. "He shouldn't have had them in the first place."

"I suppose not, but when he makes up his mind about something, there's no stopping him."

Maggie eyed him with obvious skepticism. "Funny, but ever since Caesar has been coming to us, he's been obedient, friendly, and generally a pleasure to have around. Frankly, we were surprised at how good he was, considering he seemed to be treated like an orphan."

"Orphan? Riding in a limousine? Some dog's life for an orphan."

"Was it your limousine?"

Her question went unanswered. He was struggling to keep Caesar constrained on the table, no easy feat considering how determined Caesar was to do exactly the opposite.

Maggie filled out Caesar's chart in great detail. "Will Caesar be staying with us as usual?" She tried to sound business-like. Who was this man? In spite of herself, she was suddenly as curious as everyone else especially about his connection to their beloved Caesar. And she was more than a little concerned about the dog's welfare.

"No. He'll be staying with me from now on."

That answer surprised Maggie. "I see. And where will that be?"

"Just down the beach, for the time being."

"Well, we'll miss him here at Critter Care. He was our favorite summer resident. Please call us if you'll be away and he needs a place to stay. Be sure to keep lots of water handy for him to drink. Bring him back in on Monday," she instructed. "Can't be too careful with a burn like that. You can let him down now."

The blue polo shirt strained across his back as he lifted Caesar and set the still spluttering dog down on the floor.

"What name shall I put down as contact?" When there was no answer, Maggie raised her eyes from the chart.

The man's eyes widened, then registered surprise, as the crook of his arm jerked straight out from the shoulder. Caesar, sneezing and lapping at the air, lurched forward, his leash taut, choke chain narrowing to the size of a shirt sleeve, bolted from the exam room.

"Whoa! Caesar!"

"Jolene! Help us!" Maggie shouted.

Jolene did not look up from her computer screen. "What can I do for you, Doc?"

Without answering, Maggie followed the dog down the hallway. Caesar turned sharply and lunged into the other exam room. He focused on a mop pail in the far corner and went for it. Dropping his head over the rim, he tipped the pail over and lapped frantically at the spilling water.

The only sound in the room was the echoed lapping of Caesar's tongue.

Until the man spoke.

"Tyler King."

Three

Maggie turned to him. "What?"

"Son of Swine," came the even answer.

Maggie froze. The son of the dreaded landlord was standing beside her . . . and he didn't look anything like the spoiled rich kid she'd imagined him to be. He looked like a used-up forty-something-year-old.

"I suppose this is rather awkward, isn't it?" he said. "I mean, we've hardly been introduced, and. . . . Let me take you out to dinner this evening."

"Can't."

"How can you refuse?"

"Easy. I do not consort with the enemy."

"I wouldn't call myself your enemy."

Maggie ignored his words. "Well, I certainly would. Besides, I'll be spending the evening in the Suds 'n Duds getting mop water out of my clothes, after I wash sodium bicarbonate and dog slobber out of my hair. Now, the sooner I get started, the sooner I'll wake up and this whole nightmare will be over."

"Doc?" Jolene called from her desk. "Telephone. Mrs. VanGelder."

Maggie summoned an intensely concerned gaze and leveled it into his eyes. "Priscilla must have had a relapse. I must rush to her side. It's my calling, you know."

He looked at Maggie as if for the first time. Maggie felt her face heat. She wasn't used to reading the kind of frank appraisal she saw in his eyes.

"Doc, you coming?" Jolene's insistent high voice cut in.

"Excuse me." Maggie gingerly tiptoed through puddles to get to the reception desk. She picked up the receiver and squared her shoulders. "Dr. Logan here," she said in her most professional manner.

"So sorry to interrupt you during what Jolene has described as a most auspicious occasion, my dear," Henrietta responded. "She says you were occupied with a . . .

what did she call him? A real hunk, that was it!"

"Dr. Logan? Did you say Dr. Logan?" Tyler King's voice sounded surprised. Maggie turned back toward him. "Dr. *Michael* Logan?"

She nodded. "You didn't interrupt anything auspicious whatsoever, Mrs. VanGee. Is Priscilla all right?"

"Michael Logan? Isn't that a boy's name?"

Maggie waved him away, intent on Henrietta's message.

"Well, dear, she seems a mite peak-ed."

"Perhaps Bert's fried clams were a bit rich for her," Maggie suggested as tactfully as possible.

"Michael *is* a boy's name," Tyler averred.

"I only gave her one teensy little one. I thought perhaps a bit of filet mignon might cheer her now that she's more relaxed. What do you think?"

Maggie smiled. "I see. Well, all right, just a tiny piece, cooked medium well and sliced very thin."

"How was I to know you were a girl? That wasn't fair."

Maggie spun around toward Tyler. She clamped a hand over the mouthpiece. "Fair?" she rasped. "What does your father know about fair?" She slipped her hand away. "Priscilla's still adjusting, and we don't want a repeat of the lamb kidney episode."

"Oh, thank you, dear. Now you just go right back to what you were doing. As I mentioned earlier, you just never know when a *hunk* might fall right into your lap. I'm sorry to have troubled you at such an important moment."

"No trouble at all. Anytime." With deliberate slowness, Maggie replaced the phone.

"Well, it wasn't fair, and that's all there is to it. You tricked me. Now what have you done with my dog?"

"Tricked *you?*" Maggie sputtered. "What about the dirty trick your father played on us?"

"Excuse me, miss," the voice, rich as New England maple syrup, said to Jolene, "could you tell me where Caesar may have gone? In all the confusion, he's escaped his last watering hole."

Maggie watched Jolene search for her

voice, which seemed to have departed.
The girl was positively entranced with the
man who was about to evict them and put
them all out of work. *Youth,* she sputtered
to herself.

She heard another sound of lapping
and, sparing Jolene any further strain
and wanting to get Tyler King out of her
sight before she embarrassed herself further, said, "Rest room, third door on the
right, draining the toilet."

With the power in her arms of a major
league pitcher, Maggie shoved in quarter
slots and slammed lids closed on three
Speed Queen washers, thankful the Suds
'n Duds was empty at eight o'clock on a
Saturday night. No doubt every other human being in Cape Agnes, New Hampshire, attached or not, was at the movie
theater or the weekly dance at the community center. Maggie usually chose the
opportunity to do her laundry or go to
the supermarket then. She could count
on those two places being deserted, and
only now and again suffered questions

from concerned grocery clerks about why she wasn't out kicking up her heels.

Since she'd been forced to wash her lab coat and skirt after the encounter with Caesar and Tyler King that afternoon, it seemed a good idea to do the rest of her light things. And, since she was going to the laundromat anyway, she might as well take a load of jeans and other dark things, too. The whole laundry thing had just escalated. But then, ever since she could remember, Maggie always did mega-loads of laundry when she was upset.

And Maggie was definitely upset.

She reopened one washer to add bleach and watched her lab coat twist by. The pink-and-blue patchwork dogs and yel-low-and-green calico cats tumbled up and over, covered by suds, swallowed by water, then disappeared. Just like Critter Care was going to do, disappear among free weights and stair step machines under the direction of Tyler King.

She sighed wearily and sat down in a turquoise plastic chair, settling in for a long evening with her laundry. The back door slammed, and Maggie looked up. Harry Nordquist, owner of Suds 'n Duds, came in and dropped his metal toolbox on the floor.

"How-dee, Doc."

"Howdy, Harry."

"Fourteen's been actin' up. Just thought I'd take a look. Hope I won't disturb you."

"No, go ahead, you couldn't possibly disturb me any more than I already am."

"Thought so. Too bad about you havin' to move, Wish I could help."

"Thanks, Harry. I appreciate your concern."

"I'm thinking about changing careers. Maybe this place could work out for you."

Maggie looked around at her surroundings. "You're not moving away from Cape Agnes, are you?"

Harry stared at her for a moment, scratching his balding head. " 'Course not. I'm thinking about reopening the old roller skating rink. Kids like those newfangled roller blade things, but they're scaring the bejeebers out of the old folks on the sidewalks. Be a challenge for me. Something new entirely."

"I'll say."

Harry shrugged out of his stained tan

jacket, picked up his toolbox and headed for Speed Queen number fourteen.

She picked up a discarded newspaper tabloid. Anything to take her mind off her own current state of affairs. "Grand-mother, Ninety-Seven, Weds Neighbor, Eighteen. We're in Love Say Happy Cou-ple," she read the headline. *God, where do they get this stuff?* She supposed next week the tabloid would carry an update on the birth of the ninety-seven-year-old's set of triplets. Henrietta would most certainly find nothing out of the ordinary in that story. Love finds a way was her motto, no matter how unlikely the pairing to the public.

The front door opened and closed with a squeak, accompanied by bell tinkling. Tyler King stood next to Speed Queen number one, holding a cardboard box from Fritz's Pizza and Hot Wing Empo-rium, and wearing a dazzling smile in a clean-shaven face. Maggie's fingers froze around the tabloid's edges.

"Hi." His voice came soft and quiet, as if he'd interrupted her in the midst of reading Keats or Shelley. "I felt awful that you had to spend your evening in the laundromat on account of Caesar and me, so I thought the least I could do is come by bearing a pizza offering." He strolled toward Maggie, the box held out in front of him like a gift from the Magi, and stood directly in front of her. "Speechless with gratitude, eh?"

Maggie swallowed so hard she choked. She stared up at him until the tension in her neck forced her to drop her head. She drew in a deep breath and let it out slowly along with her words.

"You're about to evict me, turn a small population of sick and boarding animals out into the streets thereby endangering their health and ruining the vacations of numerous people, force three hardworking people into the ranks of the unemployed, dissolve a service that has been important to this community, and you think I'm speechless with gratitude? Well, I think your powers of perception may be out of whack just a bit, Mr. King."

"You're right. You're not speechless."

"Nor grateful, don't forget that part."

Tyler scrutinized her across the pizza box, and Maggie grew uncomfortable. With her damp hair pulled up in a ponytail secured with a fluffy white fabric keeper, and a few loose strands falling around her face, she knew her image as the efficient businesswoman had been compromised. She now looked like a plump aging teenager in faded jeans and a denim work shirt.

"You're really angry, aren't you?" He sounded genuinely surprised.

"She sure is," Harry said from inside number fourteen.

Tyler spun around and set the box down on one of the washers. "Who's he?"

"Harry Nordquist, the magician."

"He's a magician?"

"He must be. There's no other explainable reason why these relics keep working."

"That's the swine who's gonna throw you and your critters into the gutter, ain't he, Doc?" Harry's voice echoed with a tinny ring.

Tyler's head snapped back. "I forgot how quickly word gets around in a small town. Dr. Logan, on my own behalf I have to tell you that I'm as much an animal lover as you are."

"Humph."

"You don't believe me?"

Maggie shook her head. "If you're such an animal lover, what have you done with Caesar? He's probably home alone, sick as a dog—"

"He is a dog. And I got him a sitter. Would you just let me explain, please?" His voice held no edge to it.

Maggie nodded for him to go ahead. Even the son of the villain Dorian King deserved to be heard.

"My father told me he still owned property in Cape Agnes. He told me it wasn't making enough profit to cover the taxes and had become a burden to him. All I ever saw was the name M. Logan and the address. You must believe me when I tell you I had no idea you were a woman or that I'd be asked to evict the Peaceable Kingdom. Must be why he could never do it himself and let the situation go on for so long. Guess he was just an old softie."

"Softie!" Maggie sprang out of the chair. Tyler King was easily head and shoulders over her five feet four inches, but that didn't stop her from letting loose. "I thought I had an agreement with him! He knew I wanted to buy the building!" She was practically shouting, and when Harry peeked out from behind Speed Queen number fourteen she forcibly calmed herself.

"I was behind in the rent because I had enormous plumbing and repair bills to pay, bills that he wouldn't take care of. If I didn't pay them, the place would have fallen in on all of us, and I'd never get the plumber to come as often as he's been needed. Perhaps I did bathe Ada Luddington's Saint Bernard once too often in the old tub in the back. His hair plugged the drains. Drains I might add that were already ancient. Your old softie father constantly ignored my reports and requests for new pipes until finally everything was plugged, and then it backed up and spewed out hairy sludge and other unspeakable matter—"

"Whoa! I can't take another thing!" Tyler held up both hands in self-defense.

Maggie took a deep breath and settled her tense shoulders. "I'm certain you can understand now why I just can't think of your father as a softie." Her eyes suddenly widened as she caught a glimpse over Tyler's shoulder of one of her washers vibrating violently. "Harry, quick! Number ten's at it again!"

"Jumpin' Jehosaphat, I just fixed her yesterday!" Harry scrambled out from behind number fourteen. "Open the top so she'll stop!"

Maggie pushed past Tyler and grabbed the lid on the washer, lifting it open. It didn't stop. Tyler leaned around behind it attempting to locate the plug, and suffered a splashing forceful enough to soak his blue polo and dampen her shirt and jeans. The machine banged and clattered loudly, and water gushed out of the bottom of it, soaking their shoes.

Harry came up behind them muttering. Laughing, Tyler flicked soap from his eyes with both hands. He lowered his arm and accidentally hit the edge of the pizza box lying on the adjacent washer. It flipped open and sent part of the contents, pepperoni and all, into Speed Queen number ten.

Maggie leaned over the open washer and watched stoically as tomato sauce, cheese, and triangular slices of pizza crust churned against her lab coat and other clothes.

"Jumpin' Jehosaphat! You two get away before you really break it!" Harry reached behind the control panel and flipped something. Number ten simmered down to a halfhearted bubble, then churned to a halt. Harry turned around with a sigh. "She's gonna be just fine. Just her agitator gone kaflooey again. We all have those days, don't we?" Maggie thought he was sympathizing with her. "You'll have to empty her 'fore I can fix her." He shuffled back to his toolbox.

"Of course," Maggie muttered. "Perfect ending to a perfect day." She searched her purse for more quarters. There were none. "Harry? Could you do me a favor?"

She turned and saw that Tyler King had used his own quarters and already had washer number eleven going. He was busy transferring her clothes from number ten, examining each item for pizza remnants and removing any he found before dropping it into clean water. The sight of him easily taking care of her laundry stemmed the flow of Maggie's frustration, at least for the moment.

"Wait a minute, you don't have to do that." Her voice sounded almost apologetic, and she knew she had no reason for it. He was the one who'd arrived like a cyclone that was only now winding down to a zephyr. She walked toward him.

"Yes, I do." Tyler stripped his blue polo shirt over his head and held it poised over the open washer. They watched as a lace bra disappeared seductively under the bubbles. "You don't mind if my shirt mingles with your unmentionables, do you? I mean, it could use a rinse . . . and the stimulation."

"I suppose you're implying it would be mean of me, then, to refuse it such a simple pleasure, aren't you?" Maggie's face warmed and, in spite of her irritation over recent events, she felt a smile play at the corners of her mouth. Against her better judgment, she accepted his attempt to placate her with humor.

She stood still, wondering if his denim shorts would follow the shirt into the washer, then silently chastised herself for such a giddy thought. *Act your age, Maggie old girl, or at least think like it.*

He dropped the shirt. "I'll do the shorts another time." Uncanny. It was almost as if he had read her mind. "Now, since we have to wait for all this to finish, and our supper has been washed overboard, why don't we go out and get some real dinner?"

"Without any clothes?" Maggie asked, and instantly knew what it felt like to be a comic's straight man. She'd just set him up for a great punch line.

"If you prefer it that way. I usually try to dress for a first date."

She knew it. "I meant, you're not wearing a shirt, and mine is all wet," she said as calmly as she could muster. "And what did you mean, 'first date'?"

"Implying, of course, that there will be a second." He grinned.

"I wouldn't count on it." Dating was a concept Maggie had dismissed ages ago. Why, Henrietta VanGelder had had more husbands than Maggie had ever had dates. And besides, this was *Tyler King.*

"We'll see," he said, and winked. "My

place isn't far from here. I'll get a clean shirt. You can come with me and we'll find dinner from there."

"Thanks anyway, but—"

"You're not in the habit of going out with swine-in-training, is that it?" His eyes sparked with amusement.

"It's not that . . . exactly."

"Then what is it exactly?"

"I know very little about you, Mr. King, but what I do know wouldn't exactly rate you high up on my date material list. If I had one."

"All right. Maybe I can help that. First, can we please get to a first-name basis? My friends call me Ty."

"Of which you have precious few, I'm certain."

"Ouch. For a doctor you certainly know how to inflict pain."

"I'm sorry." Maggie truly did feel sorry. It wasn't like her to behave so un- kindly toward anyone. But then, she'd certainly never been involved in such an unusual set of circumstances.

"Anyway," he continued, "ask any question you want, and I'll answer it truthfully. Perhaps that will help you decide I'm not an animal killer. Fair enough?"

Maggie shivered. She was starting to feel chilled in her damp clothes. "Maybe. What about Mrs. King?"

Tyler smiled warmly. "If my mother were alive, I know she'd approve of my taking you out to dinner."

"I wasn't thinking of your mother. I meant another, more present Mrs. King." Maggie shivered again, and her gaze shifted to his third finger, left hand.

Tyler lifted his left arm away from his side, spread the fingers, and stared at the back of his left hand. "There is no present Mrs. King . . . not anymore." When she didn't respond, he continued, "So . . . there's no excuse to prevent us from having dinner together, is there?"

"I'd say there certainly was," came Harry's disembodied voice.

Harry was right, Maggie thought. How could she possibly consider going out with Tyler King? That would be something akin to treason.

Before she had fully made up her mind, Tyler took Maggie's hand and led her toward the door. "Nice meeting you,

Harry," he addressed Speed Queen number fourteen.

"We'll see about that, too," Harry answered, straining with a wrench as long as his forearm.

"I feel funny about doing this," Maggie said into the air as Tyler led her toward an early model gold Chrysler convertible. "I've just written a letter to your father explaining why he shouldn't evict us. If I go out with you, I don't know, somehow I think I could be making it easier for him to take further advantage of me."

"You don't have to worry about my father taking advantage of you," Tyler said, opening the door for her.

She slid into the seat. "Oh? And what makes you think he won't continue with his eviction plans just because I'm having one dinner with his son?"

Tyler shut her door, came around the convertible and slid behind the wheel. He turned toward her. "As I said, it's not Dorian King you'll have to worry about from now on. As it turns out, I'm your landlord now."

Four

"Thanks, Mrs. Kowalski," Ty called down the driveway to the retreating plump figure of Caesar's sitter. "I'm sorry to hear your daughter's not feeling well." He closed the front door and turned toward Maggie. "Sorry. Looks like I can't take you out for dinner after all. I couldn't possibly leave Caesar alone in his misery. What would his doctor say, Doctor?"

"What can she say, other than I shouldn't have left my laundry alone in its misery. Thanks anyway."

She started for the door, thankful for the opportunity to make a graceful exit. Her mind was still in a quandary over what to think of this man, and she was still feeling she'd willingly entered the enemy's camp. The short walk back into town would clear her head.

"Wait a minute." Ty stepped between her and the door. "Just because I can't go out doesn't mean I can't provide dinner for us. I'm a pretty fair cook. I'll just slip into something more uncomfortable and whip up a feast for us. Don't go away." Before she could answer, he disappeared down a hallway.

Maggie gazed out the living room window toward the small bay that curved inward near the back of the house. Front of the house, she corrected herself. Shore residents always referred to the waterside of the house as the front.

She let the tension in her shoulders relax ever so slightly. Today, somehow her faith in her own strength and self-sufficiency had been shaken. Was it out of fear of losing her business and career? Her stomach had done nothing but flop around like a dying fish from the moment the bell on the laundromat door had sounded like a heralding trumpet announcing the arrival of the king. And the thought of his polo shirt wrapping around her lace bra in the washing machine—even as she stood here gripped in the throes of immobilizing indecision—unnerved her. She felt ridiculous, like a thirteen-year-old with a crush on a senior football player.

That did it. She wouldn't wait for him to return. She'd just leave right now. She turned away from the window, intent on heading for the front, no, back door.

"There, this is more formal."

Too late. Tyler King came down the hallway smiling, barefoot, dressed in an open-necked pale yellow polo shirt and drawstring-waisted white cotton pants.

"The chef can now spring into action, effecting amazing culinary artistry, while you freshen up," he said, pointing down the hallway. "Last door on the left. There's a robe in there. You can get out of those damp clothes and lay them by the fireplace. I'll get a fire going right away. Feel free to shower if you'd like. Sorry about the mess in there."

Maggie watched him walk away, not waiting once again for her answer. She wasn't certain what her answer should have been anyway. In any case, what was she doing in Tyler King's house about to take off her clothes—she wouldn't go so far as to shower—with him preparing dinner for her? She made a mental note to contact the town council on Monday. As she walked down the hallway toward the bathroom she wondered what rights she was entitled to, and if she was compromising them with the unzipping of her jeans.

When she came out of the bathroom enveloped in Ty's white terry robe, Maggie heard a fire crackling in the fireplace and smelled a delicious aroma wafting from the kitchen. In the living room she set her sneakers near the hearth and draped her jeans and shirt on a chair near the fireplace, then sat down on a low stool.

She looked around. Even in its loss of former oceanside elegance, this place was different from her upstairs apartment over Critter Care on Elm Street, where in the winter the radiators sizzled with foul-smelling water, and where curtains, wallpaper, Tad, two cats, and herself drooped from the heat and humidity during the summer. This place had definite possibilities for comfort, if one were willing to put some hard work into it and had the resources to fix it up.

Ty stepped into the living room, holding two stemmed teardrop-shaped glasses between the fingers of one hand and a slim green bottle in the other.

So it begins, she thought. *First he plies me with wine, then a sumptuous repast then . . .* Well, she wouldn't let it start. The last thing she'd do is drink wine and let her defenses down.

"Wine?" Ty asked, his rich voice slid into her mind.

"Yes, thank you." *Too quick,* she chastised herself. There were probably rules about first-dating *in,* as opposed to first-dating *out,* and she suspected she was violating at least one of them.

He held out a glass to her, and she accepted it. She saw a look pass over his face that she could only describe as positive appraisal. And she felt positively uncomfortable under his scrutiny.

"Do you like mushroom omelettes?" he asked quietly, and the tone of his voice made it sound more like he was gathering information about her rather than suggesting a menu.

"Yes, I do." She wondered if she should be saying more than that. There must be stock phrases one used on a date so one did not appear too vague. Why weren't there how-to books for this sort of thing? Or support groups for women over fifty starting to date?

Caesar lumbered in and dropped his golden head into her lap. His soulful eyes gazed up at her, and he sighed loudly. Maggie felt relieved to have him break the tension she was certainly feeling. Tyler King appeared so damned cool and relaxed.

"I guess all is forgiven, huh, Caesar?" Maggie scratched his ears. "I'm sure you've been holding a grudge against me since the sodium bicarbonate rinse earlier."

Ty laughed his rich laugh. "He drank a gallon of water the minute he got in here, and he's sworn off hot balls forever. Me, too." He stood up. "How do you like your omelette?"

"Well-done. Can I help you with something?"

"I don't think so. I'll put them on now. Salad's been tossed." He left the room.

Over her glass Maggie's eyes followed his retreating broad shoulders. She sipped the wine thoughtfully for a moment, then looked around. The spacious house appeared as if it hadn't been lived in for years. It needed painting and definite repair, judging by water stains along the wood ceiling. Patches of thick dust, spiderwebs, and peeling paint decorated the walls.

The living room was scattered with furniture that appeared to be past its prime. Two chairs covered in faded blue-and-white striped fabric flanked the fireplace. A couch in solid blue fabric stood opposite the hearth. Large faded and frayed multicolored rag rugs thrown casually around broke the expanse of bleached wide plank flooring. Muted seascapes and botanical prints framed in driftwood dotted the walls in varying degrees of tilt as if they'd either only moments before been hung, or had been there forever without a touch of alignment. A lobster trap turned upside down and resting in a wood cradle served as a coffee table.

Occupying an alcove with a pine-framed bay window was a massive antique oak partners' desk, the top of which was strewn with books and boxes and piles of

papers. Sticking out of one of the boxes
Maggie could see several picture frames.
She lifted Caesar's head from her lap and
set it carefully on the hearth rug, then
went into the alcove for a closer look at
what sort of pictures the son of Dorian
King might own.

She slipped one frame out, then another. College and law school degrees.
The last one piqued her curiosity the
most. Tyler King was a partner in a firm
that specialized in entertainment law.

Then, what the heck was he doing setting up a fitness center?

Ty came around the door from the
kitchen. He watched Maggie explore the
room, watched her body move inside his
robe. *Don't even think about it,* he cautioned himself. *That would be moving like
a bullet train on a cog track.*

She looked lovely to him in her un-
adorned way. Refreshing. He remembered how his wife, the reed-thin Sylvie,
was always perfectly groomed. Perfect
makeup, perfect hair, perfect cut to her
clothes right down to a fuchsia designer
sweat-suit in which she hadn't sweated a
drop. She was always dressed perfectly,

even on the rare occasions when she went to the market.

That was Sylvie. Perfect everything. Everything perfect. Now he knew nothing had ever been perfect, or if it had been, then perfect wasn't something he wanted anymore.

"Come and get it!" he said loudly, and startled himself. He turned quickly and went back to the kitchen.

Maggie drew away from her study of his college credentials, and padded barefoot behind him.

While the living room exuded a haphazard air, the kitchen was a cozy, organized contrast. With its arrangement of appliances, cutlery, and cutting boards, cast-iron pots and cookware hanging from a globe-shaped wrought iron framework over a butcher block topped island, it made a blatant statement that the person who assembled it loved to cook, loved living in the kitchen.

A round honey-stained pine table and four ancient Windsor chairs occupied the center of a curved expanse of windows overlooking the Atlantic. Overhead, an electrified wood chandelier flickered a muted glow from its candle-shaped bulbs onto sea-blue place mats that served as backdrops for old black-handled flatware and unmatched clear glass salad bowls. White stoneware plates held an inviting half round of omelette.

He arranged a bouquet of parsley garnished with cherry tomatoes on each plate. "My grandmother used to call these love apples," he said.

She thought she detected a provocative tone in his voice. Maybe it wasn't. How would she recognize provocative, anyway?

He refilled the wine glasses, then held the chair for her. So he was as gallant as he was a smooth-talker. She was becoming almost giddy, and it had nothing to do with the wine. She'd been without a man in her life much too long, that was it. Maybe she could ask Harry Nordquist to go to the dance one of these Saturday nights sometime. Not that she was attracted to Harry. It was just that he was, well, *safe*.

"This is a nice house. Or it could be with some work. Is it yours, too?" she asked conversationally.

He paused a moment before answering. "In a way," he said cryptically. "The furniture and all the pots and pans and dishes are mine, though."

She cut into her omelette.

"Is your father's property the only reason you came to Cape Agnes?" She took a bite of omelette and was surprised at the delicate hand in the taste of herbs.

"I was born here. I wondered what it would feel like to go home again." He swallowed a chunk of tomato and watched her through the low light.

Maggie swallowed. "Really? I was born here, too. By the way, you're a pretty good cook."

He smiled in appreciation of her praise. "Thanks. I didn't know you were born here. I don't remember you."

"I was pretty forgettable when I was a kid, anyway. All skinny legs."

"Did you go to high school here?"

"Yes. Graduated in fifty-nine. You?"

"Ah, well, you were going out just as I was going into eighth grade."

That announcement confirmed Maggie's assessment of his age; somewhere in his mid-forties. She relaxed a bit more. Since he was several years younger than she, there was no reason for her to feel nervous around him. She remembered in high school how her girlfriends always talked about the perfect boyfriend being two years older, and the notion had stuck. John Logan was exactly two years older than she.

Ty grinned slightly, as if he knew she was mentally adding up the years. "What brought you back to Cape Agnes?"

"Well, my dad died five years ago, and Mom was feeling lonely. Maybe you remember them. Irene and James Hutton."

"Hutton. The grocery store and bakery?"

"Mm-hm."

Ty smiled. "Your mother used to give me a chocolate doughnut if I swept off the loading dock in back of the store. I loved chocolate doughnuts."

Maggie set down her fork. "She made the only ones within miles of here."

"So you came back here when your father died?" Ty asked.

"Soon after. When I was divorced, and, well, I missed the ocean, so I thought I might stay and try living here again. She died a year later."

"I'm sorry. But it looks as if you got back on track after your divorce. I think when we're young we think we'll never make mistakes, and never believe that things will have the remote possibility of turning out badly." A sad note lingered in his voice.

"Divorce is painful," Maggie conceded, "even to the one who initiates it."

"I know," he said.

She studied his face for a moment. When he offered nothing more, she spoke again. "It wasn't all bad. At least I had my daughter."

"Ah, a daughter. I never had any children. How old is she?"

"Alyssa would have been thirty, if she'd lived. She and her husband were killed in a car accident several years ago."

Ty thoughtfully clasped his hands over his plate. A heavy moment passed between them. "I wish I knew what to say to you. I'm not usually at a loss—"

Maggie lifted her hand. "No need to say anything. I understand what you might have wanted to say. I am fortunate to have their son with me. Tad is ten now, and he's a joy."

"I'm having dinner with a grand-mother?" Ty teased with honest surprise and a smile in his voice that brightened the mood.

Maggie nodded, smiling in return. "Does that bother you?"

"Well, no, of course not. It's just that it's never happened to me before, having dinner with a grandmother. At least, not that I've been aware of. At least not one that wasn't my own."

"You'll note I'm capable of sitting up and taking nourishment by myself," she chided in return. Relaxing more, she dabbed at the corners of her mouth, using her napkin to conceal a smile.

"Do I detect a note of defensiveness, Granny?"

"Not in the least. I merely wished to assure you that I wouldn't embarrass myself by keeling over into the garnish. We grandmothers are a hearty lot these days."

"Consider me assured." He reached across the table and touched her glass with his own. "Now tell me, how did Critter Care come about?"

Maggie leaned back in her chair. Critter Care was a favorite subject. "When I was first married, my neighbor left his dog on a chain in the backyard and went off for a week. The poor thing was out there in rain and then heat and cried pitifully from loneliness every night. I finally climbed over the fence and brought him over to our house and took care of him. Turns out the guy decided to stay away an extra week. If I hadn't rescued the dog, it would have died of neglect and starvation. Right then and there I decided I'd provide a safe place for animals to stay the moment I could, so even people without friends would have one place they could take their animals when they went away."

"And when did that moment come about?" Ty pressed.

"We were living in Ohio then. Once Alyssa was in school I took a part-time job as a receptionist in a veterinary hospital, and took classes afternoons. And I set up a pen in the backyard and even built a small shelter from leftover lumber, and advertised that I would take in pets on weekends during vacations. My husband was against it . . ." Her voice drifted away for a moment. "Anyway, it took me almost twenty years to get my degree. I started working full-time at that hospital. And then, well, after the divorce I came back to Cape Agnes."

She rose and carried her plate to the sink. She'd been sitting there feeling as comfortable as an old shoe, but now she remembered it was only a matter of time before the proverbial other one could drop from the hand of Tyler King.

Ty pushed away from the table, and together they cleaned up the dishes and cooking utensils. Ty washed. Maggie dried, piling the clean things on the sideboard.

"Tea?" Ty asked.

"Yes, that would be nice. Do you have decaffeinated?"

"Look in that corner cupboard. I'll have you know I'm a tea connoisseur." He filled a kettle and put it on to boil.

He wiped off the preparation island, then turned and leaned his hip against it. "Tell me more about Critter Care," he urged.

Maggie took out two tea bags, decaffeinated orange spice, and dropped them into two mugs she'd slipped off a mug tree on the counter. Should she say more? Hadn't she said too much already, done too much to weaken her defense just by being there? But that's how she was, straightforward, nothing secretive about her. Her mother had once warned her that keeping mystery in her marriage was the way to hold it together. Well, it had been John Logan with all the mysteries, and eventually his secrets were what drove them apart.

Folding the dish towel and leaning against the sideboard, she once again found herself easily telling him about the pride of her professional life, Critter Care.

"I thought I could start over and figure out the rest of my life. I found this old building. The place had once been a net-making business, but had been long abandoned. I did some investigation and discovered Dorian King owned the property and that he lived in Los Angeles. I contacted him, and he seemed only too eager to rent the place to me dirt cheap. Probably because it was dirty and cheap. It was one big headache from the moment I unlocked the door, but it didn't matter too much to me at the time. I had plans. I knew I could transform it." She paused a moment, "And he did say I could eventually buy it from him. I guess I should have insisted on something in writing."

The teakettle whistled, interrupting what might have been a tense moment following her comment about Ty's father. She hadn't meant it as a jab. It just came out easily with the telling of the story.

Ty moved to the stove and poured hot water into the mugs. Maggie pulled a chair out and sat down at the table. Ty sat down across from her and handed her a mug of tea. "It looks as if you did a pretty good job on the building for the most part," he said, ignoring the comment about his father.

"I did all the cleaning and painting myself," she said with pride, "but I did hire two local carpenters to build the examination rooms and the boarding units, and to do some repair work on the upstairs for a couple of small apartments."

"Is that where you live?"

She nodded. "I have a wonderful part-

time veterinarian working with me. Elmer Everett. He has the other apartment
in the building."

"I think I may have seen him in the
restaurant."

"Yes, you did. He retired from his own
city practice some years ago. I guess he
was bored because he asked to come into
the business with me. He doesn't do big-
time surgery anymore, but he's wonderful with the everyday shots and small
injuries or digestive problems. And he
has a special place in his heart for that
old building. It's meant a great deal to
him to have something to wake up for in
the morning. He's a widower, has a
daughter who lives on the West Coast. He
doesn't want to live with her and he
doesn't want to live in a senior citizen
home. His older brother is in a nursing
home up in Sea View, and that's the last
place he ever wants to have to live. Critter
Care has kept him productive and wage-
earning. Besides, he enjoys arguing with
me over certain newfangled treatments,
as he calls them. Neither of us would give
that up for anything."

"You really care about him, don't you?"

She smiled. "He's very special."

"Well, I had no idea a trip to the laundromat could have such an interesting outcome."

"Oh my God!" Maggie sat up straight. "I forgot all about the laundromat! Harry won't know what to do with my clothes."

"Don't worry. We'll get them later."

"We won't be able to. He locks up at ten. It must be close to that now."

Ty checked his watch. "It's ten-thirty."

"I'd better go." She started down the hall for the living room where she'd left her clothes.

"And do what? If you can't get your laundry out of there until tomorrow, what's your hurry?"

Maggie stopped and thought a moment. "What about your shirt?"

"I'm sure it's been having as enjoyable a time as I have." He sent her another provocative smile.

Maggie felt her face warm. "Well, everything's going to be a mess. And I'll need my lab coat tomorrow."

"And it is charming. All those little cats and dogs cavorting all over it. Very tasteful. And most appropriate, of course."

"You're kidding, of course."

"No, actually I meant that. I've never seen a coat quite like it. It's very different, just like you."

Maggie flushed uncustomarily. "And you? What's an entertainment lawyer doing opening a fitness center? Have you been defrocked or something?"

Ty's jaw twitched. She certainly was direct. And curious enough to have discovered his past profession. "I think you mean disbarred."

"Whatever. Were you?"

"Actually I chose to leave the profession."

"Why?"

"Got sick of all that bickering."

"You mean between clients?"

"Yes, and between my wife and me. After the divorce I decided I'd had enough marital squabbling, and legal squabbling, and any other kind of squabbling, so I sold my quarter of the practice. Cape Agnes doesn't have a fitness center, and I figured I might just as well jump onto the trendy bandwagon and bring one to town. I figured it would be an easy way to make a living."

"Easy," Maggie said evenly. "Well, it's not easy for me to get out of that building." She frowned and sniffed the air. "Did you leave something on the stove?"

"No."

"Well, something's burning."

Ty sniffed. "Yep, something definitely is burning. Smells rather like roasting denim to me."

Maggie tore into the living room. "Oh my God! My jeans! How could that happen? I'm sure I hung them far enough away from the fireplace."

Caesar rose from the hearth rug and sat back on his haunches, hanging his head low.

Ty grabbed the smoldering jeans and pulled them onto the stone hearth. "I think we have the culprit; red-pawed, so to speak."

"Caesar? No-o-o, he couldn't . . . ." Maggie stopped. Caesar had, after all, dragged a trapped child from a burning log cabin in his hit series show, "Caesar, the Wonder Dog on the Frontier." But everyone knew television shows were rigged to look that way, of course. Could he have remembered that show and just reversed the action to get back at her for the sodium bicarbonate dousing? No, he wasn't smart enough to be that devious. Was he?

Ty patted Caesar's head. "Sorry. These things will happen. Naughty boy, Caesar." He pointed an admonishing finger toward the dog, but Maggie saw the twinkle in his eyes and the half smile that told Caesar his master wasn't angry with him.

"Well, it seems I don't have any jeans to wear now. I can't exactly go strolling home in your bathrobe."

"Don't worry, I'll drive you home."

"Great. And we'll be the talk of the town in the diner tomorrow morning."

He shrugged. "Has strong possibilities for my reputation." When she shot him an exasperated look, he made an attempt to act serious.

Maggie pressed her fingers to her forehead. "Oh no, I just remembered where my keys are."

"Where?"

"In the pocket of my lab coat. Now they're probably sitting at the bottom of a Speed Queen."

"Oh no," he said without a trace of sympathy.

"That didn't sound very distressed."

"It's not.' You'll just have to stay here tonight. You can get your keys in the morning when Harry opens."

"I can't stay here," Maggie said, aghast.

"Why not? It's not exactly a rat-infested dump."

"I'll call Jolene," Maggie said quickly and scanned the room for a phone. She spotted one on his desk.

Ty shook his head. "And explain your current style of dress? It would be all over town by tomorrow morning that I'd delivered you undressed to her doorstep."

"You're right."

"Well, then it's settled. You'll stay here tonight."

Maggie ran a hand through her hair. "I have a worse problem now."

"Pajamas, I know. Not a problem. I have—"

"Stop that! The problem is that I usually make a late-night check on the animals in the boarding units."

Ty nodded thoughtfully. "You still can. You can wear something of mine, I mean other than the bathrobe, and I'll drive you over there."

"But I have no keys."

"Hmm. Is it possible the animals will be all right overnight?"

"It's possible, yes, but I don't want to take the chance of not checking on them."

"Maybe Jolene could do it for you."

"No, she wouldn't know what to do if something were wrong with any of them. Then I'd have to tell her where I am, I'd have to show up like this or dressed in your clothes, and . . . how on earth did things get so complicated?" She started to pace in front of the fireplace.

"How about Elmer?"

"Unfortunately, he's away. Visiting his brother."

"I'm sure there's a logical way of taking care of all this," Ty said in an attempt to soothe her. He was serious now. He could see she truly was dedicated to her responsibilities in the animal clinic.

"The back window," she mused, "I'll just have to jimmy the back window and go in that way."

"Is that usual procedure?"

"Of course not, but neither is this, neither was this whole evening! About those clothes you offered—"

"Are you sure you have to go?"

"Positive."

Ty went to his bedroom and came back with indigo jeans and a dark green sweatshirt. "Here, try these."

Maggie disappeared into the bathroom and put them on. When she emerged, Ty burst out laughing.

"I fail to see the humor in this," she sniffed.

"That's probably because you haven't looked in the mirror."

She'd rolled up the jeans legs, but the waist fell down and rode along her hips. The sweatshirt grazed her knees and the sleeves flopped below her hands.

"I've got to go. Thanks for dinner."

"What do you mean, 'thanks for dinner'? It's a long walk into town, you know. And I'm going with you, remember? And I really think you should consider wearing your sneakers. The air's a bit nippy tonight."

Maggie looked down at her toes sticking out from under the rolled legs of Ty's jeans. "Okay, you're right about the sneakers, but you're not going with me."

"Of course I am. Who do you think is going to drive you into town? Besides, I feel a responsibility . . ." He cringed when she slid a narrow glance toward him. ". . . to those animals. After all, it won't be long before I throw them all out into the streets, lock, stock, and hair balls. I'll let this be my last act of compassion before the guillotine falls on their unspeakably cute little necks." He let out a long sinister laugh and twirled an imaginary moustache.

"Not funny," Maggie said, and walked out to the car.

Five

"Here, let me do that," Ty said peering up past her legs while Maggie stood on his shoulders in the back alley behind Critter Care.

"I can do it myself."

"I'm sure you can, but the tread on your sneakers is boring into my shoulders."

"Won't be long now." She pried at the lock with the tire iron from his car. The iron slipped through her hand, and the end of it broke through the window.

"Should be no problem," Ty observed, "now that you've managed to actually break open the window. Should be a breeze to unlock it."

"Shh," she cautioned him, "we don't want to upset the animals." She reached in, unlocked the window, then raised it. "I'm going in."

"Right, he whispered. "Why do I feel like a cat burglar? No pun intended."

"Just boost me a little more," she whispered hoarsely.

He boosted. Maggie squeezed through the window and dropped to the floor.

Ty hoisted himself up and started to crawl through the window. His shoelace caught on the corner, and he shook his foot trying to free it. At last the lace gave way and he plunged into the room landing beside her, the weight of his shoulder pressing her down. He pushed himself up on his hands. "Now what?"

She straightened his clothes around her. "Now we go down to the boarding units."

"How many are in there?"

"Three dogs and four cats. Oh, and one guinea pig in sick bay."

"What's he in for?"

"He ate a goldfish and had difficulty passing it." Ty stared at her through the darkness. "Don't ask," she added quickly, "the explanation boggles even my mind."

"What happens if they all wake up?" he whispered after a long moment.

"They won't, at least not wide-awake.

Besides, they know me. They won't panic. I just have to be sure they're all right."

The two crept in tandem down the hallway. Maggie opened the door to the boarding units. The sounds of various tones of even breathing and one snore filtered out.

"That snore's incredible. How big is that dog?" Ty whispered.

"That's the guinea pig. He also has chronic sinusitis."

"How does anyone find out that a guinea pig has sinus trouble?"

"Ask Elmer. He's the expert on that," she whispered back.

Maggie picked up a penlight from the counter and went cage to cage, peering in, touching each animal to let them know her presence.

The snoring stopped. Ty listened intently in the dim light. "Did you wake up the guinea pig?"

"Don't worry, he can't bark."

A moment later one of the cats woke up and let out a bloodcurdling meow followed by hissing and spitting. The two dogs chimed in with halfhearted barking.

"What happened?" Ty whispered loudly.

"I don't know. I'll turn on a light." Maggie got to the wall and flipped a switch. The overhead fluorescent light hummed and flickered on, bathing the room in a strobe-like eerie glow. "Oh-oh, the guinea pig's cage is empty. He's got to be around here somewhere."

"Maybe in one of the other cages."

"Maybe. I hope not. Start with the cats."

Ty peered into the cat cages. The four cats blinked up at him, alert now. The vocal one was in the corner of his cage, humped up, hair standing on end.

"Not in any of these."

One of the dogs yelped loudly. "I found him," Maggie announced cheerfully. She lifted the hindquarters of a Siberian husky and extracted a black-and-white fluff ball, his teeth bared.

"Frederick," she admonished the guinea pig, "that wasn't nice. How would you like it if Sergei had done that to you?"

The guinea pig wriggled out of Maggie's hands and jumped to the floor, then skittered along the edge of the wall and disappeared around a corner.

"Oh no! Catch him!"

Ty spun around. "Me? How? Where is he?"

"There! He's headed toward the office. Close the door!"

Ty reached the door in time and shut it quickly. Frederick changed course and skittered past on his way to the medicine storage room.

"Oh no!" Maggie yelled. "Get him before he goes in there! There's a big hole behind the sink and he could disappear down into the cellar, and we'd never find him!"

Ty dove in the direction of Frederick, and made a connecting swipe. "I've got his foot!" he called triumphantly.

"Not good enough. Get the rest of him!"

"Ow, the little bugger bit me!"

"Well, at least you've got him."

"I think it's the other way around, and I think I need help."

Maggie got down on her hands and knees, and felt behind the cupboard to where Ty grasped Frederick's back leg.

"Don't let go. I think I can get his front legs."

"Hurry up. I think I'm bleeding to death. Have you got him?"

"Almost." Maggie puffed and reached farther behind the cupboard. "Aha! Success!" She turned around and sat cross-legged on the floor, tenderly holding Frederick in her lap.

"What's going on in here?" a voice boomed into the semidarkness of the medicine storage room.

The beam of a flashlight swept over them.

"Chief Fisbee?" Maggie called.

A big blue-uniformed man loomed in the doorway. "No, Fisbee's not on tonight. O'Toole's the name. I'm new on the force. I can see I've nabbed my first perpetrators. Drop that guinea pig!"

"Please don't make her do that, Officer O'Toole," Ty begged, standing up. "You have no idea what we went through to catch him."

"Worth a lot of money, is he? Well, you'll soon find out just how big the price is. Come on, it's downtown with ya."

"Downtown?" Ty frowned.

"He means the police station three doors over. Wait, Officer." Maggie got to her feet, holding the struggling guinea pig in two hands. Sergei started to bark which set up the Irish setter in the next cage, and the four cats joined the chorus with varying pitches of meowing and hissing. An overweight basset slept through it all. "Officer, this is my establishment," she shouted over the din. "I'm the veterinarian here."

"Vet is it now? Ha! I may be new here, but I wasn't born yesterday, you know," O'Toole said, leaning into her face.

"Not only that," Ty put in, "she's a respectable grandmother as well."

"Is she now? My own sainted grandmother would be spinnin' in her grave if she heard you blaspheme against dear old ladies like that, young feller." He stepped close to Ty.

"Officer," Maggie stepped between them, cradling Frederick, "I'm Dr. Michael Logan, owner of Critter Care."

"Michael? That's a boy's name."

"See?" Ty said. "I'm not the only one who makes mistakes around here."

Maggie elbowed him.

"If you're the owner," Officer O'Toole pressed, "why didn't you just unlock the door and walk in, instead of gettin' in the hard way? Those don't even look like your own clothes."

"They're not."

"Aha!"

"They . . . I borrowed them because . . . well, that's not important now."

"Aye, just as I thought. Probably got 'em from the Salvation Army. It's my guess you two are simple thieves. Found some rich old lady's expensive pet and aim to hold him for ransom." He leaned over and snapped a pair of handcuffs over their wrists, chaining Ty and Maggie together.

"Hmm, this has possibilities," Ty whispered seductively in her ear.

Maggie gave him another sharp jab in the ribs with her elbow.

"Come on now," Officer O'Toole commanded, motioning for them to move, "it's into the black and white with you two, and bring along the victim of the crime. Way I see it, I've got a breaking-and-entering here, and a possible animal-napping as well."

"Officer O'Toole, wait," Maggie begged, holding up her two hands cradling the black-and-white guinea pig which had fallen asleep. The other animals were still voicing their disturbance, but with less energy. "If you'd just call Chief Fisbee, he'll vouch for me."

"Can't do that."

"Why not?"

"His missus is having her baby tonight, and under the circumstances, I wouldn't think of disturbin' him."

"Mrs. Fisbee's baby's coming. How wonderful!"

Ty slapped his forehead melodramatically. "We're about to be thrown into the slammer and you're exclaiming over a cop's impending issue."

Maggie shot him a disgusted glance. "Officer O'Toole, if you'd just let me explain, you'd understand that all of this is really quite simple. You see, I left my keys in the laundromat, and . . ."

"And that's where your doctor suit is, I suppose." Officer O'Toole looked askance.

"Yes, yes, that's it exactly!" Ty offered with entirely too much exuberance.

"I knew it." The officer leaned close to his face. "She'd lie and you'd swear to it. March!"

Maggie and Ty sat on a lumpy mattress on a low bunk in the Cape Agnes constabulary's lockup, Frederick in a wire cat carrier beside them, waiting for Jolene to bail them out. Maggie sat glumly, elbows resting on her knees, chin in the palms of her hands. Ty lounged back against the cement block wall, playing an imaginary harmonica and making mournful sounds.

"What a day," Maggie sighed.

"You're telling me!" Ty answered brightly. "Invigorating!"

"Invigorating? Are you nuts?"

"You take everything entirely too seriously. You ought to loosen up more. I don't know when I've had as much fun." Ty meant that. He hadn't felt this animated with a woman in a long time.

"And you seem to take nothing seriously," Maggie said, dully. "You call this fun? First a sick dog, then damaged clothes, lost keys, breaking-and-entering, accused of animalnapping, and then a jail lockup—you call this fun?" she repeated in exasperation.

"Sure do! Most fun I've had in . . . a coon's age!" Ty chuckled at his pun.

The click of Jolene's high heels echoed down the stone corridor.

"Doc? Mr. King? What happened?" Her wide eyes fell on the cat carrier. "Has Frederick been arrested, too?"

"Jolene, thank heaven," Maggie breathed. "It's a long story."

"I'm sorry I wasn't home earlier, but you know, whenever Ray gets back in town, well, we, you know. . . ."

"Yes, Jolene, I know," Maggie replied wearily, remembering that Jolene's boyfriend was a fisherman who hired on with the big boats and was gone for days, sometimes weeks at a time. Jolene could be counted on to be unreliable for at least two days following his return. "Did you vouch for us?"

"Yes, but there's some kind of fine you'll have to pay."

"I don't see why. It's my place. I'll just have to call my lawyer. He'll make them believe me."

Ty King clamped his hand over his mouth to stifle another spate of laughter.

"Now what?" Maggie sent him a weary look.

"You're locked up in here with a lawyer!"

Jolene looked from one to another, bewilderment registering on her face. She shook her head. "What about Frederick? Do I have to spring him, too, or should we notify his owner? What did he do, anyway?"

"Accessory after the fact," Ty quipped, the corners of his eyes crinkling with amusement. "He swallowed the corpus delicti, and it was pretty delectable, I understand," he said in a Groucho Marx aside, twirling an imaginary moustache. "Then he tried to make off with the evidence by sliding down the sink drain into the underworld, the rat. There's a writ out for him now. You might say it's a writ for a rat!" He convulsed into laughter.

Maggie gave him a long, weary look.

"I never did understand legal talk," Jolene sighed. "What started all this?"

Ty laughed out loud. "Hot balls!"

* * *

"I sure wish I had as much fun as you did last night," Roz Willet said to Maggie Sunday afternoon when they'd finished their auditions and were sitting in the back of Cape Agnes Central School's darkened auditorium. "I went to the dance with Harvey Angell, and he's not as light on his feet as his name would imply."

"You sound just like Mr. King. He enjoyed last night to the point of euphoria. *I* didn't find sitting in jail much fun at all."

"Really. If you're going to have the opportunity to be locked up with a man overnight, you'd think Fate might at least shine with a gorgeous hunk as a gift, now wouldn't you? Getting your landlord is a cruel trick. No one has seen Dorian King in years, and to have him show up all of a sudden. Incredible."

"It was his son, Tyler. He has control of the building, it turns out."

"Well, if the son has as much money as the father, perhaps you could work his visit to your advantage."

"This isn't a visit, Roz. Mr. King is planning to live in Cape Agnes. He's decided to turn the building into a fitness center."

"Well, we certainly could use one." Roz nodded.

Maggie snapped her head around. "Roz! What about Critter Care?"

"Gee, I'm sorry, hon." Roz squeezed Maggie's arm. "That came out too fast. Hmm. Let's just think about this. When this rich Mr. King understands how much this town needs Critter Care, maybe he could be convinced to build his fitness center someplace else in Cape Agnes and leave the clinic alone. Maybe he'd donate it for the good of the people. Think about it. What rich man doesn't want to at least pretend he's doing good for a group of people who will tell him how wonderful he is? Right? You have work to do, girl. But you can do it."

Maggie ignored Roz's comments knowing reality didn't work as neatly and perfectly as her description. She flipped through a music score. "I hope Mrs. VanGee knows what she's doing this year. *Camelot* is a pretty big production for us amateur players."

"It's so passionate, though," Roz said,

lifting her black hair and letting the long curls slip through her scarlet-tipped fingers. Maggie knew her best friend was incurably romantic. Roz always dressed in frilly feminine attire, like the pale pink ruffled blouse she now wore belted over hot pink Spandex stirrup pants and pink high heels. She had the shape for it, faithfully working out in her living room to at least three celebrity exercise videos practically every day, including one with a step bench. No wonder she was excited about a fitness center coming to Cape Agnes.

"This particular production won't be very romantic if we don't find someone else to play Sir Lancelot," Maggie whispered as Roz's Saturday night date, Harvey Angell, stepped center stage and let loose with a perfectly dreadful rendition of "If Ever I Would Leave You."

"He's even shorter than I am," Roz added, "not to mention as big around. We need someone tall and dashing to walk in here with a voice like that guy, Franco Nero, who played Lancelot in the movie."

"In your wildest dreams," Maggie responded.

Roz sucked in a sharp breath. "Dreams have been known to come true," she said in a voice filled with awe, and grabbed Maggie's arm. "Who is *that*?" Her saucy dark eyes were pinned to the auditorium door.

Maggie followed her gaze, and sucked in her own breath.

"Tyler King."

Roz's head spun toward Maggie, then back to Tyler. *"That's* your landlord?" she whispered in reverence. "Looks like Prince Charming in those perfectly fitting pants over that perfectly shaped butt. Your work convincing him to leave Critter Care alone has taken a whole new turn for the better. I'll bet you'll be paying the rent in person from now on!"

"Roz, for heaven's sake. Did you forget he's here to evict me?"

"No, I didn't. But if you try hard enough, I'll bet you can make *him* forget about it. Brother, if I'd been locked up in jail with him you can bet I'd have stuck to him like a magnet to a refrigerator. How utterly romantic. Your landlord, unknown and detested, then a surprise appearance. He turns out to be knight-in-shining-armor handsome. The two of you, thrown together in dire circumstances, forced to share body heat for warmth in a cold leaky jail cell. . . ."

"Roz, really," Maggie interrupted her friend's flow of romantic musings, "I didn't know he was my landlord till yesterday. Not that it makes a difference now whatsoever. And it wasn't a cold leaky jail cell, it was an air-conditioned carpeted room in the public safety building. The mattress was pretty lumpy, I'll say that."

"Mattress?" Roz asked suspiciously.

"We *sat* on it with a guinea pig," Maggie added quickly. "In any case we didn't do anything about body heat."

Roz leaned back and scanned her friend's face with suspicious wonder. "I won't even ask what you two were doing with a guinea pig in jail." She leaned forward and whispered close to Maggie's ear, "He's so handsome, so perfect."

"Nobody's perfect."

"He could be if he'd let me get at his hair."

There would be no stopping Roz today, and Maggie hadn't the energy to try anymore. Roz's display of interest in Tyler

King was a reminder of herself when she first became attracted to John Logan. By his own and everyone else's assessment, John was very handsome. Her attraction to his appearance had blinded her in her naivete to his lack of real inner substance. Back then, she didn't know what her own inner substance was made of either. John didn't change during their married life. But Maggie did change following their divorce. She avoided giving any handsome man—any man for that matter—a second look, thereby avoiding emotional involvement with them. She threw the resultant frustrated energy into her work.

Maggie shifted her shoulders to relieve the tension that gripped them, and shifted her gaze to the problem facing them from the stage. Anything to get the focus off her last twenty-four hours. She and Roz watched as Henrietta VanGelder handed Tyler King a music score, watched him step to center stage. At the piano Henrietta played the introduction.

"If ever I would leave you . . ." he sang a false start. Henrietta's fingers lifted sharply from the keyboard. He cleared his throat, and motioned for her to begin again.

Maggie shifted uncomfortably in the auditorium seat.

Again, Henrietta went into the introduction.

Tyler King made another start. "If ever I would leave you, it wouldn't be in summer . . ."

Maggie held her breath. Beside her she felt Roz's entire body become alert.

". . . how I'd leave in summer, I never would know," he sang in a rich baritone. Then Tyler went into the rest of the song with an easy lilt that suggested he'd been playing Sir Lancelot for most of his life.

At the end of his audition Henrietta applauded. She got up and went around the piano and talked earnestly with Ty. He seemed to be gently arguing with her, shaking his head. Henrietta spoke quietly, persuasively. Ty stopped shaking his head. He shook Henrietta's hand, then turned and strode off the stage and out the side door.

"Do you think she's convinced him to join the company?" Maggie asked.

"It didn't look like he wanted to at first, but it looks like it now."

"If he didn't want to join then why did he bother to come to auditions?" Maggie wondered aloud.

"It's a way to meet people," Roz said. "You know how it is when newcomers move in to town."

"I guess so."

Maggie had observed how some people who first moved into town had a difficult time blending into the crazy quilt of residents who made up the population of Cape Agnes. It was not that they were unfriendly. Hardly that. In fact, they were so friendly that newcomers figured they were nosy or overbearing. She was glad she'd had no difficulty adjusting or, she guessed, readjusting to her return. She needed the townspeople's support as much as they needed her services for their pets. They'd welcomed her. How would they view Tyler King's return?

"I'm in love," Roz said, sighing loudly and sliding down in the auditorium seat, dropping her head back.

"I'm in trouble," Maggie whispered to no one but herself.

* * *

When she checked the posted cast list on the village green bulletin board Monday morning, Maggie's overnight intuitions proved true. She was cast as Guenevere, Harry Nordquist as King Arthur, Elmer Everett as Pellinore, and . . . Tyler King was to play Lancelot. The chorus and other parts were filled out by various permanent and seasonal residents, including Jolene and Roz, Lloyd and Dottie, Bubba, and Harvey Angell. Even Caesar was being coaxed out of retirement to play Horrid the Dog.

She checked the list more closely for handwritten initials. Those cast were instructed to initial beside their names showing that they'd seen the posted list and were agreeing to be in the production. Several members had been by early and signed. Tyler King's initials were missing. Caesar's agreement was missing, too. Tyler owned him. Caesar could do nothing without his consent.

* * *

That afternoon, patient flow at the clinic was slow. Two cats were protesting the flea dipping she'd just given them, and Dottie Dearborn's Doberman, Hans, was sleeping in an open dog cage. Hans didn't like being home alone while Dottie was working, so he wandered over every day around eleven and scratched on the back door. One of them would let him in, talk to him for a moment, then let him take any cage he wanted for his daily snooze.

Maggie laughed. Maybe she should put a sign in the window that boasted "Home of Dottie Dearborn's Dog." That made her think of Roz, so she telephoned to see if it was all right for her to drop by.

Monday was Roz's day off from the salon. Maggie always marveled at how perfectly groomed and stylishly dressed her friend was even when she wasn't working. This day she wore rose pink shorts and matching sandals and nail polish, and a pale pink midriff-length top. Her hair was piled on top of her head with a fringe of bangs over her black-mascaraed lashes.

"Are you expecting someone?" Maggie

asked as she usually did. She shrugged out of her lab coat and pulled her yellow T-shirt out of her white slacks.

"No," Roz said, closing the front door. "I'm hoping it's a quiet day. I want to learn my lines for the play and try to memorize some of the music before we start rehearsals on Wednesday evening. Come on out in back."

They sat down on a white wicker sofa on the back terrace and sipped glasses of half-and-half, iced tea and lemonade, that Roz had set out on the matching round wicker table. Maggie kicked off her white sneakers, slouched back against the sofa, and balanced her glass on her stomach with both hands.

Roz removed cat's-eye-shaped gold-rimmed spectacles which sported her initial in tiny rhinestones on one lens, and leaned forward to peer into Maggie's face. "Something's bothering you, Doc. Tell me everything."

Maggie waited a long moment before sitting up. "Nothing's bothering me. I'll take care of everything." She fussed with the front of her hair, then the sides of it, pushing it back behind her ears then shaking it forward.

"Take care of what everything that's *not* bothering you?" Roz tilted her head, assessing her friend's nervous action.

"Well, the eviction, of course."

"You're giving up? You're looking for another place?"

"I am not. I'm going to fight for this one."

"All right!" Roz clapped her hands. "I knew you would do it. This is going to be fun!"

"It's not going to be fun at all. I've been thinking a lot about it, and I don't want to take too many chances. This is the first real home Tad's ever known. He's gotten used to things. He trusts people. He'll need that as he grows older." Maggie sipped her iced tea.

"So what are you going to do?"

"Squatter's rights prevail. An agreement is an agreement even if it was verbal with Tyler King's father. I can't help it if it's with a different landlord now. I had no control over that, and no knowledge of the property changing hands."

"Yes, but what a landlord!" Roz sighed.

"If I were you, I'd find an alternative to fighting. I always think there are, shall we say, more persuasive methods to getting through controversy."

"I'm no good at those methods, Roz, you know that."

"Well, you could be if you tried."

"I'm not interested. Besides, I'm too tired to even think about the possibility of. . . ." Maggie gave her hair a hard flip. "God, this weather makes my hair so unruly. Look at it. Does anything it wants to. And it's so dull. I hate to count the number of gray hairs left after the others keep falling out. I'm sure the total would depress me further, and I can't afford to add insult to injury by indulging in the calories in Little Bert's medicinal chowder."

Roz studied her a long moment. "Then why don't you do something about it?"

"I am. I'm talking to the town council about what civil rights and options I might have."

"Since when did the town council go into the hair coloring business?"

Maggie raised her eyes to Roz's face.

Sometimes she wondered if Roz ever followed conversations. "Roz, what are you talking about?"

"You don't need civil rights, you need highlights." Roz stood and went inside for a minute, returning with a hand mirror which she'd grabbed out of her big leather bag. "Here, hold this. Now watch. If you got a good cut in your hair it would bring out the body and make it move nice, make it freer, sexier."

"Roz, wait a minute. I don't want to look sexier . . . or even sexy. I came here to talk to my best friend about my problems, to help me find solutions."

"And that's just what we're doing. It'll be a light copper rinse. Don't want to let the color become too brassy. We'll need to work on your makeup a little. What foundation are you using? I think you need a touch more rose in it. That would solve your sallow skin problem."

"I don't wear makeup or foundation. I hate that. Sallow? I'm sallow? That sounds almost more depressing than being evicted."

"Fine, then we'll use a tinted moisturizer," Roz went on, ignoring the rest of

Maggie's comments. "And that will also get rid of some of those tiny lines you're beginning to show. You should also accent your eyes more. They're a wonderful hazel with glints of gold. They would stand out more with the right eye shadow and liner. A girl has to use everything she's got to her best advantage, I always say. Especially when she's got a fight on her hands with the town council or a Prince Charming landlord."

"Roz, wait a minute. I'm not a girl. What I've got left doesn't have any advantage. I'm over fifty and that's much too late for a make-over. I can't—"

"Can't thank me enough for arguing you out of that ridiculous notion, I know. What are friends for if they can't help friends out once in a while? It's going to be a blast for me to help you out. Let's go now! I feel inspired!" Roz grabbed her arm and dragged her toward the front door.

"Ro-ozz," Maggie groaned. But she let herself be dragged. It would take a blast, she was certain of that, but maybe looking great in a public fight *was* effective psychological warfare.

Six

Maggie knew it was only a matter of time before Darlene Thompson showed up to take photographs of the *Camelot* rehearsals for *The Cape Agnes News*. Darlene, editor of the local paper, had never taken a flattering shot of Maggie yet. It was Roz's theory that it was because Darlene felt Maggie could be competition for any available bachelor in their age group who might just happen to wander into Cape Agnes. Maggie pooh-poohed that idea. After all, Darlene did everything in her power to make herself attractive to the opposite sex. Trouble was, most of the new members of the opposite sex who came to town had families, or were twenty-year-old college dropouts, or gay, or aging itinerant fishermen, none of whom was appropriate for Darlene.

Maggie simply had never cared one way or the other.

Roz spent the rest of the day trying to convince her she should care. By the time Maggie left the salon, she hardly recognized herself.

And neither did Tyler King when she passed him on the sidewalk in front of *The Cape Agnes News* building. Of course, she'd spotted him coming toward her and had slammed a pair of large sunglasses over her face and turned up the collar of her blue chambray shirt and walked quickly by. She'd have been safely around the corner if it hadn't been for Darlene Thompson.

"Maggie?" she called from the door of the newspaper office. When Maggie didn't respond Darlene called to her again. "Maggie Logan, why I hardly recognized you. What happened to your hair?"

Maggie stopped abruptly. She knew Darlene would shout even more if she didn't respond to her, or worse, write an item for the local gossip column as Darlene often did in a thinly disguised snide way: "Maggie Logan, the only DVM for miles along the beach, was seen strolling along a downtown street in jeans and sneakers sporting the latest in 'Dottie Dearborn Do' look-alike hairstyles. When greeted, Dr. Logan did not respond. Either the remaking of her image has caused her hearing to diminish, or the good DVM's ego has become as rigid as a fifty-cent roll of brand-new pennies to match the brilliant copper coils of her brand-new hairstyle."

Maggie growled to herself, then turned back and slowly retraced her steps. "Why, Darlene, I didn't see you there. Naturally I thought you were inside composing a thought-provoking journalistic attack on the senseless painting of 'Go, Aggies!' on the park benches perpetrated by the varsity soccer players after the final championship game."

"I finished that article last night," Darlene sniffed. She nodded her head emphatically, and her short platinum bob shifted forward. She made an assessment of Maggie's hair, walking around her, scrutinizing it, looking as if she were picking out new wallpaper for the bathroom.

"I had my hair done for the first time ever," Maggie offered tentatively.

"Well, don't worry, I'm certain it will grow back to your natural . . . what color is your hair naturally?"

Maggie gritted her teeth to keep from saying something she knew she'd regret later. She couldn't remember what color her hair was naturally. It was only lately that she'd noticed it was nondescript with sprinklings of gray.

To Maggie's distress, Tyler King had also turned back and was advancing toward them. "Doc, I didn't see you," he called.

Maggie could practically see what a field day Darlene would have with that comment in her column. Halfheartedly she waved to him.

Darlene flashed a diamond-hard smile at Maggie, which softened as it swept toward Tyler. "I'm so sorry we haven't met," she said in her sweetest Carol Channing gravelly voice and held out her hand. "I'm Darlene Thompson, editor of *The Cape Agnes News.*"

Tyler took her outstretched hand. "Glad to meet you Ms. Thompson. Tyler King."

"Tyler King, Tyler King," Darlene pondered. "Ah, yes. Dorian King's son."

Tyler inclined his head toward her. "Yes, do you know my father?"

"No, I'm sorry to say I don't. That's my loss. I understand he was a man of many assets and attributes."

Maggie knew that was Darlene's pleasant way of saying she'd heard Tyler's father was rich and fat.

"Well, you know how the truth can be embellished," Tyler said.

"Indeed," Darlene agreed. "But not in my newspaper."

On that note Maggie felt her exit was just about timed correctly. "If you'll both excuse me, I have to get back to the clinic. Have a nice day." She turned and headed for the nearest crosswalk.

She was on the other side of the street and heading down Elm toward Critter Care when Tyler caught up with her.

"Wait a minute," he puffed, "I'd like to talk with you."

"Some other time. I'm in a hurry." Maggie didn't look at him, but kept moving.

"I can see that. I'm positive you were

steaming at the ankles when you left the newspaper. Ms. Thompson seemed very curious about your hasty departure. I did, too."

"Well, you can read about it in Friday's paper," she snapped. "Look in her column headed 'Cape Capers' and I'm certain she will have voiced an opinion on that."

"What are you mad at me for? What did I do?"

She stopped and spun around to face him. "As if you didn't know."

"I don't know." He spread his arms wide, palms up.

Maggie sighed with exasperation. "Then go spend the afternoon with Darlene Thompson." She stalked away.

"Why would I want to do that?" he called after her.

Maggie kept walking and called over her shoulder, "And get a haircut, for heaven's sake!"

Late the next afternoon Maggie returned to Hairoics. Oscar, Roz's aging parrot, greeted her from his perch in the corner by the mirror. "Hey, baby!" he croaked loudly. Then, "Hey, baby." That one had a lewd suggestion in the croak.

Jan, the nail technician, was just finishing up with Edith Atkins, the mayor's wife, and Terrie, the other hairstylist was sweeping up a pile of bright red-orange hair from around her chair. Maggie waved to all of them and exchanged pleasantries.

"Did you work out this morning, Jan?" Maggie asked. Jan was one of Maggie's favorite people. Always taking care of others as well as rounding up stray cats.

"Until my treadmill broke," Jan said. She put the last stroke of top coating on Edith's nails and leaned over toward a low stand to snap on a pair of electric nail dryers.

"I don't know how you have the discipline to do that every day," Maggie said with a note of envy in her voice. Jan was married with a young daughter. She was a nurturer, and she nurtured herself as well. She took pride in her appearance, was always well-groomed and well-dressed. "I'm sure your husband will fix it for you again. He's so good at that."

"He says it can't be fixed this time, and I can't afford to buy another one yet. Danielle needs braces. I went back to one of my old Jane Fonda tapes, but it's so worn out poor Jane had white streaks across her face and mumbled her instructions. I sure wish we had a real place to work out here, like a fitness club or something. I'd be the first one to buy a membership in it."

Maggie caught her bottom lip, and nodded with understanding.

"I don't think Maggie would be second in line," Roz said.

"Oh, gosh, I'm sorry, Doc," Jan said with real apology. "I forgot about your landlord. I just meant that I personally would love it if a fitness center moved into town. In some other building, of course."

"I know," Maggie said. She passed a framed color photograph of Lucille Ball in her movie days in the 1940s and knew instantly where Roz got the idea for the way she'd styled Maggie's hair.

"You just missed Mrs. VanGelder," Terrie said, checking her own long blond hair in the mirror in front of her chair. The nineteen-year-old was just out of cosmetology school and took her work and her customers seriously. "She just went on and on about *Camelot* and her brilliant casting choices. Sounds to me like she's got her cap set for our new Sir Lancelot."

Roz turned around and looked closely at Maggie. "Hey, girl, why so glum? Henrietta won't have a chance with him."

Maggie dropped into Roz's chair. "If any of that were important to me I'd try to argue with you, but I'm too tired." She pointed to her hair. "I can't stand this, Roz. You have to change me back to my former self. Even my patients at the clinic can't relate to me. And I guess I must have scared Hans yesterday. He didn't come over today for his nap."

Roz turned the lights toward Maggie's face, then paced in an arc behind the chair, finger to chin, nodding her head as she patted and examined Maggie's hair closely.

"The color looks great. What don't you like?"

"Everything. The color. The curls. I'm not the copper curl type. I spent an hour this morning brushing it out and then trying to use the curling iron the way you showed me. Look what I got. I look like I stuck my finger in an electrical plug."

"Don't talk like that," Roz scolded. "Negative vibrations will only make it worse."

"Roz, my hair can't hear me."

"No one knows that for certain. Remember what Neil Diamond said. 'I am . . . I said.' We can't take chances."

Maggie knew there was no arguing with Roz when she quoted Neil Diamond.

"Cracklin' Rosie get on board!" Oscar piped up from the corner. When he wasn't cursing, Oscar spouted Diamond lyrics often, having been coached by Roz and the constant Diamond music wafting from the cassette player nearby.

Maggie looked in the mirror at Roz's reflection. "Oscar seems in good spirits. How's his skin rash?"

"Cleared right up," Roz said. "That lotion did the trick."

"It might come back," Maggie told her. "It's a symptom of his age."

"Bottle baby! Bottle baby!" Oscar squawked with what sounded like irritation.

"I should have warned you. He's sensitive about his age."

"Who isn't? That's no reason to be insulting."

Oscar turned toward the mirror and preened his green-and-orange feathers, every now and then tapping on the glass with his beak and tilting his head appreciatively.

"When's Tad coming home?" Jan asked.

"Not for three more weeks," Maggie said.

"Bet you miss him, don't you?" Terrie asked.

"Like crazy. I think the cats do, too. They sleep together on his pillow every night."

"Aw, isn't that cute?" Edith said, moving to another chair and placing her shiny fingernails under the nail dryers. "I commend you, Doc. Not every woman your age could handle a ten-year-old boy."

Maggie flinched. She didn't want to get caught up in defending her age as being less than ancient. "He's my grandson, and he's no trouble."

"Oh, I know, I know," Edith said, settling her ample hips into the narrow chair. "I just meant, well, his affliction and all. You're a saint to take on the burden."

"Tad is losing his sight. He's not help-less," Maggie came back, not quite con-cealing the irritation in her voice. She was instantly sorry she hadn't controlled her response. She knew she was right in doing everything she could to make Tad self-sufficient, taking him to classes on how to use computers specially made for people with impaired sight. He'd balked at the Braille class, but she made him attend anyway.

"All right," Roz interrupted, cutting the growing tension, "let's make it easier on you, Doc. How about letting me work you in twice a week like Dottie? That way you won't have to take care of your hair yourself. It'd be fun to put another sign in my window, 'Home of Doc Logan's Do.' "

"I don't think so, Roz. That isn't the real me. Just please do something about toning down the color, give me a haircut I can manage, and let it go at that."

"Whatever you want. Let's just make the real you a little better. But do me and your hair a favor and speak only well of it, okay?" Roz tied a black vinyl cape over Maggie, spun the chair around, and lowered her head back toward the black sink.

"What's the latest on Maureen Fisbee's baby?" Maggie asked as Roz adjusted the temperature of the water.

"Oh, I should have told you right off," Jan answered. "She had a little girl about an hour ago. Mother and daughter are doing fine, but I heard the chief fainted during delivery. Imagine that." She chuckled.

"That's amazing," Terrie said. "When that stray cow got hit by a lumber truck last year, Chief Fisbee didn't appear to blink an eyelash at the scene. I heard it was pretty gruesome."

"That's a man for you," Edith Atkins put in. "Good thing they can't have babies. They'd never get through it. Oh, before I forget, we've formed a new town committee and we need volunteers."

"Not another one," Roz said between clenched teeth. Maggie smiled.

"What is it?" Terrie asked, peering into the mirror and wiping lipstick off her teeth with a tissue.

"The Cape Agnes Historic Landmark Preservation Committee," Edith said proudly. "We've already started petitions to the state for preservation funds."

"Which landmark are you going to save first?" Jan asked. "The old lighthouse, I bet."

"Absolutely. Had to get that on the petition first before the state started putting down their coastal scenic highway. Would have gone right through the lighthouse," Edith clucked.

Maggie closed her eyes and let the chatter about the lighthouse and the new committee fade into the back of her mind. Roz's magic fingers worked citrus-scented shampoo through her hair and massaged her scalp. There was something so relaxing, so soothing about having her hair washed by a professional. She never felt this kind of deep relaxation when she shampooed in the shower every morning. Maybe she should let Roz do it more than twice a year, she thought. The massage took away troubles, concerns, if only for a few minutes, and made her think she hadn't a care in the world. She barely registered the sound of the musical door chime as someone else entered the salon.

Maggie heard the voices of the women laughing good-naturedly. She smiled behind her closed eyes. Yes, indeed, she really should come here more often. The camaraderie among women and their local beauty experts was most enjoyable. They felt free to discuss sex, local gossip, and world events. All with an unabashed female slant.

Roz finished with a thorough application of peach-scented conditioner, wrapped a towel over Maggie's hair, and raised the chair. Maggie opened her eyes. Tyler King was seated in the waiting area—directly across from her—scanning a hairstyle magazine. He raised his eyes and looked straight at her.

"I've always wondered what women talked about in beauty salons," Tyler said with a hint of mischief.

"I . . . I didn't know you were here," Maggie said, breaking eye contact and trying to recall if the ladies had discussed his effect on the town and on her.

"I wish you hadn't discovered me quite

so soon. I have a feeling the conversation was just starting to get interesting."

"That was mild," Roz said laughing and toweling Maggie's hair vigorously. "You should come in here on a Saturday sometime. You wouldn't believe what gets talked about!"

"I just might do that," Ty returned.

Roz turned Maggie's chair around to face the mirror.

"Just comb me out," Maggie whispered, embarrassed by her wet, vulnerable appearance. "I'll go home and dry it myself."

"You certainly will not," Roz said. "Nobody leaves Hairoics less than finished. I have my integrity and reputation to preserve."

"I have my dignity to preserve," Maggie whispered.

"Then let me help to dignify you," Roz whispered back.

Maggie let out a little groan of submission. "Just don't dignify me too drastically, all right?"

"You worry too much." Roz smoothed styling gel through Maggie's hair. "So what can I do for you today, Mr. King?"

"I was told to get a haircut. So here I am."

Roz made knowing eye contact with Maggie's mirrored reflection. "Wash, cut, and blow-dry what you had in mind?"

"Not that much. Just a trim."

"Mind if I make a suggestion?"

"Do I have a choice?"

"Stop using hair spray. Your hair would move more freely if you did, and would probably stop attracting sea gnats as well."

"That's what those things are."

"How is Caesar?" Maggie asked him. She was attempting to make small talk, something she was not good at nor liked to do. But she was definitely interested in Caesar's welfare.

"Much better. He sure can drink a lot of water. I'm a little concerned about what he's doing with it. He doesn't ever ask to go outside. I have to force him to go once in awhile. At least he's able to eat dog food now. He's got expensive tastes. All he wants is that Sirloin-in-a-Can stuff."

"It's not good for him, you know. Too

many preservatives and fillers. You've got to get him off that and back onto his diet meal."

"Yes, Doctor. I will, Doctor. Any wise words on how I can convince him of that, Doctor?"

"He doesn't need convincing. He's smart."

"You don't live with him."

"Just put the meal in his bowl."

"He snubs it and goes on a fast."

"I think it's possible he misses being at Critter Care," Maggie said.

"Ouch," Ty returned.

"I didn't mean . . ." Maggie started. "I meant that his summer routine is upset. It's in his best interest to eat properly and to exercise regularly."

"All right," Ty acquiesced. "You know best. I suppose it won't kill him to go a few days without food until he gets used to it again."

"Bloody murder! Bloody murder!" Oscar squawked.

"Oscar, for heaven's sake," Roz said firmly, "it's for Caesar's own good and you know it."

"That's some bird," Ty said, and

walked over to stroke Oscar's chest. "Polly want a cracker?" he said in a parrot voice.

"You shouldn't have said that," Roz told him.

"In your beak, buster!" Oscar squawked and spit a food pellet at him.

"He certainly is moody," Ty said.

"He's been a bit under the weather," Roz explained. "We all get cranky when we don't feel well."

"Well you don't know what cranky is until you've been in the same room with my husband when he gets indigestion," Edith said, shutting off the nail dryers and examining her polish.

"Have you met Tyler King, Edith?" Roz asked. "Edith's husband is Joe Atkins, the mayor of Cape Agnes," she said turning to Ty.

"I know who *he* is," Edith said with a knowing gleam.

"It's a pleasure to meet you, too, Mrs. Atkins," Ty muttered.

"Liar, liar, pants on fire!" Oscar announced.

"Some joker, this bird," Ty said feebly.

"Dirty bird, dirty bird!" Oscar squawked.

Roz plugged in a dryer and began blowing and styling Maggie's hair with a round brush. When she finished, Maggie's hair shone with the remains of the copper highlights and fell softly around her face just grazing her collar.

"You can still pull it back for work and secure it with good clip or a soft loop. No rubber bands," Roz instructed. "Breaks the hair."

"Thanks, Roz."

Oscar gave a low suggestive whistle. "Hey, baby," he squawked in his lewd tone.

"At least he appreciates an attractive woman," Ty said with a smile.

"Slicko," Oscar muttered.

Feeling her face warm, Maggie hurried over to the cash register near the door and waited while Edith Atkins paid Jan for her silk wrapped nails. She stole a glance as Ty took her place in the chair and watched as Roz brushed through his stiff hair. She wanted to wait and see what artistry Roz would effect on him, but was too self-conscious to linger.

She paid Jan, bid goodbyes all around, and left the salon, thinking that for some reason she was beginning to feel like a stranger in all her old familiar places. And that was more than a play on words.

Seven

Caesar was stretched out on the couch, snoring as usual, while Ty sat at his desk going over his financial picture. He ran a hand through his newly cropped hair. The haircut was a steal. It cost him seven dollars and he'd tipped Roz three dollars. Smiling, he shook his head. In Los Angeles he might have gotten a breakfast at a decent deli for that. Definitely not a haircut. All things considered, he probably should have opted for a meal instead of a haircut. Caesar snorted in the midst of a dog dream. *And some dog food,* he added thoughtfully.

He shut his ledger. His finances were bleaker than he'd originally figured. He decided to push Milford one more time with his new angle on an old case they'd shared, and dialed the number in Los Angeles.

"Look, Milford, this is business," he said after a brief stilted greeting between them.

"I told you before, we have no more business," Jaris said with disdain.

"You still owe me. Check your figures on the Simpson versus Simpson case. The way I see it—"

"Ty, old boy, you're not seeing clearly at all," Jaris came back into the phone. "Not enough smog in that burg. Your lungs are too clear, and you don't have enough on your mind to think about."

"Milf, come on." Ty tried another tack. "I know you're right. I don't belong here. I wish I could be back in L.A. but I can't. I'm trying to make the best of it here for the time being. You should see the place. Not much has changed from when I was a kid. It's a throwback to another era. There's a great rib joint here called Mother Hubbard's Cupboard. It's run by a huge-hairy chested fugitive from a wrestling tag team called Little Bert."

"Hysterical. Look, Ty old man, I'd love to chitchat about your regained youth all night, but Tiffany's throwing a dinner party for some rock music group she says she's managing. You remember the types. Long-haired and bleary-eyed. I have to guard the silver. Catch you later."

"Wait, Milford. Help me out here, will you?"

"I've given you my best take on the picture. Kick the horse doctor out and get on with it. What can the old guy do?"

Ty let out a harsh breath. "The doctor's a woman."

"Ho ho, all the better! Sleep with her if you have to. Remember those famous conquests of yours? Just kick in the old King powers of seduction."

Ty ignored the last comment. "She's a nice woman, Milf. A grandmother. This time it's different."

He knew he was losing his grip with Milford. He wondered now if he'd ever had any grip on him at all. He trusted him. Once. That was his problem. He'd trusted more times than he should have and been burned for his trouble. But he'd never worried about Dr. Michael M. Logan. Before now. It was just a name on a check he cashed every month since his father had disappeared. But now this Michael Logan was a living breathing hu-

man being. A female. Dr. Maggie Logan.
A compassionate caretaker of animals. A
grandmother. And a damned fine
woman.

"A grandmother?" Milford laughed
heartily and then coughed. "Same advice.
Charm the girdle off her. Sleep with her.
Grin and bear it. God knows she could
probably use something to jog her memory. Unless of course you've lost your
edge. In that case you'll have to find another method, won't you? Should be easy.
Just pick up the little old lady and drop
her in a rocking chair someplace and take
over."

"Put a cork in it, Milford. This isn't
your grandmother we're talking about
here."

"I didn't take anything I wasn't entitled
to then and you know it. You're entitled
to this, too. Face it, King, that building is
all you've got. You still got the watch?
Pawn that, too. And what about that
mangy old mutt? You trained him, you
made him a star. He owes you and he can
pay off now. Why don't you stage a con-
venient accident for him and collect his
insurance? The premiums are paid for

the next six months and you're still the beneficiary."

"Get off it, Milford. I—"

"Hey!" Milford shouted. He put his hand over the phone and shouted some more. "Gotta run, pal. Just caught some wiseass longhair groping Tiffany's behind. Guess I'll have to show him what he can and can't touch. My best and last piece of advice. Sleep with the grandmother or help the mutt rest in peace."

Ty slammed down the phone. Caesar got off the couch and padded over, plopping down on his haunches and settling his chin on Ty's knee. He let out a long sigh. It was almost as if he'd heard what Milford said. Ty felt guilty about it.

"Don't worry, old buddy," he said, rubbing the dog's ears. "You have to go out? Hmm?" Caesar didn't move. "No, I guess."

Ty felt like more of a failure now than Sylvie had ever accused him of being. Talking with Milford had made it worse.

"I sounded like a beggar, didn't I? God, I hate that. Milford eats that up. He always did. The lower anyone could sink before asking for his help, the better."

Caesar looked up at him as if to say he knew exactly what it felt like to beg. He'd been taught to do it as a trick. At least people said that Caesar was cute and smart when he begged. There was nothing cute and smart about Ty's last ten minutes on the phone with his former partner. Emphasis on the former.

Ty reached for his wallet from his back pocket and peered into the bill section. Mentally he calculated how much he had left. Fifty bucks more or less. Probably less than more.

He opened the telephone book and looked up a name, then dialed. He hung up before the phone at the other end could ring. Caesar went back to his spot on the couch. Ty rose and turned toward the row of windows that overlooked the ocean.

"Too bad your show's out of syndication now. No more royalty checks for us," he said over his shoulder.

Caesar sighed from the couch.

Ty turned around. "I guess it's my turn to work for you now, is that what you're saying?" Caesar snored loudly. "It doesn't work that way in your kind of show business, baby, you know that as well as I do. This time we may both have to put our noses to the grindstone."

Caesar snorted.

"I'm about to do something that will save both our hides, at least for a while. I feel like a low-down dog for it, though."

Caesar's two long hairs above each eye twitched, and he raised soulful brown eyes to Ty.

"Sorry. I didn't mean it the way it sounded, buddy."

He lifted his grandfather's watch from his jeans pocket and ran his thumb over the locomotive etching that had begun to smooth over from age and thumb-rubbing meditation. He flipped open the cover and watched the second hand sweep with a rhythmic hitch around the dial where a fine sketch of another locomotive could still be seen. A tiny diamond was set into the place where the locomotive's headlight would be.

He tipped the watch back so he could see inside the cover and the inscription he knew better than he knew much of anything else these days. "To HT from LT Dec. 5, 1924." His mother's mother,

Laura, had given it to her bridegroom,
Henry Tyler, Jr., on their wedding day.
Ty's mother had inherited the watch and
given it to him when he graduated from
high school. It and that old building on
Elm Street were the only tangible memories of his mother and her family, his
namesakes, that he had left. The watch
probably was worth a lot in monetary
value, Milford had told him that on numerous occasions. In all the years he'd
carried it, Ty had never once thought of
the memento in terms of the money it
might bring.

He turned it over. The hinge was still
good, the stem in working order.

No. He wasn't that desperate. Yet.

There was still the building. Once that
whole section of the village had been
called the Henry Tyler Block, after his
great-grandfather, one of the first set-
tlers in Cape Agnes. It had been called
Tylerville then, but when Henry's beloved wife died, the residents simply decided to name it after her. They could
do things simply, back then, Tyler
mused. These days everything was more
difficult.

He owned the building now. He had issued an eviction notice to the tenants. That was before he met them. Maggie and Dr. Everett were nice people. So what? Business had nothing to do with nice people. He'd learned that from his father, and he'd practiced that theory in his own career. Yet, here he was, back in his hometown, choking on the theory. Was it because he'd been born here? Maybe all that nice people stuff had rubbed off on him.

Nah.

He leaned over and dialed the phone again. This time he didn't hang up when the ring at the other end came through.

"Henrietta VanGelder here," came the voice at the other end.

"Mrs. VanGelder, this is Tyler King."

"Yes, my boy. How are you? Have you thought about what I said?"

"Well, as a matter of fact I have been thinking about your offer. If I weren't between fees I wouldn't do it, you understand."

"Of course I do dear boy, of course I do. It will just be our little secret, won't it? So, do we have a deal?"

Ty closed his eyes for a moment. "We have a deal."

"Good! Then I'll see you tomorrow night at rehearsal."

"I'll be there. Thank you."

"Thank *you*, my dear boy. Good evening." Henrietta hung up, and he was positive he heard her chuckling before the line went to a drone.

Ty replaced the phone. He walked over to the couch and scratched the top of Caesar's head. "Well, at least we'll eat for another couple of weeks."

"I'll never get all those forsooths and zoundses and yea verilies right," Elmer complained. He shrugged into a brown cardigan at the close of the first rehearsal of *Camelot*.

"Yes, you will," Maggie reassured him. "Look how well you did in *Kiss Me Kate*."

"That was when I was a lot younger."

"It was only two years ago. You weren't that much younger," Roz said, pulling up Elmer's shirt collar from where it was trapped in the back of the sweater.

Darlene Thompson, an outdated and unnecessary press pass attached to her smart coral linen blazer, snapped a picture of them. Maggie hoped she'd use good sense when coming up with a caption for it in the *News*. Darlene was known for her printed innuendoes under the most innocuous of photographs.

"Age is relative," Elmer said. "Mentally I was a lot younger then."

"You'll do just fine. You're perfect as Pellinore." Maggie grabbed a black nylon windbreaker from a front seat in the auditorium. "You were great in rehearsal tonight, and it was only the first read-through."

"I'm not perfect."

"Are too."

"Am not."

"Are too."

"Why do you always have to argue with me?" Elmer carefully buttoned every button on the cardigan.

"Because I love a good argument and you're the best arguer in Cape Agnes." Maggie linked her arm through his. "Come on, I'll buy you a bowl of chowder at Mother's. Roz? Want to join us?"

"What are you depressed about?" Roz peered thoughtfully into Maggie's eyes.

Darlene snapped a picture.

Maggie raised her eyes heavenward. "I'm not depressed. I'm hungry. You coming, Elmer?"

Elmer patted her arm and slipped his out of the crook of hers. "Naw, you kids go on. I'm going home and watch that new lawyer show on the TV. See you in the morning. Did you make sure Hans went home before you locked up?"

"Sure did. In fact I took him home myself. Dottie's working late tonight."

Elmer's chin went up quickly. "She is?"

"Uh-huh."

"Well, maybe I could force down a little soup. Hate to miss that show, though."

Maggie figured Elmer would consider changing his mind once he knew Dottie was working late at Mother's. "Good." She leaned toward Roz. "Lawyers aren't that interesting to watch anyway."

"And have you been watching any lawyers in particular lately?" a low voice said near her ear.

Maggie jumped. When she looked around, she saw Ty grinning at her with a smug expression on his face. She was mortified to know he'd come up behind them and heard the conversation. He turned and spoke to Elmer.

"Just program your VCR to tape the program, Dr. Everett. Then you can watch it tomorrow sometime. That way you won't miss two good things." He winked at Elmer.

"Oh, dear, Mr. King," Jolene said, "you've done it now."

"Done what now?"

Maggie saw that Ty couldn't imagine what thing he'd done, and Jolene made it sound bad on purpose. Actually to Jolene it was pretty bad. Maggie decided it might be amusing for the next few minutes to watch Elmer and Ty square off.

"If they made those dad-gummed recorder things so's you could run it I'd do it," Elmer sputtered.

"That," Jolene said, and waved a good night to Maggie and Roz.

"Threw the one I had in the closet and left it there," Elmer sputtered on. "My daughter sent it to me. Couldn't get the dad-gummed clock to stop blinking twelve on a Sunday. Even if it was dad-gummed Tuesday the thing would blink Sunday. Don't talk to me about those blamed things."

"How about if I have a look at it?" Ty offered.

Darlene snapped a picture.

"What would you want to go and do that for?"

"Well, maybe I could get it to work for you and show you how to use it. It's really pretty easy once you know how."

"Well, I don't know," Elmer said, scratching his head.

"I could write out the directions for you," Ty said.

"What about the dad-gummed clock?"

"I guarantee when I'm finished the dad-gummed clock will stop blinking and will register the correct day. How's that?"

"Until the power goes off in a windstorm," Maggie whispered to Roz.

"You making fun of me, boy?" Elmer tried to sound firm but his gimlet eyes twinkled with amusement.

Darlene snapped a close-up of Ty's face.

Tyler blinked. "I wouldn't dream of it."

"Well, then, okay, I guess."

"Shall we go to your place and do it now?" Tyler offered again.

" 'Course not. Your ears lap over, boy? You heard I'm getting a late supper at Mother's with Colleague." Elmer looked up at Maggie. "What are we waiting for? Let's go."

Maggie knew he'd be annoyed if she didn't wipe the smile off her face immediately. It took some doing, but she managed. "I'm ready. You coming, Roz?" She turned to her friend.

"Can you handle it all right?" Roz was asking Ty. She circled him, scrutinizing her handiwork on his haircut. "Sometimes a day or two later is when you can have trouble with a new style."

"Oh, no. It's fine. Best haircut I've ever had."

In spite of her own feelings about him, Maggie believed Ty was sincere when he said that. He seemed open and friendly with everyone he met in Cape Agnes, and he certainly seemed to be throwing himself into this musical production. Henrietta was thrilled with his participation. Her face fairly beamed as she hurried toward them, Priscilla bouncing along in the cradle of her arm.

"Join us, Mrs. VanGee?" Maggie asked. "We're going to Mother's for a bowl of chowder."

Henrietta peered into Maggie's eyes. "You sang like an angel tonight. You're not depressed, I hope, Doctor."

Ty inclined his head. "Why do people keep asking that?"

"Well, you see," Roz began, "whenever Maggie gets down in the dumps she heads for Mother's and a bowl of Little Bert's chowder just like her mother did with Big Bert's chowder, and it always perks up her spirits, when she isn't worrying about the calories settling in her hips, and—"

"Boring story Mr. King doesn't want to hear," Maggie interrupted. "Shall we?" She walked up the aisle of the auditorium toward the rear doors.

Darlene snapped one more picture of the group. "I'll join you," she said in her gravelly voice.

"But your camera can't," Maggie said.

"Amen," Ty added.

"I'm going to call separate rehearsals for chorus, and extra sessions for the leads," Henrietta said as they headed out into the cool night air. "Keep your calendars free in the evenings, please. Most especially the two of you." She sent a glance toward Maggie and Ty.

Maggie tilted her head. If she didn't think Henrietta VanGelder was interested in Tyler King herself, she might wonder if the spirited widow was doing a little matchmaking. She had a penchant for wanting happy endings. She smiled to herself. The formidable Mrs. VanGee couldn't do anything to make a fairy-tale relationship out of the in-debt-to-her-eye-teeth Dr. Michael Logan and the rich landlord Mr. Tyler King no matter how powerful a fairy godmother she thought she was.

Somehow Maggie got through the next exhausting two weeks. Rehearsals for *Camelot* had run late three evenings a week. She'd had a rather disappointing preliminary session with the town council over her lease rights. Lack of anything in writing, they said. Somehow she'd regroup her efforts and go at them again.

During this time the clinic had been busy with a population of boarding pets all requiring attention, and she'd performed four feline spayings and one neutering, some canine dentistry, and five tail dockings on a litter of cocker spaniel pups.

She begged off from rehearsal tonight, and Henrietta agreed and gave the whole cast a breather. All Maggie wanted to do was go upstairs to her apartment, put her feet up, eat a frozen dinner, and spend a long time on the telephone with her grandson.

Tad hadn't called in several days, and she knew he wouldn't ask anyone to help him write a letter to his grandmother. He'd consider that a dorky thing to do. That was all right. She wanted him to have the experience of being on his own at the guide dog camp so he'd begin to feel he could be away from her and all his local support. Besides, the director of the camp had told her it was important for the boy to bond with the dog he'd be bringing home with him.

The whole experience would help him grow up, she assured herself. He had to do that sooner or later, and Maggie believed sooner was better than later. She wouldn't be around forever to see to his welfare. She'd have to begin to think about special education to prepare him for his future as a blind adult. And what was she going to do about college? There were things he had to learn so he could live a productive life on his own.

She went out and cleaned up the waiting area, then grabbed paper towels and glass cleaner to wipe fingerprints off the panes in the outside door. Doing a job like that made it easy for her mind to slip to other things she was usually successful at keeping at bay. Ty drove by in his convertible with the top down and honked. She waved. She suddenly thought he was better-looking than she'd originally decided. And with the late-afternoon sun reflecting off his gold car and the wind ruffling his hair, he looked especially appealing.

She recalled now the first night at rehearsal when Harry Nordquist had muttered something to her about rich kids not knowing how to act in public places like laundromats. But she also recalled that by the time the evening had drawn to a close, the two men had laughed together as Ty, his arm draped around the older man's shoulders, told the assembled cast the story of overflowing Speed Queens and the spilled pizza incident.

Since she'd met Ty, Maggie felt she was suffering from a case of acute confusion. He was a mystery to her in some ways, not exactly what she would have expected from the son of Dorian King. He'd abandoned a law practice in Los Angeles, yet she thought he was probably quite capable of being a good lawyer. He certainly had the gift of gab as well as a way of making people feel good about themselves. He was personable, she'd grant him that.

On the other hand, he was also the dreaded landlord, the evictor of woman, child, an old man, and a turnover of sick and boarding animals. It didn't seem to bother Tyler King one whit that he would be putting her out of the clinic in a few more days.

Jolene met her at the reception desk when Maggie came inside. "I'll be leaving soon, Doc," she called down the hallway.

"Anything you want me to do before I go?"

"Just seal and mail that pile of billing statements if you can. The sooner we get paid the better. And thanks, Jolene. I'll finish cleaning up in the back."

"Okay, see you tomorrow."

Tomorrow. How many tomorrows were left? Maggie looked around the place and wondered what she'd do about everything. She still hadn't found a new location for her clinic. The drains in this one were plugged again, and she hadn't even touched Ada Luddington's Saint Bernard. A vague notion nagged her. She might just have to get a job. A *job* job. And she knew in her heart no other job would compare with this, doing work she loved.

In the back room she picked up a plunger and vigorously pushed it up and down over the sink drain. With a great sucking sound, a stringy dark mass rose up and out of the drain and lay in a smelly limp heap in the sink.

"Yuck," she whispered, turning away from the odor. Maybe she should let Tyler King have this place. Let him deal with the clogged drains, the cracked plaster, and the heaving floor tiles.

"Doc?" Tyler King's rich baritone echoed down the hallway.

Maggie's hand froze over the plunger handle. She felt an unsettled tremor pass through her. Was it some sense that the other shoe was dropping? Or . . . *attraction?* Impossible. She straightened and turned around.

"Yes," she called to him.

Ty appeared around the door, smiling. "Caesar sends his apologies for his behavior the evening you were at our house. He's insisted I take you out to dinner. I thought we could go over to the Crab Shack, if it's still there."

"It's still there."

"What do you say?"

She didn't know what to say. Was he asking her out on another date? She never should have made the mistake of going out with him on the first one. Although, they hadn't actually gone out. Unless spending the night in jail together could technically be called "going out."

"Doc? Did you hear me?" Ty leaned

closer and peered into her face. "Ugh, what's that smell?"

"Excuse me?"

He grinned. "Sorry. I meant there's a pretty strong odor in here, and . . . I'm digging myself in deep here, I think. I'll just start again. Did you hear me ask if you'd like to go out to dinner?"

"Yes, I heard you," she answered quickly.

"And?"

"I don't know. I'm rather tired." She knew that excuse was feeble.

"Yeah, I know what you mean. Good thing Mrs. VanGelder gave us the evening off. I haven't sung this much since I was in chorus in high school. I'm starting to get hoarse. And that is not even a little vet humor there." He laughed good-naturedly. When she didn't respond, he tried again. "If you're feeling that low, maybe a bowl of Little Bert's chowder is what you'd rather have."

"I do not want a bowl of Little Bert's chowder!" she snapped.

Ty stepped back. "Sorry. I thought that's what you always wanted when . . . I mean, I just wanted to help you feel better."

"You may not quite understand this, but you're hardly the one to help me feel better."

Ty pruned his lips and raised his eyebrows in concession. "I know. Look, maybe if you have dinner with me you might get to know me a little better and find out I'm not half bad. What do you think?"

"I don't know how to answer that."

Maggie took the plunger to a broom closet at the back of the room, and stripped off her latex gloves. Dinner with Ty would be nice, if he was not her landlord. She had to admit she'd thought about him occasionally when they weren't together, the first man she'd wondered about since her divorce. She still had his polo shirt from the ill-fated night in the laundromat.

She should have returned the shirt to him days ago. Whenever she thought of returning it, she knew she didn't want to do it at rehearsal or in some other public place. Darlene, with her acute nose for news and her ever-present camera, could be counted upon to leap from the shadows and take a photograph for the front page of the *News*. The caption would practically write itself. How Darlene had not learned of their night in jail was a gift from the gods. She must remember to burn some incense or something in thanksgiving.

"Maggie?" His voice interrupted her thoughts. "Shall we go to dinner?"

"I don't know," she said at last. "I'm not sure I want to risk another jail sentence. It's not good for my reputation. But it was sweet of Caesar to offer. How is he?"

"His tongue's healed. He sleeps a lot now. I have a feeling it's his bladder. He's consumed enough water to float a boat. If you remember your keys, we won't have jail hanging over our heads. What do you say?"

"Oh, all right." She shrugged out of her lab coat and grabbed her windbreaker and purse.

"Try to be a bit more enthusiastic about it," he chided.

On their way out they passed Jolene at the reception desk, the phone pressed to her ear. She indicated it was a personal call and waved goodbye.

"No patients tonight?" Ty asked as they headed for his car.

"Nope. Miraculously cured."

"Ah, the wonders of modern medicine, and what I'm sure is a great cage-side manner from the lady vet." He opened the door for her.

"You didn't think so the other night when we were locked up in a cage together." Maggie slid into the front.

"I didn't know you the other night."

"And you think you know me now?"

"I wouldn't be so bold as to say that. Yet." He shut the door firmly, walked around the front of the car and got in on the driver's side.

Maggie watched him move, smoothly, surely. "You may never really know me," she said quietly.

"I can dream, can't I?"

The Crab Shack was aptly named. Its bleached and weathered wide board siding and lengthy set of stairs climbing to a spacious open dining room creaked with every step. The building overlooked the surf and as the day waned to twilight several people combed the shoreline crabbing in ankle-high water, their pants rolled up above their knees.

The old place reeked of Cape Agnes's early fishing village past. Low candlelight flickered from glass bowls shrouded in fishnet on wooden tables. The aroma of crab boil spice, steaming seafood, and wet seaweed filled the air. The bang of wooden mallets against newspaper-covered wood tables mingled with laughing voices as diners cracked crabs.

"I haven't been out here in ages," Maggie said. She dropped into a captain's chair at a table near an open window and watched the sky turn mauve and gold. "I'd forgotten what a great spot this is."

"I know." Ty seated himself opposite her. "I'm glad some things in memory remain unchanged. My mother loved this place, but my father couldn't stand the smell. He failed to grasp why anyone would go to so much trouble with those mallets, only to end up with hardly any meat."

Maggie nodded. "Mine, too. Obviously our fathers didn't understand that eating at the Crab Shack was an event more than it was a meal."

A young man in jeans and a T-shirt with a faded red lobster emblazoned over the front spread clean newspaper over their table. "Couple drafts?"

"Sounds great to me. Doc?"

"Perfect."

When the beers arrived and they'd given the young man their orders for steamed lobsters and clams, Maggie gazed out over the ocean. Worrying about Tad and his adjustments and the impending loss of the clinic had taken a toll on her emotions. She never allowed her distress to show on the outside if she could help it. It was enough that her friends and neighbors knew everything that was happening in her life; they didn't need to know how she was struggling to handle it all.

The beers arrived in iced canning jars with handles. Ty raised his and held it toward her. "Let's toast to something."

Maggie watched him with suspicion. "To what?"

"Oh, let's see. How about to Camelot?"

"The production or the fantasy?"

He laughed lightly. "Hmm. Well, being in the production is certainly something different for me. I haven't done stage work in years. They're a great bunch of people, aren't they?"

Maggie lifted her mug. "Yes, they are. Well, then to *Camelot* the production."

"Wait. What about the fantasy?"

"What about it? That sort of thing went out with medieval queens and knights, and with the Kennedy administration."

"Oh ye of little faith. Don't you know there is fantasy everywhere? It's in the air!"

Maggie sniffed. "Boiling crabs? All right, I guess by some people's standards that could be fantasy."

"You're not using the right senses."

"And you appear to have no sense at all." It was a tease, not a barb.

"You should try to have more fun."

"It's not fun if you have to try."

"You live in too much reality."

"And you seem a bit out of touch with it."

"You're right, you know," he said.

"Of course I am," she said.

"I mean," Ty said seriously, "you're right about what you said to Dr. Everett. You really do like a good argument, don't you?"

Maggie nodded. She softened. "Just as much as he does. I suppose that would bother some people. I'm sorry."

"I'm not. So, how about let's toast to good arguments?"

"Agreed."

"So much for arguing." He thudded his mug against hers and they drank.

Their dinners arrived, and Ty watched as Maggie picked the tiny sweet meat pieces out of the lobster's claws with a long wood pick and dipped them into melted butter she'd laced with the juice from a lemon wedge. She popped the meat into her mouth, savoring the taste. It had never occurred to him before this moment that watching a woman enjoy a meal was a sensual pleasure.

He ate then, enjoying the food with renewed gusto. Between mouthfuls they talked about how Cape Agnes had been when they were young, the high-school dances and steady couples, his prowess as a soccer player, her appearances in every play beginning with her freshman year. They laughed over memories of mutual acquaintances, and pondered over those they could not remember due to the few years' difference in their high-school careers.

Ty set his fork down and wiped his hands with a napkin. "I've been thinking about this problem we have."

"Which problem? The fact that we argue?" Maggie drained her beer mug. "It's no problem for me."

"No. The one concerning the building."

"Well, soon it won't be my problem. It'll be yours alone, every endearing little crack and leak in the place."

He didn't smile. "I know you probably don't think so, but I wish I had some other way to help you out."

"You're helping me *out* enough as it is. I can take care of things myself."

"I don't doubt that." His voice quieted. "I do feel bad about all this. I had no idea. . . ."

Maggie straightened. "Business is business. You've made your decision about what you want to do with the building.

But I think you should know I'm not getting out without a fight."

He frowned. "Why do we have to fight?"

"You didn't think I'd just give in and give up, did you?"

"I didn't think about it at all. Until I got here, that is. I guess I have begun to hope there'd be a workable solution for both of us."

"Then make a deal with me on the building."

Ty lowered his gaze to the table. "I can't do that."

"Well, then, there we are. Unless we can devise some kind of health club where dogs can ride stationary bikes and cats can pump iron."

"Now there's an idea," Ty said, hoping to lift the descending dark mood.

Maggie said nothing.

An awkward silence fell between them.

"For whatever it's worth, I think you're quite a lady." He reached across the small table and touched her hand.

Maggie dropped her eyes sharply and caught the look of his fingers resting on the back of her hand. They were warm, steady. She raised her eyes and looked him square in the face. Was that a compliment? A date-type compliment? She was used to compliments on her work, and compliments on her singing, but never compliments on her *person*. Maybe he was just trying to wear her down so she'd give up without a fight. She hated feeling that cynical, but she'd learned some hard lessons over time and she wouldn't forget them.

She should say something. Thank him, just in case it was a real compliment. Move her hand. Something. The look in his eyes said things, things she wished she could define correctly for her own sake.

"I. . . ." she began.

A youthful voice coming from several feet away stopped her. "Grams?"

Eight

Startled, Maggie snapped her head around. Her grandson stood near the door to the dining room, Jolene at his side. Maggie quickly drew her hand from under Ty's.

Tad came toward her, touching chairs with both hands on his way across the room. Jolene gently steered him with a hand on his shoulder when it looked as if he needed her help. Maggie was so stunned she could barely find her voice.

"Hi, Grams," Tad said, hugging her then stepping back and adjusting his eyeglasses that had dislodged from his nose in the process. He looked down at his sneakered feet.

"Tad, what on earth . . . how did you get here? You're not due back for another two weeks. Are you sick?" Maggie stood and gathered the boy into her arms.

"He's fine, Doc," Jolene said. "Ray called and said they had to put the boat in up the coast at Sea View and he was taking the bus home. He wanted me to meet him at the station. When the bus came in, Tad got off it with him. I heard you say you were coming here with . . . hello, Mr. King." Jolene smiled warmly at Ty.

"Good evening, Jolene." Ty smiled back.

"I didn't want to interrupt your date, but I knew you'd want to see him right away," Jolene said with genuine apology.

Tad pushed away from Maggie and looked up at her. "You're on a *date?*"

"It's not a date," Maggie said emphatically.

"Oh, I thought it was a date," Jolene said.

"I did, too," Ty said.

"Well . . ."

"You're on a date?" Tad asked again. "Nobody's grandmother *dates.*"

"Yours does," Ty said. "Let me introduce your grandmother's date. My name's Ty. I've heard you're called Tad. Short for Theodore?"

"I hate that name," Tad muttered.

"Which? Ty or Theodore?" Ty asked. "I think both of them are pretty good myself. Mine's short for Tyler. Tyler and Theodore. Good names for noblemen. Or maybe singing chipmunks." He laughed lightly, but Tad didn't seem to catch on.

"Thanks for picking him up and bringing him over here, Jolene," Maggie said. "You were right to find me."

"Well, I'm glad," Jolene said, checking her watch. "I have to get Ray home now. Sorry again about interrupting your date. Maybe you can schedule another one soon. Bye-bye now." She waved over her shoulder and her heels clicked across the wood floor as she left the dining room.

"Here, my man," Ty said. He dragged an empty chair over from a nearby table and motioned to the boy to sit down. Tad plopped sullenly into it.

"I think we should go now," Maggie said. "My grandson and I have a lot to talk over."

"I'm hungry," Tad said. "Didn't get nothing to eat on the way."

"Didn't get *anything* to eat," Maggie corrected.

"That's what I said." Tad drummed his toe against the table leg.

"Crabs?" Ty asked. Maggie gave him an admonishing look. "Oops, sorry . . . *Grams.*" He grinned widely.

"I'll fix you something at home. Let's go." Maggie started to rise, but Tad didn't move.

Ty watched what he figured was about to be a standoff. He could tell Maggie didn't want to make a scene in a public place, and probably not in front of him either, but it was clear Tad knew that as well and wasn't about to leave. Smart kid.

Ty signalled the waiter. "Our friend here is hungry. Crabs seem to have been vetoed. What else have you got that might interest him?"

The young waiter swept his hand wide and surveyed the room. "Fish," he said, and the tone of his voice added a "what else?" to the response.

"I see. Well, then, what do you say, Theodore, how about some fish?"

"I want spaghetti, and I hate that

name." Theodore drummed the table leg harder.

"Tad," Maggie said and placed a firm hand on the boy's arm, "you can eat here if you remember how to behave in a public place. Now please sit up and speak pleasantly to this young man."

Tad complied reluctantly. "Do you have spaghetti?" he asked the waiter.

"White or red clam sauce?" the waiter asked.

Tad sighed. "Red. And a Coke." He looked down for a moment then back up to the waiter. "Please."

"Coming up. Anybody else?"

"I'll have a cup of tea, please," Maggie said.

"And I'll have another order of crabs to keep my friends company," Ty said.

When the waiter had walked away, Maggie ventured a question. "So, how was camp? Did you pick out a guide dog to bring home?"

"I'm not bringing a dog home. I'm not gonna do it." Tad folded his arms across his chest.

"You don't like dogs?" Ty asked.

"Of course he does," Maggie said

sharply. "Tad, you know you're going to need a dog."

"I am not. I can see all right."

"But you know that someday . . ."

"I can see all right!" Tad raised his voice and kicked the table.

"Tad, now stop that. You have to face reality." Maggie waited while the waiter set down a canning jar mug filled with Coke. "We'll discuss this later."

"I'm not going to talk about it," Tad declared.

Maggie grew frustrated.

"I don't blame you," Ty said. "Reality stinks sometimes. So fill me in. What's this about needing a dog later?"

"Ty, I can fill you in . . ."

"She says I'm gonna be blind, that's why," Tad said, and took a big swig of soda.

"Oh, yeah, I heard about that," Ty said.

"If I'm blind, what do I need a dog for? I won't be able to see him or play with him. I won't be going anywhere, will I? I won't be able to go to school. I'll just sit around. Who needs a dog for that?"

Maggie wiped some imaginary crumbs from the table. "Tad, yes you will be able to go to school, maybe even the one you're in now. A guide dog can get you to school and other places you'll want to go."

"The dogs didn't like me."

"Something tells me you didn't let them like you. Caesar adores you."

"He's different."

Maggie smiled at her grandson. "You're right. Wouldn't you try again? By September you and your dog would be ready to go back to school."

Tad kicked the table again. "All the kids'll laugh at me."

"I don't think so."

"Yes, they will. And I won't be able to see or read nothin' . . . anything."

"You're going to learn Braille. And now there are computers that can do a lot of things to help you."

Tad twisted his mug around and around on the table. "I'm not going to learn that stuff. I won't need it. I'll just stay home."

"Tad," Maggie said firmly, "stop avoiding this. You can't stay home forever. I won't be able to take care of you forever."

"Why not?" Tad muttered.

Maggie's eyes filled. "Because I won't

be here forever . . . you've got to become self-sufficient, do things for yourself."

Her voice thickened and she couldn't find more words. Ty could see she was getting to an emotional point she couldn't handle in a restaurant.

"You're right, Theodore. Live like a king. Get everybody else to do things for you. Why not?" Ty crossed his forearms on the table and leaned toward the boy.

Tad looked up at him with a tentative squint. "Yeah."

"Ty, for heaven's sake . . ." Maggie started.

"I'd do the very same thing," Ty said, ignoring her.

"You would?" Tad leaned closer.

"Sure. Of course I'd have to figure a way to pay the salaries of all these people who'd work for me, but, hey, piece of cake, right?"

"Pay them?"

"Yeah, you know how it is these days. Everybody wants to be paid for volunteering. Some racket, isn't it?"

"I guess."

The waiter came and set a plate of spaghetti in front of Tad. The boy shook grated cheese over it and picked up a fork and twirling spoon and dove in. Ty was impressed at his good table manners and his prowess with the pasta.

"Besides," Ty said, "I already have a dog. Up until recently he worked for me."

"He did? What did he do?"

"Tad," Maggie interjected, "Ty is Caesar's owner."

"Caesar? Nobody owns Caesar," Tad said emphatically.

"It appeared that way," Maggie muttered.

Ty caught her smug look. "Actually, you're right. Caesar just lets me live with him. He's the star, after all."

"He's pretty brave, isn't he?"

"You mean, because he lets me live with him?"

"No. Geez." Tad sounded disgusted that a grown man could be so stupid. "I mean, all those people he saved on TV. He pulled a girl's mother out of a burning barn once. And he didn't even get his hair burned once. Just the tip of his tail. How come he didn't act so brave when he came to Critter Care?" Tad scraped sauce from his bowl.

Ty decided to take a surprised tack. "He didn't? Well, what happened? Did someone treat him badly?"

"Treat him badly?" It was Maggie's turn to be surprised. "He lived like a king . . . and please *don't* pardon my pun."

"Wouldn't dream of it." Ty chuckled behind his napkin.

"One time Frederick—he's a guinea pig," Tad began.

Ty nodded. "Uh, we've met."

"Frederick got loose one night."

"Ah, that explains his expertise," Ty said. "He practiced."

"He got loose and got into Caesar's pen," Tad continued, "and bit him right on the—"

"I don't think we need details, Tad," Maggie admonished.

"On the contrary," Ty countered, "I think we do. If my beloved pet was maimed by a vicious rodent, well, I'll have to think about the repercussions here."

Tad laughed. "Frederick's not vicious!"

"Oh really? Have you checked with Caesar about that, and what's his name, the Russian dog?"

"Sergei," Maggie said, starting to grin at the exchange.

"Sergei," Ty affirmed. "Ask him. He was a victim of that little rat. As a matter of fact, so was I." He held up one finger that had a small fading red scratch where Frederick had made his point about being captured. He wagged the finger and looked over at Maggie. "Are we amused? I think not. Do you think I should have gotten a tetanus shot?"

Tad sighed loudly. "*Anyway*, Caesar yelped and cried like a baby. I had to hug him and pet him and calm him down. I kept reminding him of when he saved that lady, but he just kept whimpering."

Ty raised his brows. "Yeah, well, I will say he knows how to milk an audience."

"Huh?" Tad frowned.

"What I mean is, Caesar had a lot of training, he did a lot of work with me in order to . . . save the lady from the burning barn."

"Training? You trained him to do that?"

"Yes. Just like those dogs at your camp. That's how Caesar was trained. He was just a two-bit canine clown on cable television until I won him . . . until I went to live with him. Once we—" Ty leaned in close to Tad. "Your grandmother will love this. Once we *bonded*, then together we made Caesar into a star."

"What does bonded mean?" Tad sent a quick suspicious look to Maggie then to Ty.

Ty looked up at Maggie then.

"Go ahead, big shot, you're doing great." With a small smile she leaned back against her chair and folded her arms across her chest.

"Gee thanks, Grams. You've had more experience at this than I have."

"Could've fooled me," she said. "Sounds like you've had a brood of kids yourself."

"You'd think so if you ever met my former partner and saw the kind of people we came in contact with."

"So what does bonding mean?" Tad asked with no small measure of impatience.

Ty took a deep breath. "It's . . . it's like what they were teaching you at your guide dog camp. How you and your dog can become good friends so you work as a team. Right . . . Grams?"

Maggie nodded. "You did that very well." She turned toward Tad. "Honey, I'm not going to force you to go back to camp right now. All you have to do is think about it for a while, okay?"

Tad's lower lip quivered, but Ty could tell he wouldn't cry no matter how he was feeling. The boy made a big production out of scraping up the last vestiges of clam sauce.

"Thinking is good," Ty said. Or not so good in some cases, he thought, but he wouldn't say that right now. He summoned the waiter for the check. "How would you both feel about a walk along the beach? It's still pretty warm, and I'm feeling the need for some fresh air."

Maggie grabbed the check. "My treat. It's the least I can do."

"Something tells me that's a warning," Ty said, pushing out his chair and rising. "Makes me wonder what's the most you can do."

"Keep wondering," she said mysteriously.

"You are a scary woman," Ty said, grinning.

Barefoot in the sand and carrying their shoes, they scuffed along the beach watching the moon and listening to the gently rolling surf. Tad had an intuitive way of touching Maggie's arm with his shoulder every now and then to keep himself on course with them. He was almost sightless at night, while still able to see some figures and light during the day.

Maggie was aware of how relaxed she felt, how this time the walk affected her differently from the many other times she'd walked the beach. The night sky was awash with stars and the moon's reflection a creamy path over the dark ocean. How many times before had she seen nights like this one? Yet, somehow tonight the sights were sharper, as if they were burning themselves into her memory.

A chill came over her. She'd had these feelings watching Alyssa play with Tad in the sunlit morning before the car crash took her daughter and son-in-law away from them forever. Tears came to her eyes. Even after all these years the memory of their deaths still hurt deeply and brought the tears that hovered just under the surface. At those times Maggie worked hard to replace the pain with a happy memory. Sometimes the pain was stronger than the happy memory she could make.

She strolled to the water and let it gently lap over her feet. There was something about the ocean cloaking her feet that often made her feel better.

Ty watched as Maggie strolled along the water's edge, Tad at her side. The salty breeze blew her hair enticingly around her neck and shoulders, and caused her long white cotton skirt to move in and out and around her legs. He drew in his breath quickly and caught up with them. He stopped abruptly.

"Look at that." He pointed down the beach toward a gnarled and twisted bleached tree trunk, barren in the pale wash of moonlight.

"Eerie-looking," Maggie shivered.

"What is it?" Tad asked, taking hold of Maggie's arm.

"A weirdly shaped old tree, all weathered and gnarled from wind and sea," she told him.

"Mmm, especially with the other trees behind it," Ty said. "Looks like a medieval castle or something."

"Is it haunted?" Tad asked in a hushed tone.

"It's possible. Everything is haunted if you let it be," Ty said.

Silently Maggie agreed. She knew that feeling.

They came upon the thick trunk of a dead tree, some of its branches curled and buried in the sand as it lay on its side.

"Shall we?" Ty motioned to the tree trunk, indicating for her to sit down.

Maggie guided Tad and they sat side by side, the boy between them, the ocean beside them, the gnarled tree ahead up the beach.

"I've always fantasized about being a knight in shining armor, and living in a castle like that," Ty mused. "What about you, Tad?"

"I dunno."

"Their clothes were constantly dirty. They didn't have laundromats, you know," Maggie responded matter-of-factly. "And I understand that at dinner they wiped their greasy hands on their dogs. I doubt Caesar would go for that."

"How unromantic of you to point out those things," Ty teased.

"Caesar would hate that," Tad said. "He'd just lick it off like he did when I spilled the chocolate milk shake on him."

"Was that a job bathing him," Maggie said, laughing. "He was a sticky mess head to tail."

"He wants to be smelly and dirty," Tad said.

"Anyway," Maggie said, "I'm sure living in a castle wasn't as romantic as the storytellers would like to make it out."

Ty turned toward her. "Maybe not, but didn't you ever want to be a queen or a princess when you were growing up? I thought a lot about being a daring knight in the jousts, saving damsels in distress, and saying things like 'What ho!' and 'Zounds!' What a time to be a man."

"If you lived long enough to become one." Maggie saw Ty's askance look of amusement. "Okay, maybe I did fantasize a little about being a princess. My dad used to call me that."

"How about if I call you Princess just for tonight?"

"Please, that's Doctor Princess now." She laughed warmly.

"And did a Prince Charming or a White Knight figure in your fantasy?" He raised his outspread hand and swept it over the velvet night in front of them. "Did he ride in, dashing in his armor, to save you from some dastardly deed, some malicious mishap?"

"Of course he did," Maggie said. "That was his job! But, that's pure fantasy. Reality doesn't work that way. There are no such things as White Knights or Prince Charmings anymore. And besides, any damsel in distress worth her bodice stays can ride up on her own horse and save herself these days."

"And you're worth your bodice stays." Ty leaned back against a branch.

"I believe so. Fortunately they don't make those anymore either, so I won't have to test them to find out."

"So, you think that you're the one who

can save you in distress. Wouldn't you need a knight once in awhile to slay all the dragons for you?"

"Not on your odds bodkins, knave." She eyed him curiously. "Do men still want to do that? I thought they liked self-sufficient women nowadays."

"I think most men still want to be a hero in a lady's eyes. Right, Tad?"

"Geez."

"More than likely it's in their own eyes," Maggie said.

"I suppose so. But it must have been exciting to have lived in the days of Robin Hood, to save the poor and downtrodden, be knighted, which is ever so much better than being besotted." Ty laughed heartily at his own joke. "Ah, to be in charge of a kingdom, pal around with Richard the Lionheart, drink mead all day, and make merry in the woods."

"How do you spell that?" she whispered.

He laughed. "What a suspicious mind you have. M-e-r-r-y, of course."

"This really is a fairy tale," she muttered.

"Did you doubt it? Picture it. Close

your eyes—you, too, Tad—and visualize
that tree castle and think hard.''

Maggie looked at Tad and saw he was
going along with Ty's game. She relaxed
and allowed herself to be taken into the
fantasy as Ty began his story in a dramatic
voice.

Nine

Once upon a time, Maid Meg, the fairest damsel in all of the shire, sat on a tuffet in a forest loudly chewing pink bubble gum and sobbing her saucerlike eyes out. Her luxurious hair, the color of toadstools at sunset, was piled to the top of her head in great coils, the better to keep it out of branches and to avoid collision with low vine-flying merry men.

Suddenly, and for no apparent reason whatever, the dashing, handsome, virile, brave, truehearted Tyler Hood, wearing a pair of forest green tights, drops out of the trees overhead.

Maggie began to hum "Greensleeves" in the background.

Ty gave her a sidelong glance. "Nice

touch." He turned his gaze back to the tree castle and continued.

"What ho, fair maiden?" quoth Hood. "Forsooth. Why dost thou cry and drop large tears on thy full breasts?"

Maggie gave him an admonishing look through the moonlight-filtered night. "Remember your audience," she said out of the corner of her mouth, and nodded toward Tad.

"Sorry," Ty whispered. He cleared his throat.

"Ist thou sad?" Tyler Hood queried.

Ty's voice cracked as he next imitated an innocent fairy-tale princess.

"Yea, verily," the beauteous maiden sobbed, blowing her nose loudly and scaring all the little creatures in the wood.

"Art thou downtrodden, sore of foot, empty of purse? Shall I rob from the rich and give to thou . . . thee?

Sayest it. Let thy desires tumble from thy ruby red lips, and thy every wish wilt be my command. I live only to serve thee. I shall brave the murkiest of moats, the dirtiest of dragons, the oldest of ogres, the morbidest of monsters, to save thee from whatever evil befalls."

"Why wouldst thou do all that for little me?" asked the maiden, knowing full well why.

"It's a good chance for me to show off my new duds. What dost thou think?" Tyler Hood walked forward on the toes of his pointed felt boots, did a runway pirouette, and walked back, striking a hands-on-hip pose."

"Geez," Tad said disgustedly.

Maggie looked over at Ty, and placed a restraining hand on his arm. "Oh, please, do let me take it from here."

"I bow to the lady's contribution to this merry tale."

While Tyler took up the job as background music, deliberately humming "Greensleeves" slightly off-key, Maggie picked up the story using a strong feminist voice:

Maid Meg, using her finely honed sense of fashion, squinted her eyes, cocked her adorable head, and assessed Tyler Hood. "Too full around the hips and I'm not too crazy about the boot points. But the tights are nice."

Tyler Hood beamed mightily. "And for all my swashbuckling derring-do thou wilt give me half your kingdom, and thy hand in marriage. Right?"

"I don't have a kingdom to give thou half of, and I need both my hands," Maid Meg said smartly. "All I have is a run-down castle in a smarmy part of the shire. The evil Count King is foreclosing. Oh woe is me, all is lost, all is lost," she wailed, then remembered that she hated wailing.

"Here now, it canst not be all that bad." Tyler Hood dropped to his knees in front of the maid's tuffet, remembered the last time he did such an act he got nasty runs up his tights, so he leapt up again.

A crunching of leaves behind them made both turn quickly.

"What goest on here?" a voice echoed from behind the faceplate of noisy armor.

"Oh yea, my heart is gladdened," cried Maid Meg, "for it is none other than Sir Harry of Nordquistshire. He will save the day."

Tad giggled, then yawned loudly.

"My turn," Ty cut in. "You're putting our audience to sleep."

"Sir Harry, my liege," Tyler Hood dropped to his knees, remembered the runs and jumped up again. "I am here to serve thee and thy fair Queen of Speed."

"On your knees, knave," quoth Sir Harry, "soon, nay, now, shall I knight thee."

"Musteth I get on my knees?" quoth Tyler Hood, still concerned about his appearance at such an occasion.

"Oh yeah, your hose, I forgot," quoth Sir Harry. "Fear not, I shall knight thee from where thou standeth." Sir Harry took out his shiny new pipe wrench and dropped it with a thud on Tyler Hood's head.

"Ow-eth," quoth Hood. "Might thou open thy faceplate, Sir Harry, the better to see me with?"

Sir Harry lifted the faceplate, but it clattered shut once again. He lifted, and it clattered; he lifted, and it clattered. At last Maid Meg removed the gum she was chewing, lifted Sir Harry's faceplate, and stuck the pink wad under the rim. Ta-da, it stuck.

Sir Harry lifted the pipe wrench, tapped Tyler Hood on each shoulder so hard he fell to his knees. "Thou art beknighted!" Sir Harry threw his head back and laughed heartily, pointing an accusing finger toward the runs in Sir Tyler Hood's tights.

Tyler Hood stood up. "We are not amused," he said in royalese. He reached over and unstuck Sir

Harry's faceplate, slamming it shut over his laugh.

"I just hate when thou doest that," Sir Harry muffled.

"That's why I do it!" Sir Tyler Hood guffawed.

Maggie held up her hands. "Wait, this tale is taking a turn for the worse. Hood and Harry are squabbling. We can't have that. One can't save a kingdom that way. My turn." She cleared her throat and picked up the tale once more.

"Well, I knewest I couldn't count on mere mortal men to save my castle," Maid Meg pouted, stamping her little beslippered foot. "I shall save the day myself, defend my castle against the evil Count King, and keep all of my bats and newts and enchanted frog princes happy as pigs in slop, and defend the honor of Caesar the Wonder Dragon who guards the entrance. And when I finisheth, I shall rewrite all of the fairy tales in the land and show how maids were the ones who saved wimpy princes from fates worse than death."

"How Grimm," quoth Sir Tyler Hood.

"The Grimmest, brother," added Sir Harry from under his faceplate.

Sir Tyler Hood turned to the maiden. *"Surely* thou canst not mean thou art strong enough to hold off Count King, please the Speed Queen, beat out Sir Harry of Nordquistshire, and do better than I?"

"Yea verily, and don't call me Shirley."

Ty leaned over and peered into Maggie's face. "Now who's turned this tale around?"

"It needed turning."

"I'll carry on from here, if you don't mind," Tyler said.

"I think not." Maggie leaned back and folded her arms across her chest. She continued the tale.

The highly intelligent and cunning Maid Meg skipped on down the path carrying a goody basket, but what she hadn't seen was the evil dragon, Evicticus Quickasawinkus, lurking in the forest.

"Lurk, lurk," quoth the dirty dragon. "I shall slither to the castle, throw a bag of hot balls at Caesar the Wonder Dragon who's a traitor to his own species, infect the moat drains with unspeakable sludge, and force the fair maiden into my waiting claws in which I clutch a castle foreclosure notice." With a great rustle of scales and switching of pointed tail, the dragon tiptoed down the path.

Ty cut in then and picked up the tale.

"Zounds! This looks like a job for Good—now Sir—Tyler Hood!" the brave and heroic Tyler Hood announced.

Maggie scoffed. "Ha! Let me run with it again."

"Sir Tyler Hood was preparing to set off on a quest to save the fair damsel from the evil Count King and that dirty dragon, Evicticus. Grabbing the nearest vine and getting a running start, he flew off through the trees in the direction of the castle. As he was on final approach, his hands slipped, the vine slipped, and Sir Tyler slipped right down along the sharp scaly tail of the dirty dragon, down to the pointed end, and into the disgusting moat. His tights were ruined.

"Help, help!" called Maid Meg from a turret window high atop the castle. Then, remembering her vow in the woods, she amended her plea. "Mild assistance, mild assistance only!"

The dirty dragon's sinister laugh echoed through the forest and his hot breath set a fire ring to circle the moat.

Tyler Hood spluttered his way out of the unspeakably polluted moat, doused the ring of fire by wringing out his pointed hat over it, and began to scale the side of the castle because there was no way he'd try to scale that dragon.

"Fair maiden, fair maiden, lettest down thy tresses!' he called.

Ty cut in. "Ah, wait, I have the perfect answer for the maiden here."

The maiden leaned out the tiny window. "I only let down my tresses with someone I'm comfortable with, not just any knave who by happenstance happens by, not one who reeks of seductive musk, and certainly not one who calls me by another maiden's name. I was never too fondest of Shirley either."

The dirty dragon laughed again, only this time in the direction of Sir Tyler Hood. The heat of his anger sent Hood skittering to the top of the turret.

"I am here to offer mild assistance, my lady."

"How mild?"

"The mildest. Wilt thou please let me in? I'm rather uncomfortable where I sitteth now."

"Mayhaps."

"Is that yea or nay?"

"I'm thinking about it."

The dragon laughed louder.

"Please, I beggest thou, Maid Meg, make up thy mind posthaste. I feel the heat of the dragon's anger close to my heart."

Maid Meg's eyebrows quirked quizzically as she leaned farther out the turret window. "Wherever. Enter, my lord."

"I shall save the day, fair maiden."

"How dost thou plan to pull that off?"

"By dropping my shredded tights and getting rid of this pointed tunic and showing thou my real worth!"

"Nay, knave! Not in front of the castle page here. Besides all knaves and knights say the same thing. How darest thou?" Maid Meg covered her eyes with widespread fingers.

"Because, when I do, surely thou wilt understand!"

Hood threw off his tunic and sent it flying from the turret window. He flipped off his soggy pointed hat and sent it flying, too. At last his soaked and shredded tights and pointed shoes came off, and he sent those flying after the rest.

"Ta-da!" Sir Hood stood with arms widespread.

"White tennis shorts, muscular thighs, and gorgeous tanned calves? I don't understand," quoth Maid Meg.

"It is I, Prince King, the White Knight, disguised as a mild-mannered, very merry man in a great metropolitan shire."

Maid Meg's incredibly wide eyes narrowed. "And art thou not related to the evil Count King?"

"Yea verily. Aye, I am the son of Count King, who in reality is really King King."

"That's redundant."

"King King has been bewitched by the bedraggled and bewildered wizardess with orange hair, VanGelder, and her toy jester named Priscilla who turned him into that nasty reptile in your moat. But look below! Subtle exposure of my own magic has turned the beast back into King King!"

Maid Meg peered from the turret. "Ugh, there he is. Thou are right. But what good canst this do?"

"The castle is thine," King King's scratchy hoarse voice echoed up from the moat. "But it must be both thines. Thous must turn it into a health spa for apprentice frog princes and call it Prince King and Maid Meg's Home for Ailing and Otherwise Out of Shape Frog Princes. Deal?"

"Deal!" Maid Meg and Prince King said in unison.

Maggie stopped Ty again. "If you're going to say the White Knight saves the day, I can't stand it. At least let me modernize the ending a bit."

"Have a stab at it." Ty turned the story back to her.

"It's a deal, except for one thing," Maid Meg asserted.

"What is that, my lovely lady?"

"The billing's all wrong. It shall be Maid Meg's and the Prince's, got it?"

"Nay verily, no more Mister Knight Guy. Surely thou canst not expect me, the most respected knight in the kingdom, to accept a reduction in title?"

"Deed I do. If it weren't for the merry maids in these tales, thou's swash would certainly be buckled, and thy derring-do . . . done in."

"Thou must be kidding," quoth Prince King.

"I kiddest thee not," vowed the fairest maiden."

Ty cut in. "My turn again."

"But what about true love?" Tyler Hood queried.

Maggie stopped him. "Cut! Stop there. I'll answer for the maiden."

"What about true love? Tell me another Grimm fairy tale."

Ty's head spun around. "Wait a minute. Fairytales are supposed to have happy endings."

"You're right, I apologize. Go ahead. Make it an ending worthy of the finest fairy tale." Maggie started humming "Greensleeves" again, and Ty continued.

"So Maid Meg and the Prince went into the animal health club business together, each with fifty percent interest in the castle once the moat was dredged, and surely, as business partners, they lived happily ever after.

Maggie looked up at him with a grin. "Yea verily, my liege, but who is this Shirley?"

The two laughed companionably, perhaps for the first time since they met.

"That was fun," Maggie said quietly.

"It was," Ty agreed. "Did you like that, Tad?"

From his nest in the crook of Maggie's arm, Tad slept soundly. Maggie smoothed the shaggy hair from his forehead.

"I think Tad says 'yea verily.' "

A cloud passed over the moon. Maggie shivered. Ty pulled her jacket up around her shoulders and smoothed Tad's tousled hair.

Maggie removed the boy's glasses and dropped them in her pocket. She cuddled him closer to her. "Real life doesn't work like fairy tales. Even with the ERA and feminism and the men's movement, women and men still struggle with their roles in life."

Ty nodded. "That's probably from the way we were raised. I have no experience to speak from, but I think it must be more difficult than ever to be a parent these days. I suppose you could teach kids the best you know, and then have it all undone by television or other kids or whatever."

"True. There's no frame of reference anymore. My parents raised me based on what their parents had taught them; for the most part, it worked. Although, they were pretty shocked when I divorced. That wasn't understood at all. I was the first in the family, the pioneer. Then, when I wanted to become a veterinarian, they were astounded. Another first for our family, a woman doing a man's job. They wanted to know why I didn't want to be a teacher or a nurse."

She could feel Ty being thoughtful

next to her on the log. In the dim light she saw him clasp his hands in front of him and continue to stare into the twisted tree down the beach. He spoke after a long silence.

"I did exactly as my parents wanted me to do, no questions asked. They wanted me to become a lawyer. I became a lawyer. Of course, they hadn't figured on entertainment law. Pure fluff, Father thought." He went quiet again for several moments. "And they never bargained for Sylvie."

She turned her head slightly. "Sylvie?"

"Someone I was married to once."

Maggie noted that he didn't say "my wife" and that his voice carried the hollow sound of loneliness. It was on her lips to ask if he'd loved her, but she thought better of it.

Ty stood up and held his open palm above his shoulder. "I think I just felt a couple of raindrops."

"It is getting chilly," Maggie said. "We should head back."

"I think so. I don't much like driving after dark."

"Me too. It never used to bother me,

but the older I get the more I can't see well at night."

Ty stared up at the cloud-filtered moon. "Yeah."

Maggie started to rouse Tad. "Come on, big boy, time to go home."

Ty touched her arm. "Don't wake him. I can carry him. Poor little guy. He's worrying about so much."

"I know. And I'm worried about him."

Maggie followed Ty as he carried Tad to the car. He settled the boy in the backseat and covered him with a sweatshirt he kept there. He turned the key in the ignition and raised the convertible top. When it was secure, Maggie got into the passenger side. Ty slid into the driver's side and pulled his seat belt over.

"I could have held the door for you," he said quietly.

"You were busy. No need for that."

When they were out on the highway and heading back toward Cape Agnes, Ty hummed the refrain from "Greensleeves."

"Too bad it can't be like it was in the olden days, you know?"

"Why, for heaven's sake?"

"Because guys need to be heroes every now and then. Helps them renew a sense of who they are, why they're here. Everybody's got to understand why they're here."

"That's not always clear. Are you speaking about yourself?"

Ty was silent for a long moment. Then, "Maybe."

Up to now it hadn't occurred to Maggie that she'd like to figure out Tyler King. Quite unexpectedly she found herself wondering about him. Wondering about personal things. Like his law practice. Caesar. Sylvie. The silence was almost deafening.

"All this because I wouldn't let you open the car door for me?" Maggie decided a little joke might break the tension filling the space around them.

"See?" Ty picked up the mood. "If you'd let me be a hero and open that extremely heavy door for you, all this philosophizing would not have come about. I hoped you've learned a big lesson here, Maid Meg."

"Tell you what," she said flippantly, "if

I'm ever stuck in a turret surrounded by a polluted moat, I promise you'll be the first person I call. Deal?"

"Deal. Just as long as you don't call me Shirley."

Maggie laughed. "This evening was fun. Even your grim fairy-tale was fun. You must have knocked 'em dead in the courtroom, Counselor."

"I wasn't bad, I'll admit. I'll also admit this was a good time. I'm not certain we solved any world-shattering problems. Or even any of our own."

Maggie turned to look over the seat and for a moment watched her grandson sleep. "No, I guess not."

"My fee was usually much more comprehensive than dinner."

"I'm sure it was." There were a hundred more things on her mind right now. For a strange reason she felt like talking with Ty about them. "Tell you what. Since you got an extra client on the docket tonight, I can offer you a cup of coffee or hot chocolate at my place as payment. What do you think?"

Ty nodded, and let out a breath through his nostrils. "That sounds nice.

I'd love to see your castle rooms, fair princess."

"Please. That's *Doctor* Princess."

"Of course. My error."

Ten

They climbed the open back stairway to Maggie's apartment, the still sleeping Tad bobbing on Ty's shoulder.

"It's not a beach house, but we've made it pretty comfortable." Maggie turned the key in the lock and pushed the door open, then switched on the lamp on the telephone stand.

"What's that awful smell?" Ty said. "I'm sorry. That was rude."

"No, it wasn't. There is an awful smell in here. Let's get Tad into bed, and then I'll investigate it."

Two cats, one yellow and the other a gray with white markings, jumped off the blue plaid couch, yawned and stretched. Maggie bent down and scratched the ears on the gray.

"This is Mouseketeer, and that yellow fat cat is Tramp."

"Good evening, gentlemen, I hope I'm not disturbing you." The cats turned and gave him cold shoulders and followed Maggie down the hall. Ty watched them walk away. "Thank you. Your welcome makes me feel right at home."

"Here's Tad's room." Maggie stepped into the small space and snapped on a light atop a painted pine bureau. "Oh my God!"

Ty sidled into the room. "What's the matter?"

And then he saw it. A pile of wet filthy plaster lay in the middle of a single bunk bed and was strewn all over the floor. A steady stream of water trickled down the wall near the corner and made a widening puddle on the floor.

"Take Tad back to the living room," she instructed. "Put him on the couch. I've got to go upstairs and see if Elmer's all right." She hurried out.

Ty followed her back to the living room, gently lowered Tad to the couch, and covered him with a colorful block crocheted afghan that had been draped over the back of it. The boy settled into the throw pillows and let out a long sigh. Oh, to be as oblivious as a ten-year-old to the troubles all around, thought Ty. Then he remembered how troubled the boy had been in the restaurant.

Maggie pounded on the third-floor apartment door. "Elmer?"

"Yeah, it's open," came an exasperated voice from the other side.

Inside she heard the clank of metal against metal coming from the bathroom. She went down the narrow hall. Elmer was in a pair of baggy boxer shorts, armed with a wrench, bending over the faucet end of the iron clawfoot tub.The tub was full and spilling over, the floor was wet, and Elmer's face was red with exertion.

"What happened?" Maggie went around him and took the wrench from his hands.

Elmer straightened with much difficulty. "The damned fool thing. I was taking a bath and the water cooled. I turned on the tap for more hot water and it came in cold. Then it wouldn't shut off. Then the tub wouldn't drain. I got out and tried everything." His voice was shaky with frustration.

"I can see that. Here, put this on." She grabbed an old flannel robe from a hook on the back of the door. It was a miracle he hadn't suffered a heart attack.

"Well, what are we going to do to get this water off? No plumber's going to come out this time of night, let alone Sid Baker." Elmer bent to pick up his slippers near the toilet. They were wet.

"We'll fix it ourselves. I'll go down to the basement and shut it off there. But you come down to my place now."

Maggie opened her apartment door and Elmer stepped inside. Immediately he screwed up his face. "What's that god-awful stink in here?"

"Hello, Dr. Everett." Ty stood near the couch.

"Oh. King. What are you doing here?"

"Baby-sitting and trying to keep from passing out from the odor. What happened?"

"That's what I'd like to know. Colleague?"

Maggie came out of the kitchen with a flashlight and a pair of pliers. "Well, Elmer," she said gently, "the water from your bathroom sort of knocked the ceiling down on Tad's bed and flooded his room."

Elmer flattened a palm over his heart. "Oh, I am so sorry. Good thing the boy wasn't in there at the time."

"Don't worry now." Maggie patted his arm. "It's nothing too terrible. I'll be right back."

"Where are you going?" Ty asked.

"To the basement to shut off the water."

"Let me do that." He started toward her.

"I can do it myself. I know just the right touch. You stay here and keep an eye on Elmer and Tad."

"Tad?" Elmer squinted. "He's home already?"

"A surprise visit," Ty told him. He motioned toward the couch.

Elmer walked over and looked down at the sleeping boy. "What I wouldn't give to be able to sleep like that. Looks like he doesn't have a care in the world."

"Looks can be deceiving," Ty said.

"Don't I know it," Elmer said.

A loud banging reverberated through the walls, and shortly afterward the sound of running water in the wall ceased. More rumbling occurred.

Elmer glanced around the ceiling. "That thunder?"

"Sounds like the rain is building into a real storm," Ty said.

"Well, we sure don't need any more water right now," Elmer said, nodding.

Maggie returned to the apartment, wrench in hand, dirt on her face and cobwebs in her hair. "That should take care of things till morning." She set the wrench on the floor and swiped a cobweb off her eyelashes. "I think this time I'll ask Harry if he would have a look at it. If he can keep the Suds 'n Duds going, he should be able to think of something to make these old pipes work. I don't think Mr. Baker will ever touch our plumbing—I mean, *your* plumbing again." She shot a glance at Ty.

"My plumbing," he said flatly.

"Well, now, what the heck am I going to do with that mess up in my place?" Elmer scratched his head.

"Don't worry about it tonight, Elmer. You can stay here with us. Somewhere."

Maggie went down the hall and

checked her own bedroom next to Tad's. It was the same. Fallen plaster and water everywhere, and a smell that would put off even the town dump inspectors. Maggie went back to the living room.

"Looks like this is the driest room in the place. You can have the couch and I'll fix something up for Tad and me on the floor."

"Now, Colleague, I'm not going to let you sleep on the floor. I can go up to my place. Fact is, you could sleep up there. My bedroom should be okay. 'Course my couch ain't so good."

"Wait a minute," Ty cut in. "We can solve this whole thing very easily. All three of you can come over to my house. There's plenty of room. Just grab what you need and we'll leave before the storm gets too bad."

"No thanks," Maggie said. "Elmer, you go with Ty. Tad and I will stay right here." The two cats leapt up onto the couch and circled and meowed. "Oh, I'm so sorry, boys, I forgot to feed you. Come on." She started for the kitchen and the cats jumped down from the couch and trotted after her.

"Why is that woman so stubborn?" Ty said. The question was more to himself than to Elmer.

"She sure is," Elmer whispered with pride evident in his voice. "She is really something. I wouldn't want her to know this, you understand, but she's a better vet than I ever was. Knows so much more. Why, if she ever went into farm animals she'd have more business than she ever dreamed of. But she's partial to dogs and cats."

"Well, if she's so smart," Ty whispered back, "how come she can't see that for one night all three of you could be in a comfortable dry place while we all figure out what to do with this white elephant I'm stuck with?"

"Because it's you offering. And because of her pride, of course," Elmer whispered with exasperation. "I'm game to go to your place. And I think the boy ought to have a dry bed to sleep in. But you gotta get her permission for that to happen."

Ty opened his arms wide, then shrugged his shoulders, sending a questioning look to Elmer.

"Figure it out, kid, figure it out." Elmer went over to Tad and pulled the afghan closer around him.

Ty understood he would get no assistance from Dr. Everett. Everybody in this town was as stubborn as a mule. Most especially Dr. Maggie Logan.

When Ty approached the kitchen door an odd smell assaulted his nostrils. It wasn't coffee brewing. It was something he couldn't define, and it grew stronger as he entered the kitchen.

Maggie was peering into the sink while the two cats rubbed around her ankles, purring for dinner.

"Lose something?" He came up behind her and peered into the sink with her, and his eyes watered. The odor was overwhelming.

"Only my mind. Look at this! The sink has been performing like Mount St. Helen. The drains in the clinic must have backed up again. It's never been so bad that it reached up here as well. The smell is atrocious."

"You're telling me." Ty frowned and wrinkled his nose. "What do you usually do when this happens? Grab a plunger?

Call a plumber? Move out for a few days? Now there's a good idea."

"A plunger has no effect. I know from experience. I *beg* the only plumber in town, Sidney Baker. Then I listen to how overworked he is, and then I barter with a bonus and free veterinary care for his two dogs and three cats for six months."

"Pretty steep rates, I'd say."

"They'll be even steeper now. I've never had to ask him to come to my apartment, only the clinic. If he honors me with a cameo appearance up here at this time of night, I'll be indebted to him for the next year." The cats meowed louder. Maggie went to the refrigerator and took out two tall cans of cat food. "Coming, guys, I know you're hungry." Using a fork, she scooped out portions from the two cans and plopped them into two different bowls.

"Selective menus?" Ty sniffed into the cans. "At least that stuff smells better than the sink drain."

"Each of them prefers a different food. I have no idea how they got that way. I've adapted to them." She set the bowls on the floor on opposite ends of the kitchen.

The lights overhead dimmed slightly, and Maggie looked up. "Now what?"

"Could be this storm is getting worse."

"I know you don't want to stay here now and have coffee. I'm sorry about this." She was apologizing to him as if everything were her fault. How ironic.

"You don't have to stay here, either. The invitation is still open for you all to come to my place. I have coffee and hot chocolate. And I can build a fire in the fireplace. And Caesar would enjoy your company. Okay?"

The lights flickered again, grew brighter, then went off altogether. "For heaven's sake," Maggie muttered. She fumbled through a drawer until she found a flashlight. She switched it on, illuminating Ty's face. He was grinning.

"What are you laughing about?" she asked with exasperation.

"I'm not laughing. Honest. I was just thinking how you seem to be a magnet for mishaps."

"Then you *are* laughing."

"All right, I do find it amusing that . . . things seem to just find you and turn into catastrophes."

"If that's true, I really don't believe I ever was a magnet for them until I met you. Well, maybe a little. Now that I think of it that's only because I moved into a building belonging to *your* father, and now to *you*. You really are laughing at me, aren't you?"

"Okay, I am laughing, it's true. Not at your expense, I hope you understand. But now that I've come clean with my confession, how about turning off the interrogation light?"

"Sorry." She moved the light away from his face and aimed the beam toward the floor. "We'd better go and see that Elmer and Tad are all right."

Ty stopped her. "I continue to have the same good idea I've had for the last hour. Why don't you just spend the night at my house? Now before you say no, let me say that you needn't worry about imposing or putting me out. It's no trouble, really. And you really should make a house call on Caesar, you know."

The rain blew against the back of the building and the room grew damp and cold. Maybe it was a good idea for them all to go to Ty's house.

Wait a minute. If she accepted his offer, that would be like setting up her tent in enemy camp. And, she accepted the creeping realization, like setting up her feminine emotions for something she hadn't wanted to contend with for years. No matter how angry she'd been at Tyler King from the moment she'd first learned of his existence, the emotion had been tempered by something else. Attraction. This couldn't be happening to her.

"Hello?" he said near her ear.

"I couldn't, I mean we couldn't," she said quickly. "I mean, it truly is an imposition. We'll be just fine here. Tad and I know the place very well in the dark. It's one of the reasons I don't want to leave, you know. For Tad. He's very comfortable here. And I'll watch out for Elmer. And then there are the cats to consider."

Ty waited a moment. "You've run out of a grocery list of reasons by now, I presume, so let me respond to each. You could. It's definitely not an imposition. Maybe you would be all right here, and maybe not. In any case, there's no need for you to stay and be uncomfortable. I understand about Tad, but he is capable of getting used to another place temporarily. As for Elmer, he's ready to go. These cats look pretty self-sufficient to me, and they'll be able to stand being here without you for one night. There. Did I hit everything?"

He felt like a teenager suddenly, and even with sweating palms it was a good feeling. He couldn't leave her here tonight. "Doctor?" he whispered. "You still here?"

"Yes." Maggie stood in the middle of indecision. "You're sure?" she asked at last. "I mean, maybe it would be a good idea just for tonight. It wouldn't be too much trouble?"

"Good. And it's no trouble at all. Can you find what you need for you and Tad with the flashlight?"

"I think so. And we should check the clinic before we go. I hope there isn't too much damage down there."

She moved around him on the way out of the kitchen, and Ty followed her. He stepped down on something soft and squirming. One of the cats let out a yell.

"I'm sorry," he said into the back of Maggie's dark form.

"He'll be all right," Maggie said over her shoulder. "Unfortunately for you that was Mouseketeer. He never forgets any slight injustice done to him."

"I'll think of a peace offering for the next time I see him."

"Make sure the pizza has anchovies."

"Mmm, this was a good idea," Maggie murmured, pulling up the collar of her aqua terry robe and sipping from a mug. She lounged against thick floor pillows strewn in disarray in front of the fireplace in Ty's beach house.

"Of course it was. I'm glad you thought of it." Ty winked and smiled at her as he reached for the black poker. He pushed at the fragrant burning logs causing an upward shower of sparks.

Outside, the wind raged and huge raindrops pelted the windows and tapped on the shingled roof. Inside, Tad was tucked into a small bedroom just down the hall. Caesar snored happily on the rug beside the boy's cot, and Elmer peacefully slept in a guest bedroom across from them. Over Maggie's protestations Ty had set her suitcase in his bedroom, and taken one pillow and an extra blanket into the living room for himself to use on the couch.

She eyed him lazily now. The crackling fire and rich hot chocolate laced with rum were comforting, and she felt herself relaxing into uncustomary languor.

"I like your grandson," he said into the fire. "And Elmer is a real gem."

"I don't know what I'd do without them," she replied. "Tad seems comfortable with you. And you hooked Elmer with his own VCR."

"He's great in the musical production, you know? In the community theaters I've worked with in the past, I've never met so many people who care about it as if they're opening on Broadway."

"Mmm. Cape Agnes is a great place to live."

"I'm beginning to think that's so."

"I hope you mean that," she said. "Capers really care about the people who live in their town. As long as others show that they care as well. Newcomers sometimes have a difficult time adjusting."

"I'm hardly a newcomer." Ty gave a light laugh.

"In a way you are. You went away a boy whom some of them once knew, and you came back a man most of them don't know."

He tilted his head. "I guess that's probably right."

"And you came back not really knowing the town anymore. Some things are still the same, but a lot has changed. At least that's the way I viewed it when I returned."

"You're right about that, I know," he said. "And I think I've been trying too hard."

"At what?"

"At fitting in."

Maggie nodded. "Mmm. Just relax. You'll be fine."

"I'm surprised you said that."

"Why?"

"Because of . . . everything."

She was silent.

He was quiet for a long time, too. "Can anything be done about Tad's sight problems?"

Maggie sighed. "Not much right now."

"What happened? Was he hurt?"

"No. It's a hereditary disease, or so

they think right now. They call it Leber's congenital amaurosis."

"I've never heard of that."

"It's a deterioration of the retina."

Ty turned to look at her directly. He wanted to know more about Tad's problem. It suddenly dawned on him how much he didn't know. He'd never heard of such a disease, yet here was a delightful little boy living with it, knowing what it meant and what he faced in the future.

"Can't it be treated?"

"They tell me that there's no cure for it based on current medical knowledge. Apparently research into the creation of a man-made optic nerve is being conducted right now. But you know how that goes." She sighed. "There's never enough money for research. And time just slips away."

Ty nodded. "I know. Has anyone else in your family had it?"

"No. Alyssa and her husband adopted Tad and they didn't know all the medical history about him, so a lot that might help him is unavailable to us. None of this has made us love him any less, I can tell you. He's the most special little boy

in the world. I've had him to Massachu-
setts Eye and Ear Hospital many times.
His doctors and nurses all adore him, too,
of course. But right now there's nothing
they can do for him. They feel just as
helpless as we do."

Ty took it all in, trying to grasp what
the boy and his grandmother faced on
their own. His own problems seemed
vastly insignificant at the moment. He
wondered if he could live gracefully with
something so pernicious. "Has he been
handling it all right?" he asked carefully.

"Up until recently. I don't think he believed anything was going to happen to
him. You know how kids are. Then the
sight really began to go."

"Tough."

"Yes, but at least he continues to hope
something will happen before he's too
old."

"What about in the meantime?" Ty
asked in earnest. "He can't go through
life waiting for a scientific breakthrough."

"We can understand that as adults, but
a child is hard to convince of that. He's
got one good friend. Robby. They used
to do a lot of things together. I'm afraid

that lately Tad is pulling back from him. Robby's been hurt by it, I think, but I can't force Tad to be with someone if he doesn't want to be with him."

"Sure, you can. It would probably be good for him."

Maggie's back straightened. "Oh, really. And just how do you think I can go about that?"

"What did they like to do together?" he pressed, ignoring the skeptical edge in her voice.

"Play cowboys. They're too old for that now."

"What else?"

"I don't know. Stuff. Whatever kids do when they hang out together. Robby's moving into something new now. The track coach has started an elementary track team and Robby's on it. This really hurts Tad a lot because whenever they would race each other, Tad always used to beat Robby. Now he can't even run."

"We'll see about that."

"What do you mean?"

"I don't know yet. I'm thinking."

"Please don't push him into anything he's not ready for," Maggie cautioned.

"You mean like the guide dog camp?"

"I believed that to be necessary."

"For what it's worth, I think you were right. Too bad Tad is so against it." He stretched out his long legs. "Maybe he just needs time."

"I hope that's it." Maggie sipped the hot chocolate. "Delicious," she murmured as Ty dropped down next to her on the pillows.

He gazed into the fire for a long moment, nodding his head. "I'll say, and the hot chocolate's not bad either."

Maggie giggled, then quickly placed a hand over her mouth. "How much rum did you put in this mug?" She peered into the dark contents with studied scrutiny.

"Enough to make you fall victim to my charms, my pretty," he laughed with mock villainy.

She didn't need a shot of rum to make that happen, Maggie mused. The dastardly deed was being done no matter how much she tried to dislike Tyler King. She wondered just how in the hell this sort of thing happened to strong-minded adults. Shouldn't there be some sort of immunity to this when one reached a certain age?

"I'm afraid you may be your own victim in this evil plot, sir," she feigned melodramatically, the back of her hand sweeping over her forehead. "Your concoction has turned into a sleeping potion, and I fear I shall not be awake enough to appreciate your advances. Should you be predisposed to make them, that is."

Ty turned toward her. "If I were predisposed to make an advance," he said quietly, "would you mind that very much?"

Maggie sipped thoughtfully. She swallowed. "I honestly don't know."

"Well, then, the only recourse is for me to make that advance. Then you'll know if you mind or not, and I'll have my question answered."

"It's not quite that simple."

"Why not?"

She balanced her mug on her bent knee. "Because of who you are."

"Who I am?"

"Yes. You represent so many negative things for me. Everything I've worked for you have the power to destroy, and you're using that power. Up until tonight, that is, when your building helped things along."

Ty understood. Once he might not have cared who got hurt in the process of his own progress, but this time it was different. He was personally becoming attached to the people involved. What else could he do? He saw no solution for himself. He was in as much of a bind as she was.

"You don't know how much I wish I could figure out how to make everything work out all right. For all of us," he added sincerely. "I'm no wizard, even if I once thought I was, fair maiden."

She waited a few moments before she was able to whisper back, "Methinks thou speakest the truth."

Slowly he reached over and took the mug from her hand. He set it with his on the coffee table behind them. Then he leaned over, his lips poised just above hers for a brief moment before he gently caught her mouth.

Maybe it was the heat generating from the fireplace, or maybe it was the rum and the hot chocolate, or maybe it was both and the touch of the soft kiss that made Maggie's skin tingle the way sun and sand did at the beach. It was easy to kiss him back. Too easy.

Carefully she drew back from the kiss. "I guess that had to happen, didn't it?" Those seemed like sane, sophisticated words when she said them, and she wondered where they had come from. At that moment she felt neither sane nor sophisticated.

"I believe it did, yes," Ty said quietly.

"I think I should say that I . . . I mean, I didn't do that . . . I hope you don't think I kissed you because I'm grateful that you took in the three of us tonight. The place was really a mess. And the clinic. . . ."

Ty moved slightly. "That never occurred to me. I thought you kissed me because you wanted to. I certainly kissed you because I wanted to."

"Why?" She said that too quickly. "God, that sounded awful, didn't it? I really don't know how to do . . . this." She smoothed her robe over her knees then hugged them to her chest, concentrating on the fire. "You're right. I kissed you because I wanted to. And I wanted you to kiss me, too."

He sighed loudly and settled back against the pillows. "Well, I'm glad that's settled."

Maggie gazed into the fire a long time. ".Nothing is settled. Far from it. It's just that it's been a long time for me. I mean, I'm not sure how I'm supposed to act, what I'm supposed to feel. I guess that probably sounds pretty naive to you, doesn't it?"

"No, it doesn't. Maybe you'll find this difficult to understand, but . . . it's been a long time for me, too."

She looked at him then. "You're right. I would have expected otherwise."

"Why?"

"Well, you do have a certain charm that attracts people. Old people, I mean. And kids. And definitely Darlene Thompson."

He laughed. "You left out dogs and crotchety old parrots."

"I was getting to those."

"What about you?" he whispered.

She laughed nervously. "I said old people, didn't I?"

He watched her face in the firelight.

"You know, of course, that you have just set me up. No matter what I say it's going to sound wrong."

"Then don't say anything."

"I have to."

"Chancy."

"I know. I like taking chances. First of all, it would be impossible for me, or anyone else, I suspect, to think of you as old."

"I've got over five years on you, and don't tell me you didn't add that up before now."

"I added it up. The answer surprised me. I've been feeling a bit like Methuselah these days. You look like the maiden in our fairy tale."

"Ha! I'd like to take that as a compliment."

"Please do. It was meant as an honest one. Anyway, the numbers just don't matter. But, let me walk on a few eggshells here and say that if you contend I attract old people—and you included yourself in that group—then it follows that I might deduce that you find me attractive? Because if that's what you mean, you should know something. I find you *very* attractive. More than that."

All was quiet, save for the drumming of raindrops against the window.

Maggie stirred slightly. "Now what? I feel very awkward right now."

"Like in high school, I know."

"You, too?"

"Yeah." He tapped two fingers against his forehead. "That wasn't cool. Guys aren't supposed to say things like that, are they?"

"I don't know. Is that what guys talk about when they get together? Whether they should be macho all the time or let their sensitive sides show through now and then?" Maggie let out a wry little laugh. "I suppose men think that's what will trap a woman. Tenderness."

"I'd hate to think it was a trap, but would tenderness appeal to you?"

"You ask very direct questions," she said.

"That's because I really want to know the answers. I sensed you were very direct, and I thought. . . ." he stopped. "No, I didn't think. I just blurted those things out."

When she didn't answer he felt her nervousness as acutely as he felt his own.

Something was happening here and they both knew it. What they both didn't know was how to handle it.

He leaned up and poked at the lowering fire, then settled back against the pillows and touched his shoulder to hers. "What do you think is going to happen to us, Doc?"

She shook her head slightly. "I don't know. I do know you're geographically unsuitable for me."

Ty was taken by surprise with that comment. "What do you mean? I'm right here in your town."

"That's the problem."

"Meaning?"

"There's too much at stake for me. More than I think you understand." She hugged her knees to her chest. "And I was never very good at happy endings."

"Me either."

The fire lowered to glowing embers. Neither of them spoke another word.

Eleven

Maggie dreamed she was the star in an animated fairy-tale film. She'd been asleep for fifty years. And she was just about to be awakened by the kiss of a handsome prince when she smelled coffee.

She stirred and nestled deeper under the blanket. Amazing. The aroma was so pungent that she practically envisioned the cup hovering just under her nose. Then she felt a mist of steam drift over her face.

"Prince Charming?" she asked sleepily.

"No, Juan Valdez," Ty said laughing, "but if you'd rather have the prince, you know I am only too happy to oblige."

Maggie blinked, and forced her eyes open. Tyler King was hunkered down beside her holding out a mug. She jumped.

"Oh, my God! What are you doing here?"

He was smiling. "I live here. Coffee?"

She sat up quickly and clutched the blanket to her neck. "This is your bed."

"Uh-huh." He indicated for her to take the mug.

She closed her eyes. "Yes, I remember now." Timidly she accepted the coffee.

"Did you sleep well?"

She eyed him suspiciously. "Why? Did you . . . did I . . . that is, did we . . . ?"

He sat down on the floor next to the bed and chuckled. She shifted her head and peered down at him. "Was it that humorous?"

"It is now. To answer all your questions, in a word, yes."

"*Yes!* Oh my God. And with Tad and Elmer just down the hall. What was I thinking?"

"Don't worry. They slept through the whole thing."

She frowned. "I don't remember anything about it."

"A lesser man might be hurt by that response. Fortunately my ego is intact."

"What was in that hot chocolate you gave me?"

"Rum. Let me elaborate. Yes, the hot

Now, for the first time...

You can find Janelle Taylor, Shannon Drake, Rosanne Bittner, Sylvie Sommerfield, Penelope Neri, Phoebe Conn, Bobbi Smith, and the rest of today's most popular, bestselling authors

...All in one brand-new club!

Introducing KENSINGTON CHOICE,
the new Zebra/Pinnacle service that delivers the best
new historical romances direct to your home,
at a significant discount off the publisher's prices.

As your introduction, we invite you to accept 4 FREE BOOKS worth up to $23.96

details inside...

We've got your authors!

If you seek out the latest historical romances by today's bestselling authors, our new reader's service, KENSINGTON CHOICE, is the club for you.

KENSINGTON CHOICE is the only club where you can find authors like Janelle Taylor, Shannon Drake, Rosanne Bittner, Sylvie Sommerfield, Penelope Neri and Phoebe Conn all in one place...

...and the only service that will deliver their romances direct to your home as soon as they are published—even before they reach the bookstores.

KENSINGTON CHOICE is also the only service that will give you a substantial guaranteed discount off the publisher's prices on every one of those romances.

That's right: Every month, the Editors at Zebra and Pinnacle select four of the newest novels by our bestselling authors and rush them straight to you, even *before they reach the bookstores*. The publisher's prices for these romances range from $4.99 to $5.99—but they are always yours for the guaranteed low price of just *$3.95!*

That means you'll always save over $1.00...often as much as *$2.00*...off the publisher's prices on every new novel you get from KENSINGTON CHOICE!

All books are sent on a 10-day free examination basis, and there is no minimum number of books to buy. (A postage and handling charge of $1.50 is added to each shipment.)

As your introduction to the convenience and value of this new service, we invite you to accept

4 BOOKS FREE

The 4 books, worth up to $23.96, are our welcoming gift. You pay only $1 to help cover postage and handling.

To start your subscription to KENSINGTON CHOICE and receive your introductory package of 4 FREE romances, detach and mail the postpaid card at right *today*.

We have 4 FREE BOOKS for you as your introduction to KENSINGTON CHOICE

To get your FREE BOOKS, worth up to $23.96, mail card below.

FREE BOOK CERTIFICATE

As my introduction to your new KENSINGTON CHOICE reader's service, please send me 4 FREE historical romances (worth up to $23.96), billing me just $1 to help cover postage and handling. As a KENSINGTON CHOICE subscriber, I will then receive 4 brand-new romances to preview each month for 10 days FREE. I can return any books I decide not to keep and owe nothing. The publisher's prices for the KENSINGTON CHOICE romances range from $4.99 to $5.99, but as a subscriber I will be entitled to get them for just $3.95 per book. There is no minimum number of books to buy, and I can cancel my subscription at any time. A $1.50 postage and handling charge is added to each shipment.

Name _____

Address _____ Apt. # _____

City _____ State _____ Zip _____

Telephone (___) _____

Signature _____

(If under 18, parent or guardian must sign)

Subscription subject to acceptance

KC 0994

We have
4
FREE
Historical
Romances
for you!

Details inside!

KENSINGTON CHOICE
Reader's Service
120 Brighton Road
P.O.Box 5214
Clifton, NJ 07015-5214

chocolate kind of knocked you for a loop. Probably because you were exhausted. Yes, I helped you to this bed."

Her eyes widened. He knew he was carrying this little game pretty far, but it was too much fun not to do it. Now she looked stricken. He supposed he couldn't have that.

"And . . . yes . . . we . . . slept in separate beds. Well, actually, you slept in my bed and I sort of slept on the couch in the living room. I never noticed how short that thing is. The couch, I mean."

Her unspoken relief was visible when her taut body relaxed.

Maggie savored the coffee then, and took a few moments to let the reality of the morning settle in. "Has the rain stopped?"

"Mm-hm. Sun was coming up when last I looked." He sat up quickly. "Oh boy!"

"What?"

"Caesar! I forgot to let him out this morning. He's probably hugging the back door crossing his legs, poor thing." He pushed up from the floor and left the room.

Maggie pulled the blanket closer around her and savored the lingering sensations from deep sleep and good coffee. There was something quite satisfying about being awakened by a man bringing her that first cup of coffee of the day while she was still in bed. Too bad he was the wrong man.

She thought back to the early days of her marriage to John Logan. They were so young and very much in love then. At least she'd thought they were very much in love. When Alyssa was born, John was as ecstatic about her arrival as she'd been. He doted on her. She was his little princess. Maggie was the perfect wife, and John was her knight in shining armor. He worked long hours. He was successful in sales for a manufacturing firm. He began to travel more. The more successful he became the harder he worked, and the longer he would be away from home.

The year Alyssa started school was the beginning of the end. Maggie thought of that now. She and John lived separate lives. There was no one thing that precipitated their breakup, she knew that.

She married him believing it was for better or worse, forever. That was how she was about everything. Committed to working through any difficulty.

By the time she and John divorced she was not feeling devastated about it at all. The marriage had been over long before the divorce was final. She chose a life of her own and a way to continue to care for Alyssa. Choices were made, and it was her action through them that made those choices continue to work.

Life was hard. Too bad no one had ever told her that while she was growing up. Losing Alyssa was the hardest and most painful event of her life. At the funeral she saw the pain John was in. His new wife seemed to be at a loss to help him. Maggie understood. No one could help.

She would never get over Alyssa's death, she knew that. If it hadn't been for Tad coming to live with her, she wasn't certain to this day that she could have gone on. Life was no fairy tale, that was sure.

"And on that note," she said out loud, "time to check on reality."

Reluctantly she pulled herself out of the warm nest and slipped her robe over her nightgown. She ran her hand through her hair and peered into the mirror over the bureau. A comb lay among some loose change, a T-shirt, and some magazines. Ty's comb. No, she wouldn't use it. That seemed so personal an act. As if sleeping in his bed had not been a personal act. She seemed to be having trouble remembering this morning what her values were all about.

Maggie shook her head. "Get it together, old girl," she said out loud.

She thought about all she wanted to do right away. First, check on Tad and Elmer, and see about getting something for breakfast for them. Maybe she could go to the market. How? Her car was back on Elm Street. It was too long a hike for groceries, and she certainly didn't want to borrow Ty's car. Darlene would have a two-page spread on that if she saw her.

And what about everything else to worry about? She'd have to call Harry and ask him if he could take a look at the mess in the water pipes. She'd have to go over to her apartment soon and feed the cats who'd be very upset with her.

She took a quick shower, dressed, and went to where Tad had been sleeping. He wasn't there. A check on Elmer's room found him missing as well. She went to the kitchen. Ty was dishing up bacon, eggs, and toast for Elmer who was saying something about having slept very well.

Anxiously she glanced around. "Where's Tad?"

Ty handed her a glass of orange juice. "Out back with Caesar. I worried needlessly about that dog's bladder control. Tad had him outside early this morning. He came back in long enough to pick up a plate of breakfast and go back out onto the porch. Wanted to watch the gulls, he said."

"Did he take his sunglasses?"

"He had them on."

Maggie checked on Tad's whereabouts and, seeing him eating breakfast and discussing something in earnest with Caesar, sat down at the table.

"That boy always did love the gulls," Elmer said. He savored a piece of egg.

"Pretty good cook for a lawyer. Remember that one with the hurt wing?"

"You knew a lawyer with a hurt wing?" Ty asked, purposefully teasing Elmer.

Elmer tilted his head back and forth a few times. "A comedian, too." He looked over at Maggie. "I worked on that bird for two hours."

"Did you save it?" Ty carried two plates of food to the table.

"Of course I saved him," Elmer said disgustedly.

"Elmer did a great job on that bird," Maggie said. "Too good, if you were to ask Tad. The bird flew away two days later. Tad meant to make a pet of it."

"Wasn't hurt that bad, anyway," Elmer said, scraping his plate. "Pretty amazing how Tad managed to catch it in the first place."

"He was always quick," Maggie said wistfully.

"This is a great old place, King." Elmer drained his coffee mug. "Been around here a long time. Used to be a carriage barn out back, as I recall."

"It's still there," Ty told him. "I haven't looked in it yet."

"Think I'll look it over if you don't mind."

"Be my guest."

"I am."

"Right." Ty laughed and watched the old man shrug on a cotton jacket and go out onto the porch. "He's a pistol, isn't he?"

"Fully loaded," Maggie said. "He's right. You're a pretty good cook. Have any other specialties?"

"Eggs are it, I'm afraid. Never had the time to cook until, well, just a few years ago. By that time the microwave oven had been invented and I learned how to prepare frozen dinners."

"I know. I never cooked much for myself when I was alone. But when Tad came to live with me, I had to do it. I'm not very good at it, I'm afraid."

"He doesn't look as if he's starving."

"He'll eat anything." Maggie cleaned her plate. "Well, I'd better bite the bullet and get this day rolling. I'll call Harry now, and then we'd better clean up and get back to town. That is, if you don't mind driving us in."

"I'll clean up. You go make your phone call."

Ty hummed as he cleared the table. He ran water in the sink and squirted in some soap to wash the dishes. This was good, having people in the house. It felt like a home. The feeling surprised him, and put a name on one of the things he'd felt was missing in his life.

He let out a long hard breath. Why hadn't his life with Sylvie ever felt this good, this comfortable? Life-style is what they called the way the two of them had lived. Life-style. If he could have just stuck to it the way it was, he and Sylvie would probably still be married. It was his fault they'd broken up. At least that's how he'd figured it. She would have gone on just the way it was, partying every weekend on this pal's yacht or that one's palatial mansion. It was he who'd grown sick of the whole scene. Maybe if he'd tried harder he wouldn't be divorced, and he wouldn't be in this financial predicament.

And he wouldn't have to wonder why he was struggling so hard to find a way to fix things so he could have his fitness center and Maggie Logan could have her animal clinic.

"I've got to get over to my apartment right away," Maggie said, walking into the kitchen.

Ty glanced up at her. Her face was flushed. "What's up? The cats can't open their own cans of food? Tsk, tsk, and I thought they were so smart."

"Harry says things are a disaster in the building. Half the town's been over there because of reports of flooding and power outages in the neighbor-hood. Seems all of it has to do with my building for some reason. I mean, your building. The village crew is there now, but they say they won't touch the place until after I see it. That means you'd better see it."

"What do they mean, touch it?"

She frowned. "Beats me, but I didn't like the sound of it. I'm really getting worried."

"Call Tad and Elmer and let's go."

When they rounded the corner of Elm Street, they were stopped by Officer

O'Toole. He bent down and peered into the car window.

"Sorry folks, this street's off-limits to vehicular traffic. Say, now, it's the animal doctor, isn't it?"

"Hello, Officer O'Toole," Maggie greeted him. "What's the problem?"

"Seems your building is about to cave in." O'Toole stood up straight and took a look down the block. "Still standing right now. But when it goes we don't want anybody down there getting hurt."

Maggie bolted from the car. "What do you mean, it's about to cave in?"

"Something to do with the roof, and all the rain last night. From what I gather, the roof was long overdue for repair. There was a lot of old damage that just couldn't take the storm, I fear. And some bad wiring. You shoulda reported that, miss, a long time ago."

Maggie closed her eyes and briefly tipped her head back. "I've got to get down there. My cats are in there!"

"Now, miss, you just take it easy now. If the fire chief says you can go in and rescue your cats, then it's okay by me."

"The fire department is there?" Tad

stuck his head out of the window on Maggie's side. "Cool."

"It is not cool, Tad. You stay here. I'm going down there."

"I'm going with you." Ty got out of the car.

"Me, too." Elmer groaned and got out of the backseat.

"Please, Elmer, stay with Tad," Maggie called over her shoulder. She ran down the street, Ty right behind her.

Elm Street was plugged with fire trucks, and the town's one police car and ambulance were parked in front of the clinic. People milled about behind yellow plastic strips. When Maggie and Ty got to the front door, they were stopped by the fire chief, Frank Reed, a short man in a yellow rubber coat, huge black rubber boots, and a brilliant yellow helmet upon which was stamped CAFD Chief.

"Hold it, Doc." He placed a restraining hand on her arm. "This place is now a designated disaster area."

"Frank, please. Let me get my cats out of there."

"Sorry, Doc, no can do. I'll send one of my men in."

"He won't be able to find them. They don't like men."

Ty shot her a quizzical glance. Maggie shrugged.

"Hold it right here," Frank Reed said. "Let me see what my men have assessed."

Maggie shivered. "Oh, please let them be all right," she said into the air.

Chief Reed returned. "All right. They say it's safe enough for you to go up there. But I'm going up with you."

"Let me go up with her, Chief," Ty cut in.

"Who're you?"

"I'm surprised you haven't heard yet. I'm Tyler King. I own this disaster area."

"Well, you've got some explaining to do, boy, if you come out of there."

Ty stopped at the entrance. "What do you mean *if*?"

"Slip of the tongue," the fire chief said. "When you come out, we'll let you know when your hearing is."

"Hearing?"

Darlene Thompson appeared at that moment from out of nowhere. Her stock in trade, Maggie thought with exasperation.

"What will you use as a defense, Mr. King?" she shouted, and held out a microphone with a long wire that led to a tape recorder strapped to her belt.

"Defense?" Ty frowned at her. "I wasn't aware I was on trial."

"Only a matter of time," Darlene said. "Were you inside when the disaster occurred, Dr. Logan?" she shouted. She whipped off her camera lens cap and snapped a photograph of Maggie and Ty with the fire chief.

"No, we were all safely out of here," Maggie said wearily, thinking that cooperating with the press, no matter how questionable that press might be, was the wisest thing to do.

"I see. And where did you spend the night?"

"I don't see how that's important. . . ." Maggie responded.

"At Mr. King's house!" Tad shouted from behind. "He saved our lives."

"Tad, it wasn't like that at all," Maggie said. "Elmer, please take Tad back to the car."

"Wait." Darlene Thompson followed Elmer and Tad. "How about an exclusive interview? How did Mr. King save you? Where did you sleep?"

"Talk about timing," Ty said, watching Darlene scurry after them. "She's better than any *paparazzi* I ever saw in action."

"Ty, forget her for now." Maggie started up the stairs. "If you're coming in, then come on."

Carefully they slogged through water and up the stairs. Ty pushed the door to her apartment open as far as he could get it.

"Oh no, look at this," Maggie groaned. She stepped into shoetop-high water in her living room. The cats meowed with annoyance at her from their perch on the back of the couch. Water dripped through the ceiling and everything was covered with fallen plaster and lath.

"Be careful," Ty warned.

Maggie squished her way to the cats. They weren't hurt, but they were frightened and cold. As she soothed each of them, she glanced around. Where to start? *How* to start to clean up the mess? Her few pieces of unmatched Salvation Army furniture were ruined, that was quite certain.

"Mr. King?" a voice echoed up the stairwell.

Ty stuck his head around the apartment door. "Yes."

"The fire chief has condemned the building. The roof's going to go sometime, and the town safety officials say you have only a few hours to get out what you can."

"Oh no," Maggie's eyes filled with tears. "My clinic, my home."

"I know." Ty pulled her into his arms.

"What am I going to do?" Maggie buried her face against Ty's shirt. She didn't cry. What good would that do?

"Come on," he said, rubbing her back, "let's salvage what we can here quickly, then we'll tackle the clinic."

With the help of many friends, by early afternoon Maggie and Ty had cleared the apartment of as much of hers and Tad's and Elmer's personal belongings as they could, along with the two cats. Jolene and Elmer supervised the cleaning out of the clinic, and Tad sat with the cats in their carriers and took in the proceedings with great curiosity.

When fire officials barred them from

going back inside, they all stood on the sidewalk and watched silently as part of the roof caved in.

Back at the beach house, Ty made coffee and dished up bowls of chowder and sandwiches for everyone. Little Bert had delivered a huge spread, including dishes and utensils, for the squad of people who'd come out to help them move and carry things. Mayor Atkins lent his pickup truck and helped them move everything they could save into the carriage barn behind Ty's beach house. They were a jovial group of townspeople, clearly feeling good about helping their neighbors.

Ty watched them. His chest swelled. Everyone from an eight-year-old child to an eighty-year-old woman carried what they could, taking direction from Maggie or Elmer or Jolene as to where the boxes and bags and furniture, what little was salvageable, could be placed. He hadn't remembered that this was how people could be. Some old chord struck in the back of his mind, and he swallowed a surprising sob that would have burst out if he hadn't caught it in time.

By the time everyone left, it was dusk. Tad and Elmer were in Elmer's room watching television. Maggie knew they were exhausted, but she noted what good spirits they seemed to be in. She slumped onto the couch, Mouseketeer and Tramp curled next to her. The cats eyed Ty with open skepticism while he built a fire in the big stone fireplace. When they weren't watching him, their eyes shifted to the far corner where Caesar lay staring at them with what could only be described as indignation in his soulful brown eyes.

"Don't worry, Doc, things will all work out," Ty said, trying to soothe her.

"I don't see how. I knew I was facing eventual eviction, but I didn't know it would be quite so abrupt."

"You probably won't think so, but neither my father nor I had anything to do with the flood." Ty struck a match and watched the fire catch.

"Maybe not you, but can you prove your father didn't put a curse on the place?" She gave a wry laugh. "I'm sorry, I guess I'm overreacting."

"I don't blame you. Fortunately Jolene and Elmer think they can make the barn do for the clinic for the time being. And just think," Ty added with an amused grin, "Elmer is talking about reviving an ancient art—house calls. They both seemed kind of excited about the whole prospect. Well, maybe Jolene isn't ecstatic about working in a barn with owls and mice for officemates." He was trying to lighten the bleakness of the dilemma for her, but wasn't having much luck.

He went into the kitchen and came back with two glasses of wine. "The old greenhouse and artist's studio at the back of the barn really are perfect for an animal clinic," he said with a hopeful note in his voice. He handed a glass to her.

"I know. I'm sorry if I sounded ungrateful. Thank you for being so generous."

"I'm glad I had the barn to offer. I just want things to work out for you, Doc." He sat down on the couch. Mouseketeer hissed at him.

"It's only temporary, I assure you," Maggie added hastily, soothing the cat's fur. "We'll be out of here as soon as we can find a place." She sipped the wine and dropped her head against the back of the couch.

"Stop fretting. You can stay as long as you like." Ty looked down at Tramp whose yellow eyes were now mere slits as he stared at him. "All of you."

He meant that. He liked the idea of Maggie being around the house. And Tad, of course. And even Elmer. Even Jolene and her boyfriend could come if they wanted to. Maybe he could see about turning the place into a condo. He'd even learn to live with the two cats. Caesar sighed in the corner. Ty guessed he'd have an easier time adjusting than the dog.

"Thank you. It really is temporary, and we'll move out just as soon as we can," she insisted again. "I do have some renter's insurance, so that will help with expenses. Whenever they get it to me."

"That could take years," Ty said.

"Why is that? You're a lawyer. Tell me why that is."

"I haven't a clue."

Ty got up to tend the fire. He set his glass on the shelf above the fireplace. He went back and lifted Maggie's feet, removed her sneakers, and stretched her legs out to rest on the coffee table. She watched him, but not as suspiciously as the cats did.

"Della Reese said it best," Maggie said.

"Whatever made you think of Della Reese?"

"She had this song out a long time ago. Something about what a difference a day makes."

"Oh, yeah. I remember that." Ty started to hum. "That it?"

"Mm-hm. I can hear her rich voice right now. Twenty-four little hours, she said. This has been more like twenty-four hours from hell."

"You think so? I don't think they've been that bad." Ty picked up his glass and drank, then peered down into the blaze.

"What? How can you say that? The building, *your* building may just fall in on itself, you know. What about your fitness center? Doesn't it bother you that your idea may become a pile of rubble along with my business and my home?"

"Not particularly."

"Don't you take anything seriously?"

"Of course, I do. But this isn't serious to me."

"Well, it is to me."

"You've lost more than I have." Ty walked over and sat on the couch, keeping his distance from the cats who wouldn't have let him any closer to Maggie anyway.

Maggie rolled her head to the side and stared at him. "I lost an apartment and a business. Elmer lost his home. You may lose an entire building. Why isn't that serious to you?"

He removed his glasses, folded them carefully, and placed them in a case on the coffee table. He dropped his head back on the couch and closed his eyes.

"Ah, Dr. Logan, don't you see? There are so many other things in life that are more important than a building, or property. I'm just beginning to learn about that."

"Meaning what? That you will just write out a check to replace the building with a brand-new one?"

"You couldn't be more wrong."

Maggie watched him for a long moment. She thought she'd begun to figure him out. A rich playboy, not a care in the world, taking nothing seriously. Money would solve everything. She was certain he thought that way. Up to now.

"Would you like to explain it to me so I'll get it right?" she asked quietly.

He opened his eyes and rolled his head to look at her. "Yes, I do. But not now. I'm too tired. And I want to be certain I understand it before I explain it to you."

Maggie rolled her head back. She stroked the two cats and closed her eyes. "Fair enough."

Twelve

Almost two weeks later Maggie stood inside the refurbished carriage barn, going over the chart of a canine patient. She looked around the place and smiled. The townspeople had moved in and cleaned and painted and laid flooring and installed lighting. Everyone with a trade offered it and those without special trades gave food to the crews and child care when needed.

The former greenhouse and its connecting artist's studio had been transformed into a veterinary clinic, filled with salvaged examining tables from the old clinic, cartons of medical supplies and instruments, and files and a typewriter. Jolene had hung plants in the many paned windows, and pictures lined the newly painted white walls. Everyone appeared relaxed and happy in the rustic clinic.

Jolene hummed as she typed up bills and records. Elmer buzzed in and out with news of this person or that, or who had purchased a new car recently, or who had a new grandchild. He'd stopped in at Dottie Dearborn's house and checked on her cat who'd had a confrontation with a squirrel, and dictated to Jolene how that particular patient was going to need close supervision. He'd have to check on her at least once a week. And he'd see that Hans made it home all right. Making house calls gave him a whole new social life and he was clearly enjoying it.

The steady flow of patients didn't let up. Just because Critter Care was no longer right in the village didn't seem to matter to pet owners wishing to board their animals or just ask for general checkups. Some visits were warranted and others, Maggie knew, were there just to be supportive of them.

Even Tad took an interest in the clinic now. He hung out for hours asking Maggie or Elmer questions. He soothed frightened cats, and replenished water bowls for boarding dogs. Wherever Tad was, Caesar was not far behind.

At the moment they were all firmly ensconced in Ty's house. At first, Elmer had seemed a little disoriented. He'd come to know his own little apartment in the other building so well that he had some difficulty settling down. Maggie hoped she would find a good place for them for his sake as well. He'd been talking vaguely about how he probably should move in with his daughter. She knew he didn't really want to do that, and she also knew how he felt about being a burden to anyone. No one, least of all Maggie, ever thought of him as such, but he was cognizant of the possibility.

Maggie wanted more than anything to get Elmer settled, get Tad settled, get herself settled. She continued to be on the lookout for a new building for the clinic.

"Nothing yet?" Jolene asked with a distinct lack of enthusiasm when Maggie came out to the desk. She knew how Maggie had been searching. Tad and Elmer stood at the end of the desk.

"Nothing yet, and nothing suitable for apartments either. I think I've exhausted every place in town. I guess I'm going to have to start looking outside of town."

"Too bad," Tad said with little sympathy in his voice.

"Yes, too bad," Elmer added.

"Try not to be so cheery about it," Maggie told them lightly. She sensed they were all quite happy with things just the way they were, and would be happier still if they all remained there.

"What about that cute little apartment across town I mentioned to you the other day? I thought you said it sounded ideal." Jolene didn't look at Maggie when she asked the question.

Maggie looked over a chart. "Way too small. Only one closet."

Maggie suddenly realized that she'd been finding fault with every apartment she looked at, even though one or two of them might have been sufficient. While she maintained she wanted to find something appropriate, she had to admit she was feeling as contented about the current arrangements as the others were. And that included living in Ty's house. Propriety urged her to move out, but she hadn't found the right place to go yet. Or so she said. And the longer they stayed the more comfortable they all became together, almost like a family. Tad loved the house and had familiarized himself with it almost immediately.

And Ty seemed in no hurry to have them leave either. She wondered about that. He refused to discuss rent with her, saying he owed it to her to have them stay there free of charge. After all, it was the disrepair of his building that had caused them to lose home and business.

When Maggie walked up to the house after the clinic closed that afternoon, she heard Ty talking as if he were arguing with someone. When she opened the back door, he was standing in the kitchen, hands planted on his hips, in the midst of a standoff with the gray cat.

"Mouseketeer won't eat his supper," Ty said as if reporting a naughty child to its mother.

"That's funny. He hasn't minded it every other night since we moved in here." Maggie went over to examine the cat's dish. "Well, no wonder. You've put Tramp's food in Mouseketeer's dish. He hates that."

"Well, Tramp didn't seem to mind the mistake."

Maggie looked around until she found the yellow cat. "That's because he'll eat anything, and right now he seems happy eating dog food." Tramp slurped away at Caesar's bowl while the big dog sat back whimpering. The gray sulked in a corner. "I don't think Mouseketeer has ever forgiven you for stepping on him that night in my apartment."

"How can anyone hold a grudge that long? I gave him a whole can of sardines, and he didn't seem to object to that."

"He probably knows it's a bribe."

"I never covered up that fact." Ty searched the inner depths of the refrigerator. "You're having dinner with your girlfriends tonight, right?"

"Right, and I'd better hurry. Roz and Jan are ready for their first glass of wine the moment they close up shop. Where's Tad?"

"In the shower. Don't worry about him." He pounded his chest à la Tarzan and said huskily, "We men can handle things in the kitchen."

"I'm glad I won't be here to observe. Where's Elmer?"

"Gone off to Mother's for the Friday night special. You probably know that means Dottie, not food. She gets her hair done at Roz's on Fridays. Her new do really brings out the diner patrons, I understand."

"You're becoming a regular Caper, aren't you?" Maggie went into the refrigerator for a bottle of grapefruit juice and a casserole dish. She poured a glass of the juice and leaned against the counter, watching Ty.

"It's important to stay up on things, you know."

"Really?"

"Yes. Did you know the Fisbees' baby has gained two pounds already?" Ty shook his head. "Amazing. And I thought only puppies grew that fast."

"Where did you hear that?"

"I read it in the society column of *The Cape Agnes News.* Don't tell me you didn't see that? Anyway, what I miss Darlene fills me in on."

Maggie stopped drinking. "Darlene? Have you . . . where did you see her?"

"I've been over to her office a couple of times. I've been reading some of the old newspapers from over a hundred years ago. Darlene has them all bound and indexed."

"I know. I helped do the work. Are you reading only the society columns, or do you find other things interesting?"

Ty gave her an enigmatic smile. "I like the history lessons I'm getting. Although, the society columns are pretty wild. Did you know that Jake Everett—Elmer's father, I'll bet—hit Lucille McClure in the back of the head with a blackboard eraser and had to clean the schoolhouse every day for a month after?"

"Yes, and later on he married her."

"And all because of a little chalk dust."

"Stranger things have happened, I'm sure," Maggie said.

"The founders of the town built a library and stocked it with their own books. Those were the Tylers, my great grandparents."

"I didn't know that."

"I didn't know about the books until I went over to the library. I didn't even know that Jolene's sister Jacalyn is the librarian."

"For the last three years."

"She looks just like Jolene. A knockout in her own way."

Maggie felt a tiny twinge and was aggravated about it.

Ty went on extolling the fine points of old Cape Agnes. "The library's in an old store that was also a fire station once. They shared it. Imagine that."

"Must have been difficult for the first librarian to be heard saying 'shh' when the fire bell clanged, I'll bet."

"Those old newspapers are wonderful. I could spend all day reading them."

"I'm sure Darlene enjoys that," Maggie said, and wished she hadn't.

"Well, I've tried to be helpful to her for letting me spend so much time there. She had some legal problem with a printer and she said she needed my advice."

"I don't doubt that."

"Hmm?"

"Nothing." Maggie rinsed out her glass. "I've put a casserole here on the counter. Tad knows how to warm it up.

Have some, if you'd like." She started for the kitchen door.

"Thanks. Have fun tonight. Where are you going?"

She turned back. "Out to the Crab Shack."

"Be careful with the hammers. I wouldn't want you to hurt your medical fingers."

Maggie grinned. "Thanks for the warning. I won't be late. Think you can survive with Mouseketeer while I'm gone?"

"No problem. I just found another can of sardines."

"Now, tell us everything," Roz said over a beer mug. "How is it living with Tyler King?"

"Come on, Roz, I'm not living with him. We're simply living in his house until I can find something suitable for all of us." Maggie felt a little flushed talking about this. She nervously brushed a hair out of her eye. "What a day. I'm starved."

"Hey, it's nothing to be embarrassed about," Jan said. "People live together without marriage all the time. No big deal."

"Right," Maggie said, "no big deal. It's a business arrangement." She rubbed her palms over the worn-thin fabric of her favorite jeans. "How about garlic crabs tonight?"

"Aren't you worried about your breath?" Roz asked.

"Not in the least."

The three of them loved to go out to the Crab Shack for dinner whenever they could manage it. They were always in jeans and sneakers and white or denim shirts and sweaters. Roz, of course, wore cranberry jeans which she had dry-cleaned so the crease was sharp. Her shirt was in cranberry silk. The young waiter brought them each a draft light beer before they even asked for it. He prided himself, they knew, in knowing exactly what his regulars wanted the moment they stepped into the place. They put in an order for three dozen garlic crabs.

"Some business." Roz giggled. "All the women in town are just green with envy."

"All?" Maggie said. "Are people talking about our living arrangements?"

"You didn't honestly think you could do this and no one would notice, did you?" Jan said. She started in hammering on the first of the crabs from the big basket the waiter brought them. "Half the town helped you move in with him."

"I didn't move in with him! Why don't people understand that?" Maggie took a napkin from the pile on the table.

"Michael, my dear, it's you who doesn't understand." Roz grabbed a crab and began to crack it.

Maggie grabbed one and hit it so hard the thing shattered. "I understand things the way they are, not the way people want to think they are. Ty is still my landlord."

"More like lord and master." Jan giggled. "Now before you go getting all huffy I was just teasing. Anyway, how are you going to handle it with Tad when your romance . . . heats up? If it hasn't already."

"Jan!" Maggie fell back against her chair. "Stop it! There is no romance.

There isn't going to be any romance. This is a business arrangement, pure and simple."

"Well, if you're smart you won't let it stay pure, or simple," Roz said smiling.

"Why are you two doing this to me?"

The two looked at her for a long moment. Finally Jan spoke. "To be perfectly direct, as you know we both are, when was the last time you had sex?"

Maggie gave them an amused frown. Her bottom lip twitched. "I don't think that's anyone's business but my own."

"Can't remember, hunh?" Jan said.

"I'm not that senile."

"It would do wonders for your skin," Roz said knowingly, "not to mention your mental and emotional outlook. Ty is sure good to look at, and I bet he'd feel good to the touch, too."

"There can not be a romance, my friends."

The two looked at her. "Why not?" Roz asked.

"Well, I'm at least five years older, for one thing."

"As if a little thing like age should be a factor," Jan said.

"Yes, you're just making excuses, and you don't mean any of them," Roz added.

"Why would you think that?" Maggie shook her head.

"Because," Roz said, "you can eat a dozen crabs in the first go-round and you haven't even touched the first one you splattered all over the dining room. Classic case of romantic dilemma."

"I give up," Maggie said.

"It's about time," Jan said.

The three laughed and clinked beer mugs. By the time Maggie made her way through the work of cracking and picking out the meat from one crab, she'd lost her appetite.

"Yes, ma'am," Roz underscored, "classic case of romantic dilemma."

"Yo, Tad!" Ty called from the kitchen. "Ready for some supper?"

Tad came in from the porch, Caesar at his heels. "What have you got?"

"There's some kind of casserole your grandmother made."

"Yuck."

Ty gave him a sidelong glance. "Oh,

I see. How about if I just stick it in the freezer? We'll fire up the grill and cook us some hot dogs. That okay with you?"

Caesar barked and crawled under the kitchen table.

"He prefers you to call them something else," Tad told him.

Ty went out and piled some charcoal in a little grill and lit a fire. He came back in and found Tad setting the table.

"Pretty good," he said to the boy. "You'll make some lucky lady a good husband some day." He took off his glasses and wiped them on his sleeve before putting them back on.

"Husband? Yuck. I'm never getting married."

"Good idea. Stick marriage in the deep freeze along with that casserole."

Tad laughed.

"You got a girlfriend yet?" Ty asked.

"Geez, no!" Tad wrinkled his nose.

"How come?"

"I don't want a girlfriend."

"That's a very good reason," Ty said.

"You got a girlfriend?" Tad asked.

Ty waited a moment. "Not now."

"Did you once?"

"Yep, more than once," Ty told him. "And I had a wife once, too." He saw the boy's mouth drop, and his bright blue eyes widen. "Before you get any ideas, it wasn't at the same time."

"Where are they?"

"In California."

"How come you're here then?"

"You might not understand this, but part of the reason I'm here is because they're there." Ty grinned. "I'll explain it someday. Let's talk about something else. Tell me about your eyesight."

Tad ran his hand along the edge of the countertop. "I can't see good."

"What can you see?"

"Most everything, but not very clear. Kinda blurry. I can make out colors and shapes. Some days it's almost like it always was, but some days it's worse. And I can't see anything at night."

"And the doctors say this is how it is for a while, hunh?"

Tad shrugged. "Guess so. Maybe they'll invent something someday and then I'll see good again."

"Maybe. Bummer. I know how you feel."

Tad grabbed a can of root beer out of the refrigerator. "You want a beer?"

"Yeah, thanks. And grab the hot dogs, I mean the wieners while you're in there."

Tad hauled things out of the refrigerator including jars of mustard and relish and set them on the counter. He handed Ty a can of real beer. The kid sure surprised him.

"You don't know how I feel," Tad said. "You're not going blind."

"Maybe not yet. But I've got a disease, too." Ty popped open the can and took a long swig.

Tad looked at him, surprise on his face. "I didn't know that. What kind of disease?"

"One that's not as bad as yours but that affects my vision, too. It's called glaucoma. It's nothing to worry about."

"Does Grams know?"

"No."

"How come?"

Ty gave him an exasperated look. "I didn't tell her, that's why, and I hope you won't tell her either."

"Why not?" Tad got out a knife and opened the plastic on the package of wieners.

Ty watched him. So what could he say to the kid? If his grandmother knew about his disease she'd feel different about him? Obviously she wouldn't feel different about her grandson, and he wouldn't want to make the kid feel that way or wonder about it.

"Because."

"Because why?"

"I don't know," Ty said, feeling irritated. He grabbed the package of wieners and went outside to the grill.

Tad followed him, and Caesar banged the screen door open and came out with them.

"I know anyway," Tad said with a little pout.

"Oh? You think you know something?" Ty dropped four hot dogs on the grill and spaced them out in a line. "Okay, smart guy, suppose you tell me what you think you know."

"You won't tell Grams you're sick because you like her and you wanna be her boyfriend and you're afraid she won't like you and be your girlfriend if she knows you got eye problems."

"C'mon, that's baloney."

"Is not. You do like Grams."

Ty took a pair of tongs and rolled the hot dogs over on the grill. "I mean the part about her not liking me if she finds out I've got this problem. She isn't that kind of person. What I've got isn't catching, you know, just like what you've got. That's not any reason for somebody not to be somebody's girlfriend. Or boyfriend."

"Gotcha!" Tad laughed uproariously.

Ty hung the tongs over the grill handle. "Whaddaya mean by that?"

"You like Grams, you like Grams," Tad singsang.

"Hey wait a minute. You trapped me."

"Pretty good, hunh?"

Ty finished cooking the hot dogs and went in for a plate to carry them on. "You want to eat out there or in here?" he called to Tad.

Tad held the door for Caesar and they both came into the kitchen. "In here. The skeeters are coming out now."

Ty opened a can of pork and beans, dropped a long-handled spoon into the middle of it, and stuck it in the middle of the table.

"Cold beans. Yum," Tad said. "Grams would never let me eat them like that."

"Yeah, well we men like 'em like that," Ty said in a he-man voice.

They fixed up their hot dogs just the way they both liked them, and plopped beans on their plates. Caesar saw that he wasn't about to get a bit of it and chose to snooze.

"I like living here," Tad said.

"Yeah?"

"Yeah, better than that old apartment. It smelled funny. But this house is great. I wish I could live here forever."

"I wish you could, too. I wish I could, too," Ty said. He took another helping of beans.

"Why can't you? It's your house, isn't it?" Tad asked in direct typical kid style.

"Only sort of. I have an arrangement with a bank."

"Why don't you just buy it?"

"I'm lucky I could buy these wieners and beans."

Tad looked up at him. "Everybody says you're rich."

"Can you keep a secret?" Ty leaned across the table. Tad nodded. "They're wrong."

"Maybe you better get a job," Tad said. "Grams says work is good for something, I forgot what."

"Well, it's good for getting money," Ty said, "but I'll bet your grandmother said it was good for the soul."

"That was it."

"Why am I not surprised? She works very hard, doesn't she?"

"Yeah. She says she does it because she wants to, but I think she does it because she has to for me. I told her to get married," Tad said. "That would help with money. Maybe she wouldn't have to work so hard. But she said she doesn't want to again. She was married once to my grandfather, but I don't remember him."

"Marriage is hard," Ty said.

"I guess."

"So," Ty ventured, "does your grandmother have a boyfriend already?"

"Nah."

"How come? She's pretty and she's nice. She should have a boyfriend."

"What for?"

Ty gave him a long look. "Someday I'll tell you."

Tad shrugged. "She doesn't have to have a boyfriend if she doesn't want to, you know. She can do everything herself."

Ty inclined his head and set his fork down. "How old are you, anyway?"

"I'm ten and you know it."

"Well, then quit talking like a thirty-year-old. It scares me."

Tad giggled. Ty laughed with him. What a great kid, he thought.

"You know something, Tad?"

"What?"

"I think you're one of the best friends I've ever had."

"Yeah? How come? An old guy like you's gotta have a lotta guys to hang out with."

Ty screwed up his mouth to keep from laughing out loud. "I'll try to forget you said that so we can still be friends. I think you're one of my best friends because we can talk about everything to each other. What do you think?"

"I guess."

"Let's toast to that." Ty lifted his beer can.

Tad giggled. He put down his fork,

pushed up his glasses, and lifted his root beer can. Ty clanked it with his.

"To us," he said.

"Yeah," Tad said. "To us."

When Maggie got back to the beach house it was after ten. Ty lounged in a chair near the fireplace reading a novel. Summer nights could be damp and cool near the ocean, and Maggie loved the way Ty made the house cozy and inviting on such nights. The fire crackled comfortingly. Caesar was stretched out in front of it on the hearth rug, snoring. A Beethoven sonata was playing on the radio.

"Hi, I'm ho . . . back," she called. She hung up her jacket in the hall closet.

"Ah, yes," Ty mimicked W.C. Fields, "it's the little woman returning from bridge club, or was it PTA?" He put down his book. "How was dinner?"

"Very funny as usual. I always have a good time with Roz and Jan. Tad in bed?"

"Yes. You know he really works hard around here, doesn't he?"

"He sure does. I wish he'd play with his friends, though."

"I know. I'll try to figure something out. Can I get you anything?"

"I think I'll get a glass of juice." She went out to the kitchen and returned a couple of minutes later with a tall glass. "So what did you men find to talk about?"

Ty chuckled. "Private manly things. What did you girls talk about?"

Maggie sniffed. "We *women* talked about. . . ." She suddenly felt very warm. "Womanly things you wouldn't be interested in."

"How do you know? You tell me what you talked about and I'll tell you what we talked about. Fair?"

Maggie stood at the window and watched the surf roll in under the glow of moonlight. "I'm not really interested in what you talked about."

"Oh, I think you would be."

She sipped her juice. He was right. She was interested in what he talked about with Tad. Maybe the boy did share his feelings with someone at last. But, no way in hell would she tell Ty what she and her friends had talked about at dinner. The subject must be changed immediately.

"Did you make up with the cats while I was gone?"

"Not exactly."

She looked around. "Well, what did you do with them?"

"I didn't do anything with them, or to them for that matter. They're a couple of turncoats, if you ask me."

"Why?"

"See for yourself." He pointed toward Caesar.

Maggie walked toward the sleeping dog and leaned over. Mouseketeer and Tramp purred contentedly, curled up in the protective embrace of Caesar's four thick paws.

"Made themselves at home finally, as you can see."

Even the cats were taking advantage of a temporary situation, and acting as if they'd moved in forever, Maggie mused. It was a total conspiracy. She was convinced of it.

Thirteen

Ty went out on the back porch with a cup of coffee and *The Cape Agnes News*. He'd donned a pair of ragged cutoff jeans, a faded blue T-shirt, and a pair of beat-up leather sandals. He loved early summer mornings on the beach before too many people were up. The two cats lazed on the porch railing at the sunny end. The gulls were fishing seriously. At least they had jobs. He knew he had to get serious as well.

He leaned against a porch column and watched the sun bathe the waves in a golden wash. A kind of alien contentment had settled inside him lately. He shook his head. Weird. The last thing he should be feeling was contented. His life was a mess. The Elm Street building's cave-in and the delay in having it demolished had put him in even more dire straits than he'd been in before. The contentment had to do with something else. It was this whole sense of . . . family, that's what it was. Here in this little seaside community a little magic had been performed. If one didn't like the family they had, or if they no longer had one, they could simply make a new one right here. And there seemed to be willing participants almost everywhere he looked.

What had Maggie said he was becoming? A regular Caper, that was it. It was more than that. He knew it now. It was as if he'd been born into a new family, or adopted into one. Or he himself had adopted a family for himself. Several townspeople. Henrietta VanGelder. Harry Nordquist. And Elmer and Jolene. Definitely Tad. And Doc. She was at the center of it. He felt more . . . what? *Married*. More married to her and this family than he ever had to Sylvie or than he'd ever felt with his parents.

"How come I had to get this old before I found out about it?" he muttered. "I suppose that's better than finding out at eighty-five."

Feeling married. Whoa. What about

love? Ty's conscious mind argued with his subconscious. He'd been through marriage counseling and individual therapy. That's what people did in their circle of friends out in California. The last therapist had told him he was probably incapable of ever understanding real love. He'd believed that was so even before he paid that shyster a hundred and seventy bucks for an hour of psychobabble that he could have authored himself.

Ty turned and leaned his back against the column. "Holy cow," he breathed. "Snuck right up on me when I wasn't expecting it. Talk about eerie. I didn't even know it happened. Tad did. Think of that." He drained his coffee mug. "Holy cow. I'm in love. This is really it. I know it. I ought to call up that jerk therapist and give him an earful. I'm in love. With her. With that kid. With all of them. With this town." His breath grew ragged and he stood up straight. "With that ocean and sky and those hardworking gulls, and. . . ."

He grew dizzy with the realization. "I gotta tell somebody about this. No. I can't tell anybody. Nobody'd believe it. Maybe

I can tell her. No, I can't tell her. She wouldn't believe me probably. She thinks I'm not serious about anything." He turned around in a circle twice, both hands plastered to his head. "Man, I've really cracked. I'm talking to myself."

He started to sit down in the wicker armchair when he heard a voice coming from the side of the house. He walked to the end of the porch and peered around. Tad was sitting on a long piece of driftwood talking to Caesar. Ty stepped off into the sand and walked slowly toward them.

"What's up?" he said a few feet away from them.

Tad jumped. He shoved his sunglasses up against the bridge of his nose. "Hi," he said glumly.

"And a cheery good morning to you, too. What are you doing up so early?" Ty dropped down to the driftwood next to the boy.

"Caesar had to go out so I came with him."

"I'm going into town later. I'll give you a ride in if you want to hang out with some of your buddies."

"Nah." Tad took a stick and doodled aimlessly in the sand.

"What about this guy Robby? Heard you two were best buds once upon a time."

"Not anymore."

"How come?"

"We're not, that's all."

Tad got up and kicked some sand with his bare toes. He hiked up his baggy surf shorts. The oversized T-shirt blew in the breeze, plastering itself against his visible ribs. The kid didn't have an ounce of extra fat on his body. Tentatively Ty felt around his own waist and ribs. If he didn't start working out himself pretty soon, his extra ounces were going to turn into flabby pounds.

Ty peered around into the boy's face. "You know, sport, it takes two to keep a friendship going. Maybe it's your turn this time to call Robby. How about it?"

"No. He's not home."

"How do you know that until you call him?"

"I know that's all."

Ty set down his newspaper and set the mug on it. He rose and kicked his sandals off and walked over to the boy. "Hey, we're friends, remember? We drink beer and eat cold beans together. And we tell each other everything. I need to talk to you about something, too. But you talk first, okay? So what's up?"

"Robby joined the new track team," Tad said finally without looking at Ty. "Today is first practice."

"Oh. That's why he won't be home later." Tad didn't say anything. "You want to go into town and check him out? See if he's any good?"

"Nah. I know he's good."

"I heard you're better."

"I beat him lots of times." Tad backed up as the surf came in with greater strength and slapped his ankles.

"So why don't you just go out for the track team, sport?"

Tad looked at him disgustedly. "You know I can't run."

"Something wrong with your legs?"

"No. Geez."

Ty scratched his head. "Your lungs bad?"

"No." Tad kicked at a fluff of surf foam.

"Oh, must be you've got a bad heart then, right?"

"No! What's the matter with you?"

"Me? Nothing, Theodore. And there's nothing wrong with you either, sport."

"There is, too, and you know it. And don't call me that name again."

"Which name? Sport or Theodore? And what's wrong with you? Give me a clue, would you?" Ty knew he was badgering the boy, but he kept it up on purpose. This was the most fire he'd seen in him since they'd met.

"Theodore! I hate that name. And you do, too, know what's wrong with me!" he shouted.

"What?" Ty shouted back.

"I can't see!"

"Oh, big deal. You're not totally blind yet."

"But I'm going to be."

"Maybe. But you're not yet. Geez, man, there's no reason why you can't be on that track team. Unless of course you don't try."

Tad kicked the sand. "I won't be able to do it so why should I try?"

Ty waited a long moment before speaking. Tad didn't walk away so he guessed the kid wanted to be talked into trying out for the track team. How was he going to do that?

"I guess you're right," Ty said finally. "Just sit around, get your grandmother to wait on you hand and foot, get fat, lose all your friends. You're right, Theodore. I don't know what I was thinking, Theodore."

Tad seethed as much as his little body would take. "Don't call me Theodore!" he shouted in frustration.

"Why not, Theodore? It's a great name for a couch potato."

"Damn you!" Tad yelled.

"Here now," Ty said coolly. "I'll bet your grandmother wouldn't approve of you cursing your elders. Tsk, tsk."

Tad jumped up and took a slug at Ty. Ty dodged.

He swung again. Ty dodged.

"You deserve to have me around needling you every now and then, Theodore. And I still like you, Theodore, even if you don't like me. So I guess I'll just have to bug you, Theodore." He gave a playful punch to Tad's arm.

"Don't." Tad pulled away.

The kid was madder than a banty rooster, and it was all Ty could do to keep from laughing. But he didn't want to add that kind of insult to a constructive kind of energy he hoped was taking shape. He had the urge to grab the kid and hug him, tell him not to worry, that he'd protect him. But Tad didn't need protection. Just like he didn't need it. What they both needed was to break out.

Ty gave him a playful punch again. "Oh yeah? You gonna stop me?"

"Yeah, I'm gonna stop you!" Tad yelled.

"Gotta catch me first!" Ty said, laughing. He tapped Tad on the arm again. Tad took a swing. "You missed me." He tapped him again.

That last one goaded Tad far enough and he lunged. Ty took off on a half-hearted run. *Come after me, Tad, come after me. You're so mad you want to clobber me. Come and get me.*

Tad started to run after him. His sunglasses fell off, but he didn't stop to retrieve them.

"Caesar!" Ty called. "Push!" He stayed

just enough ahead of Tad so the boy couldn't touch him.

Caesar ran and caught up to Tad and bumped his leg. That knocked the boy off balance but he caught himself and then caught Caesar by the collar. The two ran side by side and Ty, far ahead of them now, turned around and saw the two running like a team right toward him. His eyes filled in spite of what he thought was his hardened heart. Is this what love did to a man?

Caesar veered a little, and Tad said, "No, he's this way!"

When they caught up to Ty, Tad grabbed his shirt. They both fell down in the sand and rolled over and over. Tad sputtered and then started to laugh. And then Ty was laughing and spitting sand out of his mouth. Caesar sniffed the two of them over and over, then flopped down next to them. They lay spread-eagle in the sun.

"You thought you could get away from me, didn't you?" Tad said breathlessly.

"Yeah, I did," Ty said, even more breathless.

"I could see your shadow, you know.

And I followed the sound of your feet. You didn't know I could do that, did you?"

"No, I didn't know you could do that. You're sneaky. But you had help. Caesar helped you."

"Yeah, well, he almost went the wrong way. I had to show him."

Ty caught his breath. God, he felt good. Better than he could ever remember. "You're pretty smart, sport," he said. "And you're one damned fast runner. You know it, too, don't you?"

Tad didn't say anything. Ty jumped up and grabbed him by his hand and pulled him to his feet. Tad squinted up at him. Ty picked him up off the sand, hugged him, and spun him around. Caesar barked.

"I figured you could do it, sport. In fact, I knew you could. You just didn't know you could. I had to make you mad enough to find out how good you are. You're a fast little monster!"

"What?" Tad kicked out. "You did that on purpose!"

"Yes, I did. Now stop kicking and I'll put you down. I'm proud of you, Tad, old man. Damn proud of you." Caesar

barked. "You, too, you mangy mutt!" He
scratched the dog behind the ear.

"You're good, Theodore, really good.
Do you know that?"

"Don't call me Theodore!"

"Okay, okay, never again if you say to
me right here and now, 'I, Tad, ...'
What's your last name anyway?"

"Mills."

"Say it. 'I, Tad Mills, am a great runner.' "

"I'm not saying that."

"Suit yourself, *Theodore.*"

Tad gritted his teeth. "I said don't call
me that."

"I'll stop calling you Theodore when
you say what I told you to say, Theodore.
Okay, Theodore?"

"Okay!" Tad's fists clenched. "I, Tad
Mills . . . ."

"Am a great runner."

Tad sighed loudly. "Am a. . . ." He
looked down at his feet. "Runner," he
muttered barely audibly.

"What? I didn't hear you, Theodore."

"Runner," Tad said. "Runner!" he
yelled.

"What kind of runner?" Ty yelled
back. "What kind of runner are you?"

"A great runner!" Tad yelled. "Okay?" His voice cracked.

Ty grinned down at him. "More than okay. Great! Now you've got a lot of work to do," Ty told him.

"Work? What do you mean work?" Tad gave him a skeptical glance.

"I mean real work. Yes, sir. We're gonna make you into a first-class runner. And Caesar? You're gonna have to slim down, pal, or you'll never keep up with your job."

"Caesar's got a job?"

"You bet. He's your assistant coach."

"The teacher isn't gonna let him do that."

"Yes, he will."

"How do you know?"

"'Cause your trainer's gonna tell him that's how it is if he wants the best runner in the ten-year-old age group in Cape Agnes to be on his new team."

"I don't have a trainer."

"Yes, you do."

"Who?"

"Geez, kid, I thought you were smart. Me."

* * *

Tad flopped down on the bed in his room. He threw his sunglasses on the bedside stand. He was careful to keep his feet hanging over the edge of the bed like Grams had told him so the sand would fall on the floor instead of in the bedspread. He let the tears come into his eyes this time because nobody could see him.

He was scared. Scared of a lot of things. Scared to go run on this team his teacher had put together. Scared he'd fall down or run into trees or people and look like a goof. He remembered seeing a high-school runner once wearing glasses that were tied on with a black band. Maybe that wouldn't be so bad.

A knock came to his door. "Hey sport, you ready?" Ty called from the other side.

"Ready for what?" Tad jumped up and opened the door.

"We got to get to town. Track practice starts today, right? Well, you gotta be there early so you can show the coach your stuff."

Tad turned around. "I don't think I want to be on a team. I just wanted to show you I could run fast, that's all."

"And you did. And now you're going

to show everybody else. Shake a leg. We got to get moving. And change those loud shorts, will you? Put on something a little more subdued." Ty started down the hall. Then he turned and came back. "We'll get some team shorts if they've got them. And a matching collar for Caesar. He's going to try out for the team, too."

"Geez," Tad muttered, but he obediently hopped up to rummage through his dresser for a conservative pair of swim trunks.

"Well, I don't know," Mr. Hanson said. "It doesn't say anything in the track rules about letting a dog run with an athlete."

"I know," Ty said, "but this isn't NCAA here. These are kids. You know how they are. They have to feel they can do what everybody else can do. You have the option as the coach to adapt the rules to your league here, or whatever it is."

Russell Hanson scratched his balding head. "I know it's kids we're dealing with. And I'm no coach. I'm a fourth grade teacher. Somebody had to do something. Some of these kids were starting to be troublesome. The girls as well as the boys. Superintendent thought they had too much energy. It wasn't my idea for a track team, but here I am."

Ty noted his rounded girth. He looked unfit, just like a lot of coaches he remembered in his youth. But his coaches were willing and enthusiastic, this guy wasn't.

"Well, then, be a hero, would you? Look at them out there. The kids want Tad, and he needs them. And he needs Caesar, too. Don't worry about him. The dog, I mean. I'll keep him in check. You just train the boy."

"Look, Mr. King, I'm no trainer," Hanson said. "I feel I'm doing my job if I just get these kids to run around a track and keep in their lanes. The superintendent is talking cross-country, too. Cross-country, fergodsakes. With my luck these kids'll get lost somewhere along the way. Well, I got to get going. Your kid can stay and the dog, too. What the hell?" Hanson walked away blowing a whistle and getting the sound to come out with every other puff.

"He's not my kid," Ty started to say. "Thanks," he replied instead. Ty stood on the sidelines and watched Hanson get the kids running. The guy was right. He was no coach. The kids didn't pay attention half the time. The girls talked in a small group. The boys teased them. They all ran into each other. All the fathers and mothers on the sidelines groaned or yelled at their own kids and other people's kids. It was one big fiasco for one excruciating hour.

One of the mothers got into an argument with Hanson. She said she didn't want any girls to be on the boy's team. The teacher grew red in the face and yelled at her that it wasn't *his* idea to allow girls. One of the other mothers said her daughter had every right to be on the team. She threatened to go to the superintendent if Hanson tried to prevent it. The other mother said she'd report him if he *didn't* prevent it. He told her to take her rotten son and go home. The rotten child in question kicked Hanson in the shins.

"You little shit!" Hanson bellowed.

"Oh, oh," Ty muttered.

"What's happening?" Tad said as he and Caesar came up to Ty.

"World War Three, I think."

"My Susan is going to be on this team," one of the mothers yelled.

"It doesn't matter, Mom," the girl with the bouncy blond curls said. "I can play field hockey or something."

"You said you wanted to run track, honey," her mother said, calming down. There were tears in her eyes. "If that's what you want, there's no reason you can't have it."

"Well, I'm going to report you today," the boy's mother yelled. She was built just like Hanson except she had more hair. "You can't swear at my Richie and get away with it. You'll be fired unless you apologize right this minute."

"I will not apologize. Your cretin kid kicked me. I could have him suspended."

"Of all the nasty tricks," the woman yelled. "If Richie isn't made captain of this team today, you're out of it."

"You're too late, madam," Hanson yelled, "I quit. You can have Richie and you can be coach of this team for all I care. Tell that to the superintendent!" He tried to throw down the whistle. But he struggled too hard and got hung up

in the string which made him embarrassed and madder.

"Looks like there isn't going to be a
track team, hunh?" A young friend of
Tad's came up to them.

"Looks like it," Tad said wistfully.
"Hey, Ty, this is Robby."

Ty stuck out his hand to the boy. "Hi,
Robby. You're pretty fast. You and Tad
could make this team hot."

"And Caesar, too," Robby said.

"Caesar, too."

"If there was a team," Tad said. "It
figures."

"There goes Mr. Hanson," Robby said.

"Boy is he mad, hunh?" Tad said.

"Did you see his face?" Robby said.

"No. What did it look like?"

Ty noticed there wasn't a trace of reticence in Tad's voice when he asked his
friend to describe the teacher's face.

"Redder than the table in the cafeteria
that time we turned all the ketchup bottles upside down on those arithmetic
cards and the cooks had to pick them
up!" Robby laughed and Tad laughed out
loud.

"Oh, boy, that's really red!" Tad said.

"If Mr. Hanson was our coach it would be really fun watching him get mad, wouldn't it?" Robby said.

"Really fun."

"You two are real monsters," Ty said.

The parents were now arguing among themselves. He saw some of them call their kids and start to walk away.

"Well, that's it," Robby said. "No track team. Wanna go to the movies, Tad?"

"Nah. I guess I'll go home."

"Yeah."

"Nobody's going to the movies on a beautiful day like this," Ty announced. "And nobody's going to go home and sulk around the place either."

"What should we do then?" Robby asked.

"Get out on that track. You monsters are going to run some of that energy off." Ty started to walk toward the dispersing group of parents and kids.

"But the coach quit!" Tad yelled.

"They just hired a new one, sport. Me!"

"All right!" Robby shouted. "Come on, Tad. You better get in shape, Caesar!"

The two boys and the dog ran after Ty.

"Wait a minute, folks!" Ty called to the parents. "We have a track team here that needs to get into practice." He bent down and picked up Hanson's whistle, wiped off the end of it on his shorts, and blew it loudly. "Gather around for a team meeting."

The parents reluctantly walked toward him, kids in tow.

"Here's the scoop. I'm Coach King. We're gonna whip this team into shape and have our first exhibition meet in two weeks. We'll have a team photograph taken for the newspaper so everybody wear a pair of decent shorts and T-shirt next week. If we work this out well, we'll get uniforms or at least matching shorts. There will be no parents at track practice, but I expect them all here at the meet."

Some of the parents started muttering among themselves.

"This is how it is," Ty said. "If some of you don't like it, feel free to form a rival team and we'll get some competition going." Nobody said anything.

"That's what I thought. Right now I'm going to appoint captains and other key officers of the team." Ty looked at the woman who'd been arguing with Mr. Hanson. "Which is your son, madam?"

She beamed proudly and pointed out a boy with an expression that asked to be smacked. Ty took in a deep breath. A troublemaker, if he ever saw one. He'd have to be diplomatic about this.

"Richie, right?" The boy nodded and gave a smug look to the other kids. "You're the uniform steward. As soon as we get uniforms, that is."

"What? He should be the captain," his mother argued.

"The co-captains have been appointed. Susan and Robby, you're co-captains," Ty said with authority.

"Yeah!" yelled both the boys and girls.

"The manager of the team is Tad Mills."

"Me?" Tad said with surprise.

"Co-manager is Caesar the Wonder Dog."

Caesar barked, and Ty thought he heard a question mark at the end of it.

"Do I make myself clear? Anybody want to dispute any of this?" Ty said loudly.

Nobody said anything.

"All right, then. Let's get to work. Parents?" Ty looked at his watch. "Come back at noon and pick up your team member. You will receive new instructions then."

They all checked their watches and wandered away.

"Wow!" Tad whispered. "How did you do that?"

"Geez," muttered Ty. "What in the hell did I just get myself into?"

Fourteen

"Good morning, Mrs. VanGelder, Priscilla," Jolene greeted them cheerily, then her voice lowered to a soft coo. "Oh, is Priscilla not feeling well today?"

"I'm not sure, dearie. Looks a little listless, don't you think?"

Jolene peered over at Priscilla. The poodle cocked her little head and looked all around. "She looks fine to me, Mrs. VanGelder, but Dr. Logan should take a look at her just to be sure."

"Actually . . ." Mrs. VanGelder leaned toward Jolene and whispered, "I'd like to have a second opinion. No offense to *the* doctor, you understand. She's first-rate. But, I do think," she cleared her voice, "it never hurts to have a look at someone else. I mean, have someone else look at her. You understand, don't you, dearie?"

"Oh, yes ma'am," Jolene nodded vigorously, humoring the older woman. "We're extremely busy this morning, but I'll see what I can do for you."

"Thank you, dearie. Can't be too careful, you know."

"Yes, ma'am. Would you like me to see if Dr. Everett can see her along with Dr. Logan, if need be?"

Mrs. VanGelder beamed. "Why, what a good head you have on your shoulders, young woman! Sort of a medical team examination. I knew you'd understand."

Jolene smiled. Priscilla took that moment to leap from her mistress's arms and scamper down the hallway to Maggie who was just emerging from the examining room.

"Priscilla!" Maggie scooped up the little bundle of squirming curls and scratched her ears. "Where've you been? I haven't seen you in such a long time." She looked up as the flush-faced Mrs. VanGelder hurried down the hall after her dog. "Morning, Mrs. VanGee."

"Good morning, Doctor." She gently took the poodle from Maggie's arms. "Here, Priscilla, you naughty girl. Might have suffered a relapse in all your excitement."

"Relapse? Has Priscilla been feeling ill?"

"Possibly. I think our trip might have been too taxing for her delicate constitution."

"Ah, yes," Maggie said, nodding. "Where did you go? I heard you were going to take a trip since the production rehearsals had to be postponed."

"I finally decided on the Bahamas."

"How nice. Is it really better there as their ads proclaim?"

"Not in my opinion," Henrietta sniffed. "We're both glad to be back."

"You took Priscilla with you? Were there no restrictions against taking her?"

"I don't know. I suppose there were. But Priscilla enjoys vacations, so she just snuggled down in her luggage and slept until we arrived."

Maggie touched the tip of Priscilla's delicate nose. "What are her symptoms? Did she eat something that disagreed with her?"

"Could be," Mrs. VanGelder patted Priscilla's topknot. "Can't get much to eat there except conch—conch chowder, conch salad, conch burgers, conch fritters, conch fingers, whatever they are. Didn't know they had fingers, but then I didn't know what a conch was till I went there."

Maggie smiled. "Well, let's have a look at her." She started back toward the examining room. "How do you like our new digs?"

Henrietta gazed around the greenhouse as she walked. "Very nice. I like what you've done with the place. Looks a lot different than I remember. Cleaner, for one thing."

"Here we are. This is a very nice examination room. Very bright." Maggie motioned for Henrietta to go inside and place Priscilla on the table.

"Uh, Doctor," Henrietta began, stopping at the doorway, "I hope you don't mind, but I've made an appointment with your colleague this time. I have nothing against your doctoring as you know, my dear, but I believe it's always best to get another opinion in such matters."

"Ah, yes, of course," Maggie nodded knowingly. "Fine, Mrs. VanGee, I understand. We can't be *too* careful. I bow to my colleague's opinion. He and I can have a consultation later." Maggie patted Priscilla, and started to walk away. She couldn't wait for that "consultation"!

Chances were that Mrs. VanGelder was shopping for another husband. For a moment Maggie considered warning Elmer, then changed her mind. It was good for him to be pursued by the richest unmarried lady in town. It would be good for his ego. It wouldn't hurt if Darlene Thompson got a tip on this one. No, she couldn't do that to Elmer. He'd be mortified if he read that in the paper.

Ty came down the hallway just as Maggie and Mrs. VanGelder were parting.

"Mrs. VanGelder, hello," he greeted her warmly.

"Hello, Tyler, my dear."

"How was your vacation? And Priscilla's, too, of course." Ty patted Priscilla on the topknot.

"Fine, I guess. I hope you all didn't forget your lines or the music in all these goings-on. We're going to get right back into it Sunday night and work extra hard."

Maggie observed that Mrs. VanGelder seemed a bit nervous at seeing Ty, but she dismissed it as excitement over the impending consultation with Elmer.

"I didn't forget," Ty told her. "I can't speak for the others. They've had a lot on their minds lately." He shot a glance at Maggie.

"So, I've heard," Henrietta said. She leaned toward Maggie. "You must take care that the gossip doesn't hurt little Theodore."

"Mrs. VanGelder, I. . . ." But there was nothing Maggie felt like saying about their circumstances at the moment.

"And you, young man," Henrietta said, turning to Ty, "take care you don't hurt yourself playing track with those children. They can be a handful, you know."

"Yes, so I'm learning. Don't worry. I'll be careful."

"Is there something you need, Ty?" Maggie asked.

He gave her a long direct gaze. "Indeed there is."

Henrietta eyed them with open suspicious curiosity.

Maggie felt her cheeks warm. "And would you mind telling me what that is as carefully as you can?"

Ty grinned. "Ah, yes. Caesar's new supply of vitamins."

"I'll get them," Maggie said, grateful for the chance to retreat from Mrs. Van-Gelder's intuitive gaze. Jolene came down the hallway toward them. "Wait right here, Mrs. VanGee. Jolene, would you let Dr. Everett know Mrs. VanGelder would like to see him as soon as possible?"

"Yes, Dr." Jolene grinned with an air of complicity. "Should I ask his new assistant to join them as well?"

Maggie turned her head to question and then remembered. "I think that's a splendid idea. I hope you get the kind of opinion you need," she said to Henrietta. "I'll get those pills for you, Ty."

Maggie and Ty walked down the hallway together. Henrietta thought they made a rather handsome couple. She liked young King, but she had decided early on that he wasn't the businessman his father was.

Jolene went around the corner and knocked on a door. Henrietta thought she was gone rather a long time, but then she was back and beckoning her to follow her toward another examination room. Henrietta felt a fluttering in her breast. She smiled to herself. That little fluttering always told her she was about to have an auspicious meeting. And she just knew she would be in fine form this morning.

She entered the examination room eager to see Dr. Elmer Everett. He was there standing by the stainless steel table, hands thrust in his lab coat pockets. Beside him stood Dr. Logan's grandson, Tad. He was wearing a white lab coat that almost reached his ankles. Henrietta forced a smile.

"Good morning, Doctor."

"Mrs. VanGelder," Elmer greeted her.

"And young Tad. Why what a pleasant surprise. How nice to see you. What are you doing here?"

"Tad's my apprentice," Elmer told her. "He stays at my side wherever I go. Only way to learn, you know."

Henrietta frowned. "I suppose so."

"Now then," Elmer said, "what's troubling little Priscilla? Shall we have a look, then?"

Tad lifted the poodle from Henrietta's arms and gently placed her on the examination table.

Henrietta watched the two of them from across the stainless steel table. They chattered quietly between themselves, poking at Priscilla's ribs, peering into her ears, and listening to her heartbeat.

"Hmm," said Tad.

"Mm-hm," agreed Elmer. He felt Priscilla's stomach and shook his head. "Un-unh," he declared.

"Too fat," Tad announced.

"Excellent diagnosis. Bordering on obese, I'd say," Elmer declared.

"What? How dare you say such a thing? My little Priscilla is not overweight, not a bit. Are you, baby?" She adjusted her corset under her knit dress and gathered Priscilla against her full bosom.

"May I suggest . . . ?" Elmer started.

"No, you may not!" Henrietta cut him off.

"Might I offer a word . . . ?" Tad began.

"No, you may not," she huffed. "I've heard all I need to hear."

With a flip of her orange hair, she spun

around toward the exit and marched into the hallway, slamming the door behind her. She ran directly into Maggie.

"Imagine the nerve of those two," she sputtered, "saying my little baby is . . . is *plump*. How dare they?" Not waiting for an answer, Henrietta stepped smartly down the hall, chin held high, jutting into the air.

Maggie peered around the door of the examining room with a questioning look at her two colleagues. "Did you two say that dog was fat?" she demanded.

"Who said anything about Priscilla?" Tad asked innocently, palms outward.

"Anything at all?" Elmer responded with a wink.

Maggie laughed out loud.

"Boy, a guy really has to look out that some woman doesn't trap him. Right, Elmer?" Tad said, peering up into the old man's face.

"That he does," Elmer said with amusement. "Let that be a lesson to you, young man."

"You're both bad," Maggie said to them, and headed down the hallway to the reception area.

At the counter, Henrietta tapped her foot while Jolene wrote up her bill. "How do you like being in this old place?" she asked, scanning the room.

"We like it a lot," Jolene responded brightly, "although I think Dr. Logan would rather move back to town."

"Why would she want to do that?"

"I think she wants to move back for Tad's sake." Jolene kept writing. "But she hasn't been able to find a new place. She's been looking for quite a while."

"Does she really need that other veterinarian?"

"Dr. Everett? Oh yes, ma'am, she does need him. The practice has grown by leaps and bounds, you might say."

"I see. Well, I don't see why she doesn't just stay here. The place seems to get more business than it did in that terrible old building."

Jolene stood and leaned across the counter and whispered, "That's what we want to do, but Doc is determined to move. Has to handle things on her own, you know. Says she can't feel indebted to anyone, least of all Ty King. But we don't even know who owns this place. He's renting it and he's never said who he pays the rent to."

"Hmm," Henrietta nodded. "I do admire the doctor's independent spirit. But, could her resistance be because she's attracted to him and she doesn't want to put herself in a compromising position?"

Jolene looked down and fiddled with her ledger. "Well, I wouldn't know about that, Mrs. VanGelder. I think they like each other, but Doc says she can't take advantage of their friendship."

"Oh, but *surely* she can't be that stubborn. This is business."

"Oh, but she can," Ty came around the corner. "And I wouldn't call her Shirley to her face if I were you, Mrs. Van-Gelder." He laughed and went out the front door.

Mrs. VanGelder frowned. "What did he mean by that?"

"I never know what they mean half the time," Jolene said, handing the bill to the older woman.

Henrietta took her receipt and put it in her bag. "The doctor should take a tip from me. Even if I've made a decision about something, I exhaust every other possibility I might wonder about. When I'm satisfied I'm right, I act." Jolene nodded while Henrietta talked. *Twit of a girl doesn't get a thing I'm saying,* Henrietta thought. "Would you please tell Dr, Logan to tell the rest of the musical cast that they have another week off? I have some things to take care of."

Jolene jumped. "Yes, Mrs. VanGelder. You take care now."

"Oh, I plan to take more than that," Henrietta said. She hurried out.

"How's practice going?" Maggie asked Tad at breakfast. The two of them were alone this morning. Elmer was already out on a house call and Ty had left early. She didn't know where he'd gone.

"Good." Tad finished a bowl of cereal and then set the dish on the floor for Mouseketeer to finish the milk.

"I can't wait to see your exhibition meet this weekend. How do you think the team is doing?"

"Good." Tad chomped a slice of toast.

"How is Ty working out as coach?"

"Good."

"Is something wrong, Tad? I think I could use a few more details about your team besides good."

"Well, it's good. Everybody likes Ty. 'Specially the girls." He chewed rapidly.

"Oh, they do, do they?"

"Yeah, they said for an old guy he's cute." Tad wrinkled his nose.

Maggie chuckled. "The main thing is that the kids like him and that they practice hard. They do practice hard, don't they?"

"Yeah. Ty says we can have real uniforms if we work hard and help each other out."

Maggie wondered briefly where Ty was going to get the money for uniforms. She had begun to suspect that he didn't have the money everyone thought he had, but she didn't know that for certain.

"And do you all help each other out?"

"Pretty much. Caesar helps me. But he gets tired sometimes."

"What happens then? Do you run on your own?"

"A little. Sometimes." Tad drained his milk glass then got up and put it in the sink. He waited for Mouseketeer to stop licking his cereal bowl, then picked that up and put it in the sink, too.

"Well, you know, Caesar is getting older. Maybe you'd like to think about going back to guide dog camp," Maggie ventured. "You could get a dog of your own. A young dog you could work with."

"I don't want one of those dogs, Grams. And besides, it would hurt Caesar's feelings." Tad went to the screen door and looked out on the porch.

"Is he out there?" Maggie asked.

"Yeah, he's asleep under the hammock."

"Tired out, I guess. Does he have to go to the track with you today?"

"No," Tad said. "We have a day off. Ty had to go somewhere."

"Do you know where?"

"Nope. Grams, I heard Jolene say you want to move back to town."

"Well, I do, eventually. I haven't been able to find the right kind of place for the clinic, or an apartment for us. So it won't be right away. You can still enjoy the summer here."

"I don't want to move."

"You will later. Especially when winter comes. It will be better for us in town. You'll see." Maggie got up and put her cup in the sink along with his dishes. "Besides, this is Ty's house, and he'll want it all to himself again soon."

"He likes us all living together."

"We're not actually *living together,* Tad." She watched him running his finger absently over the screen. "Did he say that?"

"The kids say you and Ty are living together."

"Tad, now listen. There are several meanings to the term 'living together.' Ty and I are *not* living together in the sense that some couples do."

Tad turned around and cocked his head. "Well, he lives here, right?"

"Right, yes."

"And you live here, right?"

She knew where this was going. "Ri-ight."

"Then you're living together."

"Tad, we're just guests here. You and I along with Elmer, and even the cats. We're just guests until we can move back into our old place, or a new one. *Guests.*" Maggie sighed. She couldn't figure out any other way to explain it. "Now stop saying that we live together. I've got to get out to the clinic now. You coming?"

"Why? It's not a bad thing. Danny Trink's mother lives with her boyfriend."

"I don't care what Danny Trink's mother does, and Ty is not my boyfriend. God, that sounds like sixth grade. I'm too old for boyfriends." She started out of the kitchen to go change her clothes.

"That's not what Ty said." Tad made that sound like a tease.

Maggie turned around. "What did Ty say?"

"I can't tell."

"Why not?"

"Because."

"Well, you better tell me, young man. If people are saying things about me, then I'll have to set them straight."

"Not people. Just Ty. And besides, it's man talk. We're best friends and we keep secrets."

Then suddenly, Tad changed his mind. "Okay, if I tell you, you can't tell him I told you. Promise?"

"I promise I won't tell him you told me. It will be our secret."

"He's got an eye sickness, too, and I think he thinks you won't like him because of it."

Maggie was stunned. She clung to the chair tightly. "Did he . . . actually tell you that?"

"Yeah. He told me he's got a vision problem."

"That's terrible."

Tad watched her for a long time. "You mean you wouldn't like him if he was blind?" His voice was thick and shaky when he asked the question.

Maggie went around to him and dropped down on her knees. "Oh, Tad, of course not. I mean, that wouldn't matter to me at all. It's what's inside a person that counts. You know that. I've always taught you that. If a person has a good heart and is kind then that's all that really matters."

"So you would like him even if he was blind?"

"Of course."

"And you like him when he *isn't* blind."

"Yes, of course I do." Maggie tilted her head.

"I knew it!" Tad clapped his hands.

"Tad, just what are you up to? Was this all a trick? Ty isn't going blind, is he?"

"It wasn't *all* a trick. He did tell me he's got a sickness. So, Grams," Tad ran a finger up and down his grandmother's arm, "if he likes you and you like him, why can't we just go on living together right here?"

Maggie stood up and kissed him on top of his head. "It's pretty complicated for a ten-year-old, Tad."

"Ty says I think like a thirty-year-old." Tad got up from the chair. "Guess I'll go out and see Elmer now."

"I think you'd better before you tell me anything else I don't really want to know. Tell Elmer I'll be out there in fifteen minutes."

"Okay." Tad started out the door.

"Hey," she said.

"What?" He turned around.

"I love you."

"I love you, too, Grams." He ran off the porch and headed around toward the path to the clinic.

Maggie stood in the kitchen shaking her head. If she thought she was spinning from indecision before this, she could expect to be drawn into a whirlpool at any moment. The only question right now was, did she want to climb out of it?

Fifteen

On the day of the exhibition track meet, Maggie sat in the bleachers amid a group of chattering parents waiting nervously for the first event. It was the hottest day of the summer thus far, but she still felt shivers every now and then.

Parts of her life that she'd thought were all neat and clean and honest were being chipped away by circumstances. And more. By growth, she suspected. Tad's growth of course. Her own? Difficult for her to say. You'd think that when you passed the half-century mark, you would have it all together, as some young folks used to say. Had what all together? The rest of life?

She shaded her eyes with her hand, her gaze pinned on the back door of the high-school gym from which the team would emerge. And the coach. The self-appointed coach. Ty. She knew the school board and the superintendent were already discussing what to do about his taking over the team when they'd already appointed someone to the post. Mr. Hanson had taken ill quite suddenly and had withdrawn from the program before the start of the fall semester. Maggie found it all rather amusing, having been a member of the parent-teacher group in the last three years.

The school was extremely proud of its championship senior high-school track team. They'd brought home the regional trophy three years in a row, and the brand-new track had been built just for them. State-of-the-art, at least as much as they could afford in Cape Agnes. One-quarter-mile oval of rubberized asphalt with clearly painted lanes and starting lines. The whole idea of this youth track team was to justify the track for every child in the central school district, of course. But it also meant that it was possible for Cape Agnes to lead the way in elementary school sports teams, and gain additional funds for other sports equipment.

Maggie wasn't certain she agreed with the current thinking. She didn't much like the idea of kids eight to eleven competing the way the high-school football or baseball and soccer teams did. But, if it helped Tad the way it had seemed to these last couple of weeks, then she knew she'd have to reconsider voting against such a proposal during the next budget election.

She shifted in the hard bleacher seat. Anyway, wasn't she supposed to have her life all mapped out? The life-expectancy age for women was now seventy-seven point seven years. That meant she had another quarter century, give or take, to do with what she wanted. Right. What was that anyway? And if you allowed for maybe ten or fifteen years of being ill or even senile, well, that certainly cut things down a bit.

A cheer went up from the people around her, and she looked up and saw the team running out to the track. Tad was in the middle of them, Caesar at his side, and Ty brought up the rear carrying a clipboard, sunglasses shielding his eyes, a whistle dangling from a cord around his neck, and a billed cap on backward.

She'd always hated that when Tad did it, but somehow the backward hat on Ty's head was almost endearing.

She watched him closely. He wrote things on his sheaf of papers attached to the clipboard. Was he wearing contact lenses? Prescription sunglasses? Why would he even think for a moment she couldn't be his girlfriend just because his vision might be failing?

Embarrassed, she looked at the people around her, almost worried that they might have overheard her thoughts. That was foolish. He may be losing his sight, but she was losing her mind! What about that? Would he be her boyfriend if he knew about that?

"All right, teams!" Ty yelled.

Maggie sat up straight, watching Tad as closely as she watched Ty. The twenty-or-so boys and girls stood still, gathered around him, and listened intently. They wore arm bands, some in crimson and some in white. She presumed that was a way for them to split their exhibition teams. She could not make out Ty's words from her perch in the bleachers, but she saw the kids nodding their heads, saw Tad grasp the fur at the back of Caesar's head.

"Everybody together for personal reinforcement," Ty said firmly.

The group grew close together in a circle, arms around each others' shoulders, boys and girls without any show of embarrassment. "Hooroo!" they yelled together, and then they all patted Caesar and shook his paw.

"Take your places!" he called.

Then a shot from a starter pistol in the hand of one of the fathers, acting as an official, signalled the start of a series of events. Dashes and sprints. Maggie thought that's what they must be. They were fast runs by four kids each, and they were over very quickly. She saw Tad taking care of the borrowed equipment at the side of the dirt track. He had plastic water bottles in a plastic crate, a pair of foot blocks, and a roll out tape measure. He'd proudly told her that the senior high-school track coach had lent them to Ty.

Maggie's eyes filled. Tad was so happy to be a part of all this, she knew it. And Ty had somehow managed to draw him out. She could see the boy felt useful.

Someone touched her arm. Maggie jumped.

"Hey, Colleague, how's he doing?" Elmer sat down next to her.

"Just great. It's amazing what he's done with these kids. I haven't seen one boy tease a girl or vice versa. And look what he's done with Tad! He's thrilled to be a part of all this."

"That's who I meant when I asked the question, Colleague." Elmer chuckled. "I was wondering how Tad was doing. Did he run yet?"

Maggie warmed with the realization of her mistake. "Run? What do you mean? Tad's not going to race."

"Oh?" Elmer shaded his eyes. "Then what's he doing at the starting line?"

Maggie peered over at the yellow line painted across the track. Five kids were there, two girls and three boys. And Caesar. And Tad was in the outside lane. He was wearing a black elastic band around his head that held his glasses snug. The adjustment strap was so long it flopped down the back of his neck.

The gun fired.

The kids started running, Tad wearing

his swim trunks and a crimson arm band along with them.

Maggie stared. The whole event passed by her in slow motion. The kids were all together, running in a knot, Tad bringing up the rear. His lean little legs stretched out. Caesar loped next to him, now and then nudging his thigh. They rounded the curve in front of the bleachers, and then the runners began to spread out. The parents were on their feet, and then the cheering started.

"Go, Robby! Keep going!"

"Susie! Look that's my Susie gaining speed!"

"Danny, get in there!"

"Betsy, don't fall down!"

Then Tad picked up speed. He went down the straightaway flat out with Caesar keeping pace at his side. Slowly, Maggie stood up. She grabbed Elmer's arm and he stood with her. Across the field she saw Ty standing tall, rigid, his eyes pinned to the five runners. At the finish line, one of the fathers held a stopwatch, and behind him stood a mother with another one.

"Tad," Maggie whispered.

"Would you look at him go?" Elmer remarked.

"Tad!" Maggie yelled. "Go, Tad, go!"

The race was down to two, three if Caesar were to be counted. A girl with blond curls and Tad. The others lagged behind, and one boy dropped out and limped to the side. The girl and Tad crossed the finish line almost at the same time, but she was ahead of him and won the race.

They both stood on the side bent over, breathing hard.

"Susie! That's my Susie!" a woman yelled behind Maggie.

"That's my Tad," Maggie whispered. She could only think how much she wished his mother could see him now. Alyssa would be so proud of his accomplishment.

Maggie and Elmer left the bleachers with the rest of the small crowd and went down to the finish area. Maggie ran over to Tad who was now walking around in a circle, breathing hard.

"Here," Ty said. He held out a water bottle to Tad and grabbed his hand and thrust it around it.

Tad squirted the bottle and a stream

hit him in the face. Maggie cringed. He was probably embarrassed to do that in front of his friends. He handed the bottle to the blonde girl. She took a drink and handed it back to him. He squirted again and this time managed to get the stream into his mouth. Then he went to Caesar who was lying down, panting heavily. He took a bowl out of his gym bag and a bottle and poured water into the dish for the dog. Caesar looked up gratefully and drank deeply. Tad grabbed him around the neck and hugged him while he drank.

Maggie had tears streaming down her face. She couldn't let Tad know that. He'd think that was another dorky grandmother thing to do. And Ty was surrounded by kids and parents, and the school superintendent. He kept looking up and catching her gaze now and then. The whole thing was almost too much for Maggie to take in all at once. She hung back and tried to control herself when Elmer went forward and grabbed the boy.

"Tad! You were really great! You know how to hit shins, or whatever it is!" He hugged him hard.

"Thanks, Elmer. You mean kick butt," Tad said against the old man's shirt.

"Kick butt. Yes, indeed, you can kick butt," Elmer said.

"Did Grams see me?" Tad said, stepping out of Elmer's bear hug.

"Of course I did," Maggie said, wiping her eyes and coming around from behind Elmer. "You . . ."

"Me and Caesar kicked butt, Grams! Did you see us?"

"I saw you run a great race. I'd prefer you say it that way." She hugged him and bit back a renewed flow of tears.

"I got beat by a girl," Tad muttered against her.

"Yes, but you beat Robby again," she whispered.

"Yeah, but it's not cool to get beat by a girl." He looked up at her.

Ty came up to them then. He heard the last sentence Tad had uttered. He put a hand on the boy's shoulder.

"You did a great job, Tad. All of you did a great job. You've got a great team. I knew you could do it, my man, I knew it!" Ty was grinning as proudly as if Tad were his own son.

Maggie could feel the affection he held for Tad. She looked up at him and mouthed "thank you." He held her gaze and smiled so widely she was almost undone by it.

"I was okay," Tad said, "but geez, I got beat by a girl."

"What do you mean okay?" Ty said. "You were fantastic! The runner who came in ahead of you beat you by a fraction of a second. She happens to be *very* fast. Be glad you're on her team. She will help you be the best runner you can be just because she shows how it's done." Ty leaned closer to Tad. "And she's gonna be a high-school track star someday, you just wait. And another thing, she told me she thought you were hot." Ty winked.

"Well, I am hot. And I probably stink, too. Is that what she said?" Tad plunked his hands on his hips. "I'm going home and take a bath."

"Geez, you make it so hard to give you a compliment," Ty said with mock disgust. "She means you're a good runner."

Tad looked down and scuffed his running shoes along the side of the track.

"Did I hear you volunteer to take a

bath?" Maggie blurted. When Tad gave her one of *those* looks, she closed her mouth.

"Now, listen," Ty said to Tad, "you have to take care of your partner before you take care of yourself. Remember? We went over Caesar's post-race needs. Got it?"

"Got it. I will. He was awesome, wasn't he?"

"Awesome is right. He was really into it."

"Hey Grams, Robby asked me to come to his house for supper and stay overnight. Can I?" Tad peered up into Maggie's face.

"Of course. I'll drive you over there after you take care of Caesar. And your bath, of course."

"Thanks!" Tad started to run off.

"Wait a minute, Manager," Ty called after him, "you've got work to do. Gather up that equipment."

"Yes, Coach," Tad called back.

He gathered up water bottles and put them in the crate. Robby helped him and Susie carried the foot blocks. The three chattered among themselves as they headed toward the gym door, Caesar tagging along behind them.

Maggie looked up at Ty. "Yes, Coach. And thank you. I don't know how you did what you did, but that is a changed boy."

"I'll say," Elmer said. "Never saw such a light on his face."

"Aw shucks," Ty said, pretending modesty, "t'weren't nothin'."

"I don't know what to say," Maggie said, shaking her head.

"You don't have to say anything. Just keep encouraging him. He's got a lot of heart when he taps into it, and a lot of confidence. But this was a lucky race for him. If he sticks with it and the school decides to form a team, things are going to be a lot tougher. That's when the real test will come."

"I'll be there for him."

"I know. I believe you always have been."

Maggie and Ty stood still, the waning afternoon air still warm between them.

Elmer cleared his throat. "Guess I'll head back to the clinic for an hour or so," he said, then added, "in case anybody cares."

Maggie turned her head quickly. "I'll

be there as soon as Tad is ready to leave.
Got any preferences for supper tonight?''

Elmer stood still for a long time.
"Won't be home for supper tonight. Going up to Sea View to visit my brother in
the nursing home.''

"Tonight?'' Maggie was surprised.
"You were just there last week.''

"So? I can't see my brother two weeks
in a row? He's eighty-six, you know.''

"I know Elmer. It's just that you only
go every other week and you were just
there last week. I'm just surprised that's
all. Will you come in on the ten o'clock
bus?''

"Since that's the only night bus, I
guess I will.'' Elmer started to walk toward the gym. "I'll see what's keeping
the boy.''

"I'll be at the station to meet you,
then,'' Maggie called.

"Good thing,'' Elmer said over his
shoulder. "Mrs. VanGelder said she'd
drive me all the way up there sometime,
and I don't relish the thought of that.''

"I gather she's over her snit, then,'' Ty
said, laughing. "How did you get out of
that one?''

Elmer just smiled enigmatically and kept walking.

Maggie and Ty stood silently for a long moment. "Well," she said, breaking the silence, "I'd better get him home and in the bathtub before he gets chilled. Robby's mother likes them to have supper early."

"Yes, I guess you'd better. Please make sure he sees to Caesar first. He's got to get into that habit."

"Right." She started to walk away.

"I'll be home by six. Have to go face the superintendent in his office right now. Unless you want to do something else, maybe we could eat supper together tonight?" He spoke quietly.

Maggie suddenly felt nervous or something. "Uh, sure. Do you want to go out somewhere?"

"No. I just thought it might be nice to be around the house tonight. I think the sunset will be magnificent, and that porch is the best viewing place on the beach. Is that okay?"

She nodded. "It's fine. I don't know what's in the refrigerator, but I could. . . ."

Ty lifted his hand. "Don't worry about

it. I'll pick up something on the way home after I get a tongue-lashing in the principal's office." He laughed.

"Thanks for what you did for Tad," she said. "No matter what happens he'll have today to start from. You have been great for him. I wish. . . . Thanks." She turned and walked quickly toward the gym.

Ty watched her go. His mind spun with wishes of his own, with regrets, with wonder.

He looked at his watch. Better get to the school office pronto, and get this over with. He knew what they were going to say. Thanks, but you aren't a teacher and you can't continue this once school starts. No money in the budget. He understood that. He had to do something about a real job. He had to do something about that building in the middle of town, too.

He had to do something about himself.

He sighed, then walked toward the school door.

After Maggie dropped Tad off at Robby's house and spoke to his mother for a few minutes, she took the long way from town out to the beach house. Her stomach fluttered, her mind reeled with a myriad of thoughts all blending together. What was going on? What was she so nervous about?

A wild thought jumped into the entanglement of questions in her mind. *When was the last time I shaved my legs?*

She checked the rearview mirror and, seeing no traffic behind her, took a quick turn onto Beach Road.

"Oh God," she said to the passing scenery. "I'm really crazy now, aren't I? Thinking about my hairy legs at a time like this."

A time like what? She didn't have to ask that of herself. She knew what she meant by the "time." She'd been skirting the issue in her head while trying to keep as much space between herself and Tyler King whenever they were in the same room. All the while she'd been coping with the mess of her eviction notice, the broken water pipes, Tad's surprise return from camp, and the subsequent moving into the beach house and temporary placement of the clinic in a barn behind it, all that time she'd been working to keep at bay her escalating feelings about Ty. She couldn't possibly be in love with him, whatever that really meant anyway, so that left only one thing. *Lust.*

"Oh for heaven's sake." Admitting that was alien to her upbringing. Wanting a man physically was something only "women of a certain type" felt. How did a woman become a "certain type"? Was she born that way? Did she have it in her genes? There was no way she could have been born like that.

Yet, she simply flat out wanted this man in bed. "There's nothing simple about that," she muttered.

Her suspicious nature—her practical nature—suggested that perhaps he'd been subtly manipulating her for his own gain. Why not? That happened all the time. She'd seen it and heard about it. He wanted her out of that building without a fight. Just go and make everything easy. Well, she sure as hell wasn't going to do that. She'd had an agreement with his father, and by God she had planned to make Ty honor it. Of course, with the shape everything was in now, forcing him to honor an agreement he didn't even know about in the first place seemed ludicrous.

She came to the corner of Beach Road and Ocean Way and stopped the car. She'd be at the house in five minutes. Not much time to settle her thoughts, get hold of her emotions, and stop thinking in such base ways.

What was there to fight for now? A mess of a building. Even if it did belong to her, it would take thousands of dollars to make it habitable again. Fortunately the walls were still good, and the foundation still pretty sound. The roof was gone for all intents and purposes, the gaping hole in it covered over with a silo cover and strapped down. It belonged to Ty. But what about all the money she put into it? Money she was never reimbursed for by his father? Well, he was letting her live in his house rent free, and giving her his barn rent free. He'd even done a lot of work on it himself, painting and building along with the rest of them. Still, it was his fault she was even in this predicament. Or his father's fault. The sins of the father?

Of course, she should have been more forceful herself. She should have carried through on her threat to take Dorian King to court for repayment of her money and an order to make the building safe. She'd started the proceedings, but never carried them through. She felt pretty wimpy about it, but then, she much preferred peace over battles. Look at what reticence got her. She had to learn someday to beat that kind of behavior.

When? It wasn't as if she had another half century to play with.

She put the car in gear and headed down Ocean Way. Maybe they could talk tonight. Really talk. Everything had been on the surface up to now. What he did with Tad touched her so deeply. Why hadn't he said anything about his own vision problem? Maybe he didn't really have one. Maybe that was all a ploy to win Tad's confidence. That wasn't a good thing. Tad was as much of a realist as she was. If the boy found out Ty was lying about that, he'd be angry and would never forgive him. Tad could not stand being condescended to.

She pulled into the driveway and shut off the car. "Talk," she muttered. "Just talk. Control your lust. What would Mother say?"

She walked out back and checked the clinic before going into the house. Everything was fine. She knew it would be. Elmer had taken care of things.

"Procrastination is a way of life," she said. She'd tried to shake that all her life. That's why she believed she was a late bloomer. She'd procrastinated using every trick in the book. "There are reasons for that." She looked around. "I have got to stop talking to myself. That's what people do when they get old."

Was that it? She was feeling she was getting old? So she was a few years older than Ty. What difference did that make? Well, it would to some people. She reached down and felt her legs under her slacks. Not bad. Just a tiny soft stubble. One good thing about getting older was that hair didn't grow so fast.

She shut the door to the clinic and started up the path to the house. What did she think she was going to do? Burst through the door, grab him, throw him on the floor, and make violent love to him? She sucked in a sharp breath. Boy, did that sound good!

On the porch Caesar was sleeping near the screen door. He opened his eyes when she started up the steps. "Hi, big dog," she said affectionately. He flopped his tail a couple of half-hearted times. "Tuckered out, aren't you?" She hunkered down and gently stroked his head. "You were wonderful. And you made Tad feel wonderful. You and Ty." Caesar sighed and closed his eyes.

In the kitchen she could hear him opening and closing drawers, moving pans, rummaging for some cooking tool or other. And humming. Ty was humming. He sounded happy. Maggie tilted her head and listened for a few seconds. What a comforting sound that was.

Comforting. What an alien word that was to her.

She opened the door and went in quickly before she changed her mind and went over to Roz's house.

Ty stopped humming and turned around quickly. "Honey, you're home! Did you have a hard day at the office?"

She laughed lightly. "Have you been taking Donna Reed lessons? Where are your pearls?"

"They didn't go with my apron."

He brushed his hands over a towel he had tied over his denim cutoff shorts. He was barefoot. His legs had a light dusting of sand-colored hair. Why hadn't she noticed that before? That was silly. Men were supposed to have hairy legs. He wore a T-shirt so old and worn it looked soft, like that sand-colored hair. Would the hair on his chest be the same color? God, she had to stop this.

"Doc? Everything all right? No problems with Tad, I hope."

She shook her head. "No, of course not. He's on cloud nine. You gave him a great day, an accomplishment he can be proud of."

"He did it himself. Just needed a push. Speaking of pushing, go get changed into something comfortable. We have things to talk about." He gestured with two hands.

"Talk. What a good idea," she said, and headed down the hallway. Past the opening to the living room, something yellow

caught her eye. She backed up and looked
in. The living room had been rearranged.
The focal point was the fireplace. The
sofa, chairs, pillows, and coffee table were
arranged to best advantage. All Ty's
books were out of their cartons and up
on the shelves. And in the middle of the
coffee table was a huge bouquet of yellow
jonquils and daisies spraying out of a
heavy clear glass vase.

"For heaven's sake," she whispered.
What was he doing? Was he displaying
his own possible lust by setting a lovely
trap?

Nah.

She went down the hall to her room.
His room. Well, his room with her stuff
in it. She'd tried to be careful not to just
take over the whole space. He still went
in there to get clean clothes and shoes.
And he dressed in there when she was in
the bathroom. They'd worked it out quite
smoothly she thought without even planning it that way. It had just evolved easily,
without discussion. She wondered at that
occurrence now. It was as if they'd been
on the same wavelength from the very beginning. Of course, they both knew that

couldn't possibly be true. Never were two people more opposite.

She scanned the room. It was neat. Her things and his things. So they were of the same mind in one thing. Neatness. They both liked to know where everything was so they could find it the moment they needed it. Lots of people were like that.

She changed into jeans shorts and a T-shirt. No shoes. She loved going around the house barefoot. She could never do that very often in the apartment. But living in a beach house almost demanded shoeless attire. Okay, so that was something else they had in common.

She took life seriously, paid attention to details, was careful to keep a realistic eye on everything.

He wasn't serious about anything. Everything was a joke to him.

They both liked to laugh. Maybe they both needed to laugh. She knew why she needed to. She only sensed he did, but didn't know why. Maybe they had a lot more in common than she realized.

Sixteen

"I have news," Ty said as Maggie walked into the kitchen.

"What kind of news?" She looked over what appeared to be a bushel of cut vegetables and into a pot steaming on the stove. "Mmm, that smells good. What is it?"

"Bouillabaisse."

"I thought you said you could only cook eggs."

"And bouillabaisse. News I never thought I'd have in my life." He reached into the refrigerator and extracted a bottle of champagne. "Here." He handed the bottle to her. From the freezer he took out two chilled stemmed glasses. "Come on out on the porch." He opened and held the door for her to pass through.

"Champagne?" she said as she slipped by him.

"Of course, champagne. This is a celebration."

He motioned her to the wicker armchairs and set the glasses on the table. Then he took the bottle and with his towel apron finished opening it. The cork popped sharply. Caesar raised his head for only a moment, then dropped it back to the floor and returned to sleep.

"What happened?" she asked, holding the two glasses while he poured. "Did the building collapse completely and the town crew pave over it?"

"Nothing that mundane, my dear," he said cryptically.

"Mundane? I would think that would solve all your problems."

"It's going to take much more than the mere collapse of a building to solve my problems, but I'm working on them." He set the bottle under the table in the shade and held his glass toward her. "To a new start."

He gave her the most direct gaze she'd ever seen, and it took incredible strength for her to hold it and give him hers.

"I'll drink to that," she said and touched his glass. They drank. "This is very good," she said. "I don't usually care much for champagne, but this is very light and smooth."

"I aim to please." Ty flopped down in the chair next to hers and draped a leg over the arm.

The action stretched the crotch of his worn shorts, and Maggie caught the hint of a swell there. A warmth spread up her chest and over her face. A hot flash. Yes, a flash of heat because she realized Ty was not wearing underwear.

"I have a job. Can you believe it? For the first time in my life, I asked for a job. That's a shock. But the biggest shock of all is that I got it!" He laughed and took a long swallow of champagne.

"A job?" Maggie sat up and scrutinized him. "Why would you need a job?"

"Everybody needs a job."

"But . . . you're Tyler King." Maggie feared her suspicions were true.

Slowly Ty turned his head toward her. He had to tell her. It was time. He couldn't keep up this wealthy entrepreneur facade any longer. This moment had been long coming. Bit by bit every layer he'd used as insulation against reality had been chipped into and weakened. He knew now it was because of Maggie Logan. Not because she'd deliberately set out to do that to him. No. It was because of her that he'd started the chipping away himself. Guilt over what his father had started with her and what he'd continued at her expense? Partly. Especially in the beginning. But now as he looked at her, saw the kind of open honesty she displayed, he knew the rest of the reason.

"Did you know you look like a teenager sitting there in shorts and a T-shirt, barefoot?" he said, his voice suddenly thick.

She moved uncomfortably. "I'm hardly a teenager. I can barely remember when I was one." She watched him watching her, and drained her glass. "Don't change the subject. Why does Tyler King need a job?"

Ty reached under the table for the bottle. He refilled their glasses. "Because I'm broke."

Maggie slowly set her glass on the table. "Broke."

"Yes."

"Because of the building?"

Ty sat forward and rested his elbows on

his knees. "No. At least not directly. Chalk it up to high living and divorce, bad business deals with my partner for which I was as much responsible as he was. My mother had a lot of medical bills. But that was all right. I'd have paid anything to make her feel better. And then there's the mess my father made, including that building. If it hadn't been for Caesar's residuals up until last year, I'd have been registering for food stamps."

Maggie stared at him. "I . . . I can't believe this."

Ty nodded. "I didn't want to believe it either, which is why I've been in the predicament I've been in."

"And why you kept cashing my checks and ignoring my pleas for assistance."

He nodded again. "I'm not proud of that. Then, well, it was the frame of mind I was in. I'm sorry for what I put you through, and I will find a way to make it up to you."

Maggie rose and walked over to the porch railing. She leaned against it and gazed out over the ocean and the rose-and-purple cloud-streaked sky. He watched her.

"I know you've hated me for all of this," he said. "You've had good reason. I've hated myself. I've felt sorry for myself. I figured somebody owed me something. It's only since I've been back in Cape Agnes that I've begun to see things differently. It's me who owes. I owe you and Caesar. And it's time I started paying my debt."

Maggie turned around and glared at him. "Well, I'm really happy for you. But what about Critter Care and Elmer? What about Tad? I don't know what I'm going to do about them. They're my responsibility. You've got yourself and Caesar to worry about, that's all. Good for you. That's all you've got to think about. Yeah, you do owe me. I won't let you get off the hook about that. But I can see you're in no position to make any of it right. I'm out a lot of money personally, but I'm also out of a home and a business. And unlike you, I don't know what I'm going to do about it. Tad is going to need a lot of emotional and financial support. And I'm out of the financial part. As for the emotional part it's getting thin." She set the glass down on the table. "What in the hell am I celebrating?" She started to go for the door.

Ty stood up and stopped her with a hand on her arm. "Wait a minute. I deserved all that, I know. I'm glad you vented on me. I know I've been selfish. I never knew how good it could feel to think about somebody else for a change."

"Don't you dare tell me you're thinking about *me,*" Maggie breathed. "You're still thinking about you."

"I won't deny that. Don't we all think about ourselves? Aren't you worried as much about you as you are about Tad? And Elmer?" He held her arm and her gaze, knowing how much she wanted to get away from him. He couldn't let her go. He wouldn't let her go. "Please, stay and listen, stay and talk. Something's been going on between us that has more than a dispute at its heart. You know that. I've been a screw-up, I admit that. You've had some bad knocks. Both those things brought us together, along with a thieving dog and a brilliant kid. There's a reason for all that."

She continued to stare at him, her body rigid. Then he felt her slightly let go of her tension. She turned back to face the ocean and he saw her shoulders lower. "All right, I'll listen," she said at last. "What job are you celebrating?"

Ty stepped back. He suddenly felt prouder of what he was about to announce than he had almost anything in his life. "You, Michael Logan, Doctor of Veterinary Medicine, are drinking champagne with Tyler King, the new elementary-school track coach."

Maggie turned around. "They hired you? They're paying you a salary?"

"I wouldn't go that far. Shocking as that is to you, they've hired me. But salary?" He chuckled. "More like an allowance. Four thousand for the year. But, hey, I'll take it. Beggars can't be choosers. But you want to know something? I think I'd have chosen this job if I'd ever thought I had the opportunity for something like it. It's been the best couple of weeks of my life working with those kids."

Maggie stared at him. "You're the elementary track coach," she said in disbelief. "Who would ever have figured that would happen?"

"Certainly not me. Seems like Della

Reese was right. What a difference a day makes. Or even two weeks."

"You probably don't know that four thousand dollars isn't enough to live on."

"It will have to suffice for the moment. The superintendent and principal told me if I wanted to teach and could get a certificate, there would be more money. Fourteen thousand, I think. That's not bad."

"I suppose not, considering what you've been operating on for the last few years. You do realize that if you teach you'll be with children for several hours a day."

"Yes. Could that be so bad?"

"Maybe you should ask some teachers who've been teaching for the last ten years. Ask Mr. Hanson. I'll bet he can educate you." She shook her head then broke into a smile. "Actually, I think this is just great. The kids really seem to like you."

"Don't sound so surprised."

"I'll try to temper that. I'm beginning to see how you could make a difference in their lives. You certainly have made a big difference in Tad's life in a short span of time."

"He's the one who's made a difference in my life. And you."

"Me?" Maggie's stomach fluttered again.

"I admire you, Doc. I respect you. You've worked hard for everything you've ever achieved in your life. You've taught me a lot."

"Me?"

"Yes." He pointed out across the ocean. "Look."

She turned and saw the sky had turned golden mauve, and the ocean waves had metallic tips. The day was rapidly drawing to a close and nature was not going to let it go out without fanfare.

"Isn't that spectacular?" she whispered.

"Yes," he whispered into the back of her hair. "And because of you I've taken the time to appreciate evenings like this. And mornings. And every day." He braced his hand against a porch column, his arm brushing her shoulder.

Maggie's pulse raced. This man had a way of grasping her emotions and turning them inside out. But she'd learned something, too. She'd given him the power to do just that. She'd let go of her control and allowed his very presence to do that to her. She turned around and faced him. "How did this happen?" she whispered.

"I don't know," he answered. He leaned toward her upturned face, closed his eyes, and placed the brush of a kiss against her lips.

She opened her eyes. "That's not enough," she said thickly.

"What?" he whispered.

"That's not enough. I want more." Maggie had never said those words to a man in her life. But the truth was she did want more, and she wanted it right then and there, if need be. "Put these glasses somewhere."

"Your every wish is my command, your highness." He took her champagne glass and his own and placed them on the porch railing.

"I hope you won't be sorry you said that."

"I don't believe sorry is what I'm going to be."

She slipped her hands up and felt his chest through the thin T-shirt, and encircled his neck with her arms. "Kiss me again, and this time I want to feel it in my toes."

"With pleasure."

He placed his hands over her hips and drew her close to him, fitting her pelvis against his. Then he ran his hands up her spine, flattened one against her shoulder blades, and slid the other into her hair at the back of her head.

Ty's lips touched hers lightly, igniting the flame of desire in Maggie. Then he kissed her deeply. She couldn't remember feeling so swept away by a kiss before. She kissed him back with as much fervor.

When their lips parted, she opened her eyes and looked up into his. She opened her palms and fitted them over the back of his neck and pulled his head down to her. And then their lips met again with a fury that overwhelmed them both. The need was strong, the desire to give and to take just as strong.

They broke apart and he clasped her to him. "I've wanted to do that for so long," he said hoarsely.

"So have I, but I didn't know it," she said. "And I want more, now."

He opened the door and they squeezed themselves, still embracing, through it. Then he pressed her back against the refrigerator and kissed her while his hands ran over her, grasping her waist, her shoulders, her hips, her buttocks, her thighs as if he'd never felt their like before.

She pushed at him and broke the kiss. "In the bed, in the living room. Somewhere," she said breathlessly.

"Everywhere," he countered.

She slipped away from him, then grasped his waistband and started to pull him toward the hallway.

"The bouillabaisse," he said.

"Too hot," she giggled.

He laughed and reached out to turn off the gas under the pot. "It was going to be so good, too."

"This is going to be better." She pulled him down the hallway to his bedroom. The room she'd been living in since she'd moved in.

She yanked on the snap and zipper of his cutoffs and pushed them over his slim hips. She was right. He wasn't wearing any underwear. They fell to his ankles releasing him.

"Turnabout is fair play," he said, and did the same with her shorts. When they fell to her ankles, he slipped his hands over the silkiness of her panties. "They're the same color as the sky was tonight," he marveled. And then in a deft move, he peeled them away to fall at her feet. Before she could move he slid his fingers between their bodies and slipped gently inside her.

"Oh, God," she breathed and dropped her head back. She scraped her fingernails over his back than pulled at his T-shirt. The fabric was so thin that it gave. She ripped it from him and threw it on the floor.

He circled his arms under her buttocks and lifted her high. Suspended above him she looked down through her hair as he kissed her breasts through her T-shirt and bit at the bra closure beneath it.

"Take it off, take it off me," she commanded.

He set her firmly on the floor, then whipped the shirt over her head and flung it on the bed. Then he pulled open the front closure of her bra and let her breasts fall free, catching them in his hands and pushing them up to meet his lips. He dropped to his knees leaving a trail of kisses down her stomach and abdomen until he reached the part of her that was aching for his entry.

"Oh-h," she moaned as his tongue found the place it sought. She twined her fingers through his hair and pulled him hard against her.

"I can't wait any longer." He stood and lifted her, dropping her carefully on the bed. "You're ready. Are you ready?" He slipped his fingers inside her again and covered her mouth with a wide, deep kiss.

She writhed against him as her answer. And then they were on the bed and he was inside her, grinding, pushing deeper. She strained against him, unable to breathe under his crushing kiss and pressing weight. He wasn't all the way inside. What was she supposed to do? It didn't matter what she was supposed to do. She did what she wanted to do. She grasped his buttocks with both hands, bent her knees with her feet flat on the bed, and thrust up as hard as she could.

And then he was inside her, plunging deep and moving fast. "Damn it, damn it, damn it!" he said into her ear.

His body convulsed and she felt him pulsing inside her. He pushed faster, harder, then stopped almost in mid-thrust before falling against her. She slid her hands up the small of his back and clasped his shoulders. A chill went over him and she felt the little bumps raise on his skin. His breath came in ragged gasps.

"God, Doc, I'm sorry. I . . . that was so good. So good for me. I couldn't . . . help myself. I should have waited for you."

"Sh. Don't say that. You thrilled me. You just don't know. I've never been . . . no man has ever gone wild over me like that." She tried to calm her racing pulse and erratic breathing, but it wasn't working. "I hope it was me," she added, "not just *it*."

He rolled over on his back and rolled her with him, still locked inside her. "I don't know what I could possibly say that would tell you that without a doubt it was you. I tried to hold back, but the moment you lifted against me and I was so deep inside you, I lost all control. It was you. And me. Us."

She lowered her head and kissed him. "I'm glad."

"I'm sorry I didn't get you there first."

"That doesn't matter. I barely know what that means anyway."

He stopped caressing her. "Is that right?"

She nodded. "You don't miss something you never had, right?"

An enigmatic smile played over his lips. "Oh, lady, you are about to learn what you've been missing. And if I have anything to do with it, you'll never miss it again."

"What?" She arched her back.

He rolled her over, slipped out of her, and gathered her close, then kissed and licked her breasts. He pulled up her knees then slipped his arm between them and pulled her hip close to him. She could feel him still hard against her. He caressed her gently, touched between her thighs, touched below her navel, moved surely inside and found what he was looking for. He nuzzled her breasts and kissed them, moved them with his lips. And his fingers kept up their relentless thrumming until her breath came fast, her senses climbed, and her mind broke free. At her peak the spasms came quickly, deliciously, one after the other after the other. She moaned. She couldn't take any more. She tried to break free, but he wouldn't stop. And then when she thought there was no higher place for her senses to soar, she was wildly flying again.

The landing was inevitable, but they came down together and she felt a warm syrup spill out of him and slowly drip down her thigh. Her racing pulse began to slow. She caught her breath and forced it to become even again.

"Wow," she breathed.

"Yeah," he said.

"Tell me you didn't make up what just happened."

"I didn't make up what just happened. I never could have fabricated that." He slid his arm over her rib cage and nestled his lips against her hair.

"I didn't know such a thing could happen. I feel like Sleeping Beauty lying dormant for a hundred years." She took a deep breath, and let out a low laugh. "Sleeping Grandma is more to the point."

He kissed her hair. "Well, I'm glad I was the prince who awakened you."

"Did you really tell Tad you thought I should have a boyfriend because I was pretty?"

Ty lifted his head sharply. "That little stool pigeon. He blabbed."

"Yes, he did. Did you say that?"

"Yes, I did. Are you fishing for compliments?"

"Of course."

"Well, okay. I'm surprised you don't have men pursuing you constantly."

"Ha!"

"I mean it. You're warm, compassionate, giving."

"Old."

"Aged well like fine wine," he countered. He gave a playful tap to her naked behind. "And built for exquisite comfort."

She leaned over and planted a light kiss on both his nipples. "You're not so bad yourself."

"Speaking of wine, we've left some perfectly fine champagne out on the porch. I think I should rescue it, don't you?"

"Capital idea," she said, pushing him to get out of the bed. "And what about your bouillya-whatever-it-is? I'm starved."

"You should be." He got out of the bed and went in search of his clothes. He lifted the shredded T-shirt off the floor. "Look what you did to my best shirt. One would think you were also love-starved."

"One would be right. Get to that kitchen and get supper on the table before you find out just how hungry I am right here and right now."

"Harrumph. One good tumble in the sheets and she becomes a demanding monarch. I can see my work will never be done." He zipped up his jeans with a flourish.

When he was gone she stretched out, luxuriating amid the sheets and blanket and the scent of their lovemaking. It was good. Better than she could ever have imagined. What a wonderful slice of life to have lived without for so long.

By the time she came out of the bathroom, fresh and dressed in her robe, Ty had a fire going in the fireplace and had set out bowls of his aromatic concoction on the coffee table. Two lighted candles flanked the vase of flowers, and the champagne bottle was protruding from an ice-filled plastic bucket, the two glasses stuck among the cubes.

"Your highness, your feast awaits you," he said, bowing low, naked except for his denim shorts.

"And what a lovely feast it is. Oh!" She glanced up at the clock above the fireplace. "Do I have time to eat it?"

"Yes. Don't worry about Elmer. He's staying over in Sea View tonight."

"How do you know that?"

"He told me just before he left. You were taking Tad over to Robby's when he came in. Here, sit down and have your dinner." He pulled out a pillow for her.

"Why do I get the feeling you helped Elmer decide to stay in Sea View?"

"Because your woman's intuition is so strong. I won't deny it." He sat down next to her.

"You mean you knew we were going to . . . make love?"

"I didn't know it. But I was sure as hell hoping."

She smiled while he poured what was left of the champagne. "It's lost a little of its pizzazz," she said, holding her glass up to the candlelight. "Just like me."

Ty leaned over and kissed her. "My magic soup will restore all the pizzazz that you need."

"What about you?"

"I intend to have two helpings."

Later, they snuggled side by side in the pillows, under a quilt, in front of the fire.

"Doc?" he asked hoarsely, his eyes telling her how much he wanted her, yet asking if it was all right with her to go on.

Maggie's heart quickened with her own desire. Much as she'd tried to ignore it or push it out of her mind, she knew she had fallen in love with Tyler King. She'd thought that was reserved only for brash youth, yet here she was a grandmother and falling in love again.

She gave to and took from this man as

if it were the most natural thing in the world. To let go this completely, to be lost in the arms of this man, felt so right, as if she'd always known this was the way it should be. He pushed himself up to lean on his hands above her. Loving fingers of firelight moved over his glistening body in gentle caresses.

Maggie's breath caught in her throat. "You are a beautiful man," she whispered.

With a sigh Ty sank down over her, gathering her warmth and softness against him. How right this felt, how right Maggie felt in his arms. He loved her. What a surprise this was! Was it too soon to declare it? He remembered something he'd read somewhere long ago, "Faint heart never won fair lady." *Do it*, an inner voice urged him. *Do it!*

He opened his eyes and took in the loveliness of her in the cocoon they'd made for themselves. "I love you, Doc. I love you, and I want to be with you all the time." He kissed her tenderly.

"I love you, too, Ty." The words sounded as if they came from a shy young girl, not the sensual woman who lay beneath him. "I love you," she whispered it over and over. She said it as if she didn't quite believe a fantasy had come true.

He didn't doubt that it had, for both of them. He sank against her body and wrapped his arms completely around her, sighing deeply. For the first time in his life he was feeling truly married,

Hours later, in the special velvet darkness just before dawn, they made love again, slowly, savoring the moment as new lovers do. Afterward, Ty pulled the quilt over them as Maggie lay against him sleeping soundly. The fire had long gone out, but the white-hot glow of ashes remained. He kissed the top of her hair, gathered her even more closely into his arms, and sank into a contented sleep.

Seventeen

"Maggie, I believe you have no choice," Bob Marshall told her. "As your attorney I'm recommending that we take Mr. King to court and sue him for damages. Chances are he'll be willing to settle out of court. He owes you a lot of money for all you did to keep his building together all these years. And I also think we can get him on misrepresentation."

Maggie sat in an antique oak chair in Robert Marshall's law office on the third floor above *The Cape Agnes News*. Maggie trusted Bob Marshall. He had the oldest law practice in Cape Agnes. She knew he had her best interests at heart. But what he was proposing now was not something she could readily agree to. Not now. Not after the weekend with Ty.

"I don't really want to do that, Bob," she said. "He doesn't have any money. He just got a job recently, and I know for a fact he's only making four thousand a year. What do I want with that? There has to be a better way."

"There isn't. Listen to me, now is your chance. We sue him. Maybe he hasn't got any ready cash. How can you be certain he's leveling with you? You don't know about everything he may own. What we do know right now is that his name is on the deed to that Elm Street building, and he hasn't paid the taxes on it in almost four years. It's going to public auction anyway. We'll get that. The only other thing he owns is that has-been television dog and the dog's insurance policy which is about to run out. That and his car are about it. The time is ripe. You'll come out of it with the building which you'll use for collateral to secure a loan. Then you can rebuild the place and get your business and home back in place."

Maggie hedged. "I don't know about this. I don't feel right. I don't want to take anything away from him. I just want it to work out for all of us. There must be some other way."

"Maggie, this is not a win-win situation

here. One of you is going to win, and the other is going to lose. It's as simple as that. As your attorney I rather like the idea of you being the winner. Look at it this way, I win, too. You'll keep my wife's three Himalayan cats in shots and grooming and boarding for the next five years." He smiled warmly.

"I know you're right about the business end of it. But, we've got to think of something else. I just can't sue him."

"Look, I know you and the boy and Dr. Everett have been living with King since the building caved in." Maggie wasn't going to argue the "living with" point. "And I suppose it's possible you may have, well, developed feelings for him. But you've got to set these feelings aside, or you're going to be in a very difficult situation in the not too distant future. And you can't count on him to help you out. What about college for Tad? You're going to need money and a lot of it. This is a start. At least if you own the building you'd have something to sell. Think of it as an investment. And what if a breakthrough comes in Tad's medical treatment? Your health insurance won't cover the extent of that kind of thing."

Maggie nodded. "I know. I believe you. I just hate doing it this way."

Marshall leaned back in his leather chair. "All right. Suppose you give it some more thought. We have a little time. The mayor and the town council are trying to come to a decision about what to do with the building anyway. And if they work the way they usually do, we should gain several weeks of waiting time. All right?"

Maggie pushed herself out of the chair. Suddenly she felt very weary. "Yes, thank you, Bob. I don't want to think about much more right now."

"Ah, yes, you must be going into dress rehearsals for *Camelot* soon, aren't you?"

"Next week."

"Well, it's good for you. You've always enjoyed being in Henrietta's productions."

"Yes, I have, but I can tell you I'll be glad when this one is over."

"I see. Tyler King is in it, too. I forgot about that. That must make it difficult. And if we were to go into a court proceeding right now that would make it all the more tense for you, I know. All right. As soon as the production is over, we'll meet again and discuss what you can do. Fair enough?"

"Thanks, Bob. I'm glad you understand."

Maggie walked down the stairs from the law office and past the glass door to the *The Cape Agnes News*. She saw Darlene sitting at her computer terminal engrossed in the composition of her latest feature. With any luck she could sneak by the door and not be seen.

She was almost to the front door of the building when the flash of a blue polo shirt in the *News* office caught her eye. She gave in and looked. Ty was walking from the back storage area, carrying two of the heavy bound old editions of the newspaper. Back when it had been called *The Cape Ledger.* She considered going in there, thought better of it, and kept moving. She got out onto the street before either of them saw her.

At the clinic Elmer seemed to be in less of a jovial mood than he had been in recent weeks. Maggie noticed a distinct slump to his back and a frown that didn't relax. They were cleaning up after setting a broken leg on a German shepherd and getting the dog settled in his cage. The procedure had gone without a hitch and without one argument from Elmer. Not even a tiny criticism.

"You feeling all right, Elmer?"

"Just tired," he said without looking up.

"Don't forget Hans is back there before you lock up," she said.

"I don't need reminding about Hans," Elmer snapped.

"I know you don't. I guess I need reminding now and then, so that's why I said it." Maggie hoped that would soothe his ruffled feathers.

"Keep your mind on business and you'll remember what you're supposed to remember." He grabbed his brown sweater from the hall tree by Jolene's desk, and started out the door.

"What do you mean? Wait a minute, Elmer. I'll walk up to the house with you."

He didn't respond, but kept moving.

"What's the matter with Elmer today?"

Maggie asked Jolene when she stopped at the reception desk.

"Don't know, but he seems more crotchety than usual." Jolene finished the last of her filing and straightened the desk.

"I'm worried about him. I think his brother's all right. He didn't mention that anything was wrong when he got back from Sea View. In fact he seemed in good spirits last night. This isn't like him to change so radically in so short a time."

"Maybe it's Dottie's new beau."

"Dottie has a new beau?"

"So I hear. He's Joey Something, I can't remember his last name. New man at the post office. Joined the fire department and he's a volunteer ambulance driver. Everybody likes him. He and Dottie went to the movies on Saturday night, and it was the talk of Mother's this morning at breakfast."

"Was Elmer there for breakfast?"

"Yep. He came in with Ty late in the morning."

"Oh yes, Elmer did say he was going to the dentist's office. Something about a loose filling. You know what pride he takes in the fact that those are all his own teeth."

"I know. He seemed all right then. Don't know what's got into him." Jolene started for the door. "See you tomorrow, Doc. Gotta run. Ray's coming in tonight and I'm cooking a special dinner. This might be the big night." She lifted her left hand and waggled her third finger.

Maggie smiled. "Oh, I hope so, Jolene. I get to throw the first wedding shower for you."

"Terrific! 'Night."

"Good night and good luck. I'll be thinking of you."

Maggie went to the back of the clinic and checked on the German shepherd. He was sleeping. She turned on the baby monitor she kept near any overnight patients so she could hear in the house if the animal awoke. She was about to leave when she heard scratching from the other side of the door of the boarding pens. She opened it and Dottie's Doberman walked out.

"Hans, come over here. Looks like I'll have to drive you."

The big dog followed her out and she

locked up. He jumped into her car when she opened the door and she drove him home. Dottie came out on the front porch still in her waitress uniform from Mother Hubbard's.

"Hi, Dottie." Maggie walked up the sidewalk to Dottie's little cottage, Hans trotting beside her like a small horse. "Here's your errant boy."

"I wondered where he was. Usually Elmer brings him home and puts him in the kitchen if I'm not here. I thought they were just late tonight. Where's Elmer?" Hans waited by her for the usual smooch on his nose then went inside for his dinner when she opened the door for him.

"I don't know. He left the clinic before I did. He seemed kind of moody. He forgot about Hans even though I reminded him."

"Must be the moon," Dottie said knowingly. "Have a seat." She motioned to two lawn chairs on the porch.

"Dottie, does Elmer know about your new boyfriend?" Maggie probed.

"New boyfriend? Who? Joey?"

"I guess."

Dottie giggled. "Joey's not my boyfriend. We're just friends. I'm old enough to be his mother!"

"Oh. Does Elmer know that?"

"I don't know. Why would Elmer care about Joey and me?"

"Because he cares about you."

"Me? Elmer?"

"Yes. I thought you knew." Maggie instantly felt she'd violated Elmer's privacy.

"No. I had no idea. I just thought he was being nice to me because he's just naturally nice." Dottie smiled. "Elmer likes me."

"Well, then I just can't figure out what's bothering him," Maggie said, rising. "Guess I'll just have to make him tell me. I hope he's not sick."

"I don't think he's sick. He was sure mad this morning, though."

"Mad over what?"

"Why, over what's happening with your old building on Elm."

"What do you mean what's happening with the building?"

"Well, the county safety commissioner says it has to be torn down within fourteen days. He says it's a safety hazard for people walking by, and he said something about it attracting rats which, I can tell you, didn't make Little Bert none too pleased. You know the back of that building is just across the alley to our back door at the restaurant."

Maggie was too stunned to take in the part about Little Bert's distress. "Torn down? When did this happen? I never heard anything about it."

"Just this morning. Darlene came in for coffee and blabbed it all around that she was writing the big feature story. She took pictures and everything. It'll be on the front page in this week's paper." Dottie scrutinized Maggie's face. "Gee, Doc, naturally I thought you knew about this."

"No, I didn't know about it. I wonder if Elmer thinks I knew about it, too, and he's mad because I didn't tell him. Was Ty there when Darlene was talking about this?"

"Oh yes. They were all at the same table. Lloyd was there. And Mrs. Van-Gelder. Jan from Hairoics. She was shocked, I can tell you. Well, we all were. We were positive you or Mr. King or somebody was going to rebuild it. Elmer really cares about that old place, you know."

"I know. He worked there as a boy making nets. His father worked there, too."

"He said something about once something gets old, people just think it's worthless and throw it away. You know, Doc, I think I'm going to invite Elmer to supper one night soon. What do you think?"

"I think that would be a very nice idea, Dottie. I think Elmer might like that." Maggie started down the sidewalk for her car. "I'll see you tomorrow, Dottie. You're not working tonight, are you?"

"No. Worked a long enough day as it was. See you. Thanks for bringing Hans home."

"Anytime."

Maggie got into her car and drove away. She wasn't certain where she should go. Back to the beach house? Would Ty be there? No. He should be at school with the track team. That's where Tad was. Suddenly Maggie felt like watching the practice.

* * *

Maggie turned the car down Elm Street. The last time she'd been past the building the sight of it almost broke her heart. Everything was the same as when they'd moved out. Nobody had touched a thing except for placing the plastic over the part where the roof had caved in. Now as she neared it she felt a surge of old memories flood back. Maybe she should have tried harder with Dorian King instead of giving up when he didn't respond to her letters. Maybe she should have called her attorney in then instead of waiting so long. Maybe he could have done something about it. Maybe she should have tried harder to secure the place for herself once and for all.

All the maybes in the world wouldn't change what was now. She hadn't been brought up to take the bit in her teeth and run with it. She'd been taught to take things as they came and accept them. Her only rebellion against her family's values had been in getting a divorce and becoming a veterinarian. She'd thought those were major obstacles to have overcome. Now she believed she hadn't carried the rest of it through to closure. Other people were making all the decisions, and she had no recourse but to watch.

She took a long look at the building as she slowly drove past. Time to find out just what was going on. She pressed the gas pedal and drove around the corner and out to the school parking lot.

She walked over and stood by the fence to watch Ty with the children. He waved and smiled, and she felt the fluttering in her stomach again. As she watched Ty move and interact with the runners, a wave of love swept over her. *Love.* What a wonderful feeling, yet a scary one.

Tad didn't seem to be among the children. She shaded her eyes and scrutinized the group. Where was he? She finally saw him sitting on the far end of the bleachers, elbows on his knees, chin propped in his palms. He looked glum. Where was Caesar? She didn't see him anywhere and he wasn't at the clinic when she left. She started to walk around to the gate so she could go and talk with Tad.

Ty went over to him. He seemed to be encouraging Tad, or talking him into something. Tad got up, reluctantly, Maggie observed. He went out onto the track with Ty. And they started to run. Ty was in the side lane where Caesar usually ran, and she could see him talking the whole time as he ran next to Tad. What in the world was going on?

When practice was over and the kids started to run back into the school, Maggie went to meet Ty.

He leaned down and kissed her cheek. "You look great. And I know you feel great," he said, teasing.

"It's all I've thought about all day." Maggie felt her cheeks warm. "We have to talk seriously. But first, I'm worried about the way Tad looked out there. What's the matter? Where's Caesar?"

"That's what's the matter. We can't find him," Ty said, and there was worry in his voice.

"What do you mean you can't find him? He's always around the house or the clinic. If he's not there, he's wherever Tad is."

"I know. He wasn't around when I came over to the school. I thought somehow he might already be here with Tad. Maybe Jolene brought him in or something. But Tad said he hadn't seen Caesar since just after lunch. You know Robby's mother picked him up so the boys could go to the pool."

"Yes. And Caesar was home then?"

"Yes. According to Tad he was with Elmer on the back porch. He was fine."

Maggie bit her lip. "Strange. Elmer isn't around either. He was in a cranky mood this afternoon when we closed up. He forgot all about Hans. That surprised me. You know he likes to take Hans home so he can talk to Dottie if she's there."

"Yeah, I know." Ty grinned sheepishly. "I hear tell she's got a boyfriend, though."

"He's not her boyfriend. You heard that in Mother's this morning, didn't you?"

"Well, yes. Poor Elmer. He didn't take that too well. He tried to cover it, but I could see it bothered him."

"Among other things, I gather."

"What other things?"

"What do you know about the county safety commissioner saying the Elm Street building has to be demolished in two weeks?"

Ty looked down at his running shoes. "So you heard about that?"

"Of course I heard about that. You ought to know by now everybody in Cape Agnes hears everything, and they talk about it because they just assume everybody else has heard about it, too." Maggie tried to soften her agitation, but she didn't do a very good job of it. "I want to know why you didn't tell me about it."

"I only heard about it myself this morning. I didn't want to call you and ruin your day before I did a little more investigation into it." He scrutinized her face and his expression told her he was bothered by this conversation.

"And so you went to *The Cape Agnes News* office to do what, investigate?"

Ty shook his head in disbelief. "Man, things really do get around this place quickly."

"I saw you in the office with Darlene."

"I wasn't with Darlene. She's the editor. She has to be there. I wanted to look into something in the old issues of the newspaper." He narrowed his eyes. "Wait a minute, do I detect a note of jealousy in your voice?" He smiled then. "Believe me, you have nothing to be jealous about when it comes to Darlene. Or to any other woman for that matter. When did you go by the *News*? I didn't see you."

"You were too busy to see me," she said, and realized she still had an edge of irritation in her voice. "I didn't go by. I was coming down from the third floor of the *News* building."

"What's on the third floor?"

Maggie waited a long moment. "My attorney's office."

"Hi, Grams," Tad called as he and Susan walked over to them.

Ty gave Maggie a questioning frown, but said nothing.

"Hi, honey. How was practice today?" Maggie bent to hug him but saw him give her a silent admonishing look. He clearly didn't want her to do anything dorky in front of Susan.

"Susan was great," Tad said. "I didn't do so well without Caesar with me."

"He did, too, Dr. Logan," Susan said. "I clocked him and he was just as good as he was when Caesar was here."

"That's because Ty ran with me," Tad said glumly.

"And I could hardly keep up with you," Ty told him. "And you were good. You stayed in lane easily."

"Grams, where is Caesar?" Tad pushed up his sunglasses and peered around her.

"I don't know," Maggie said gently. "We were just talking about him. I haven't seen him all day."

"He wasn't sick," Tad said, a small sob in his voice. He bit back the tears that threatened.

"He is getting old," Susan said. "My grandfather's dog got old and he went away to die by himself. Grampa said it was an ancient tradition among the wolves to go away quietly and just go to sleep forever. He says dogs are descended from wolves—"

"Caesar isn't dead!" Tad cried then. "He's not sick. He's not even old."

Ty hunkered down in front of him. "Actually, Tad, Caesar is getting old. He's worked hard all his life. It is possible that he decided—"

"You shouldn't have made him run with me!" Tad shouted. "That made it worse for him."

"No, it didn't, Tad," Ty said gently.

"He loved that. I could tell. So could you. He wanted to do that."

"But maybe he shouldn't have done it. Elmer said when we had to put Mrs. Treen's old cat to sleep last week that she still had a couple of good years in her. But Mrs. Treen wants to move to Florida to a 'tirement place and didn't want the cat. Elmer says soon as things are old or hurt people just throw them away. Soon they'll be doing it to people, he said. Maybe Caesar heard him and got scared." The tears poured down Tad's face then, and he didn't care if Susan saw them.

Maggie threw her arms around him and cradled his head against her.

"I guess I better go home," Susan said. "I hope you find Caesar."

"Thanks. Maybe Tad can call you later and let you know," Ty told her.

Abruptly Maggie stopped comforting Tad. She held him away from her and looked into his face. "When did Elmer say those things to you? About throwing old things away, I mean."

Tad sniffed and wiped his nose on the sleeve of his T-shirt. Ty took a bandanna from his back pocket and gave it to him.

The boy wiped his nose again and handed the bandanna back to Ty.

"Try to remember, Tad. When did Elmer say those things?" Maggie pressed.

Tad sniffed. "When we put Mrs. Treen's cat to sleep."

"Is that the only time he said anything like that?"

Tad thought a minute. "And this afternoon he said it just before I went to the pool with Robby."

Maggie looked up at Ty. "Oh no."

Ty saw the pained look in her eyes. "What? No. You don't think Elmer would. . . ."

"I think I'm beginning to have an idea where he might have gone." She took Tad's hand. "Come on, we'd better hurry."

"Where are you going?" Ty asked to her retreating back.

"To the building on Elm Street. You'd better meet us there."

Eighteen

Maggie drove to the Elm Street intersection. Officer Fisbee was just getting out of his patrol car, which he'd used to block entrance to the street. Maggie stopped the car and rolled down the window.

"Vincent, can I drive down there?"

" 'Fraid not, Doc. Fire trucks are there and Chief Reed isn't letting anybody down there."

"Is there a fire?" Maggie began to panic. Her intuitions were growing stronger that something was very wrong with Elmer.

"Not yet. It's your old building again. Somebody heard some timbers falling in there and called us. We came right over."

Maggie pulled the car over and parked it. "Wait right here," she said to Tad.

"Grams, what's wrong?" Tad asked in a frightened voice.

"I don't know yet, but I'll find out." She got out of the car and went over to Officer Fisbee.

"Vincent, what else do you know?"

"Well, the fire boys are seeing what they can do to make the place safe. Chief Reed called the safety commissioner to tell him what happened. He's on his way over here. My guess is they'll want to start demolition right away. Maybe even today."

"Oh my God! Vince, please let me go down there, please."

"Sorry, Doc. I know you care about the place, but I can't let you go near it. It's against the rules right now. My orders are to direct everybody around the other block. Nobody's allowed down there."

Ty pulled his car up behind Maggie's. He parked it and ran over to them. "What's going on?"

Maggie's eyes filled. "Something fell in the building. Somebody was walking by and heard it and called the fire department. Nobody can go down there. Vincent says they might start demolition right away."

"They can't do that."

"Oh God, Ty, I have the worst feeling that Elmer's inside the building. And Caesar."

"What?" He grabbed her hand. "Do you know that for certain?"

Officer Fisbee reached in his car window for his radio. "You have reason to believe Elmer's in the building, Doc?"

Maggie shook all over. "Not for certain," she said in a tearful voice. "It's a feeling. He's missing and so is Caesar. Maybe they're just out for a walk, but he was feeling bad about things, and I . . . oh, I don't know."

Suddenly Tad ran by them. He screamed, "Elmer? No! Don't let them knock down the building! Caesar's there!" He ran down the street toward the fire trucks.

"Oh, God, I didn't see him get out of the car!" Maggie screamed. She took off on a run after him. "Tad, Tad, stop!"

"Wait, Doc, stay here!" Vincent Fisbee called after her.

"I'm going after them," Ty said and started to run.

Fisbee grabbed him by the arm. "I said

nobody's allowed down there.'' He pressed the button on his radio. "Chief Reed, Fisbee here." He released the button.

"Reed here. Go ahead Fisbee."

Fisbee pressed the button. "We have reason to believe—"

Ty broke away from him and started to run down the street.

"Get back here King or I'll be forced to arrest you!" Fisbee yelled.

"You can do that later!" Ty yelled back. "I'll even turn myself in." He kept moving.

Maggie couldn't catch Tad who'd sneaked under the yellow plastic strips strung around the site by the fire department, and disappeared behind the building. She got to the fire chief who was talking on his radio.

"Chief Reed, my grandson just ran inside the building. Somebody get him! I think Elmer and Caesar are in there, too."

"Calm down, Doc. Fisbee just told me."

Ty ran up to them. "Where is he? Where's Tad?"

Reed opened his radio again. "Fisbee,

I told you to keep people out of here, now do it!" A crackling came back over in response. "I don't care what they did. Just don't let anybody else do it! Roger."

"Please let me go after them," Maggie pleaded.

"No," Reed said. "We don't need anybody else wandering around in there. Stay here." He walked to two of the other firemen and spoke to them.

Maggie trembled next to Ty. He put his arm around her shoulders. "Don't worry, they'll figure out a way to get them out. If they're in there."

"They won't know where to look," Maggie said. "They don't know the place like I do. And now Tad's inside."

"Where do you think they'd be? Where would Tad be likely to go?"

"Up to Elmer's apartment on . . . oh, God, on the third floor. That's where all the damage is. What if it starts to fall again? Dear God, they'll be hurt or. . . ."

Ty leaned near her ear. "Keep the chief busy. I'm going inside. Don't let them send anybody until I signal." He held up the whistle that still dangled from a string around his neck.

"Ty. . . ." Maggie was almost going to tell him not to go in, but she didn't. She walked immediately over to where the fire chief was talking to two of his men. Ty slipped away at the same time.

Inside the building, Ty wandered toward a back stairwell. He had no idea where it led. He'd only been in the building briefly since he'd been back to Cape Agnes and remembered nothing about it from when he was a boy. It was different back then anyway. More like a big open warehouse.

He waited. Listening. Footsteps. He could hear them. They moved slowly. The feet were sliding as if inching along somewhere above him. They sounded light. It must be Tad. He didn't want to call out for fear he'd scare the boy. He moved through some fallen plaster and timbers to the boarding units of what used to be the clinic. Another stairway. He looked up it. He could see daylight above, but it looked sound.

Wires hung everywhere. Water stains spread over walls. He felt a stab of guilt like none other he'd ever felt in his life. Why hadn't he paid attention to the letters he'd opened that had been directed to his father? Had he been so damned full of his own life that he hadn't cared about what other people were going through? It was just like his father to ignore her requests for aid or to even acknowledge her letters. Just like him to take off again and not tell anybody where he was. He'd been doing that all his life. Ty realized now he'd been almost following in his father's footsteps.

Ty started up the stairs. They moved when he put his weight down on each one. His hand shook on the railing. He was shaking himself. He'd never forgive himself if anything happened to that boy or that old man. And even Caesar. He loved the dog. That dog had been the closest friend he'd ever had. When everything else went to shit he still had Caesar, and Caesar loved him unconditionally. He hadn't known a human being to compare to that.

Yes, he had. His mother. Never his father. It would serve the old coot right if he were dead someplace. He'd been dead to him for years. Even before he disappeared.

He got to the landing and looked around. Overhead was daylight masked by thick plastic that drooped with water. There was a door at the end of the hallway and what appeared to be another stairwell going down. That must be Elmer's apartment. Carefully he walked along the wall. The floor creaked beneath his feet. He waited.

Footsteps again. "Elmer?" Tad's voice a bit above a whisper.

Ty jumped. Where was he? It was difficult to tell from which direction the voice had come. He didn't want to call out and scare him. And he didn't want to let Elmer know he was looking for him. He was liable to hide even deeper into the building and put himself in more danger.

There. Another sound. What? Whimpering. *Caesar!*

"Elmer!" Tad's voice, stronger than a whisper now. "Don't worry. I can take care of you. Where are you?"

The whimpering again.

"Elmer? Please. Are you here? Is Caesar here?"

Ty could hear Tad inching along a

floor somewhere. He admired the boy for his courage. He knew he understood the layout of the building. When it was whole. Things were different now, though. Partitions had fallen in. Tad could be in serious danger. Ty didn't know which to do first, find him or follow Caesar's moans.

The whimpering came louder. Ty followed it. He came to the door and tried to push it open. It wouldn't budge. Either it was locked from the inside or it was jammed. He thought a minute. He hoped for the jammed option. He looked around for something to pry it apart with. There was a loud sniffing from the other side.

"Caesar? Is that you, boy?"

Caesar barked once. Then he barked in high-pitched spurts.

"Okay, okay," Ty said. "Calm down. I'm going to get you out."

"Caesar?" Tad shouted.

Caesar barked again.

"Shh," Ty said to the door. "You're going to cause a cave-in."

He found an old broom. He broke the wooden handle and used the splintered end to wedge between the door and the jamb. It moved. He was able to get his hands around it and push it in. Caesar jumped up on him, and Ty caught him around the neck and calmed him.

"Down, down. You're liable to make the floor give out, and we'll be on the street faster than we plan." He stroked the dog's head. "Am I glad to see you, too, pal. Where's Elmer? Where is he?"

Caesar cocked his head, then padded through water to another door that was ajar. Ty followed him, carefully picking his way over boards and plaster and overturned furniture. Caesar went into the room. Ty looked around the door. Elmer lay on the bare bedsprings. Ty got to him quickly. There was a small cut on his forehead. Ty took the bandanna from his back pocket and dabbed at the blood.

"Elmer, Elmer. Wake up." He placed two fingers against the carotid artery in the old man's neck. A good, strong pulse. "Elmer, come on." He slipped an arm under Elmer's shoulders and lifted him to a sitting position.

"Go away," Elmer muttered.

"Okay, but you're coming with me."

"Am not."

"Are too."

"Am not."

"Jesus, Elmer, this is no time for one of your arguments. Maggie's in the street frantic with worry. Tad's somewhere in this damned place looking for you and Caesar."

"Well, go get him out of here. They're gonna knock the place down today, and I'm going with it. Me and Caesar." Elmer tried to push Ty away.

"Why would you want to do a thing like that?"

"Nobody likes anything old."

"Yeah, well, as soon as the both of you get old then ask me whether I like you or not. Come on."

"I'm not going, I tell you."

"Elmer!" Tad's voice echoed.

"We've got to get to Tad," Ty said. "But I'm not going without you." The blood started running from Elmer's cut. Ty dabbed at it again, then made a strip from his bandanna and tied it around Elmer's head. "How'd you cut yourself?"

"On a goddamned board in the clinic."

"Why didn't you look where you were going?"

"It fell while I was under it, you jack-ass."

"Sorry."

"Hey! Dr. Everett!" A bullhorn carrying Chief Reed's voice came up the hollow of the building.

"Shit," Ty muttered.

"Who's that?" Elmer said.

"It's your buddy, the fire chief. He's going to screw up everything and get us all killed if he isn't careful."

"Well, you get out of here and find Tad. Caesar will stay with me."

"Look, I won't let you kill my best friends in this lousy old building. Now come on." Ty stood and tried to pull Elmer to his feet.

"See? Lousy old building. That's what you said. Then there's me, a lousy old man. And Caesar will kill himself trying to keep up with the boy on that track. That's the kind of heart he has. He'll be a lousy old dog."

Ty ran his hand through his hair. The boards beneath his feet groaned along with him. He couldn't leave Elmer and

Caesar, and he couldn't let Tad keep wandering through the rubble. And once those firemen started rummaging around, no telling what might happen to the building.

"Now listen and listen closely. There is a way I can save this building. I'll do it if I have to throw myself in front of the wrecking ball. But I need you to back up my findings. If you're dead, you can't do that. I need your memories. I need your strength."

Elmer looked up at him, weariness on his face, but a flicker of interest in his eyes.

"And besides that," Ty dropped down to his knees in front of Elmer and took both his strong hands in his own, "I love you, you stubborn goat." His voice broke. "I never said that to my father. I never could. But you've come to mean something to me that I didn't understand until now. I've turned you into a . . . a father for me. You've been one to Tad. I've seen how you've been with him. I wanted that for me, too. You've even been a father to Caesar in some ways."

On cue, Caesar nudged Elmer's arm.

"This is a real thin trick you're pulling here, King. All this talk about father. What in hell do you think you're pulling?"

"It's not a trick. I know it sounds kind of mushy. I'm probably not saying it right. I don't have any practice." Ty shrugged his shoulders.

"Elmer!" Tad's voice was filled with panic. There was a banging sound.

Elmer and Ty went rigid. Caesar ran out of the room.

"Caesar!" Elmer called him.

"Here, boy, here!" Tad said. Relief was evident in his voice.

"Don't tell him I'm here," Ty whispered. "Listen, here's what I want you to do."

"Just a minute." Elmer stopped him. "Before I do anything, boy, you're going let me say something about what you just told me," he said, still holding Ty's hands.

"We'll talk later. I have to get out and . . ."

"Later may be too late, for all we know," Elmer said. "I'll get out of here, but first I want you to know something.

I never had a son. Got me a wonderful daughter. But if I could have asked for a son, it never would have been you."

"See?" Ty said. "I told you we can talk about this later. You can depress me when we're down on the street. Now come on."

Elmer stood up. "Just wait a minute. You should know something. I knew your mother and your father years and years ago when we were all young. I was real sweet on her."

Ty tilted his head and a smile spread over his lips. "Yeah? You liked my mother?"

"I liked her, but I was kind of shy back then. Dorian got to her first. He rushed her and took her to the prom. I didn't have a chance."

"He did have a way of talking people into things, I know."

"You don't know the half of it. Anyway, when I first saw you, I wouldn't have given two cents for you. But after living with you these last weeks, well," he stopped, his voice grown thick. The boards creaked louder under their feet. Elmer spoke fast. "Now I couldn't have enough money in the world to pay you for all you've done for me and for Maggie and the boy. And you remind me so much of your mother. You've got her eyes, you know. And her smile. She was the sweetest girl in the world. Not that I didn't love my wife, you understand. But your mother always had a special place in my heart."

Ty couldn't help himself. He threw his arms around the old man and held him close. A sob caught in his throat.

"I wish you were my son," Elmer said into Ty's shoulder. Then he pushed away. "But since you're not, I'll just treat you like one. Get me the hell out of here, you young fool!"

Ty raised his eyes heavenward. "What the hell do you think I've been trying to do?"

"Well, stop arguing then and tell me what you want me to do."

On the street Maggie waited. When the sound of falling timbers came, her fear turned into uncontrollable frenzy. The fire trucks' engines continued to hum. A crowd of people had gathered. When

Chief Reed discovered that Ty had gone into the building as well, he became angry and organized his men into a search team. They were busy working at the weakest part of the building, trying to shore it up with ropes and scaffolding. Darlene Thompson ran over to her.

"Maggie, is Ty really in there trying to find Elmer and Caesar?"

Maggie's tears spilled over then. "Tad's in there, too."

Roz came through a knot of firemen and embraced Maggie. "Oh, honey, where are they? Have you heard anything?"

"Nothing yet," Maggie cried into Roz's shoulder.

"Is it true Tad is completely blind?" Darlene said, pencil poised over her notebook.

"Darlene, for heaven's sake, can't this wait?" Roz said, glaring at her.

"It's news, Roz," Darlene said, "and sometimes a reporter has to forget about emotion and just write the facts."

"It's okay, Roz," Maggie said. "I'll talk to her. No, Tad is not completely blind yet. He can see some lights and colors, some shapes. He's very resourceful. He's very smart. He'll find his way out of there. Ty will find Caesar and Elmer, and everyone will be all right." Maggie talked fast, assuring herself more than giving a story.

"And what about the building?" Darlene asked.

"I don't care what happens to the building," Maggie said. She accepted a tissue from Roz and wiped her eyes and blew her nose.

"I thought you were going to fight for it, take it over. The town council report said you had grounds to sue Dorian King or his heirs for all they owe you for repairs and mental anguish. As you know, the taxes haven't been paid on it. Do you feel then that you are responsible for the property at this time?"

Maggie stared at Darlene. "I don't own this property. And even if I did that's not important now. What's important are the lives inside there."

"Grams! Grams!" Tad's high-pitched voice came from behind her.

"Tad!" she shrieked. "Tad?" She ran in the direction of the voice.

Tad came toward her, a big grin on his face defying the tear streaks down his dirty face. Leaning on him was Elmer holding a bandanna to his head. Beside them Caesar limped, whimpering.

Maggie ran to Tad and threw her arms around him. "Oh, thank God. I was worried sick about you." She jumped up and threw her arms around Elmer. "About all of you." Caesar whimpered loudly and she grabbed him, too.

Darlene ran over to them. "What happened? Why did you go into the building, Dr. Everett? Did Caesar find you? How did you find them, Tad?" She snapped a photo of all of them together.

"Well, it was really great!" Tad said, excitement in his voice. "Caesar found me and he led me to where Elmer was. He had to walk on a beam to get to me, and he told me how to find the right boards so I wouldn't fall."

"How did he do that?" Darlene asked.

"He stuck his nose in my face so I'd know where he was. Then I took a hold of his fur on the back of his neck and he pulled on me. Then he showed me where

Elmer was. He was lying on the bed, and I thought he was dead."

"Oh, God," Maggie moaned.

Elmer tapped Darlene on the shoulder. "Let me tell the rest. The boy here, Tad Mills, saved my life and Caesar's, too. He got me out of there and helped me down the stairs and then he helped Caesar get out. We couldn't have done it without him. We'd still be in there when the wreckers came, and we'd be dead now. Why, this is the most courageous boy in all of Cape Agnes."

That's when Maggie got suspicious. She looked around the crowd. "Where is . . . ?"

"Officer Fisbee?" Elmer said a little too quickly. "He's right over there. You'd better go tell him the boy's all right." He pushed her shoulder.

Narrowing her eyes suspiciously at Elmer, Maggie went over to Officer Fisbee.

Ty came from out of nowhere it seemed and joined them. "What's going on?" he asked as if he'd only just come on the scene. "Is everybody all right?"

"Everybody's just fine," Maggie said, peering closely at him. He avoided her eyes. "I just wanted you to know, Vincent, that Tad and Elmer and Caesar are out of the building. They're a little scraped up, but they're in good shape."

"I'm mighty glad to hear that," Officer Fisbee said.

"So am I," Ty said, acting extremely relieved.

"How'd you get that cut on your arm?" Maggie asked with some alarm.

Ty looked down. "It's just a scratch. Got it on the beach this morning. That's what I get for climbing around the rocks barefoot. They're really slippery."

"They're not the only thing that's slippery," Maggie muttered.

Elmer came over to them. The bandanna around his head had slipped a little and he pushed it up. Maggie stared at it. She recognized it then. It was Ty's bandanna. She'd seen him give it to Tad on the track earlier. How was it that Elmer had come out of the building wearing it if they hadn't seen him? She saw Elmer and Ty pass a look between them. Saw Tad hug Elmer. Saw Caesar sit and lean against Ty's leg. And then she knew. They all had a story to tell, but there was only one that had been placed into public record.

She felt a little stab of pain inside. Tyler King was an enigma to her. One minute she figured he was a self-centered thoughtless man out for his own gain, a man she could never care for, and the next minute she was filled with love for him.

"Well, as long as everyone's out in one piece, I'll take off now," Tyler said.

"Going home?" Elmer asked him.

"No, not yet. I've got some business to attend to."

"Anything I can help with?"

"No, thanks, Elmer. Not yet. I appreciate the offer." Ty started to walk away.

"Well, call me if you need me . . . *son.*"

Ty stopped and turned around. He didn't say a word, but his smile told Maggie there must have been a lot that transpired inside that old building, more than she would probably ever know.

"Doc," Edith Atkins said into the phone the next morning, "have you heard?"

"Heard what?" Maggie was dressed

and just on her way out to the clinic when the phone rang.

"There's an emergency meeting this morning. You've got to be here."

"Why? What kind of meeting?"

"They're going to discuss your building. Or Mr. King's building. It doesn't matter. But this is going to be great!" Edith seemed gleeful at the other end of the line.

"Great? Why? I think it's going to be one big mess. Ty should be at that meeting, too. He certainly should have a say in what's going on since he owns the property."

"He's at the town hall already," Edith told her.

"He is?" Maggie was surprised. Ty hadn't said a word about going to a town meeting. Why hadn't he told her?

"Yes. He was going to make a presentation of some kind. But I walked in with some information of my own, and all hell broke loose. And is Joe ever mad at me!"

"Edith, what are you talking about? Why is your husband mad at you? What kind of information?"

"You'll be pleasantly surprised, I think. Even if there is going to be a big fight. The county safety commissioner is here, too. He didn't like it much when Ty secured a court order last night to prevent him from wrecking the building."

Maggie knew that Ty had done that. To what end she couldn't be certain. All he'd told her was that he wanted to buy a little time. He had some work to do, he'd said, and some important promises to keep.

"Ty didn't know that my dear husband, the mayor, would call an emergency town meeting," Edith continued. "He's reading over all his notes now. You get in here. I'll stall them until you arrive. But hurry." Edith hung up.

Bewildered, Maggie replaced the phone. She ran out back to the clinic and found Elmer in the medicine storage room with Tad.

"What do you know about what Ty's doing regarding the Elm Street building?" she asked.

Elmer was checking medicine inventory and didn't look up from his list or the bottles Tad handed to him. "Not a thing," he answered finally.

"Something tells me you do."

"Don't."

"I don't have time to argue with you, Elmer," Maggie said, impatience creeping into her voice. "If you know something, I wish you'd tell me."

"Haven't a clue, as Tad says," Elmer said, not looking at her. He smiled over at the boy who kept straightening jars and bottles and boxes.

"All right. But I'm not through with you. You'll have to take care of things here this morning. Edith Atkins just phoned and said an emergency town meeting has been called regarding the demolition of the building. Ty is already there, so he must have known something was going on." She waited for Elmer to rise to the bait.

He continued to check bottles and write on his lists. He spoke after a long moment. "You'd better get moving then. He'll need all the help he can get."

"You *do* know something, don't you? Just what happened in there with you and Ty?"

"You know all there is to know, Colleague. Now get a move on it. Jolene and

I will handle everything here. And Tad, too."

"Tad? Is there anything you want to tell me?" Maggie touched his shoulder.

"Good luck, Grams. Whatever's going on, I don't know. I'm just a kid."

"Yeah, you're a kid going on thirty," she said.

"That's what Ty told me," Tad replied.

Maggie turned to leave. "For once, he and I agree on something."

"You agree on more than you know," Elmer said just as she closed the door.

Nineteen

Maggie hurried down the corridor in the town hall to the town council chambers. She could hear shouting before she even got to the door. Taking a deep breath, she opened it and stepped inside.

"I've told you a hundred times that old place is a hazard to the personal safety of the citizens of Cape Agnes," Jerome Fine, the county safety commissioner shouted.

"Not to mention an eyesore to the beauty of our town," Mayor Atkins added.

"I've ordered it demolished," Fine said, "and demolished it will be."

"Yes, before we have another tragedy," Mayor Atkins added again.

"What tragedy, Joseph?" Edith Atkins asked. "There's been no tragedy. You're dramatizing again."

"Edith," Joe blustered, his face turning beet red, "you know Dr. Everett was in there, and Caesar, and the boy, Tad Mills. You were there."

"Yes, I was there. And I agree with the stand they took," Edith said.

"What stand are you talking about, woman?" Atkins yelled.

"Do not speak to me in that tone of voice, Joseph," Edith said with studied calm. "You will find yourself sleeping in the guest room if you're not careful."

Mayor Atkins sank back against the railing.

"Ah, Dr. Logan." Commissioner Fine saw her and relief flooded his face. "I'm so glad you're here. After the ordeal you went through when your grandson was missing inside the building, I'm certain you'd like to add something to these proceedings."

Maggie walked forward. "I'm afraid I don't have any idea what these proceedings are for."

"Why, to raze the building on Elm Street, of course," Mayor Atkins told her. "Your old clinic. The King Building."

"The Tyler Building," Edith announced.

"The what?" Maggie breathed. She looked over at Ty who was standing over at a side table. He had piles of papers spread over the top, and she recognized two of the bound volumes of the old newspapers.

"The Tyler Building," Edith repeated. "The Cape Agnes Historic Landmark Preservation Society, of which I have been named president, has recently been apprised of something very important about our town. Something many of us didn't know. I'm sorry to say the Society has a great deal of work to do to record everything about Cape Agnes. In the meantime no buildings will be torn down without our being consulted first."

"What is this all about?" Maggie asked. "Where is the Tyler Building?"

"I believe I can best answer that," Ty said, stepping forward.

"You've said enough," Mayor Atkins said.

"Now, now, Joseph," Edith admonished, "this is an open meeting. Anyone can speak."

The door to the meeting room opened, and Darlene Thompson walked in with another bound volume of the old newspaper. "Here's the one you were looking for, Ty," she said and slid it onto the table with the rest of the copies.

"Go ahead, Mr. King," Edith said.

"Wait," Darlene said, slipping a canvas bag off her shoulder. "I want to record every word." She opened the bag and took out her camera. She reached in again and withdrew a tape recorder, plugged it in, and set up a microphone on a little stand. "All right, go ahead."

Maggie took a seat. She was feeling a little weak in the knees.

"The building on Elm Street which housed Dr. Logan's animal clinic and two apartments," Tyler said, "the one you are all so quick to tear down, is the oldest building in Cape Agnes. My great grandfather, Henry Tyler, the founder of your fair village—check your history—erected that building and started the first industry in the area. Net making. His nets were famous all along the coast for their strength and their flexibility. Fishing is what eventually made this town grow and prosper even more, but what originally brought the people here was the net industry and a growing community."

Maggie watched Ty as he carefully chose his words. He was presenting his case calmly, intelligently, without talking over their heads or beneath them. And she was flabbergasted at his report.

"Thanks to Ms. Thompson of *The Cape Agnes News*, I was able to research much of my findings through her files and these wonderful bound volumes of *The Ledger* and *The News*. And did you know that your village library has some interesting information about Cape Agnes? Cape Agnes, I might add, was renamed from Tylerville in honor of my great-grandmother, Agnes Tyler. Anyway, your library, which is in very cramped quarters, holds some wonderful old photographs, documents, and ancient books. I even found several of old Tylerville's famous fishing nets in the attic. Made me wonder if my grandfather's fingerprints were on them."

Maggie heard the note of awe in his voice. She swallowed a small lump.

"Just what are you getting at, King?" the commissioner asked.

"I can answer that," Edith Atkins piped up. "Mr. King presented his findings to the Preservation Society yesterday. It is our ruling that all plans for demolition of the Tyler Building be stopped." She held up her hand as the commissioner started to say something. "We do recommend that some sort of safety precautions be taken at cost to the village. Upon further investigation we know that it will be our recommendation that the building be completely restored and a plaque be installed bearing the title and date. Mr. King has agreed to be completely cooperative."

"Cooperative in what way?" Mayor Atkins asked.

"I will donate the building to the village," Tyler said.

"Thereby getting yourself off the tax rolls, of course. Not that you've paid the taxes in several years," the mayor said. "You're not fooling us, Mr. King. If you give the building to us, you will probably reap a healthy tax deduction and no longer be obligated to pay property tax. In the meantime, we inherit a building that will cost more than the town can afford to rebuild, and we lose the revenue from taxes that a responsible owner would normally pay. I'm sorry, Mr. King, but on behalf of Cape Agnes I am telling you that we are refusing to accept your gift."

"What?" Edith said in shock. "You can't refuse to accept it."

"Oh, but we can."

"Well, the Historical Landmark Preservation Society can block your nonacceptance."

"All right," Mayor Atkins came back, "we'll accept the building on the condition that it is returned to its last state. The animal clinic must be restored and rent paid to the village. The two apartments upstairs must also be restored and rent from those paid to the village. We will establish rates at that time. What do you think of that?"

"Fine," Edith said. "That's fine. We accept."

"Wait a minute," Ty said. "I don't like to see an argument between married people, but there are other opinions you need to seek."

Both Edith and Joe Atkins looked at

him, puzzled. Commissioner Fine sat down. He appeared no longer to be a part of the proceedings and didn't seem to know how to get back into them or how to exit gracefully.

"Who else could possibly have anything else to say about this?" Joe Atkins asked.

"Dr. Michael Logan for one," Ty said. "The clinic and one of those apartments were hers. And Dr. Elmer Everett for another. He had the other apartment. What if they have made alternative plans by now?"

"If they have," the mayor retorted, "then that is your fault, Mr. King, for delaying so long in doing something about your building."

"Nevertheless, they still have a voice," Ty said quietly.

"Well, then, Dr. Logan, just what do you intend to do?" the mayor said, turning to Maggie.

Maggie stood. Darlene snapped another photo. Maggie looked at Ty for a long moment. Then she scanned the faces of Edith and Joe Atkins. Jerome Fine was leafing through a magazine.

"I don't have any idea," she said, and left the chambers.

Maggie was into her second bowl of clam chowder when the lunch crowd began to fill Mother's.

"Hey, Doc, how are you?" Roz took a seat beside her and waved to Dottie. "I hear the town is going to present Tad with a medal of courage for saving Elmer and Caesar."

"I know. Tad is beaming about it. Can you believe he's invited little Susan Mayfield to the ceremony?"

"He's come a long way. I thought he didn't like girls," Roz said. She scanned the chalkboard that listed the daily specials.

"He didn't until Susan and the track team." Maggie dabbed at her lips with a napkin. "Light day today?"

"Yes. And am I glad. I keep thinking any minute now Mrs. VanGee is going to call us back to rehearsals and I'll be exhausted. I'm trying to rest up. Where is she these days? She didn't make her usual appointment."

"I don't know. Jolene said she left instructions for all of us to take another week off. She's acting mighty peculiar, even for her."

Dottie came over to the table, pad and pen poised. "What'll it be, Roz?"

"Number three and a cup of tea. How's your hair holding up?" Roz scrutinized Dottie's carefully placed coils.

"Perfect, as usual. You're a real artist, Roz. Say, Doc, did you know I invited Elmer over for dinner tomorrow night?"

"No," Maggie said, smiling. "Did he accept?"

"He accepted and asked if he could bring Tad with him."

"Tad? Hmm. Sounds like he thinks he needs a chaperone."

"Not a bit," Dottie said. "She's a little slow, isn't she, Roz?"

"I'll say."

"Slow about what?" Maggie looked from one face to the other.

"Guess we have to spell it out," Dottie said.

"Looks like it," Ros concurred.

"What are you two talking about?"

"The reason Elmer wants to bring Tad

to dinner," Dottie explained, "is so you and Ty can have some privacy."

"That's ridiculous. Elmer doesn't think like that."

"He does now. Of course, I think Tad's been prompting him."

"Tad just doesn't want to leave that beach house," Maggie told them emphatically.

"That's one of the reasons," Dottie said. "Number three coming right up." She headed back to the kitchen.

Maggie shook her head. "The people in this town think they know everything about everybody."

"They think that because they do," Roz said.

"Well, they don't know everything."

Roz looked at her friend for a long moment. "Two bowls of chowder. What's bothering you?"

"Oh, Roz. Everything. This summer has been so crazy, I don't know what I'm doing anymore. And it's worrying me. I have to have things settled before school begins. I want Tad to feel secure once the semester starts."

"I think he feels secure already. By the

way, he dropped in at the shop the other day and asked to make an appointment to get a cool haircut."

"He did? He never said anything about that."

Roz giggled. "I know. He said he'd tell you after the haircut was finished."

"As if I wouldn't notice, I suppose." Maggie chuckled.

"He told me that Ty told him to come over and talk to me about it. So we sat down and got out my page magnifier and looked in some hairstyle books. He picked out the one he thought was the coolest."

"Ty told him to do that, hunh? I'm afraid to ask what it is. Please tell me it's not one of those with the little tail hanging down the back."

"Of course not. Those aren't cool anymore. Besides, as he put it, he needs something 'aerodynamically suitable.' "

"Aero . . . what?"

"I gather this is for his role as manager of the elementary track team. Don't worry," Roz said easily, "we can make this haircut grandmother suitable as well as aerodynamically suitable as well as cool.

It's short and very trim. You'll like it, I promise."

"All right. I guess I can let him take this responsibility on his own."

"This table taken?" Lloyd Fitchen plopped his mailbag at the end of the table.

"Yes, and you're included," Maggie said.

Lloyd slipped his leg over the picnic bench and joined the two women for lunch. "Before I forget, here's those perm samples you've been waiting for, Miz Willet." He extracted a brown padded envelope from his bag and handed it to Roz. "Oh, and here's Elmer's mail and one for Mr. King. Do you mind taking this, Doc?"

"No, not at all, Lloyd. I'd be glad to."

She glanced down at Ty's letter. She couldn't help but notice the return address. It was printed in big block letters. Guide Dog Trainers of America. It was mailed first class. She was curious, no doubt about that. Lloyd was curious, too, and she could tell he wanted to talk about it.

"Hope it's not bad news," Lloyd said, probing.

"Nothing important at all," Maggie said.

Dottie came over with Roz's lunch order and Lloyd gave her his. "When's Henrietta coming back, anybody know?" he asked when Dottie had left. "It isn't like her to just up and leave twice right in the middle of a production. Of course, the mess with your building and all had something to do with it the first time."

"No," Roz said. "We don't even know where she went. She's been very mysterious these days."

"Well, I just happened to notice some time ago that she received a lot of letters from some hotel in the Bahamas. Didn't she go there on vacation recently?"

"Yes, she did," Maggie answered. "Maybe she met a man there. You know, she told me she'd like to get married again."

"Wouldn't that be something?" Roz chuckled. "What if Henrietta has taken up with the hotel bellman or something?"

"She wouldn't," Lloyd said. "I took her out to dinner one night, and that was it.

She only went once. I make a good living at the post office. I think that's not enough for her. A rich man has to support her, and that's not me."

"Well, then, maybe she's met a rich man and has gone to the Bahamas to snare him," Roz said.

"How's Tad doing?" Lloyd asked next.

"He's just great. Doing fine."

"Tyler King going to buy him a guide dog?"

"What?"

Lloyd waggled his head. "Just wondered if Mr. King was getting Tad a guide dog." He motioned to the letter.

Maggie straightened and pushed her chowder bowl to the side. "Tad has no interest in getting a guide dog at the moment. That's far in his future if he does that."

"Oh, well, maybe Mr. King is just gathering information, then."

"I have no idea what information Mr. King is gathering," Maggie said, a little too icily.

"Well, I can tell you about that," Lloyd said.

"You don't have to," Maggie said.

"I want to hear about it," Roz put in.

"Well," Lloyd leaned across the table, "Miz Thompson says that he's taken a big interest in the history of Cape Agnes."

Roz bit into her sandwich. "We all know that, Lloyd."

"And he's been looking into grants from the state to get his building restored."

"That should make a lot of people happy," Maggie said.

"You?" Roz asked.

Maggie didn't answer.

"And there was a big scandal in the law firm he used to be in. His partner turned out to be a real crook."

"How'd you find out about this partner of Ty's?" Maggie asked.

"It was in one of those California papers Miz Thompson receives. We read about it one morning. Then Mr. King has been receiving registered mail from his partner. I bet he's got a payoff of some kind."

"What do you mean by that?" Roz sounded annoyed by Lloyd's inference.

"Well, I don't know. Isn't it possible Mr. King is as guilty as his partner? We don't know anything about him really, do we? He doesn't seem to have a job, but he seems to live all right."

"Not that it's any of our business," Maggie said. "Besides, he's started a new job with Cape Agnes Central School."

"Really?" Roz said. "Doing what? Is he a teacher?"

"He's the elementary track coach," Maggie said proudly.

"Only pays four thousand a year," Lloyd said.

Even Maggie was amazed this time. "How do you know that?"

"I'm on the school board. We have to approve new hires and any expenditures, don't we?"

"True."

"Anyway, he won't receive a pay check for a month. So what's he been living on all this time?"

"What difference does it make?" Roz asked.

Lloyd shrugged.

Maggie had wondered about that herself all along. And he had admitted he was broke. She wasn't paying rent anymore, so he didn't have that to use. She had to stop this. Lloyd had planted seeds of doubt in her mind, and she wasn't going to let them grow. It was all just the usual Cape Agnes idle gossip.

"Well," Roz said, taking out her purse and putting some money on the table, "I have to be getting back to the salon. Oscar was rather unruly this morning, and Terrie can't handle him when he uses profanity in front of the customers."

"Mind if I walk over with you?" Maggie asked.

"Come ahead. If you've got time I'll give you a trim. Your ends are getting uneven. Take it easy, Lloyd. See you later this week."

"Have a fine day, ladies. Don't forget your mail, Doc." Lloyd shoved the pile across the table to her.

"Thanks, Lloyd. Nice talking with you." Maggie left money for her lunch and followed Roz out onto the sidewalk.

"You fibbed," Roz said.

"What do you mean?"

"You did not enjoy talking with him. You were very disturbed by what he said. I saw your face."

Maggie pursed her lips. "I was. I hope what Lloyd implied isn't true. If Ty's former law partner is crooked, I hope Ty isn't in on it."

"He probably isn't," Roz assured her.

"He is Dorian King's son."

"Character doesn't have to be inherited," Roz reminded her.

They walked into Hairoics and found Tad going through Roz's hairstyle book again.

"Tad. What are you doing here? Don't you have practice right now?" Maggie sat down beside him.

"Yep, but Ty had something to take care of, he said, so we got out early. Robby's mom dropped me off here. Jolene's got an appointment later so I figured she could take me home."

"You certainly are keeping up with people's schedules," Roz observed.

"Well, Grams gets all tizzied if she doesn't know where I am or how I'll get someplace," Tad said, flipping pages.

"I can't help it if I worry about you sometimes," Maggie said.

Tad looked up from the book. "Grams, I can take care of myself. I saved Elmer and Caesar, didn't I?"

Maggie gave Roz a look that said there

was some question about the validity of that statement. "I know. But heroes need to be taken care of sometimes themselves, you know."

"That's what Ty said."

"What did he say?"

"He said it's tough being a man all the time, and sometimes we just want to be taken care of. Not all the time, he said, 'cause we're supposed to watch out for our women and our 'sponsibilities."

"He said that, did he?" Maggie said quietly.

"That guy sure talks a lot," Roz said.

"I found the haircut I want," Tad announced.

"Let's see." Maggie leaned over his shoulder. "What's all this about a new haircut anyway?"

"I have to have one that doesn't slow me down."

"I see."

"Can you do it today, Roz?" he asked, his wonderful open expression as endearing as ever.

"Let's see." Roz looked over her appointment schedule. "I guess I could squeeze you in."

"It doesn't have to be today, does it?" Maggie asked him.

"Well, yeah, it does." Tad swung his feet. "Why?"

"Because if I like it, Dottie told me I could ask Susan to go over to her house for dinner with Elmer and me."

Maggie blinked and looked over at Roz.

"It appears to me your present haircut hasn't slowed you down one bit," Roz said, smiling. "If it's okay with your grandmother, I'd be happy to cut your hair today."

"It's all right with me," Maggie said.

"Good," Tad said. "But could you go someplace else while she does it?"

Maggie gave a feigned dejected look. Then she hugged him. "All right, I'll go someplace else. There's an apartment I want to look at anyway. It's in a house on Dewey Street. It might be good."

"That's not a good street," Tad said.

"There's not a bad street in Cape Agnes, Tad," Maggie said gently.

"I like it fine right where we are."

"I know you do. How long do you think he'll be, Roz?"

"We should be finished in an hour, I

think, what with the shampoo and blow-dry."

"Blow-dry?" Tad said, screwing up his mouth.

"Of course," Roz said. "No one leaves my salon less than completely finished. What if you ran into Susan on the street and you looked unfinished?"

"Oh, yeah," Tad said. He got up and went over to the shampoo chair.

Maggie started to leave.

"Doc, don't worry so much. I get good vibes about all this. You'll see. You'll be pleasantly surprised when all this comes out just right."

"I wish I could believe that," Maggie said.

"Wishing can make it so sometimes," Roz said.

"I deal better with facts," Maggie said, and left the salon.

She was just turning the corner when she ran into Ty.

"Hey," he said, "where you going?"

"Over on Dewey to look at an apartment? Where are you going?"

"In to Hairoics to see if Tad got there all right."

"He did. I was just there. I have to go back and pick him up in an hour."

"Great. I have to go out of town overnight. I just wanted to be sure he was taken care of."

Maggie frowned. "Out of town? Where?"

Ty looked at his watch. "I can't tell you right now. If all goes well, I will have big news to tell you about tomorrow night. Speaking of that, we can have dinner by ourselves tomorrow night, I hear. Elmer and Tad have dates. Can you beat that?"

"I wouldn't call what Tad's doing dating."

"You wouldn't call what we're doing dating either." He grinned widely.

"We are not dating. And what Tad's doing better not even be in the same ballpark as what we're doing." She couldn't help but smile herself.

"Those are all just words anyway. I don't want to put definitions on our relationship right now. So, dinner tomorrow night, just the two of us?"

"Of course. There are things I have to talk to you about. Can't you tell me where you're going right now?"

"No. If it doesn't work out then it won't matter. If it does, then I'll tell you. Trust me."

Maggie looked at him skeptically. "Oh, I almost forgot. Lloyd left a piece of mail with me to give to you." She rummaged in her bag and found his letter. "He was very interested in it, as usual."

Ty looked at the letter. His face colored slightly. "Nothing for him to be concerned about. As usual."

"Should I be concerned?"

"Not yet. Don't try to wheedle things out of me. You know I can be persuaded so easily by you."

It was Maggie's turn to feel color rising over her face. "I know nothing of the kind."

"The heck you don't," Ty said, planting a kiss on her cheek. "Play your cards right and I'll let you have your way with me tomorrow night after dinner. Or before. Or during, even."

"Not in broad daylight," Maggie gritted, pushing him away. "Here comes Darlene."

"Why not?" Ty whispered suggestively. "Morning, afternoon, night, dark, light.

I could make love with you anytime, anywhere."

"Geez," Maggie said, quoting Tad. "I can see this week's headlines forming in her brain right now."

"Gotta run, babe." He squeezed her arm and took off across the street.

"I'm not a babe," she said as he moved away from her.

"Are, too!" he shouted from across the street.

"Are too what?" Darlene asked, stopping at Maggie's side.

Maggie thought hard before answering. After all, this was Darlene Thompson, a femme fatale in her own mind. Oh well, might as well tell the truth to the press. "A babe."

Twenty

"You feel wonderful," Ty said, holding Maggie close in his arms.

She snuggled against him and pulled the sheet up over them. His heart pounded against her cheek and she enjoyed the comforting thrum of it. "You feel fabulous," she said.

He lifted her chin and gave her a long satisfying kiss. "This was all I could think of last night in that motel room. It had one of those old coin-operated vibrators in the bed. Looked kind of rusty, but I tried it anyway. I almost got motion sick! I think the thing needed adjusting. Of course if you'd been there I wouldn't have adjusted a thing."

Maggie laughed, deliberately dirty.

"I don't like the sound of that," he said, giving her bottom a love tap. "What sinister thought is roaming around in your mind?"

"I just had this picture of you and me and the vibrating bed and wondered if we ever would have connected!" She began to giggle.

"Oh, baby, count on it!" He rolled over on top of her. "Just like this."

He seemed to be everywhere at once with his hands and his lips and his hard heat. She wrapped her legs around him and brought him inside and held onto him. They rocked and clung until they were both gasping for breath. Carefully he lifted and slid off her.

"You're right," she said, breathing heavily. "No erratic bed could thwart our erotic activity!"

"You know it." He stretched and yawned.

"I suppose we should think about dinner," Maggie said. "You didn't even give me the chance to tell you what we're having."

"I knew what I wanted the minute I walked in the door tonight."

"And you just helped yourself, didn't you?" She leaned over and kissed his chest.

"Didn't I though? I kept thinking positively all the way home that Elmer and Tad would be gone."

"Good thing they were."

"I take it the haircut turned out all right, and Susan Mayfield got invited to dinner."

"Yes, she was."

"Well, then, I guess we have a little while left before they get back."

"Yes. So, are you going to tell me where you were and what you were doing?"

He pulled her into his arms. "Yes, I am. And I hope you're going to be pleased when you hear it."

Maggie leaned her head back and looked up at him. "Is there a chance I wouldn't be pleased?"

"Well, there are extenuating details that need to be worked out and you are part of them, or at least you will be if you agree."

"Tyler?" a male voice came from somewhere in the house.

They both jumped. "Who is that?" Maggie whispered, blowing a lock of hair off her forehead.

Tyler was rigid. "I don't know."

Maggie started to rise and reach for her robe. The bedroom door was pushed open wide. She dove back under the covers.

A tall, portly frame of a man filled the doorway.

"Well, well, what have we here?" he boomed in a loud voice.

Maggie was dumbfounded at first, but finally found her voice. "Who are you? What are you doing in this house?"

Tyler sat straight up and pulled the blanket up to his chin. "Father. You're back."

Maggie snapped her head around and looked at him. "This is your father?"

Tyler nodded woodenly.

"How astute an observation." Dorian King barged into the room, past the bed, and looked out the window. "I can see that I've taken you by surprise. Well, no matter. We need to talk."

"You're Dorian King?" Maggie breathed.

"We've established that."

"But, I assumed you were dead. Was I wrong?" she asked Ty.

"Obviously that was a wrong assumption. If I'm here I'm not dead." Dorian

King turned around and looked at them. "And who might you be?"

Maggie grew annoyed with Ty. He wasn't saying a word. In fact, he was utterly motionless. She could see he wasn't going to, or couldn't say a word. He just sat there clutching the blanket under his chin and staring at the door. She sat up and pulled what she could get of the blanket up around her own chin.

"Dr. Michael Logan, Dee Vee Em."

Dorian King stared at her. "Whatever." He scanned the room.

"I am . . . was . . . your tenant in the building on Elm Street," Maggie said as firmly as she could. She elbowed Ty, but he didn't move.

"Doctor? Oh, yes, the animal girl who complained constantly. So this is what you look like?"

Maggie fumed. She wanted to blurt out that she wasn't surprised he didn't know what she looked like because he didn't know what his building looked like, either. But he was an old man, and he appeared to have been very ill. And, of course, he was Ty's father. She believed she ought to try to be civilized. She took a deep breath and spoke as calmly as she could.

"Well, you won't have to hear me complain any longer, Mr. King. Your building has fallen in on itself, and the authorities have condemned it. Isn't that right, Ty?"

Ty didn't move.

"Condemned!" Dorian boomed. "What did you do to it? Well, never mind. I knew renters would not take care of the place as well as I could do it myself."

"Now just a minute, Mr. King . . ."

"You probably didn't even know what was happening in the place. Girls are never aware of such things."

That did it! "Mr. King, I am the *woman* who repaired that place constantly, at my own expense I might add, to keep it together. And while you might call it complaining, I call it responsible reporting. I called you every time the sink drains backed up, or the heater died, or the roof leaked, or the power failed. I thought perhaps you'd like to know, thought you'd want to take care of things before they really got bad."

"Yes, yes, I remember," he waved her away. "Drove me crazy with your insignificant complaints. Couldn't be bothered, couldn't be bothered.''

"Well, you'll have to be bothered now because the place looks like it's been through World War II."

"If you let that place fall in, I'll sue you for damages."

"Sue *me* for damages! I lost all my furniture and appliances in that mess. If anyone should be suing anyone, it's *I* who should be suing you!"

"Now just a minute, you snippy girl, you can't talk to me that way."

Maggie squared her shoulders under the blanket. She felt like a little girl, and it bugged the hell out of her. And her big strong hero was just sitting there under the blanket, mute. "I'm sorry but I must talk to you this way, Mr. King. I've never had your attention before now. You've never listened to me."

"Remember, Miss, you wanted to buy the place. You begged me to let you buy it," King reminded her.

"Oh, *now* you remember that I spoke to you about that. I can only thank my lucky stars that you ignored me long enough to keep me from going through with it."

Dorian King turned his back on her and said defensively, "My son needs the place for his exercise room, or whatever it is."

"Fitness center." She looked over at Ty. She looked back at Dorian King. "What in the hell are we doing having this conversation right at this moment? Mr. King, you will kindly get out of this room right now. Go and wait in the living room."

"You're very bossy," Dorian sniffed.

"It appears I have to be. Neither one of you has the sense to get out of here on your own. Please."

"Fine. I won't wait longer than ten minutes. You'd best be in that living room pronto." Dorian King turned and huffed from the room, slamming the bedroom door.

"Ty, for heaven's sake, what's got into you?" Maggie jumped out of the bed and grabbed her clothes. "I've never been so mortified in my life. To have your father walk in on us like this. And when I think that Elmer and Tad could have been here, my blood runs cold."

Ty moved then. "If they'd been here we wouldn't have been doing this." He got out of the bed and began to put on his clothes in an almost stilted robot-like fashion.

"What's wrong with you? I thought you'd gone into cardiac arrest. I had to hold the most ridiculous conversation with that man while I was in a . . . rather compromising position." She finished dressing and brushed her hair, then pulled it back in a rubber band, completely ignoring Roz's instructions.

"I thought I had gone into cardiac arrest myself," Ty said dully. "You have to understand, I believed he was *dead*. I truly believed he was dead this time. He was always disappearing. But this was the *longest* time he'd been away without *any* word. I'm stunned."

"Well, you'd better get unstunned fast. He's waiting in the living room for you. For us, I guess." Maggie hastily made up the bed. "You first." She pointed toward the door. She followed him down the hall to the living room.

Dorian King stood in front of the windows overlooking the ocean, hands clasped behind his back. Ty noted again what a big imposing man he was. He'd almost forgotten that. He guessed now that in his mind he'd reduced his father to a withered thing.

"I'd have met you, Father, if I'd known you were coming back," Ty said after a long pause.

"Didn't need meeting." Maggie saw that Dorian King seemed a bit nervous now that Ty had spoken. "What's this woman doing half-dressed in my house? Where's your wife?"

"Father, it's my house now. I took over the deed. You signed it over to me, remember?"

"Of course I remember. Do you think I'm going dotty or something?"

Ty tried again. "Sylvie and I are divorced." He waited again. His father did not turn around. "Where did you go? You never did tell me where you were going, you know. I didn't have a number where I could reach you."

"I know. Planned it that way." Dorian seemed to grow more unsettled.

"Why so secretive, Father?"

Dorian turned and shot a glance toward Maggie. Warily she watched the way Ty and his father related to each other. This was nothing like the way she'd been with her parents. These two seemed to keep their distance, physically and emotionally.

Dorian King turned to leave. "Well, I have things to do. Just wanted to let you know I was back. We'll talk soon."

"Father, we should talk right now."

"We will talk, but not right now," Dorian said gruffly. "All right. Meet me at the Cove Inn for dinner in an hour. I have some things I want to discuss with you. Miss, uh, what was your name again?"

"Maggie Logan," she gritted through tight teeth.

"Yes, of course. I don't know why you're in my son's house, but if you want to come to dinner with us tonight, I suppose it would be all right."

Before Maggie could answer, Ty moved between her and his father. "We'll be there."

Dorian King turned and strode away, and the vibration of the slamming door left a hard memory of him in Maggie's mind.

"I can't believe what just happened," she breathed.

"Then you wouldn't believe how I feel." He returned to the bedroom.

An hour later Maggie and Ty pulled into the Cove Inn parking lot. She'd called Dottie and spoken to Tad and Elmer to let them know where she'd be. They sounded as if they were having a grand old time. She wished she was there instead of where she was right now. The atmosphere in the car was tense.

"Why does he want to talk in a public place?" she asked.

"He doesn't like being alone with me," Ty answered evenly.

"Why not?"

"I think I make him feel guilty. He wasn't much of a father or a husband and he knows that."

"Oh."

He leaned over and kissed her tenderly. "I know this is difficult for you, but I hope you know how much it means to me that you came with me."

"I'm here for you, that's true. I just wish we'd had the chance to talk before he arrived. There is so much we have to discuss."

"I know, and we will." He opened the car door. "Let's go in now. Father is probably pacing and wondering what's taken us so long."

Inside the Cove Inn the hostess directed them to Dorian King's table. The atmosphere inside this restaurant was very different from the Crab Shack. The lighting was darker and the decor more formal. As they moved through the room, Maggie noted that even the patrons were much different from those in the Crab Shack. She hadn't started to relax since Dorian had stormed into the bedroom, and she could see she would not find it easy to relax here either.

Dorian was seated at a table set for four drinking a Manhattan. He did not stand up when they approached. After Maggie and Ty sat down, Ty called the waiter over and ordered a martini for himself and a glass of chardonnay for Maggie.

"There's something I have to talk to you about, Tyler. You can hear this, too, Nellie."

"Maggie."

"Whatever." Dorian drained his glass and signalled the waiter for another. "While I was away, I got to thinking about things. I've not been happy all my life. I was never a good father, I know that now. And I was not a good husband to your mother. I've regretted that, all of it. I haven't been able to live with myself. I don't expect you to understand that. I'm not even asking for your forgiveness. I just wanted to have the chance to say I'm sorry for all I've done to hurt you. It's too late to apologize to your mother."

Maggie looked at Ty while Dorian was speaking. He listened to his father without showing emotion. She ached for Ty, but couldn't help but feel her heart soften just a little toward Dorian King. There was no accounting for the way in which human emotions could change.

Ty cleared his throat. There was a thickness there he had difficulty getting around. "She loved you right to the end."

Dorian did not look up. His second Manhattan arrived, and he took a swallow. "I know," he whispered, "I know. The memory of that haunted me wherever I went. I couldn't get away from it.

More important, I couldn't get away from myself. I sank real low, Tyler, real low. I don't even want to explain it. I was considering suicide."

"Father," Ty said, struggling to stay in control, "no matter how bad things got, you could have talked to me about them."

"No, I couldn't. I wanted to be a big man to you. And I knew I wasn't."

"You were once."

"When you were little, maybe. Then I got too big for my own good. I went crazy, I know." Tears came to the old man's eyes, but he was too stubborn to let them fall.

Maggie watched the two men struggle within their personal turmoil. She guessed it might be better to have this talk in a public place, sensing they might both shatter under the tension of the painful history they shared.

"What kept you from . . . suicide?" Ty asked, and the word was barely audible.

Dorian cleared his throat and nervously adjusted the knot in his tie. "While I was away, I ran into a former high-school mate of mine. We sort of renewed our friendship, that is, I was resistant at first, but she kept at me, drove me crazy talking and asking questions. She made me see that my life was worth living, told me I owed it to you and to myself to start over. Start over. Imagine that at seventy-six."

Maggie waited in the tense atmosphere around the table. Would Ty just let that confession fall, or would he give his father the break he was clearly begging for? She watched Ty's face, saw the conflict in his eyes. He needed to give himself a break as well, and she wasn't certain he knew how to do that.

Ty spoke then. "She sounds like a wonderful person. I'm glad she helped you."

Dorian nodded. "She did help me, a lot. And . . . we spent some, uh, time together, and . . . now, Tyler, I wouldn't want you to think I could ever forget your wonderful mother, but you know, I was very tired of being with too many of the wrong women, and I felt very alone, and. . . ."

Ty lifted his head and leveled a strong gaze on Dorian. "Get to it, Father. What have you done, eloped or something?" He laughed lightly, nervously.

Dorian relaxed into a wide grin. "Don't I have a smart son, Millie?"

"Maggie."

"Whatever."

"You did elope," Tyler said, the realization of it setting in.

"Not exactly eloped. I mean, I wanted to talk to you about this first, but, well, we went to see Judge Humphreys this afternoon. I wanted to get married while we were in the Bahamas, but it seems the lady had to be sure she was marrying the right man. Didn't want to rush into anything, I guess."

"The Bahamas?" Maggie asked. She sat back against her chair, thoughtful for a fleeting moment. The Bahamas were certainly enjoying a wave of popularity lately. A new kind of realization dawned on her.

"Yes. She came back here, she said to think things over. Said there was one more thing she had to do. Then she came back to the islands and got me. Made me come here, home, with her."

"Do you love her, Father? Does she love you? I've learned only recently that that's the only important thing there is.

Everything else comes much easier after that."

"I know I love her. Imagine that? Me saying I love her. She says she loves me. I hope someday I'll believe her. I'm so lucky. She's a lovely woman. Likes to do nice things for people." He turned toward Maggie. "And she even likes animals, Aggie."

"Maggie. Whatever you want. I'm happy for you, Mr. King," she said, and knew she meant it. She enjoyed watching him feel the first rush of a new love.

"I'm sure she is a wonderful woman, Father," Ty said. "When do we get to meet her?"

"You mean it's okay with you?" Dorian sounded like a kid who'd just brought home a pet turtle.

"Of course it is. I do want you to be happy, Father." He turned toward Maggie. "No one likes being alone. Life is so much more wonderful when you can share it with someone you love." Tyler lifted Maggie's hand, and kissed the tips of her fingers. She smiled at him with love in her eyes.

Dorian cleared his throat again. Ty

scanned the room. "All right, Father, where is she? Bring her out of hiding."

Dorian stood up, excited as a boy. "I'll be right back."

"Are you all right?" Maggie asked Ty.

"Shaken to the core. I think I'm just coming out of shock." He let out a long shaky sigh. "Yeah." He drained his martini glass. A smile slowly spread over his mouth. "Can you beat this thing about him getting married? That blew my mind, I can tell you." Ty turned toward Maggie. "That sly old fox."

Maggie looked over Ty's shoulder toward the door to the dining room. She tapped him on the shoulder. "I'm not sure just exactly who's the slyer fox," she said with an amused laugh.

"Hmm?"

"Take a look."

Tyler turned around. His father was coming through the dining room with the fur-caped Mrs. VanGelder on his arm, Priscilla in his other arm.

Ty scratched the back of his neck, and a grin tilted one corner of his mouth. "The word 'swine' seems to be coming back to me as if in a dream."

"Shh." Maggie spoke quietly through barely moving lips, "Smile, now, and forget everything you ever thought or heard." She stood up quickly. "Mrs. VanGelder! How wonderful! Congratulations!"

"Mrs. VanGelder-King, dear Doctor. And how lovely it is to see you two together in public." She clasped Maggie close to her, and whispered in her ear, "Well, I've gone and done it again, haven't I, dearie? Took another attractive bachelor out of the running, except for Junior King, here, of course. But I trust you'll take care of that situation."

Maggie's face warmed. "I'm so happy for you."

Ty stood up, beaming at his father and then at his father's wife. "Congratulations to you both. Welcome to the family Mrs. King," he said, planting a kiss on her plump cheek.

"No need to be so formal, Tyler." The new Mrs. King patted his cheek. "Now, I would never expect you to call me Mumsy, but you can certainly call me by my first name. Would you do that? Especially under the circumstances. All of them."

"Of course," Ty said, and looked nervously over at Maggie. "Henrietta."

When they'd all sat down, Ty ordered champagne. "I'd like to offer a toast to the newlyweds. To my father, welcome home. I hope this time you stay forever." He touched his father's glass. "To my father's lovely bride, thank you for being persistent. I wish you much joy and the strength to show this guy what a good life can mean."

They all touched glasses. Maggie beamed upon them all. "I'm very happy for all of you," she said.

"Now, my dear," Henrietta said, "tell me of your progress in finding a new clinic." She turned toward Dorian. "That building was a terrible mess, Dory. And now it's causing a safety hazard. You're going to have to do something about it."

"I suppose so." Dorian sighed.

"Father, I had no idea you were coming here," Tyler said, "but quite without knowing I've made a philanthropist out of you."

"A what? What did you do?"

"Don't worry, this is good. You've just donated the building to the town, Father.

Did you know it's the oldest one in Cape Agnes?"

"Of course I do. Built by your mother's people. Gave? What do you mean gave?" Dorian's eyes narrowed.

"What a wonderful idea!" Henrietta said. "Pillar of the community, that's you, Dory."

"There's a catch," Ty said.

"I knew it." Dorian sat back and folded his arms across his chest. "Go ahead. What's it going to cost?"

"Four years back taxes for one thing. I've secured a partial grant for restoration, but it has to be met by equal funds from the outside or I can't have it. I thought I had it worked out, but everything didn't pan out the way I thought it would."

"Your old partner Jaris," Dorian said. "Read about that scandal in the papers. Did you get what he owed you?"

"Some of it. He won't be good for the rest of it, unless his wife doesn't get everything she's asking for. Poor Milford will go to prison for certain. Anyway, I have some attorneys working on it for me."

"All right," Dorian said, "I'll pay the

taxes, and I'll more than match the grant. I suppose you'll want me to fund that fitness center in there as well."

"And don't forget my darling Doctor's animal clinic," Henrietta said, patting her husband's hand.

"Of course. I owe Margaret that."

"It's Michael," Henrietta said.

"That's a boy's name," Dorian returned.

"See?" Ty said, giving Maggie a toast with his champagne glass.

"What an interesting idea," Dorian said. "A fitness center and an animal clinic in the same building."

"Yes," Henrietta said, "isn't it?" She raised her hand and swept it in front of her, as if reading an imaginary sign. "Logan and King—Health and Fitness for Human and Beast. It has a nice ring to it, don't you think?"

"Welcome to the family . . . Maggie," Dorian leaned over and kissed her cheek.

"Whatever," Maggie whispered, kissing him back.

"Actually," Ty said, "I agree with the Historic Preservation Society's idea to restore the building to its former state."

"What about your fitness center?" Dorian asked.

"And the animal clinic?" Henrietta asked.

Maggie stayed silent.

"I have changed my mind," Ty said. "I don't want to run a fitness center. And I think the town library should move into the building. They need a lot more space. And there would be room for a museum on the upper level. So much that relates to the history of Cape Agnes is just stored in different places. It should be on display. People should know what a wonderful place this is. And you can do it, Father. You and Henrietta. You can make the people of this town proud to live here and proud to have you for neighbors."

Maggie watched them all smiling and nodding. For the first time, Dorian smiled at his son, full-out with eye contact. Maggie hadn't said a word through Ty's speech.

Ty turned quickly toward her. "I know I haven't discussed this with you, Doc. It was one of the things I wanted to talk with you about. We never got the opportunity . . ."

"I know," she said. "I just want to say right now that I agree with the plans for the Tyler Building. I believe in it and I believe it's the best and most wonderful thing to do." She raised her glass and swirled a gentle arc around them all. "And I believe Cape Agnes may have the first resident fairy godfathers."

Twenty-one

"This is my grandson Theodore. We call him Tad." Maggie placed her arm around the boy's shoulders and looked down at him. "This is Ty's father, Dorian King."

Tad took a long look at the imposing man who seemed to fill the kitchen in the beach house. He looked over at Ty. "Are you glad he's back? Elmer says he gave you a hard time."

"Tad!" Maggie could not contain her shock.

"He did give me a hard time," Ty said truthfully. "But that's in the past. Yes, I'm glad he's back."

"Okay." Tad walked over to Dorian and stuck out his right hand. "Pleased to meet you, Mr. King."

Dorian reached down and grasped the boy's hand. "And I'm pleased to meet you, Theodore."

"I hate that name," Tad said.

"I hate the name Dorian, too. Shall I call you Tad?"

"Yes, sir."

"The you can call me Dory."

"You like that better than Dorian?"

Ty laughed at the boy's comment and Maggie's chagrin.

"As a matter of fact, I do."

Tad shook his head and sighed, disbelief written on his face. "Okay, Dory."

The elder Mr. King chuckled.

Caesar came into the kitchen and sat down next to Ty's foot.

"Oh for the love of Pete, is that Caesar the Wonder Dog?" Dorian's mouth dropped open. He bent down to pet Caesar. The dog growled at him.

Tad went over to him. "It's okay, Caesar. Ty says he's glad he's back."

Caesar looked up at the boy then at Dorian. Then he lifted his right paw and allowed Dorian to shake it.

Henrietta came through the back door carrying Priscilla, who had to attend to her business outside.

"Hi, Mrs. VanGee. Hi, Priscilla," Tad greeted them.

"Hello, Theodore, dear."

"He hates that name," Dorian cued her.

"Oh. You haven't heard the surprise, have you?"

"What surprise?" Tad picked up Priscilla and sat down.

"Mr. King and Mrs. VanGelder were married today," Maggie told him.

"Holy cow! So now you're Ty's stepmother! Cool!"

Henrietta laughed. "Oh my. It is cool, isn't it?"

"Dyno, hunh, Ty?" Tad looked over at him.

"Yes, it's pretty dyno, sport. And before I forget in the festivities of the evening, I owe you this, Henrietta." Ty withdrew an envelope and handed it to her.

Henrietta stared at him. "Dearie, there's no need for you to do this."

"Yes, there is. I feel kind of sheepish about the whole thing."

Maggie watched them, an unspoken question on her lips.

"I was literally without any money. The bank was all over me about paying for this house if I was going to live in it. Henrietta and I made a bargain. Through her generosity, I was able to borrow money to get me through. I'm now able to pay it back and I'm happy to do so. Thank you." He kissed her cheek.

"He had to work for it, though," Henrietta said. "This is the part that bothered him. I told him I'd lend it to him if he'd be in my production of *Camelot*. He didn't want to do it that way. It bothered him that other people would not be paid, that they were all giving of their time willingly. But I insisted, and he finally agreed."

"From now on it's for free," Ty said. "That is, if that production ever opens. There've been too many interruptions already."

"We'll get serious soon," Henrietta told him. "Perhaps we might make it a fall production."

They laughed over it, and then Maggie got busy preparing tea and setting out cookies. The others went into the living-room while Ty built and lit a fire. Maggie brought in the tray with the tea things, and milk for Tad.

"Where's Elmer?" Ty asked. "I want to call a kind of family meeting."

"He's in his room watching television," Tad said. "He's not gonna come out here."

"Why not?"

Tad shifted his eyes toward Dorian and said nothing.

Ty felt a little stab of pain. "Oh. I'll go talk to him. He's part of this family we've been constructing whether he likes it or not."

He went down the hallway and found Elmer watching television in the dark. "What are you watching, Elmer?" He snapped on the light on the bedside table. Elmer looked up but said nothing. Ty sat down on the bed next to him. "Hey! That's Caesar in Dodge City! How'd they get that?"

"Cable," Elmer said dully, "they get everything."

"Then Caesar should get a check. I'll make some calls tomorrow." Ty watched the screen for a minute, then looked over at Elmer. "Would you come out and join us for tea? I'd like to call a family meeting."

"Then go meet. You got your family out there."

"It's not complete without you."

"It's complete. Your father's back, isn't he?"

"Yes, he is."

"Then you don't need me."

"Elmer, I will always need you, regardless if Dorian King is back or not."

"He's your father."

"And you're like a father to me. You're one of my best friends. I feel like you're family." Ty took the old man's hand and rubbed the back of it. "Please come out."

Elmer rolled up and grabbed the remote control. He aimed it at the television and pressed the button. The room went silent. "You mean it?"

"With all my heart."

Elmer got up and straightened his sweater. Ty stood and watched him come around the end of the bed. Tears came into Ty's eyes. Geez, he was becoming emotional, he thought. Tad would probably give him a jab for that.

"Thanks," Elmer said.

Ty walked close and gave him a hug.

"I should thank you," Ty said.

"You bet you should, you jackass," Elmer said. "I gotta go out there and face the guy that stole my girl fifty years ago. How do you think I feel?"

Ty chuckled. "I'll try to keep the two of you from killing each other. Come on."

In the living room, Dorian and Henrietta were telling stories about when they knew each other in high school. Maggie heard Ty and Elmer coming down the hallway. When they came around the corner, Henrietta gave Elmer a bit of a haughty smile, no doubt remembering the exchange she'd had with him in the clinic the last time she visited.

"Oh, Elmer, I'm so glad you joined us," Maggie said. "We have a lot to talk about."

"C'mon over here, Elmer," Tad said, indicating a seat on the couch next to him.

"Elmer?" Dorian said, recognition on his face. "Elmer Everett?"

"That's me," Elmer said. "Hello, Dorian. How've you been?"

"Well, all right, all right," Dorian said. He crossed the room holding out his right hand. "How have you been? You look great. The years have been good to you."

Reluctantly Elmer shook Dorian's hand. "Not so good to you, eh, Dorian? But, looks like you're doing all right now." He nodded toward Henrietta.

"Yes. You know, I owe you an apology," Dorian said.

"For what?"

"The night of the senior prom over at the high school."

Elmer nodded. "Accepted. Let's get on with it."

Maggie thought she detected a collective sigh around the room. Everyone sat down and helped themselves to tea and cookies. Ty stood by the fireplace mantel.

"I wanted us all together tonight, so we could talk about what's happening in our lives," Ty said.

"What's happening?" Tad asked.

"That's what we're going to talk about, sport," Ty said.

"Are we going back to Elm Street?"

"I'm afraid not. You won't be able to go back to Elm Street," Ty told him.

"Yeah!" Tad cheered.

"You're going to tear it down, aren't you?" Elmer started to get up to leave.

"Elmer, don't go. No, we're not going to tear it down."

Elmer watched him, suspicion on his face.

"They're going to restore the building," Maggie told him. "They're going to try to make it the way it once was. Ty hopes the library will go in there. Wouldn't that be a great spot for it?"

Elmer smiled then. "Sure would. Jacalyn will be so happy when you tell her. She's been wanting to move her library to a better place. Oh, I forgot to tell you Jolene and Ray got engaged tonight."

Maggie smiled back. "I knew it. She must be walking on air right now!" The assembled "family" chattered loudly about how matrimonial news was certainly in the air today.

"Anyway," Ty said over the din, recapturing their notice, "the top floor will be a Cape Agnes museum. There are even some of those authentic nets available, Elmer. Can you believe it? Somebody had the good sense to save them."

Elmer grinned. "This is all wonderful,

but there are a couple of snags, aren't there? Like where's the animal clinic going to go, and where are the three of us going to live?"

"Right here, can't we, Grams?" Tad looked over at Maggie.

"Well, Tad, that's something we have to discuss. You know I'm still looking for a place."

"What's wrong with this one?" Dorian asked. "Needs some work, but it's sure big enough for everybody."

"We are going to be living in town, Dory, dear," Henrietta said. "I may consider becoming more than just a summer visitor."

"I have more to say," Ty put in, "and then I hope you'll all say what you want."

"I want to live here," Tad said.

"Sounds good to me," Elmer concurred.

"Tad, now wait a minute," Maggie started.

"Could I finish?" Ty said.

They all fell silent.

He produced a letter from his chest pocket. "I've just been granted license to open a Guiding Eyes school."

Maggie sucked in her breath. Ty left

the room and went outside for a moment. They all looked at each other wondering what he was doing. When he returned, he had a golden Labrador puppy on a leash.

"This is Kelly, our first star of the school. Six of his cohorts will arrive next week."

Caesar pushed up from the hearth and walked over to the new puppy. Tramp and Mouseketeer came out from behind a chair and circled him. Kelly dropped down on his front paws and woofed. Caesar barked and the two cats ran to the kitchen.

"Won't this be fun?" Elmer said.

Ty turned in earnest toward the boy. "Tad, Caesar and I have given this a lot of thought. We've discussed it at great length, and while he's still your buddy he wants you and Kelly to be partners. And I'm asking you to be my partner in my new venture. I'd like you to think it over. You don't have to tell me tonight."

Maggie bit back tears. "So that's what you've been up to."

Dorian and Henrietta both looked at her at once.

"Yes," Ty said. "Now this is where things are going to get sticky."

Henrietta and Dorian switched their gaze to him.

"I know," she said. "But don't worry. I will find a place for the clinic. I know you'll want to use all of this for your school, and I think it's just wonderful."

Dorian watched Ty. Henrietta watched Maggie. Tad stared at Kelly. Caesar watched Tad and Kelly. Elmer watched everybody.

"There are a lot of options. The old roller rink. If Harry Nordquist doesn't want to turn in his Speed Queens for roller blades, I can take that and turn it into a training facility. If he does want it, then I'll find something else. Build something new."

"Don't be ridiculous, Ty. This place is perfect for what you want to do," Maggie said.

"Sure is," Elmer said.

Tad kept staring at Maggie. He hadn't said a word since Ty announced his plans.

"But I think your clinic should stay right here," Ty said. "People like coming out here. There's a lot of room. You're all set up here and you're comfortable. Why go?"

"That's a good idea," Elmer said.

"Well," Maggie said, "I'd like to be near the clinic. I'm certain I'll find the right spot again so we can have an apartment close by."

"That's good, too," Elmer said.

"So then," Ty said, getting nervous, "this is still the best place, isn't it?"

"But we can't live here," Maggie said. "You're starting a new life and a new business. This is your place. This is the right place for it."

"Exactly," Elmer said.

"And you'll be starting a new life, too," Ty said.

"Sort of. Just in a different place."

"Oh, I get it now," Tad said brightly.

"Wish I did," Dorian said.

"I understand," Henrietta said.

"Me, too, and it's great," Elmer said.

"What are you all talking about?" Maggie became a little annoyed.

"Geez, Grams," Tad said. "This is it. See, Ty is asking you to be his girlfriend and move in with him. He wants to be your boyfriend because he really likes you. So that means you can live together. And then I can live here, too. And Elmer wants to stay. Even the cats like it here. And I'm thinkin' I might like to be Ty's partner, you know, with the guide dogs, long as it's okay with Caesar and everything."

"Simple," Elmer said.

"Great idea," Dorian said.

"I'm so happy," Henrietta sniffed.

"No," Ty said, "that's not what I meant. Not exactly, anyway."

"Oh," they all sank back against the chairs and couch.

"I mean, part of it's right, Tad. Just not the part about all that girlfriend and boyfriend stuff."

"But, you said—" Tad began.

"I know what I said. Just don't put words in my mouth or you can never have cold beans again. There's still that casserole in the freezer, you know."

"Yuck."

"Tad," Maggie admonished. She was feeling very uncomfortable and wished she could make some kind of graceful exit.

"What I was getting at and wasn't doing a very good job at," Ty stammered.

"Oh, for heaven's sake," Elmer said. "Do I have to do this for you?"

Ty colored deeply.

"This is it, Colleague. The jackass here wants you to move in with him. He wants us all to keep living here. But he wants to get married. Can you believe it? Wouldn't you think he'd avoid that? But no. And besides that, he wants to run this dog school thing with you as his partner as well. I can see it'll be all up to me to take care of this clinic. Not that I'm not up to it, you know, but I want some ground rules set down right off."

"Elmer," Maggie put a hand on his arm, "you're embarrassing all of us. Please."

"Well, then, just say yes, so we can all relax," Elmer said.

There was a heavy silence.

Ty crossed the room and got down on his knees in front of her. "Everything Elmer said," he whispered. "I love you, Doc. And I love, Tad, and this cranky old goat you came in here with. And I want you all to stay and be part of my family, and let me be part of yours. And let my father and Henrietta be part of us, too. And, another thing, will you marry me?"

"Yes!" Tad shouted, jumping up and down.

Maggie's eyes brimmed. "What Tad said," she said. Then she whispered, "I love you, Ty. I never thought I'd say yes to a marriage proposal again, let alone hear one. But yes to everything."

"Well, well, well," Dorian said. "It's been quite a day, quite a day."

"Twenty-four little hours," Maggie said.

"I knew it. I just knew it!" Henrietta crowed.

Tad came over and hugged both Maggie and Ty. He looked over at Elmer. "You're next!"

"Get outta here," Elmer said.

"You know something?" Ty said to Elmer. "It's worth it to swim some murky moats at times. If you can find a Princess Charming like I have to save me from the dragons, then try it."

"I agree," Maggie said laughing.

"I'm too old," Elmer said.

"Are not," Maggie said.

"Am too."

"Are not."

"Geez," Tad said. "Here we go again."

WATCH AS THESE WOMEN LEARN
TO LOVE AGAIN

HELLO LOVE (4094, $4.50/$5.50)
by Joan Shapiro
Family tragedy leaves Barbara Sinclair alone with her success. The fight to gain custody of her young granddaughter brings a confrontation with the determined rancher Sam Douglass. Also widowed, Sam has been caring for Emily alone, guided by his own ideas of childrearing. Barbara challenges his ideas. And that's not all she challenges . . . Long-buried desires surface, then gentle affection. Sam and Barbara cannot ignore the chance to love again.

THE BEST MEDICINE (4220, $4.50/$5.50)
by Janet Lane Walters
Her late husband's expenses push Maggie Carr back to nursing, the career she left almost thirty years ago. The night shift is difficult, but it's harder still to ignore the way handsome Dr. Jason Knight soothes his patients. When she lends a hand to help his daughter, Jason and Maggie grow closer than simply doctor and nurse. Obstacles to romance seem insurmountable, but Maggie knows that love is always the best medicine.

AND BE MY LOVE (4291, $4.50/$5.50)
by Joyce C. Ware
Selflessly catering first to husband, then children, grandchildren, and her aging, though imperious mother, leaves Beth Volmar little time for her own adventures or passions. Then, the handsome archaeologist Karim Donovan arrives and campaigns to widen the boundaries of her narrow life. Beth finds new freedom when Karim insists that she accompany him to Turkey on an archaeological dig . . . and a journey towards loving again.

OVER THE RAINBOW (4032, $4.50/$5.50)
by Marjorie Eatock
Fifty-something, divorced for years, courted by more than one attractive man, and thoroughly enjoying her job with a large insurance company, Marian's sudden restlessness confuses her. She welcomes the chance to travel on business to a small Mississippi town. Full of good humor and words of love, Don Worth makes her feel needed, and not just to assess property damage. Marian takes the risk.

A KISS AT SUNRISE (4260, $4.50/$5.50)
by Charlotte Sherman
Beginning widowhood and retirement, Ruth Nichols has her first taste of freedom. Against the advice of her mother and daughter, Ruth heads for an adventure in the motor home that has sat unused since her husband's death. Long days and lonely campgrounds start to dampen the excitement of traveling alone. That is, until a dapper widower named Jack parks next door and invites her for dinner. On the road, Ruth and Jack find the chance to love again.

IT'S NEVER TOO LATE FOR LOVE AND ROMANCE

JUST IN TIME
by Peggy Roberts

(4188, $4.50/$5.50)

Constantly taking care of everyone around her has earned Remy Dupre the affectionate nickname "Ma." Then, with Remy's husband gone and oil discovered on her Louisiana farm, her sons and their wives decide it's time to take care of her. But Remy knows how to take care of herself. She starts by checking into a beauty spa, buying some classy new clothes and shoes, discovering an antique vase, and moving on to a fine plantation. Next, not one, but two men attempt to sweep her off her well-shod feet. The right man offers her the opportunity to love again.

LOVE AT LAST
by Garda Parker

(4158, $4.50/$5.50)

Fifty, slim, and attractive, Gail Bricker still hadn't found the love of her life. Friends convince her to take an Adventure Tour during the summer vacation she enjoys as an English teacher. At a Cheyenne Indian school in need of teachers, Gail finds her calling. In rancher Slater Kincaid, she finds her match. Gail discovers that it's never too late to fall in love . . . for the very first time.

LOVE LESSONS
by Marian Oaks

(3959, $4.50/$5.50)

After almost forty years of marriage, Carolyn Ames certainly hadn't been looking for a divorce. But the ink is barely dry, and here she is already living an exhilarating life as a single woman. First, she lands an exciting and challenging job. Now Jason, the handsome architect, offers her a fairy-tale romance. Carolyn doesn't care that her ultra-conservative neighbors gossip about her and Jason, but she is afraid to give up her independent life-style. She struggles with the balance while she learns to love again.

A KISS TO REMEMBER
by Helen Playfair

(4129, $4.50/$5.50)

For the past ten years Lucia Morgan hasn't had time for love or romance. Since her husband's death, she has been raising her two sons, working at a dead-end office job, and designing boutique clothes to make ends meet. Then one night, Mitch Colton comes looking for his daughter, out late with one of her sons. The look in Mitch's eye brings back a host of long-forgotten feelings. When the kids come home and spoil the enchantment, Lucia wonders if she will get the chance to love again.

COME HOME TO LOVE
by Jane Bierce

(3930, $4.50/$5.50)

Julia Delaine says good-bye to her skirt-chasing husband Phillip and hello to a whole new life. Julia capably rises to the challenges of her reawakened sexuality, the young man who comes courting, and her new position as the head of her local television station. Her new independence teaches Julia that maybe her time-tested values were right all along and maybe Phillip does belong in her life, with her new terms.